REBEL MATCH

REBEL MATCH

THE ROYALE VAMPIRE HEIRS, BOOK THREE

by

GINNA MORAN

SUNNY PALMS PRESS

For Inquiries Contact:
Sunny Palms Press
9663 Santa Monica Blvd Suite 1158
Beverly Hills, CA 90210, USA
www.sunnypalmspress.com
www.GinnaMoran.com

For Yvonne, Thanks for your enthusiasm and friendship.
You're awesome!

1

A LITTLE COMPROMISE

I SNAP MY TEETH, MISSING Bronx's shoulder by an inch. He shoves me away and growls. The vibration of the deep, throaty noise sinks into my bones. Stumbling backward, I land on my ass with a thump. Bronx strides toward me to grab my ankles, but I throw my legs up to somersault back to my feet before he gets a chance to drag me to him to pin me to the floor.

Dashing away, I concentrate on getting my body to keep up with my mind. If I try hard enough, I can run for a few feet inhumanly fast. Especially with the hunger burning in my stomach. The fact that Bronx stalks me helps. He sets off my human fear instincts, and in doing so, he pisses off my dhampir half. It takes everything in me not to spin around and throw myself at him. I know if I do, my deep-seated nature will realize how much it enjoys Bronx, and I might let him pin me just for the fun that might ensue. As much as I like the thought, I can't let him win.

Bronx materializes in front of me. If I use vampire speed, so can he. Those are the rules. He blocks my knee as I thrust it up to hit his gut, and I swing my arm out a second later, managing to clock him in the ribs. My hand aches from the force, but it was just enough to make him stagger back. I launch at him without giving him the chance to react and hook my arm to his neck to swing my body around to his back.

I fail miserably. My ass can't manage the task, and I end up stuck on his arm.

Bronx grabs my leg and hoists me off my feet upside down in front of him. He dangles me a foot off the mat and shakes my body, causing my shirt to hike to my chin to show off my workout bra.

He chuckles as I grumble in annoyance, trying to mimic his growl. I swing my body a few times, but all it does is bring my shirt over my eyes so that I can't even see. I rock in his tight hold until my shirt comes off completely. A loud cat-call whistle cuts through the air from the back of the small gym where Mikkalo watches the two of us practice.

"Don't let him win, Gwen," Mikkalo says, standing up from his chair. He rubs his hands together, flexing his deliciously muscular arms. "Think about how sweet it'll be when you get to bite him anywhere you want."

Just the thought sets off my dhampir nature.

Bronx senses my oncoming strength and releases my leg to drop me to the mat, but I surprise him and swing my body forward, hooking my arms to his waist. I throw my legs at him, locking them to his neck, and the two of us fall together. I land with my knees on both sides of Bronx's head, and he purrs the sexiest noise.

"This doesn't count as you pinning me," Bronx says, hooking his fingers to my sides.

I squeeze his head between my thighs and grab his wrists, yanking his arms to the mat before he throws me off him. "How about now?"

He has the bravado to turn his head and nip me with his fangs. I clench him harder, his damn mouth taking full advantage of my closeness. A shiver runs through me, tingles blossoming every spot he kisses.

"Gwen, get it together," Mikkalo calls. "He's distracting you."

Bronx growls at him deep in his throat, the vibration causing my knees to weaken, and I sink my body onto his face. Fuck. Me.

I hunch forward and rest my head on his torso. "It's working."

"Mmm," Bronx murmurs. "I can't wait for my prize."

Jameson claps his hands, trying to get my attention. "Damn it, Gigi. Remember what's at stake."

Chuckling, Bronx rolls me off of him to get on top of me. I don't even fight. My damn vagina refuses to let me get myself together. "You will love losing to me, dandelion. I promise."

The second my back hits the mat, I remember what the hell I'm supposed to be doing and what's on the line if I don't succeed. If Bronx pins me, I get to co-star with him in a movie for our private collection, allowing him to bite me wherever he pleases. But if I pin him, I get to enjoy a strip-tease from him, a full-body massage, a bite wherever I choose, and he has to let Jameson drive us the next time we go somewhere. Mikkalo said I shouldn't make it a win-win for Bronx, so he came up with the last one.

"Aw, man." Jameson's loud-ass groan sounds through the air, cutting over the sound of Bronx's humming as he continues to distract me. "Gigi, we were counting on you."

Bronx laughs and kisses my thigh, shifting off me to turn his body to look at his brothers. The second his weight eases up, I pull my brain from the lust clouding my judgment and hook my arms around him to roll him to his back.

He's not the only one who can play this game.

Stretching forward, I slide my hand into his shorts. Bronx freezes and relaxes as I lace my fingers around his cock as it hardens under my touch. I murmur a hum under my breath and sink harder onto him. He totally lets me.

"And he's down," Mikkalo says, chuckling. "I'm calling it. Gwen wins. Her distraction is far more effective."

Jameson's shadow stretches next to us. "I swear you better not use that move on anyone else."

I giggle and twist on Bronx, turning myself around. Bronx grins at me, letting me tug his arms above his head. Smiling, I tip my head up to look at Jameson. "Not even on you, Jamie?"

Jameson play-growls at me. "Hell yeah, you will...in approximately eight hours."

Bronx tightens his hands on my waist. "So until then, get to work, brothers. If you can't find something to do, I'll tell Everett to find something for you."

Mikkalo and Jameson look from me and Bronx and then to each other. They disappear a moment later, leaving us alone. Bronx flips me off of him and tugs my hands over my head. He straddles my waist and bends down to trail his lips to my jaw.

"I think we should call it a tie tonight, dandelion," he murmurs. "You technically didn't pin me."

"Is that so?" I say, drawing my mouth to his.

"Mmmhmm. I'll give you what you want. You give me what I want..." He rolls again, taking me with him. "A little compromise."

"You'd still have to let Jameson drive next time," I say, grazing my teeth to his bottom lip.

He eases away and glares. "Not happening."

That's what he thinks. I smirk and close the space again, kissing him deeper for a moment. "I guess I'll have to call Mikkalo back to judge our re-match. I won't go easy on you," I tease.

Bronx moans, feeling me rub my body to his. I can't help myself. Our wrestling often turns into more, and I already anticipate what's to come. Hopefully both of us. "Fine. Jameson drives. One way only."

I laugh and shake my head, stopping him from trying to distract me again. "Round trip or nothing."

Sighing, he cocks an eyebrow, trying to see if I'm joking.

I lick my lips. "Just think about it. You'll be able to give me your undivided attention."

His dark eyes search mine. "Hmm."

"Play lapsies. Maybe a little blood exchange if it's a distance away."

Sitting up, Bronx catapults to his feet with me still clinging to him. His mouth captures mine, kissing me with a deep-seated passion that exudes from his soul. He slides his hands down my lower back and strolls with me to an elevator that'll take us to his suite on the top floor of the Blood Match Center in Crimson Vista.

Silence greets us in the hallway where we pass by Everett's suite. Now that we were forced to relocate from Night Palms Castle, things seem to have settled more as my guys get back to their regional duties. The only difference is that they take the nights off during my time with them, doing their best to keep me out of view of practically everyone they can manage.

I don't mind it though. I grew up in a bunker, and our floor is far larger than that. I have access to the roof where I can visit the garden and enjoy the city lights. We have the gym to exercise in. My guys easily entertain me. The only ones missing are my brothers, but I can't even stand to think about Grayson and Silas. Other than that, my life is far better than I could have asked for or imagined.

"So, what's your answer?" I ask, grinning at him. "Is it a tie or do I win?"

"Tie...if we start now."

Bronx stiffens before we reach the bend in the hallway that leads to our room. Without saying anything, he flips me from his arms and onto his back. I hook my arms around his neck without squeezing and snuggle my chin into the crook of his shoulder.

"No need to get defensive. It's me, Mr. Royale."

I groan at the low rumble of Corona's voice.

"This better be damn good, Mr. Anderson," Bronx says, linking his fingers to mine instead of reaching for the hidden weapon strapped under his shirt.

Bronx carries me toward our suite, where Corona leans against the wall outside our door. He runs his fingers through his wavy brown hair, keeping his gaze trained on Bronx while I blatantly glower at him. I'm nearly certain Bronx only holds my hands to stop me from rushing the asshole vampire to try to rip his heart out. Because I'm so not okay with his presence nor will I ever be after he murdered Kyler.

Corona straightens his back and tugs out his com device from his pocket. "Would a sighting of one of the Baron brothers be considered good?" Tapping the screen, he lights up the wall with a projection.

My blood cools at the sight of...Cortland, I think. His eyes lack any real color, giving him a creepy-ass appearance that even the rest of his ruggedly handsome features can't save. I tighten my fingers around Bronx's, making him wiggle his hands against my strength. We both stare in silence as Cortland appears right in front of the security camera and smiles before it blinks off.

"Send me the coordinates of that," Bronx says.

Corona taps his com device. "Would you like me to

send out security?"

"No, Mikkalo will handle it."

"Are you—"

I slap Corona across the face from over Bronx's shoulder. "He *said* Mikkalo will handle it."

Corona blinks in surprise, as shocked as I am over my rebellious hand, but he doesn't react or look at me. I'm tempted to do it again for a reaction. Because damn. It felt good as hell.

Corona steps back like he reads my mind about smacking him. Instead of chancing my wrath, he nods at Bronx and vanishes too fast for my eyes to follow.

The world blurs around me, and I screech as I fly from Bronx's back and onto our bed. Bronx doesn't give me the chance to move before he's on top of me, his lips crashing into mine, his fingers combing through my hair.

"I can't believe you just did that," Bronx says, leaning up on his elbows. His eyes search mine, flashing silver with his lust and approval.

I tighten my jaw. "He's lucky it was only a slap."

"And I'm lucky to have such a fierce, feisty dhampir watching my back," he says, cuddling me close.

I smile. "Always."

A tap on the door draws our attention away from each other. Sighing, Bronx pushes off the bed to answer it. If we weren't just ready to give in to each other, he'd have just called out for one of his brothers to come in. He knows me—and them—well enough that I wouldn't kick any of them out...so, he's stopping them from coming in.

I scoot to the edge and watch him cross the suite, furnished like a small apartment with an open kitchen, sitting room, dining area, and our sleeping quarters tucked past an archway with the privacy curtain drawn open.

Bronx swings the door open, and I catch sight of Everett in the hallway. I slide off the bed and pad my way closer to assure neither of them tries to whisper. Everett greets me with a smile, and I hold open my arms for a hug.

Bronx clears his throat. "We'd invite you in, but—"

"No worries, brother. I just wanted to stop by as to not risk word getting out that we have a solid lead on Ashton." Everett glances from Bronx and back to me. "He's been registered in the Vaduva Region as a gen. pop. donor."

"What?" Confusion pinches my brows. "I don't understand. He was a convicted criminal."

Everett's jaw tightens. "Technically not. Zaire never signed off on your brothers before his death, which is how Corona was able to sell them as fake blood debtors without going to auction. Only you and Kyler were on record."

"Oh."

Bronx hooks his hand to my side and pulls me close. "Which is good."

I shift and look at Bronx. "I just thought you'd remove

me from the system."

The two of them look at each other again. Bronx tightens his jaw, his eyes flashing silver. Neither of them has to say anything for me to know that whatever thought they silently share isn't going to be something I like.

I narrow my eyes. "Okay, one of you spit it out. Why are you looking at me like you're going to run for cover?"

Everett chuckles and shakes his head. His blue eyes sparkle at me, and I can't resist losing myself in their blue depths. I love the way he looks at me. "I'd never."

Bronx nudges me toward him. "Good. You tell her."

I scoff and laugh. "Seriously, Bronx?"

Everett takes me into his arms and nuzzles his face to my throat, not even caring that I'm still a bit sticky with sweat from my workout session. "Only if I get the rest of your night, Bronx," he says through kisses to my heated skin. "You also have to follow up on my lead and make the arrangements to visit the Widows."

Bronx groans. "Decisions. Decisions."

I swivel in Everett's arms. "All right. That's it, you two."

Hooking my fingers to Everett's shirt, I yank him with me. I snatch onto the front of Bronx's shirt next and tug the two of them into the suite and kick the door behind me. Neither of them says anything as I drag them by their shirts toward the sitting area. They fail miserably at remaining expressionless. Everett's eyes crinkle in the corners, showing he's on the verge of laughing at any second.

I push them back on the couch and stand in front of them with my hands on my hips. Bronx breaks first, his lips curling into a half smile as he drinks me in, loving every second I boss him around. Everett rests his elbows on his knees, propping his chin on his hands. Hell, if it takes everything in me not to plop my ass between them and sprawl across their laps to bask in all their attention.

I lick my lips, shifting my weight on my feet. "Whoever tells me first gets to feed me," I say, meeting each of their gazes.

"Deal," Everett and Bronx say at the same time.

I tip my head back and laugh.

They growl at each other and then Bronx says, "You know there is nothing more we want than to erase your record..."

The tone of his voice wipes the smile from my lips. I purse my mouth, sighing through my nose. "But?"

"You had Blood Matched to Zaire. The contract was submitted to Donor Life Corp the minute after he signed it." Everett reaches for my hand and tugs me to him. He looks as pained as I feel at the information. Not only have I been registered to the Royale Region, but I have been put into the Donor Life Corp territory's database. The dumb contract is legit, which makes me nervous.

I plop down on the middle of the couch, and Bronx and Everett automatically close the space to squish me between them. "I guess I shouldn't be this upset. I knew it was happening. I just forgot since..." I can't finish my sentence. Too much has happened since the night they found me in the city. It almost feels like a lifetime ago. More like another life completely.

Bronx surprises me by biting his arm. The sweet scent of his blood wafts through the air, seducing my senses. Everett follows Bronx's lead and sinks his fangs into his arm next. I release a hum in my throat, my body tingling in anticipation. I hadn't realized how hungry I was until this moment.

Everett slides me across him to take my spot in the middle. He coaxes me to lie down, and I rest my head on Bronx's thighs, feeling his arousal stiffen under my head. They smile at me, looking so hot with their rising desire. I didn't expect them to both feed me, but I love that they do. Moments like this, just being together and facing the bullshit of our lives with the support of one another gets me in a good way.

"You guys," I murmur, licking my lips.

Bronx hovers his bleeding arm above my mouth. "Open up, dandelion. Let us make you feel better. Your eyes are starting to flash."

I link my fingers to his wrist and pull his arm to latch

my lips around his bite. Bronx releases a soft moan the harder I suck. My body tingles with lust, and I can't stop my body from squirming. Everett slides his hand between my legs, distracting me with his touch before I lose control with Bronx. I gasp and release Bronx's arm to bring Everett's offering to my mouth next.

"So good," I say, kissing Everett's puncture wounds, using my lips to staunch the bleeding.

"Need more?" Bronx slides his arm around me to prop me up.

I snuggle to him, listening to the sound of his heart beating. "Nope. I'm pretty perfect. The only things that could make this night better are—"

Bronx and Everett's com devices beep, the noise cutting through the air to silence my thought. I sneak my hand into Bronx's pocket and pull it out before he can stop me. It blinks on under my fingerprint, displaying the silliest picture of me and Jameson sticking our tongues out at the camera.

I can't stop from smiling as Jameson's face pops into view. "Miss me already, Jamie?"

"Always, Gigi." Jameson forces his mouth to smirk with the words, but his eyes don't light up like usual. Something must've happened in the short time since I saw him in the gym. "And I'll come bring you lunch in a bit, but first, can I talk to Bronx?"

"I'm here," Bronx says, pressing his cheek to mine.

Jameson tightens his jaw, his eyes flashing silver. Everett scoops me onto his lap, letting Bronx get to his feet. Bronx disappears into the bathroom and shuts the door. I scrunch my brows and meet Everett's expressionless gaze.

"Seriously?" I ask, staring at the closed door.

Everett touches my chin, getting me to look at him. "You know Bronx will tell us once he has a chance to process whatever news Jameson has to share. He likes to have complete control over how stuff gets delivered, especially if it's in regards to you."

I purse my lips. "I know, but I can handle whatever it is."

Leaning in, Everett brushes his lips to mine. "We know that, but can you blame us for wanting to protect you?"

I shrug and puff out my lip more. "Yeah, yeah. I'm such a damsel in distress."

Everett mirrors my dramatic pout and then fake-glares at me. I close my eyes, trying to listen to Bronx's conversation with Jameson, but I can only make out an occasional growl and the thunk of his head hitting the door in frustration.

I nearly make it to my feet to rush to where I can listen. Everett flips me off his lap and onto the couch, caging my head in with his elbows. His eyes flash silver as he leans in, looking so determined to distract me from the curiosity that wants me to dash to the bathroom door to press my ear to it.

"What do you think you're doing?" I ask, hooking my fingers to his shoulders. "Distracting me isn't going to work. We don't have nearly enough time."

He bites his bottom lip, drawing my gaze to his mouth. "Wanna bet?"

"Mmmhmm." I dare him even to try with my eyes.

"If I manage to prove it, you have to wear a dress every night for a week," he says, running his finger across my jaw to sweep strands of my blond hair away to see my throat better.

"You have until Bronx hangs up," I say, arching into him to feel his weight against me. "And if he catches you, then I'm wearing pants during your time for the next month."

Everett doesn't even hesitate and says, "It's on."

I don't get the chance to react before he rips the strap of my tank top with his teeth and kisses my shoulder, grazing his fangs over my collarbone and down to my chest. I stretch my back, sinking my head into the couch cushion, enjoying the sensation of his tongue gliding between my breasts.

I comb my fingers through his hair, my breathing picking up pace as he shifts my bra away from my boob so that he can suck my nipple into his mouth. A moan escapes my lips, and Everett breaks away to smile up at me.

"I wish I could continue," he says, sneaking his hand between my legs to tug my workout shorts out of his way to tease me a little. "But Bronx just hung up, and I have to meet Jameson and Mikkalo."

I narrow my eyes at him. "You're lucky you did distract me."

He flashes his fangs with a smile. "Don't forget to pick out the dress. There's no way I can wait another four days to ravish you. The next time we're alone—"

The door to the bathroom swings open, stopping Everett from whispering his words. Bronx rubs the back of his neck, drawing his gaze to the two of us on the couch. A strange expression crosses his face, but it's not because of me or Everett. I can't stop a blip of fear from igniting in my heart.

Bronx clears his throat. "Be ready in an hour, Everett. We'll meet in the lobby."

I blink a few times, letting Everett help me to my feet. "You're leaving?"

He nods. "All of us."

Everett kisses my cheek and motions to Bronx. Leaning in, he whispers, "Looks like he could use a little distracting."

Vanishing, Everett leaves me standing near the couch. Bronx closes the space to me and hugs me, lifting me a bit off my feet in the process. He doesn't say anything right away, making my nerves even worse.

"Why would you need distracting?" I ask, tilting my head up to meet his gaze.

He presses his lips into a line. "It seems that the Barons weren't joking about trying to seize the region."

"Fuck," I say. "What do we do?"

Snuggling his chin into the crook of my neck, he breathes in the scent of my hair. "We need to face them head on."

I was afraid he was going to say that.

"Tonight?"

"Yeah, the sooner the better. For everyone's sake."

I straighten my shoulders and ease away from him to meet his gaze. "Their hearts are mine."

"They won't even know what hit them."

2

UNEXPECTED VISITOR

"RELAX," I WHISPER, MASSAGING MY fingers into Bronx's taut shoulders.

There was no way I was just tossing on clothes after my workout, so I insisted Bronx join me in the lavish glass, tile, and metal shower. His handsome, brooding face can't seem to soften as he runs strategies through his mind.

I should be more worried about leaving the safety of the Blood Match Center and our high-security suite, but it's been a month since we've arrived and days since I've gotten fresh air since Jameson's the only one to take me to the roof. I kind of look forward to seeing something else, even for only a bit.

Bronx turns around to face me, shower steam glistening across his chest. "I'm sorry, dandelion. I didn't mean to get lost in my thoughts."

I smirk and run my fingers across his slippery chest. "Maybe I should do a better job at reminding you that I'm here, feeling super hot...and still a little hungry."

Bronx closes the space, pushing my naked body against the shower wall. I love how easy it is to steal his attention to focus on me. Everett was right about Bronx needing some distracting. Standing on my tiptoes, I meet my lips to his, slipping my tongue into his mouth. He reacts with fervent passion, sliding his hands to my ass to pull my hips to his. I shift my body, allowing his erection to rest between my legs, but I don't go any further. Instead, I break from his lips and kiss his neck, sucking my way down the planes of his chest.

"I do owe you a bite, don't I?" Bronx murmurs, shifting my sopping hair from my shoulder to watch me work my way down.

I peek up at him. "I'm saving that for later. I'm not hungry for your blood. I'm starving for just you."

He hums in his throat. "Is that so?"

I lick my lips. "Can I show you how much?"

Bronx lets me push him back until I get him to sit on

the shower seat to enjoy the heat of the steam wafting through the air. He watches me with a hot intensity as I ease to my knees to kneel in front of him. He's always so focused on assuring my pleasure that I want nothing more than to reciprocate.

I spread his legs to get between them and suck my bottom lip between my teeth. Lacing my fingers around his prominent shaft, I stroke his erection a few times, feeling it flex in my hand. Bronx releases a soft breath and digs his fingers into my shoulders. I start slow, kissing his thigh and trailing my tongue all the way to his balls to lick them softly.

"Gwen," he whispers, my name sounding like a sexy plea from his lips. His body relaxes, and he links his fingers through one of my hands.

I work my mouth over him, listening to his heart beating and his breath turning into quick pants as I glide my tongue up the length of his shaft and suck his tip into my mouth, massaging my tongue over it. He moans, tightening his fingers through mine, and shifts to lean his back on the shower wall.

I suck a bit harder and inhale a deep breath as I draw him into my mouth. I take my time licking and sucking and kissing, using his moans to let me know what he likes the most. His fingers comb through my wet hair, playing with the strands. He never takes his eyes off me though I don't look up at him. I can just feel his gaze devour every second as I please him in a way that turns me on, knowing how much he enjoys it.

Bronx moans again, his hands trailing from my head to my shoulders. I pick up speed, sucking and licking until his body tenses and flexes with his oncoming orgasm. He bows forward, releasing a sexy cross between a growl and a purr, the sound reverberating through me as he cums, the sweet, sugary flavor not unlike his blood.

"You're so amazing, Gwen," Bronx says, massaging his fingers into my back as I kiss my way up until I climb onto him to straddle his lap. "Have I told you that enough lately?"

"You don't have to say the words. The looks you give me speak volumes. Your kisses. Your embraces. Even wrestling with me. You make me feel so incredible all the time." I adjust myself on his lap, his body already aroused again and ready for more.

He graces me with a gorgeous smile that lights his eyes and makes me smile just as wide. Wrapping his arms around me, he hugs me close, kissing my collarbone, just enjoying the taste of my skin.

I moan at the sensation of his mouth caressing my nipples. Bronx eases my body onto his until pressure builds between my legs. I sink down on him and gasp, tingles bursting through me. He grazes his fangs to my shoulder and moves his hands to my hips to help guide my body up and down.

Everything about this moment feels so amazing, so hot and sexy. My body slides against his as I rock, our passionate lovemaking the thing we both needed after the news we got tonight. I roll my body against Bronx's, clinging onto him as he stands up and presses my back to the shower wall. He thrusts so deep that I can't stop my loud-ass mouth from shouting just how good Bronx's motions feel. Our lovemaking turns into something wild and untamed, something deep-seated and delicious that every inch of my body hums with desire.

Tingles burst through me, his body hitting me just right, getting me off from the constant friction he creates. He shifts my weight to one arm and uses his hand to rub my clit, his fingers stroking just hard enough to make me orgasm. I gasp through the intensity of my muscles tightening and then rest my head to his shoulder, holding on to enjoy our bodies as close as our souls.

Bronx kisses my throat and nips my skin, using the hand not holding me to protect my head from banging into the wall. I give up on suppressing the volume of my moans, my voice coming in quick bursts with each of his deep penetrating thrusts. He finishes with the sexiest noise that vibrates across my skin. Slowing down, he pants and hugs me, just listening to the water and our hearts racing. He kisses me softly, resting his head to my shoulder, and doesn't let me down for a minute while we both catch our breaths. My legs tremble a bit as I find my footing, and I reach up and hook my fingers around his neck, pulling him in for another kiss.

"Tonight's going to be fine, you know," I say, standing still as he runs the bath sponge across my skin to help me clean off. "I'll not only protect you, but I'll also make sure everything goes to plan."

He releases a soft chuckle. "Do you know how hard it is for me even to consider leaving this shower? I want more of you. I can't ever get enough. You're so—you're everything to me."

"I hope it's torture," I tease, trailing my fingers over his bulging muscles.

He groans and turns off the water. "The worst. I had big plans for us tonight."

"Big plans, huh?" I ask, grinning. I drink in his naked body and reach out to play with his building erection. "If we hurry, we might have enough time for you to give me the strip tease you promised."

He chuckles. "And feed you in bed. My brothers don't have to join us for dinner since we'll be hanging out with them."

"Whatever you want."

Bronx opens the shower door and grabs a towel to wrap

around me. We stroll together into our suite where we're surprised by Mikkalo, Everett, and Jameson. They were supposed to meet us in the lobby. The only time they'd dare come in without an invitation on each other's nights would be because something happened.

Fear trickles through me, stealing the warmth from my skin, making me shiver and tighten my towel around me. Their intense gazes rove over me and drink me in despite the fact that I'm sure I'm seconds away from hearing Bronx lose his shit.

"Nice shower?" Jameson asks like this is all sorts of normal. "Sounded fun."

I narrow my eyes. "What's wrong? I know you guys didn't come here to ask to join in," I say, beating Bronx to the question.

That makes all of them look at each other, making me blush. "You know nothing, Gigi," Jameson says. "I'm nearly certain the whole city wants to take a shower with you."

Bronx releases a growl, shutting Jameson up. "Get to it, brother."

"We have an unexpected visitor," Mikkalo says before Jameson can answer, tugging his com device from his pocket to hold it out to Bronx.

I lean forward to glimpse the video feed of what I think is the security post that monitors the select few vampires able to come and go as they please during the quarantine that traps both donors and shadow dwellers in Crimson Vista for the unforeseeable future.

"Who are they?" I ask, staring at three gorgeous female vampires waiting in their vehicle for the guards to motion them through.

No one answers my question while the five of us stare at the screen.

The red-haired driver flicks her gaze right at the security camera. I nearly duck out of the way, feeling suddenly nervous as all get-out like the woman could actually see me, even though she can't. Bronx slides his arm around my back, pulling me closer to him. Jameson closes the space on my other side, draping his arm over my shoulders to sandwich me to Bronx in the best way possible.

"Did Viorica announce her arrival?" Bronx asks, lowering his voice.

Mikkalo taps the screen and pulls up a list of notifications. "Not with me. All alerts from Zaire's private line have been forwarded to you."

Bronx groans and crosses the room to his bed, leaving me with his brothers. Everett motions for me to go with him to the wardrobe, and Jameson follows along, keeping his arm around me. Mikkalo joins Bronx to look over his com device. No one has to say anything for me to know that they're trying to stay calm. Whoever the hell these women are have them on edge. It's worse than when Corona comes around or even thinking about the Baron Coven.

"Put her in a gown," Bronx calls from outside the wardrobe. "High heels, jewelry, perfume. Arm her too. And fast. We have about fifteen minutes."

I stand in surprise as Jameson lifts my arms while Everett slips a white gown over my head. The strapless dress hugs my curves, leaving me very minimal range to move my legs. I watch in the mirror as the two of them complete my look with ruby jewelry to add to the single bracelet Jameson gave me with a tracking device that I never take off.

Spinning me around, Jameson meets my gaze, scrunching his nose. He swipes a glass bottle from a small built-in vanity and spritzes my throat with a floral perfume that nearly overwhelms my senses. Everett hikes up my gown and hides a thigh holster with a dagger and then helps me step into glittery stilettos pointy enough to impale someone.

"Makeup or no?" Jameson asks Everett, looking at the collection of products I haven't touched.

"That's up to Gwen." Everett shifts to stand behind me and combs a brush through my hair. He fastens a few pieces out of my face with a ruby clip.

I raise my eyebrows. "Can someone please tell me why you're dressing me up like a doll?"

Jameson picks up a lipstick. "The Vaduvas are coming." The way he says it makes it sound like a war heads to our doorstep.

Holding still, I let Jameson apply the lipstick but bat his hand away before he tries anything else. "The Vaduvas? Why does that coven sound familiar?"

"Viorica is the head of Donor Life Corp's board." Everett's voice remains even as he stands next to Jameson to drink me in. They nod at each other in silent approval. Usually, I'd laugh this weird experience off, especially because of how effortlessly they put my look together, but something about their eyes pushes me on the edge of losing my shit with nerves. How can they not be freaked out? The head of the whole territory is here, and Zaire is dead. She will surely ask about him.

I grimace. "Fuck."

Jameson tightens his jaw, his green eyes darkening. "Don't panic. If you panic, they'll think something is up. We shouldn't have anything to worry about in front of Viorica. Unless Everett crossed one of her daughters in the last few months."

Everett punches Jameson hard enough that he has to step to catch himself. "I'd never touch a Widow. That was Mikkalo."

Mikkalo growls at Everett's revelation, and I wonder if one of the tattoos Zaire gave him on his side was due to one of these so-called Widows. Why they have such a nickname? I have no idea. I'm not sure anyone will tell me either.

"Relax, Mikkalo," I say, strutting from the wardrobe.

"I'm not jealous of something that happened before me."

He closes the space and touches my cheek, peering into my eyes. "I love you, you know. Thanks for saying that. You're it for me."

I smile and kiss him, risking smearing the lipstick Jameson applied. "The way I want."

"All right, brothers. Five minutes. Go get dressed and meet us downstairs. I'm taking Gwen." Bronx materializes in front of me, taking Mikkalo's place.

A cool whisper of a breath blossoms across my cheek with Mikkalo's kiss goodbye, and I shift on my feet, gathering the skirt of my gown in my fingers. Bronx takes a moment to drink me in. He caresses his fingers to my jaw, his eyes flashing silver.

"You look beautiful, Gwen," he says, pushing my still damp hair behind my ear.

I grab the lapels of his suit jacket, wishing I got to watch him dress. It's one of my favorite activities to do with all my guys apart from watching them undress. "I want you to rip this dress off already."

He releases a purr from his throat. "Save that thought. The second we leave this room, I can no longer touch you. You must act the part of a Blood Match. Don't speak unless spoken to. And be prepared. I'll do my best in handling Viorica, but if she suspects that anything is up, she will try to manipulate your mind. I'm counting on you not to react."

I bare my teeth at him. "Can't I just stay here? I don't like any of this."

He shakes his head. "You've been put under my care while Zaire is supposedly away—at least to the board. Something came up with Blood Rebels that will prolong his absence. When he returns, he'll request another few weeks with you."

I blink a few times, mulling over his words. I just hope that it works out like he plans. The last thing I need is to fail my guys by messing up. I'm not even that great at hiding my reactions to things I shouldn't be able to hear.

"Fuck, Bronx. I'm nervous," I admit. "What if I fail?"

"It wouldn't be you who fails." He pulls me in close and kisses me. "Now, come on. The sooner we greet Viorica, the sooner we can leave. We still have things to take care of, remember?"

I shut my eyes, breathing into his lips, letting our breath mingle for a moment. "I nearly forgot."

He scoops me up and cradles me in his arms. "Give me another few minutes to handle this, and I'll assure you forget again."

I don't have the chance to respond as the world blurs around us. Bronx sets me on my feet in the elevator, and I hold his gaze until the door beeps on the ground floor. I bow my head and lace my fingers together, keeping my hands in front of me. Stepping forward, I pray that my legs get their act together to walk properly in these too-tall heels. It's the first time in a while that I've had to walk on my own in death-trap shoes.

Bronx leads the way to the lobby, and it takes everything in me not to lift my head to peer in the direction where I hear a few feminine, nearly musical, voices whisper through the air. I train my gaze on the three pairs of stilettos not unlike the ones I wear. Two of the female vampires show off their smooth, muscular legs—one in a short dress and the other through a slit up to her thigh in a gown. The third woman wears tight black pants with a blazer, much more business-like than the other two.

"Misses Vaduva. What an honor it is to be graced with your presences," Bronx says, stopping in front of me, keeping his muscular form between me and the three vampires. He takes a deep bow. "I do hope this is more of a social call. Can I get you a donor?"

Whoa. Bronx must be nervous as hell to be laying his nicety on so thick. It takes everything in me not to react and touch him. If one of these vampires is head of the board, she must be extremely powerful.

"Actually, Mr. Royale. If you could please call upon Zaire. I'd like to have a quick meeting with him," the tall, gorgeous redhead says. Her eyes burn into me as she acknowledges my existence with an arched brow.

I dart my gaze to the floor, silently kicking myself for looking up at her. I couldn't help myself. Her voice practically commanded my attention.

"We'd love a donor and some company, though," the brunette next to the woman says.

"Perhaps the pretty thing behind you," the last woman, another redhead, says. She risks stepping closer to me, giving Bronx a foot of space. "What's your name, Miss?"

"Ms. Royale," I say, flicking my gaze up to meet the sharp features of the woman now standing uncomfortably close.

She looks a bit younger than I'm used to, almost like she transitioned as a teen, but her fierce gaze says there is nothing young or inexperienced about her. "What's your first name, darling? There's no need to be formal with me."

"Gwen," I respond.

"Step back, Heidi," Bronx warns.

The other woman grins, showing off her fangs. "Oh, Bronx. We wouldn't dare hurt her." She wiggles her fingers at me. "Would you like to join my sister and me for a little fun?" Turning her attention to Bronx, she adds, "Is Mikkalo around? I'd love for him to join us."

Bronx doesn't react, keeping himself in check, though I know her words get on his nerves. He hates that she shows me attention at all. Stepping more in front of me, he says, "Unfortunately for you, Merrick, Ms. Royale is unavailable for donations. She Blood Matched to Zaire. I'm only watching her in his absence and can't grant you permission."

"Absence?" the first redhead asks, tilting her head. She steps closer like she can intimidate Bronx, and I guess she does, because he steps back a little.

"The board was notified, Viorica," Bronx says, using the woman's first name. "Zaire followed the necessary protocols."

I should've known she was the leader of the board. She exudes authority, her very presence screaming that we must abide to her whims. Releasing a small breath, I try to keep calm. All three of the women scrutinize my every gesture, even if Bronx blocks me.

Viorica hums under her breath. "It must've slipped my mind. Oh, well. The trip to see the growth of the Royale Region has been interesting. Your coven has done an excellent job."

"Thank you, Viorica. Is there something else I can do for you while you're here? I'm acting head of our region during Zaire's absence. I can arrange a tour of the city. Perhaps a trip elsewhere?" Bronx remains straight-backed, even-toned. It helps with my nerves.

Viorica shifts her eyes from Bronx and to me again. "Since we've come all this way, I suppose you can provide me a region update. Any more problems with the Blood Rebels? It's rare for a female to travel alone, you know. I'd think Zaire's Blood Match would have an army searching for her."

Fear sneaks up to clench my chest as Viorica unexpectedly acknowledges my past. Her attention turns to me to gauge my reaction. Of course she would know I was a Blood Rebel. My matching information was given to the board, which means she knows I'm not a normal applicant.

"She had a brother and a blood source. Both now deceased." Bronx glances at me. "From what we know, she had no personal ties to any nests in the last few years. The vampire assisting her and her brother hadn't actually been involved with rebels."

I clench my jaw as to not react.

"I'm assuming Zaire took all necessary precautions in handling her?" Viorica's voice lowers to a pitch I shouldn't be able to hear. "It sounds like he extracted the information appropriately."

"Yes, Viorica. Gwen is not a threat. She's been surprisingly obedient and has adjusted well. I think she enjoys the lavish life Zaire bestowed upon her." Bronx turns to me with a smile. "Right, Ms. Royale?"

Ugh. I wish he didn't ask me a direct question, especially in regards to anything to do with Zaire. I get heated just thinking about him. Though, now I'm glad he tried to get all bitey with me. If he hadn't, who knows where I'd have been with my guys.

I nod my head. "Yes, sir. Very much so."

"And what about Zaire? Do you enjoy him?" Merrick asks, speaking up. I nearly forgot she and Heidi were listening.

Heidi looks from Viorica to Merrick. "How could she, Merrick? Mr. Royale isn't here. He must not have been fully interested in Blood Matching. Probably testing to see if she attempts to murder one of his brothers. I mean, that's what I would do."

"I would never." My. Dumb. Mouth. I just couldn't take them talking in front of me like I'm not here. It doesn't help that I want to defend myself.

Merrick raises her perfectly arched brow. "Hmm. Just what I expected. Their leader's away so the Royales will play. Which one do you favor, Gwen? It couldn't possibly be Bronx. He doesn't...do donors."

Heidi laughs. "It's most surely Everett. He has rather low standards."

Ah, hell no.

I clench my hands into fists, my body reacting without my mind's consent. Merrick devours my reaction, parting her perfect plum lips in a dazzling smile that makes her even more gorgeous.

Bronx steps back to block me, puffing his chest out to create a solid wall of muscle. I can't tell if he's protecting me or these so-called Widows. "Enough. You will show me and my brothers respect in the Royale Region, Ms. Vaduva. Gwen is a part of our household and nothing more. Because of the sensitivity of the situation, I want to make it clear that Gwen is Zaire's personal blood source. He was not going to risk losing his investment after so little time. So please, keep your ideas to yourself. I don't need my brother getting unfounded thoughts upon his return."

"Which will be?" Viorica asks, directing his attention to her. The silent woman hasn't moved an inch from her spot, though Merrick stands so close to Bronx that she can brush her fingers to his hand. And then she does.

He crosses his arms. "I'm not sure."

"Call him and ask. He hasn't returned a single message I've left him." Viorica snaps her gaze from Bronx to the archway that leads to the hallway.

I spot Jameson, Mikkalo, and Everett standing nearby. I have no idea how long they've been there, but it takes a lot of effort not to react to them. They must sense my desire to run to them, because they all materialize around me and Bronx, which cages me in between their bodies. I don't know if it was instinctual or what, but my tight nerves relax, especially feeling Jameson's chest press into my back.

"I'm sorry, Viorica. Due to a breach in security, Zaire is off the grid. He'll not check in for another two days." Mikkalo tugs out his com device from his pocket and hands it to Viorica. "As you can see, he's gone out of the Donor Life

Corp territory."

Viorica tightens her jaw. "He did not discuss these matters with the board."

"He didn't want to raise any alarm. Zaire is plenty capable of ending any threats to our region." Mikkalo puts his com device away.

"I suppose you're right. But please, the next time he checks in, I want you to inform him that he's needed in Midnight Valley. It's mandatory. One week from today." Viorica turns to the other women. "Now, if you'll excuse us, we'll be on our way. My daughters and I still have time to make it home before dawn."

And like that, the three of them disappear.

Bronx releases a deep growl and slams his fist into the nearest wall. "She knows. She fucking knows."

I inhale a small breath at his words. "What?"

Mikkalo closes the space to Bronx and rests his hands on his shoulders, stopping him from taking out his rage on the building. "We don't know for sure."

"Even so, if she requires his presence, she'll find out." Jameson keeps his voice even, but his frown says everything.

"We're screwed," Bronx says. "We're going to lose it all. Then what? It's our influence and power that protect Gwen."

I close the space and wrap my arms around him. "That's not true. It's you." I turn to Jameson, Mikkalo, and

Everett and motion them closer. "And the three of you too." I attempt to hug my arms around all of them, smothering their heads in the process. "Plus, we're going to take care of the Barons tonight."

"Hell yeah, we are," Mikkalo says.

"And I don't care about power. All I care about is being together. The four of you and me. I'd be happy even in the shadows."

"Mmm, I can't ever get over how perfect you are," Everett whispers, bringing his lips to mine.

I smile. "Good. Because you're stuck with me."

"How we want," Jameson says.

"Now, someone get me out of this dress," I say, swirling my finger.

Bronx sweeps me off my feet, lifting me up before his brothers can even try. "Gladly. I'm in desperate need of a little more stress relief."

I giggle and pat his chest. "Then you better hurry."

Bronx turns to his brothers. "Get the car ready. Make sure the Vaduvas leave the city. We'll meet you in thirty. I'm going to give our girl whatever the hell she wants."

Nothing has ever sounded better.

3

AFTERMATH

THE SCENT OF VAMPIRE BLOOD fills the air, permeating from the open door of a brick house. Bronx tightens his hold on me, choosing to carry me against his chest to assure his arms never leave me. Mikkalo leads the way with Everett beside us and Jameson watching our backs.

Mikkalo stops at the front door and holds up his finger. "Do you hear that?"

I close my eyes, trying to hear what Mikkalo does. A soft whimper cuts through the air. I've never heard anything like it—maybe a hurt animal. Possibly a cat. It's not quite loud enough to distinguish.

"It's a child," Everett says, stepping forward. He swivels to look at me. "Doesn't sound hurt. Just in need of care."

My heart seizes, my breath quickening. What the actual fuck? "A k-kid?"

Mikkalo grabs Everett by the shoulder, stopping him from rushing inside. Everett flashes his fangs, fully ready to fight to enter the house. The two of them square off.

"You can't just charge in there, brother. It could be a trap," Mikkalo says, tugging his com device from his pocket. He taps into a nearby security feed and studies it for a minute. "All the feeds are down in the area. The last thing recorded was a Baron douche." He replays the same video that Corona showed Bronx earlier.

"Cortland." I can't stop his name from escaping my lips.

"You know his name, Gwen?" Bronx whispers, confirming that's why I say the name.

I bob my head. "He was the one who wanted your head." I swallow, my heart aching at the memory. "I'd never forget a horrible threat."

"That's great, dandelion. The more information we can gather, the better." He hugs me tighter.

"Maybe tell us sooner, next time." Jameson wraps his arms around both me and Bronx.

"We agreed to let her process at her own speed," Everett says, chiming in. "That night was awful. I don't know about you, but I don't like reminding our girl of our shortcomings when it comes to these assholes."

"That's enough," Bronx snaps. "Mikkalo, sweep the perimeter. Jameson, back me up. Everett, stay with Gwen. Gwen, protect Everett's ass. You're the better fighter."

I don't even get to touch my shoes to the ground as Bronx hands me over to Everett. Mikkalo disappears around the side of the house, and Jameson leads the way with Bronx right behind him. I feel utterly useless, just hugging Everett. I know my safety is my guys' number one priority, but whatever they can handle, I know I can handle too.

"Don't take it personally," Everett says. "Bronx knows what a badass you are, but he also knows that a room full of dead vampires might trigger your wild side."

I crinkle my nose. "So, this isn't about protecting me?"

He shakes his head. "Bronx would rather have you back him up."

"I can hear you," Jameson says, appearing in the doorway. "Not cool."

Bronx smacks Jameson on the back. "He's only speaking the truth, brother."

Holding his hand out, Bronx motions for Everett to put me down. I link my fingers through Bronx's and let him lead me inside the house. Everett slides past us, following behind Jameson as he guides him to the soft cry of the supposed child. I tug Bronx with me to follow behind them, but Bronx stops me.

"No, Gwen," Bronx says. "I need you to come with me upstairs."

I stop in my tracks, a dozen questions flitting through my mind. "It's bad, isn't it? How many?"

Bronx turns his gaze away from me like he doesn't want to see my reaction. "Nine vampires, at least."

"And humans?"

"None. That's why I need you. They're locked up on the second floor." He clenches his jaw, stopping himself from mirroring my frown.

"Before or after the attack?" I ask, staring at the streak of blood running up the pristine carpet. At the top of the landing lies the beheaded body of a male vampire. I try to remain expressionless. I know if I react, Bronx will relocate me outside in case. It's like he thinks I might lose my shit and start licking some stranger's blood off the floor. I mean, I'm a little hungry but not *that* hungry.

He rubs his lips together. "I don't know."

I groan. "Fuck."

He tugs me closer, hooking his fingers to my side. "Are you up to it? I think it'll be less traumatizing if you approach them than me. I'm not exactly—"

"A dandelion?" I say, interrupting him. "You're right.

You're definitely more of a big, hard-ass beast with a soft spot right here." I touch his chest. "Just keep your fangs in check and don't stand so straight, and we'll be fine."

He releases a soft chuckle and smiles. "You know I love you, right?"

His admission, while I'm aware of because he's admitted as much in front of me to his brothers, catches me a bit off guard. I freeze and turn to him, staring at his handsome face, totally devouring my reaction.

"I do now," I say, biting my lip. "And I love you too."

"Yeah?" he asks.

I nod and kiss him. "Yeah."

Bronx scoops me up, taking the stairs two at a time. He hops over the dead body and doesn't set me down until the floor is clear of blood. I stand with him in the middle of a hallway and peer around, trying not to look inside all the open doors. I can smell the potent, slightly rancid smell of a dead vampire coming from the door at the end on the left. If it weren't for the soft breathing coming from the room across from it, I might turn around and rush back down the stairs.

Bronx clasps my shoulders, pressing his chest into my back. "All you have to do is tell them that you're the head of the Daylight Donor Division of the Royale Coven and that you're here to relocate them to the nearest city until we can go over their contracts."

I stiffen and turn, forcing him to let me go. "Why can't we just let them go?"

His brows pinch together. "Go where exactly?"

I shrug. "I don't know. A place that'll make them exempt? I know what happens to people who lose their work contracts, Bronx. If the Barons did this because of me, I—"

Bronx leans in and cuts me off with a kiss. "Okay. We'll figure out how to get that done, even if we have to create our own exempt community."

"Really?" I smile in surprise. "You'd do that?"

"Might as well do something unheard of the last week we're in charge." His words wipe the smile right off my face, and he sighs, turning me back around. "Go on, Gwen. The faster we get them situated, the faster we can move on. The last thing I want is to get trapped in this damn town for the day, especially since the Barons seem to have ravaged the place."

I study his hard features for another moment and then twist around to face the mess the Barons left behind. Sucking in a deep breath, I steel my nerves and enter the room on the right. I stop in my tracks and cover my mouth, my stomach heaving. Nausea rolls through me, paralyzing my limbs. Gross things don't usually bother me, but something about seeing the five guys and one woman latching onto the torsos of two dismembered vampires grosses me the hell out.

My world spins, and I throw up blood in the hallway.

Everett materializes next to me, taking Bronx's place. He combs my hair up with his fingers and gently rubs his hand into my back. I clutch my knees, waiting for the rolling in my stomach to stop.

"Go relocate the body, Bronx. Quickly. They will have less time to react that way," Everett says. He squats down to look at me. "Just take a few breaths, Gwen."

"I don't know what's wrong with me," I say, closing my eyes and breathing through my nose. "I don't usually get grossed out."

He chuckles. "Well, you've also never seen something like...this."

I manage to stand upright, a weird-ass noise drawing my attention to the stairs. Jameson holds a little human on his hip, and I can't stop staring at how weird it is. I have never been around a child before except for my brothers growing up, and back then, it wasn't weird.

"I brought you some water, Gigi," Jameson says, holding up the glass in his free hand.

I twirl my finger at him. "Looks like you found a friend."

He chuckles. "Maybe we can keep him."

I raise my eyebrows. "And then do what?"

Shrugging, he says, "Feed him? I was thinking we could name him Jameson the Third." Jameson adjusts the little guy in his arms, flashing his fangs in a smile. "What do you think tiny human? Jameson Jr.?"

The kid's face scrunches a second before he wails, gushing big tears from his eyes. Jameson frowns and holds him away from him, dangling the kid out like he'll explode at any second. The sight is far more hilarious than it should be. Jameson looks totally offended that his charm didn't work on the little guy, though I'm pretty sure the baby doesn't understand a word Jameson says, or he does, and is freaked out.

Everett steals the kid away and whacks Jameson on the back. "Keep your fangs in check, brother. The Barons probably scared him." Carrying the kid closer, Everett holds him out to me. "Here, I want you to take him with you into the room. It might stop the people in there from attacking. I already hear them searching for weapons."

"Yeah, the disappearing corpse set them off a bit," Bronx says, strolling from the room on the left where the putrid smell wafts from. "And I no longer think our girl should approach them. I'll call the nearest city to send human security in the morning."

Everett links his fingers into his hair. "We shouldn't leave them here alone. With the child, I think things will be fine with Gwen."

"You expect a snotty, crying little dude to protect our girl?" Jameson asks. "Yet you flip your shit over any of us letting her get out of arm's reach? What the fuck, Ev?"

I raise my free hand, trying not to look at the child. It feels incredibly strange to hold another person. I'm used to being carried and not the other way around. "Chill out, Jamie. Everett's right. There's no way they'll attack me or whatever if I'm carrying a child. Humans are fiercely protective of kids."

Bronx sighs and motions toward the room. "I can already tell your mind is set, so go on. Hurry up. If you're wrong, we'll be here to back you up."

"And remember what Bronx said. Make it clear that you're here to help on behalf of the Royale Coven's Daylight Donor Division," Jameson reminds me. "Though, I hate the title on you."

I don't even know how to respond to his musing, so I don't.

Everett swipes his sleeve to my mouth, probably wiping off any remnants of the blood my body expelled in horror. He pats my cheek and nudges me to get my legs to start working on their own, even though I really don't want to do this.

It was always Ashton or Grayson who dealt with the people we rescued from terrible vampire households. They were much better at taking charge and handling those who were frightened.

Stopping outside the now closed door, I take a moment to listen to the people shuffling around inside. I raise my hand and knock a few times. "Hello? Please don't attack me. I have a child with me." Silence falls over the room, and I crack the door open and try to peer inside. "I'm unarmed and here to help you. The Royale Coven sent me. I'm head of the Daylight Donor Division. Are any of you injured?"

A guy clears his throat. "Y-yes."

I gently kick the door open, instinctively turning the kid away instead of holding him in front of me just in case they react violently. "I'm coming in."

"Gwen, use the baby as a shield," Bronx says, keeping his voice low.

I glower at him.

Jameson backhands his shoulder. "That might be our future kid you want Gwen to endanger." He releases a soft growl, narrowing his eyes.

Before the two of them go at it, I swing the door open all the way. And damn. Even though Bronx removed most of the dismembered vampire, he forgot an arm. What makes it worse is that a man clutches it, prepared to use it as a weapon.

"Please don't try to slap me with that thing," I say, adjusting the kid on my hip so that the small group of people can see him, but he's still safe enough on my side.

The man flares his nostrils, his eyes darting to the child. "Put my son down."

I tighten my jaw. "I will when you drop the arm.

You're going to scare him more."

The only woman in the room snatches the arm away from the glowering guy and proceeds to whack him with it. She then tosses it on the floor and rushes to me. I brace for her to collide into me or some shit, but all she does is hold her arms out.

"Thank you for saving my Timothy," the woman says. "I was so scared."

I hear Jameson grumble about the kid's name under his breath. His voice is too low for the woman to overhear, but I can't help glancing at the door. "You guys are safe now. The assholes who did this are gone."

The woman takes the child from me and snuggles him close, releasing a soft cry of relief. "It happened so fast. The Yorks couldn't even draw their weapons."

"So they were ambushed?" I ask, trying to think of the questions my guys would want to know. "How long ago?"

"Just after sunset. A man arrived at the door looking for shelter from the night. My partner, Clive, took pity on him and snuck him in through the back." The woman glances over her shoulder at the five silent guys huddled together. "I—I don't remember much of what happened after. We woke up locked in here. I thought they took Timothy. He was with his big sister..." Tears explode from the woman's eyes, and she starts sobbing. Turning, she looks at the guys again. "Oh, no, Clive. Daphne. She'd have tried to fight."

"Daphne?"

"Gwen," Everett whispers. "The child was alone."

"Did you see her...she just turned eighteen. Mr. York offered her a contract that would allow my husband and me to retire early." She sucks in a deep breath. "Daphne!" The woman's voice rips through the air, startling me.

"Tell her that she is not here, Gigi," Jameson whispers.

Bronx clears his throat. "Also tell her that finding her will be our priority."

I lick my lips and swallow, turning my attention back to the woman. "You are the only humans here. My...team didn't see any dead humans, either. All vampires. I think she might've been taken."

The woman gasps. "No."

Reaching out, I touch her shoulder. "But don't worry. We're going to find her. We'll get the monsters responsible for this."

The woman thrusts her arms around me, making Jameson, Everett, and Bronx all release quiet warning growls. I pat her back with one hand and wave the other to get them to chill out. I'm nearly certain the last thing on this woman's mind is hurting me.

"What's going to happen to us?" The question comes from one of the guys. The woman clutches me too tightly with the baby between us that I can't see who the voice belongs to.

"Well, I'll introduce you to my team, and we'll go from there." I glance at the doorway. "I have to warn you. They are vampires. The Royales."

The people gape at me. "The region's ruling coven is *here?*" another one of the men asks.

I nod. "Is that a problem?"

"No, of course not," the woman says. "Just surprising. Usually the Grey Coven would handle disputes or attacks."

"Oh, well, this is a personal matter." I don't know how else to respond. These people seem to be much more aware of vampire infrastructure, probably because they're not part of the general population. Either way, it's better to keep things short. "And if you're ready, I'd like to introduce you to my guys."

"Your guys?" the man, who I think is Clive, asks. He steps forward and puts his arm around the woman.

"My team," I say, trying not to react. No one responds to my comment, so I wave at the door. "Misters Royale, the humans are ready to meet you."

"Damn, Gigi. So formal," Jameson says, popping his head into the doorway.

A strange, guttural noise rips through the air, coming from one of the silent guys. I don't have a chance to respond as the people yell and rush toward us, fully set on attacking.

Jameson shoves me out of the way. "Gwen, watch out!"

The six people tackle him.

4

ATTACK

"SHIT, BITING IS NOT FUN unless it's our girl," Jameson says, shoving Clive so hard that he flies across the room.

I rush and pick up Timothy from the floor as he wails his head off. Bronx and Everett enter the room, yanking off the remaining people. Jameson jumps to his feet and closes the distance to me. I gape at the deep bite mark bleeding on his throat.

I inhale a sharp breath and hand him Timothy. The humans launch back to their feet and rush my guys again.

"What the hell?"

The woman manages to close the space to Everett, sneaking behind him to jump on his back while he attempts to keep the men away without hurting them. The second she sinks her teeth into his shoulder, something inside me snaps. Shadows crowd my vision, and I charge at her. Linking my fingers to the back of her shirt, I haul her off with my dhampir strength and throw her into the wall.

"They've been manipulated to attack us," Bronx says, punching Clive in the face.

"What do we do?" I ask, intercepting one of the other guys before he can sneak up on Bronx. I jump up and hook my arm around the man's throat, pulling him back. He doesn't attempt to fight me but tries to break away to continue his mission to bite Bronx.

So I kick him hard between the legs.

The guy howls. He drops to the ground, falling onto his side. He remains in his spot and clutches his most definitely injured cock. I realize the woman curls in on herself, pressing her back into the wall, covering her face. She doesn't continue to fight like the four yelling guys.

Everett grabs a guy and shoves him into the wall, hoisting him off his feet. "Stop fighting," he commands, attempting to lock him in a gaze.

I jog up to him, intercepting Clive's attack by ramming into him. He skids across the floor and hits the wall, but it wasn't hard enough to keep him down. He stumbles back to his feet and throws himself at Everett again.

"They consumed blood," Bronx says as Everett drops the guy to the floor when his mind manipulation doesn't work.

Everett elbows Clive in the jaw. "We're going to have to knock them out."

"Gigi, get over here," Jameson calls. "You could get hurt. My brothers can handle it."

"They weren't manipulated to attack me. I can help," I argue, grabbing another guy by the back of his shirt. Spinning him around, I knee him in the gut, and he drops to the ground. It takes a kick to his groin to keep him there.

"Damn," Jameson says. "Ouch."

The guy blinks a few times, his face softening as he catches his breath. "Don't hurt me. Please, I don't know what's wrong."

"I never thought I'd encourage such behavior, but Gigi, I think you're on to something," Jameson says. "Hey, brothers. Aim for the nads. The severe pain breaks the manipulation."

Both Everett and Bronx look at each other like the last thing they want to do is kick someone—especially someone technically innocent—in the groin. Me, on the other hand? Desperate times.

I strut forward. "Grab them."

Bronx locks his arms around Clive, holding him in place. He turns his head, totally squeezing his eyes shut. "Sorry, man," he mutters under his breath.

I swing my leg and kick him right in the junk, making him holler. Like the others, he drops to the ground and stops fighting. "So you can sever someone's head but not kick them in the balls?" I ask.

"Yeah, pretty much," Bronx says, grabbing onto the last guy.

I narrow my eyes at him and turn to Everett, letting Bronx restrain the bucking guy. Bronx releases an annoyed growl at me, and all I do is smirk. I can't help it. Messing with him is the only thing stopping me from thinking about what the hell I'm doing. These poor people never deserved to be treated like this. But it's better to cause them some discomfort than having them stuck in the mind prison of sadistic assholes determined to fuck up my life.

"Close your eyes, Everett," I say, shaking out my hands at my side.

Everett raises his brow at me but does what I say. I swiftly kick the man hard enough to break the mind manipulation. Everett lets him fall to the floor and comes to my side. Bronx grumbles at me, and I finally turn my attention back to him with the remaining guy.

I close the space. "Just a few seconds longer. I love seeing your muscles put to work."

"Damn it, dandelion," Bronx snaps.

Rolling my shoulders, I step closer. Bronx braces the guy and closes his eyes. I kick up with all my strength.

"Gwen!"

Something crashes into me, and I accidentally kick too far forward, kicking both the man and Bronx. Bronx yells out and reflexively thrusts the guy at me to cup his junk. I hit the floor as the man falls on top of me. Jameson growls and hoists the guy off. Everett grips Clive as he continues to thrash, trying to attack.

"Ah, hell," I say. "It didn't work on him."

"Same with this asshole," Jameson says, locking the man in a headlock.

After a minute, the guy passes out. Everett knocks out Clive at the same time, and Bronx manages to compose himself to help tie them up. I guess it couldn't be as easy as I hoped. If it were, more people could break from mind manipulation.

"I thought you were done being a pain in my damn balls," Bronx says, resting his arm on my shoulder.

I shift and frown at him. "Want me to kiss them and make them feel better?"

My words shock the hell out of him, and a few indecipherable expressions cross his face. Jameson groans from his spot, clearly not as amused as I am at my teasing of Bronx. Everett takes a few minutes to examine the four people I managed to break out of the mind manipulation.

The woman cradles Timothy in her arms. "Please don't perform their final donations. Clive would never purposely hurt a vampire."

Bronx looks from me to the woman. "We understand the problem. Unfortunately, we're going to have to keep them restrained until the vampire blood leaves their systems. We'll do our best to ensure their safety."

Mikkalo materializes in the doorway, startling the woman. She releases a yelp and twists to hide Timothy. Mikkalo ignores her reaction and strides into the room and peers around, assessing the situation. He comes to my side and touches my cheek, like he just needs a second to make sure I'm okay.

"What's up? You're supposed to be on watch," Bronx says gruffly.

Mikkalo turns his head, cracking his neck. "We gotta go. I got something on the feed just outside of town."

"Is it the Barons?" I ask.

Mikkalo shakes his head. "No, it's one of your brothers."

Jameson hits the throttle, picking up speed in the car. I grip Bronx's hand, kind of regretting that I pushed to get him to allow Jameson to drive. The guys teased that I drove like him, but he's far more daring, pushing the car to its limits. And I don't know. Something is different about being a passenger with a crazy driver than being the crazy driver.

"I bet you wished you'd have listened to me and stayed back with the humans," Bronx says, wiggling his fingers in my death hold. "Mikkalo and Everett would've protected you just fine."

I dig my fingers into Everett's leg. "No, I don't. I know they would have, but the last thing I want is to be separated. I can't protect you all otherwise. I was worried about you and Jameson."

Jameson flicks his gaze to me in the mirror. "Don't worry, Gwen. We're almost there."

"Then slow your ass down," I snap, my voice rising. I don't mean to yell, but we drive awfully close to a block wall. It freaks me out.

"And waste my one opportunity to drive Bronx in our eternity? No fucking way." He flashes his fangs at me in a smile.

Bronx pulls me onto his lap and brushes his lips to mine. "I don't want to waste my first opportunity to distract you either."

His words make me smirk while Jameson sighs. I sink more into Bronx feeling the goodness of his arms around me, restraining me despite Everett wanting to seatbelt me in. Mikkalo had made a good point about needing to quickly escape the vehicle, which trumped Everett's fear of a car crash. So with the threat of the defanging of his brothers if something happened to me, Everett gave in and agreed that Bronx would be my seatbelt with Everett as my backup.

"Then try harder," I say, nipping his lip.

He kisses me deeper, shifting me so that I straddle his lap. Everett scoots closer and rests his hand on my lower back, like my position freaks him out just a bit.

"Damn," Mikkalo says from the front seat, speaking up for the first time. He's been consumed in watching all the nearby feeds on his com device, though I know he's kept some of his attention on me.

"Damn is right," Jameson says. "You're lucky we're not on autopilot or I'd climb back there."

I laugh against Bronx's mouth. "I don't think so, Jamie. I'm going to assure this won't be the last time you get to drive."

"Make it worth it to Bronx, so I can drive next," Mikkalo says.

"I can get on board for that," Everett says, sliding his hand to my ass.

I rock a bit, feeling Bronx's body react to my closeness. He hums under his breath and breaks from my mouth to kiss my throat, totally taking advantage of our current position and his brothers' ridiculous encouragement.

Bronx hooks his fingers to my hips and sucks my earlobe into his mouth. He whispers, "It might take a little more than this to convince me."

Leaning back, I meet his playful smirk. "Be careful about what you suggest."

"If you guys start boning, I'm going to remember that for my night and insist we go on a road trip," Jameson says.

I tip my head back and laugh. "Nu-uh. The last time we got naked in a car..." Shaking my head, I push the thought away. "No car sex. With any of you."

Bronx continues to kiss my neck, rocking me against him. "I bet I could change your mind."

I groan and slide off him, getting Everett to scoot back over. "Most definitely, which is why no more distracting. I'm not risking such a rude interruption or getting caught naked."

Everett touches my leg and leans in to whisper, "Impossible in that dress."

I shiver under his soft breath. "Everett."

"What the hell did you say to our girl?" Jameson asks.

Everett chuckles without responding. "Can't give all our secrets away."

"Definitely not," I say, grinning.

Shifting in the seat, I sprawl my legs across Everett's lap and nestle into the crook of Bronx's arm. Tilting my head up, I kiss him softly again. I can't help it. Bronx links his fingers through mine and snuggles me, showing me the attention I need. He's far more relaxed than usual, and I gobble up his attention.

Jameson releases a growl, drawing my attention from Bronx. Stomping the brake, Jameson sends the car screeching to a halt. He and Mikkalo exit the car, slamming their doors. I sit up straighter to peer out the windshield.

"Shit," Bronx says, lowering his voice. "More humans."

The second Bronx says the words, I spot a man stumbling onto the road. Another follows behind him, walking weird as hell, like his legs work against his mind. A dozen more humans push and fight to exit a house half the size of the York Coven's. Jameson materializes in the road and releases a whistle. He waves his hands toward us, and Everett slides his arm through mine and tugs me from Bronx.

Bronx swings his door open. "Looks like the fucking Barons mind manipulated every damn human in this town."

"There are more people coming from the other houses," Everett says, stretching his arm to point past me. "Might be too many to handle."

Bronx hops from the car. "We just need to clear the road. Gwen, we'll lead them away. You drive."

I nod and let him pull me to my feet only to slide behind the wheel. "Be quick. I don't like this."

Bronx leans in and kisses me. "Everett, stay here with Gwen."

"Was already planning on it," he quips, joining me in

the front.

Everett taps the navigation screen, brightening the headlights. The humans moving toward us squint but don't stop. Bronx shuts my door and closes the space to them. Mikkalo and Jameson help him surround the people and then they split up, jogging at a human pace. I ease my foot down on the throttle. My palms sweat against the steering wheel, and I maneuver the car to go around the crowd.

"Gwen, just floor it," Jameson calls.

Sucking in a breath, I stomp the throttle, jolting the car forward. I clench my teeth, my nerves bunching in my stomach.

A man lurches away from the crowd, turning his attention to me. Another guy yells incoherently and pushes him into the street. I attempt to jerk the wheel to avoid him, but another man falls into the road. Everett taps the navigation screen, turning on the autopilot instead of relying on me to hit the brakes.

The car slows to a stop, and a man slams his hands on the hood. Everett jumps from the car. Bronx, Mikkalo, and Jameson all yell at him not to leave me. Everett growls and tugs the man off, throwing him a few feet to the side.

"Gwen, turn off the autopilot and ease forward," Everett says, staying close enough to the car to hop back in.

I do as he says and glide the car forward. He pushes men out of the way as I continue driving. I flick my gaze to the area around us and spot my guys keeping most of the humans occupied in their mind manipulated haze of rage that has them attempting to attack.

"They're triggered by me," Everett says, growling and pushing the men back. "I need to put some space between us."

"The hell you will!" Bronx shouts.

A man scrambles onto the hood of the car to climb over it to try to attack Everett.

He falls off, and Everett rushes in front of the car and drags him out of the way. The guy flails and manages to sink his teeth into Everett's arm.

"Just ten feet," Everett says, disobeying Bronx's command.

Bronx growls. "Gwen, floor it as soon as it's clear. We'll catch up."

I grip the steering wheel, my knuckles turning white. "Got it."

Everett puts distance between him and the car, sneaking around to the trunk to stop what feels like hundreds of guys from blocking my way.

I haven't seen a single woman since we left the lady at the York's. It freaks me out just a bit. The Barons are psycho assholes, and I wouldn't put it past them from taking the women to keep for themselves.

They're unregistered, so they obviously don't care

about Donor Life Corp's laws.

"Gwen, get ready," Mikkalo says, dodging the swelling crowd.

I inhale a breath.

"Go!" all four of them shout in unison.

I stomp the throttle, jolting the car forward. A blip of fear rushes through me, and I try not to glance at the mind manipulated men.

If one of them gets in my way, I can't stop. I won't stop. I have a terrible feeling now that two dozen feet stretch between me and my guys.

Flicking my gaze to the rearview mirror, I check on my guys to make sure they're following me.

"Gwen!" Everett yells. "Stop!"

I snap my attention back to the road in front of me. Shock washes over me at the familiar guy stumbling into the street to block my way.

Slamming the brakes, I burn rubber to stop. A cloud of smoke wafts through the air and hazes my surroundings.

Something crashes on the hood of the car, and I jump.

My door flies open, and Bronx tries to grab me, but I don't let go of the wheel. I can't take my eyes off the hooded figure in front of me.

"Come on, dandelion. We'll take care of him," Bronx says, trying his best to coax me from the driver's seat. "We have to go."

Mikkalo and Jameson materialize in front of the car, preparing to fight my brother.

Silas jerks his bowed head up, meeting my gaze.

He flashes his fangs.

5

BROTHERLY BETRAYAL

"HEY, LITTLE SIS—"

The sound of my brother's deep voice triggers a wave of darkness to collide through me. Without thinking, I floor the throttle and send the car barreling forward. My action catches Silas by surprise, and he hits the hood and smashes into the window. The force fissures the glass, and I slam the brakes again, sending him crashing off and under the vehicle with a couple of thumps as I run him over.

Mikkalo and Jameson stand in shock, the car a mere

foot from the both of them. I heave a few deep breaths, my nerves shattered. I can't believe my eyes. I can't believe that Silas was transformed into a vampire.

Thrusting the door open, I hop out. Bronx gathers me into his arms, not letting me get far. I thrash and yell, punching his shoulder in an attempt to make him put me down. I've never been so annoyed to have been swept off my feet in my life.

"Silas! You asshole!" I screech, my voice cutting through the air. "I'm going to kill you!"

Bronx releases a growl into my hair. "Calm the hell down, Gwen."

"Then put me down!"

He heaves a breath as I elbow him in the clavicle. "Fucking fine."

I don't get the chance to brace myself. Bronx drops me, releasing another guttural noise from his throat. My knees hit the hard ground, and I curse. Everett materializes next to me, but instead of helping me up, he swings his arm and punches Bronx in the stomach, knocking him back a couple of feet.

"Gigi, shit," Jameson says, trying to approach me next.

I snap my head up and look at him. He raises his hands, freezing in place. Something in my eyes causes his hesitation, but I take advantage of it and crawl toward the car. Lying on my stomach, I search beneath the vehicle for

Silas, fully set on kicking his ass.

Two hands lock to my sides, hoisting me off my feet. Mikkalo tosses me onto his shoulder, and I swing my arm down and slap his ass. He flips me into his arms and raises his eyebrow at me.

"Where is he?" I ask, narrowing my eyes.

Mikkalo doesn't answer me right away. Instead, he strides to the car and slides into the backseat with me on his lap. His brothers follow suit, and Bronx plops into the driver's seat, barely giving Jameson a moment to hop in back with us. Everett swivels in the front seat and looks at me, giving me a long once-over as he tries to assess my body to make sure I'm uninjured from my fall.

Bronx floors it, managing to swerve around the few guys who caught up with us. He glowers at me in the rearview mirror, looking like he wants to chew me out. I meet his heated gaze with my own.

"Gwen." Jameson breaks the heavy silence first. "Are you okay?"

I scrub my hands over my face, finally breaking Bronx's glare. "What the hell? What the—ohmyfuck. My brother is a vampire." The realization sinks deep into me, twisting my insides. I bow forward and hang my head between my legs. "I don't understand."

Mikkalo kneads his fingers into my back. "The Barons are going to try to use your family against you, Gwen."

"This is so screwed up. They threaten and pretend to kill my brothers but then they go and transition Silas? What's the point?" I groan, trying to wrap my mind around it.

"Maybe to convince you to leave us. You don't know the Barons but you know your brothers. It's actually rather strategic," Jameson says, twining his fingers through mine.

Everett rotates in the seat to face me completely. "But I doubt they expected you to react by plowing into him."

Mikkalo wraps his arms around me, pulling me close. "Which, fuck. I'm sorry you felt you had to, but I'm proud as hell. Our badass."

"He betrayed me," I murmur, replaying my actions in my mind. I never in a million years thought that I could hurt my brother, but he killed our mortal bond the second he joined the Barons. I wonder if this is what Bronx feels like with Brooklyn. "So did Grayson. We should just give up on the rest of my brothers. What's the point? They're obviously going to pick each other over me."

Grief sweeps through me at the realization, and I squeeze my eyes shut. I'm not going to cry. I can't. Not for them. They sure as shit wouldn't cry for me. Not now at least.

Jameson hugs his arms around both me and Mikkalo, squishing me between them in a way that helps me keep it together. "I'm sorry, Gwen. I know how much you care about them."

Bronx clears his throat. "And we're still going to go after them."

I turn my attention to him. "No. It's fine, really. We have too much other shit to worry about." And in all honesty, I'm not sure I can even face them.

I hadn't known it at the time, but our familial bond died with Dad. Rochester assured it, and Laredo? I don't even know. All my memories of him are a jumbled mess. I know he manipulated my mind. I know he pretended to be working for the elders. But what I still can't figure out is why. His brothers seemed pretty pissed that he kind of stole me away.

"Gwen, for our sake, it's better if the Barons don't get their hands on the rest of your family," Bronx responds, tightening his jaw. "Or anyone else for that matter. Your brothers need to be with us, even if we have to lock them up."

I rest my head on Mikkalo. "Because of the dhampir gene."

He doesn't even have to agree for me to know that's the reason. I never thought about the extent of it until recently. All those times my brothers claimed to have sex? What the hell? Why risk it? I never thought about the consequences of their actions until now. Some poor, unsuspecting woman could end up like my mom. Except at least she knew what she was getting into. At least I think.

"This is so messed up," I murmur, trying to suppress my thoughts of the bunker and my brothers. "You don't think..." I can't even finish my thought.

"If your brothers passed on the dhampir mutation, I'm sure the Barons would know about it. They seem far too concerned with you that I highly doubt it. Not to mention the likelihood of actually having a symptomatic female...we'd have heard about dhampirs if it was easy." It's like Everett knew what was on my mind. But it's not the first time we've discussed the possibility. Still, it's better not to leave it to chance.

"One of the assholes did mention he didn't want to have to wait a few more decades for the occurrence." I absently link and unlink my fingers with Jameson's.

"Well the fucker's going to have to," Jameson mutters.

Bronx turns on the car's autopilot. "So why transform Silas?" His question digs into me. "Why lessen the possibility of more dhampirs by assuring a carrier can't pass on the mutation?"

"Gwen still has four brothers," Mikkalo says. "Either that or they're confident that they're going to get our girl."

I groan. "Never going to happen."

"Damn straight," Bronx says.

Reaching out, I clasp his shoulder. He rests his hand on top of mine, searching my face for a moment. I relent to his pleading eyes and ease between the seats to climb into his lap. He gladly accepts me, sliding back the seat a bit to make space.

I rest my head on his shoulder. "Thanks for not being pissed off that I fought you."

He snuggles me close. "Oh, I am, dandelion. You're in so much trouble."

I scrunch my nose. "If I'm in trouble, you're definitely in trouble."

"Is that so?" He lowers his voice, totally getting turned on at any sort of punishment I come up with. "The good or bad kind?"

I take his bait. "Depends. Which one will it be for me?"

Jameson releases a purr from his throat, sticking his head between the seats. He brushes my hair off my shoulder, using his nose, and kisses my skin. I tip my head back so he can reach my throat too. "Definitely the good kind. And by me. My time's coming in an hour. Any freaky thing Bronx wants to participate in will have to wait."

"Or he could join us," I tease, full-on giggling at the thought.

"Careful, dandelion. I lost half my night to this bullshit. I might take you up on the offer," Bronx murmurs, kissing the other side of my throat. He shifts me on his lap, rubbing my body to his boner.

I shiver at his words. "Bronx."

"I'm only teasing, but I can tell you like the idea." He whispers the words in my ear, kissing my earlobe. "Maybe we can discuss it sometime. When we return to Crimson Vista."

I shift to meet his gaze. "What do you mean when?"

"The sun will rise before we return. The windshield has been compromised, and it's probably not a good idea to try to brave the way back. The daytime gives too many people an advantage," Mikkalo says, drawing my attention to him.

I blush, realizing that even though Bronx whispered the suggestion, he still didn't whisper it quiet enough to keep between us. That, or he let his brothers hear on purpose, testing all their reactions. Or mine.

Shifting on Bronx's lap, I look at Mikkalo. "So where will we be staying?"

Everett taps his finger to my leg and motions to the windshield. "Here."

I gape at the road ahead of us that ends right before the stretch of ocean. I've never been so close to such an endless body of water that I can't take my eyes off the gradient of colors from the gray of the night darkened water to the purpling of the sky.

"Whoa." I lean forward as if the few inches could give me a better view. "Who lives here?"

At the end of the road and before the ocean towers a building a few stories tall. It's the only one around that I can see. Dozens of balconies extend from tinted-glass doors. I stare at the glass like I could see through to who's inside, but it's pointless. I think curtains cover the doors for additional privacy and protection.

"Technically us," Everett says. "We have properties all over our region. This one is a bit too far from Crimson Vista, so Zaire always treated it as a getaway spot. It is cared for by the Crescent Coven, allies of ours from before the divisions. They run a nearby city."

Bronx turns off the autopilot, hooking his hands to the steering wheel while caging me in. I rest my head on his chest, listening to the silence that falls through the car apart from our soft breathing and hearts beating.

Five figures materialize outside a set of glass double doors as Bronx drives the car under the covered drive. None of them approach us, standing tall and expressionless, just watching us. I squirm a bit, my nerves getting the best of me. I don't think I'll ever get used to meeting new vampires.

"Relax, Gwen. Try not to punch out any hearts while we're here. The Crescent Coven might be the most tolerable out of all of our city heads." Bronx swings the door open and takes me with him.

Everett, Jameson, and Mikkalo take their positions around us, caging me in as a way to protect me. Silence fills the air apart from a strange noise that sounds almost like a hum. I've never heard anything like it.

"What is that noise?" I ask my guys, stretching to peer around from Bronx's arms.

"Lovely, isn't it?" A soft, almost melodic voice draws my attention to the five guys waiting for us to close the space. "I've always found the ocean soothing. It's a shame Donor Life Corp doesn't allow us to enjoy it."

"Huh?" I ask, nearly forgetting that I should most definitely not be engaging in a conversation with a strange vampire.

"Now where did you find this gorgeous little thing, Bronx? She looks delicious." A man with neatly styled brown hair, expressive brows, and a boxy jaw with a few days growth of stubble steps forward to greet us.

"Smells delicious, too." Another guy—a fiery auburn-haired vampire with blue eyes and light freckles across his nose—steps forward, flaring his nostrils. I can't stop my eyes from gawking at him. I've never seen freckles on a vampire.

"The best I've ever tasted." Bronx's words shock the hell out of me, and I bat his shoulder, twisting my mouth. He chuckles and plants his lips to mine, cutting off my complaints. "But don't tell Zaire. He'd have my head."

Okay. What. The. Fuck.

"And I'm about to kick you in your balls for not preparing me for this weird-ass introduction," I say, wiggling in Bronx's arms. "Now put me down."

The man howls a laugh. "No wonder you like her."

Bronx relents and sets me down, and the first man whacks him on the back, sliding his arm around his shoulders. The two of them start walking, not even acknowledging me or anyone else for that matter, and I turn and look to Everett, Jameson, and Mikkalo.

"Later," Jameson mouths to me.

"So let me guess. The five of you need a place to stay for the day?" The man strolls with Bronx and pushes open the door. The other guys quietly follow behind him, and we finish the line with me safely tucked inside a muscular circle.

Bronx nods. "You bet your ass I wish we didn't, Ronan. There was an attack on Twilight Peak. Both the Grey and York Covens were massacred. Many others."

Ronan stiffens. "Another region?"

"Unregistered," Bronx responds. "The place was a mess, but they left the donors unharmed."

"They must plan to return then." Ronan glances at his coven mates. "Do you need any help?"

"A daylight security detail could be beneficial. I'll give you first priority on transfers." Bronx keeps his voice even without looking at me.

Ronan shifts on his feet. "Nash, get on it."

"Yes, brother." The auburn-haired guy disappears without a second glance in our direction.

"Dodson, Conrad, and Malabar, why don't you meet

us in the dining hall while I show the Royales to their rooms." Ronan looks at Bronx. "I'm assuming the donor will require her own suite?"

"Not a chance," Jameson says, speaking up. "Don't think we forgot what happened the last time we stayed. If anything happens to Zaire's Blood Match, he'll cast our asses to the shadows."

Ronan smiles, showing his fangs. He darts his attention to me and back to Jameson. "Perhaps I could offer you a place in my coven."

"Ugh." I can't stop my rebellious mouth from making the sound.

"What, gorgeous? Worried about losing all the attention? I'd let you come too." Ronan licks his lips. "Been a while since we've had any good entertainment."

My guys don't even get the chance to growl as I shove past them.

I slap Ronan across the face, sending his head jerking sideways.

It's me who roars.

6

THE CRESCENT COVEN

"YOU DO REALIZE THAT I'M going to kick your ass if you ever fail to suppress your bullshit adventures." I stare at myself in the mirror, using a damp cloth to wipe the blood from my lips.

Laredo hooks his fingers to my hips and rests his chin on my shoulder, pressing into me. I don't react to the hard-ness of his excited body, turned on because I just finished sucking the deep bite I left on his shoulder.

"You say that every time, yet here you are, enjoying

what I have to offer you." Laredo eases back and spins me around. Lifting me up, he sets me on the sink and slides between my legs. "You know, you're not going to be able to resist me forever."

I bow forward and glide my tongue over his shoulder. "Wanna bet?"

"Mmmhmm. If you see the alternative to the life I've presented you—"

I press my index finger to his lips. "But I never will."

"As long as you're a good little dhampir."

"Oh, you mean if you're a good little vampire," I tease, giving him a shove back to get to my feet. "You know what will happen if you're not."

He smirks at me. "We'd have to sustain each other."

I roll my eyes. "You act like you're the only one who can satisfy my...needs. I bet I could saunter into any shadow and find your replacement before you could even blink."

He play-growls at me. "You'd never."

"I guess we'll see."

Something crashes outside the bathroom door, and Laredo stiffens. He sneaks his hand into my jacket and tugs out my silver stake. Fear buzzes through me, standing my arm hairs on end. I shuffle as quietly as I can to the tub and step into it, pulling the curtain across to hide.

"Little brother, I know you're here." I tense at the sharp tone of a man's voice erupting through the door. "I caught one of the Gallagher boys sneaking into the grove. He confirmed you have the Baron intended."

Laredo tightens his jaw and flicks his gaze to mine, looking at me through the crack in the curtain. "Get ready to run," he mouths without a sound.

I swallow, my nerves tightening my chest.

Turning the doorknob, Laredo flings the door open and charges out. Glass shatters, probably the coffee table, and a few growls sound out. Hustling from the bathroom, I dart into the living room without looking. Laredo lies beneath a guy with long, light brown hair. He pins him, the stake a few feet away.

"I should kill you for treason," the guy snaps.

"Come on, Thaxton. You know I haven't committed treason. The contract was never signed. You can thank Rochester for that fuck up." Laredo jerks his hand up and locks his fingers around Thaxton's throat.

Thaxton growls and punches him, sending blood spraying from Laredo's mouth. "A verbal agreement is good enough. Now, where is Gwen? I don't want to scare her."

Anger rushes through me seeing my blood source bleeding. It takes everything in me not to rush the asshole and jump on his back.

"She's in her room," Laredo says. "Asleep."

Thaxton hops to his feet, letting Laredo up. The two of them fix their clothes, assessing each other. The front door *to our small house flies open, and I freeze at the sight of Grayson and Porter.*

Thaxton's too slow to react, and Grayson pulls his gun out and shoots the vampire. I run toward the glass slider and manage to escape unnoticed. More gunfire bursts through the air, but I don't stop. I can't.

"I got you, my dhampir," Laredo says, scooping me off my feet to sling me onto his shoulder. "No one is taking you today."

"Laredo, my brothers."

He heaves a breath. "I guess we'll see how good they really are. Sorry Gwen, only you're important to me."

"No!"

My hand hits something solid, sending pain swelling through my fingers. I groan and curl in on myself, cradling my fist. Cool arms wrap around me, and I breathe in Jameson's familiar scent. Everything comes back to me in a wave of panic. I try to sit up, but Jameson rolls me over to face him, bringing my hand to his lips to kiss.

"You're okay, Gigi. You were having a nightmare." Leaning in, he combs my hair from my face and meets me for a sweet kiss. "Are you hungry? Can I feed you?"

My stomach growls at his words. He pulls me closer until my lips caress his sweet skin. I let him settle between my legs and moan at his major morning wood pressing against me through our underwear. I don't remember what happened, but right now, feeling Jameson's arms around me feels more important than thinking about the shit show of my life.

Reaching between us, I slip my hand into his boxers and lace my warm fingers around his hard-on. He moans and nips me with his fangs pricking me just enough to get a taste of my blood. I sink my teeth into his shoulder, my body humming with lust and need, and I can't stop myself from rolling on top of him.

I shift my panties out of the way and guide him to enter me. And fuck, does it feel good. I roll my body, still sucking his shoulder, and ride him so hard that he stretches up to press the headboard to the wall so it doesn't bang against it.

I ease my lips away and straighten my back, resting my hands slightly behind me on his legs. He sits up a bit to pull my shirt off and grazes his fingers across my naked breasts, his eyes flashing silver as he watches me bounce on him, moaning and panting every time I sink down.

Neither of us says anything, just watching each other. His breathing matches mine, and he curls up and glides his tongue across each of my breasts. He nips my skin, drawing a pinprick of blood to tease him again. Hunger flashes in his eyes. I can tell he wants more of me, all of me.

"It's okay to bite me," I whisper, my voice coming out low and sultry, the idea of him doing so in this moment turning me on even more.

He glides his tongue over his lips, drinking me in for a moment. "Are you sure?"

I brush my hair from my shoulder and nod. "Here, sit up."

Jameson does what I say, resting his back on the headboard. I continue to rock my body to his, resting my hands on each side of his head against the wall for better leverage. He kisses me softly, letting me taste the sweetness of his mouth for a bit longer. Breaking away from my mouth, he trails his lips down my throat while sliding his hands to my ass to pull me harder to him over and over again.

His fangs graze over my skin, sending tingles through me. "Take a breath, Gwen."

I inhale a small breath, the pressure of his bite fading as quickly as it came. He sucks on my shoulder, the feeling of his tongue leaving tingles blossoming across my skin. Shifting one of his hands, he draws it between us to rub my clit to increase the pleasure cascading through me. I moan against his shoulder, picking up speed, my body now dying to find release from the hot intensity of our passionate lovemaking.

He works me over for a few minutes longer with his fingers. I pant so hard, my body wanting to explode until it finally does. He moans as I climax, feeling my muscles clench. I muffle my loud mouth, sinking my teeth into his shoulder again.

Pushing me back on the bed, he grabs my legs and flips them over my head. He rips my panties off completely and lays on top, thrusting so hard and deep that I can't stop my voice from yelling out in pleasure. Jameson releases a throaty noise as he cums, his face scrunching with his own ecstasy.

Slowing down, he spreads my legs to nestle between them and holds up his weight with his arms. He kisses me again, sliding his tongue into my mouth like he can't get enough of me. I savor the weight of him, the feeling of his desire still radiating from him.

"I've missed you," he whispers into my hair, only pulling back from my mouth to gaze into my eyes.

I smile at him. "I've missed you too. You always make my nights so perfect."

"You think I'm the reason for the perfect start of our day? No. That's all you. I mean, so insatiable. I love everything about it. You didn't even waste time to undress." He kisses me again.

I giggle and slide my hands to his ass, squeezing it. His boxers remain halfway down his hips. "I couldn't help myself."

"Good. Maybe you won't be able to help yourself again."

He flexes his erection between my legs, and I moan and

pull him to me by his hips. Voices trickle over the subtle music humming in through the door, drawing my attention away from Jameson. He gently pinches my chin, turning my face to look back at him, kissing me so that I can't focus on anything else.

"Let's relocate to the bathroom," he murmurs into my mouth. "It'll buy us at least thirty more minutes."

I grin and nod my head. "Hurry, they're getting closer."

Jameson eases away and holds his arms open for me. I jump from the bed, letting him catch me, and he kisses the laughter from my mouth, strolling with me to the bathroom. He kicks the door closed at the soft knock and covers my mouth with his hand, making me laugh harder at his determination.

With one hand, he flicks the water on, closing us in the opaque glass shower. Steam fills the air, and he presses my back to the cold wall. I screech in surprise, the tile like ice on my hot skin.

I land on my feet in the stream of hot water, sighing at how incredible it feels cascading over the two of us.

Jameson drops to his knees and attempts to lift one of my legs on his shoulder. My hands slip on his wet skin, and we both laugh. Without somewhere to sit, there's no way my body's going to cooperate through standing. I pull him back to his feet instead and cut off his soft plea to let him try anyway with my index finger.

I drag down his bottom lip and trace my finger over his chest and along the line of his bone-hard abs until I get to my knees and smile up at him. I lick my lips, and he inhales a soft breath with silver flashing eyes.

"Can I find out if you taste as good as your blood?" I ask, stroking my fingers over the length of his cock.

"Gwen," he says, releasing a soft moan.

I smile again and lick the underside of his shaft, working my way to his tip. He gently cups my head in his hands when I suck him into my mouth, moaning with pleasure. I enjoy the hell out of his reaction and peek up to catch him staring at me. He looks so sexy with his damp hair sticking up all over the place and the shower steam glistening on his chest.

I hum under my breath, digging my fingers into his hips as I find the motion that gets the most noise out of him. He combs my wet hair with one hand, holding onto my shoulder with the other. I suck a bit harder, bobbing my head, and slide my fingers from his hip to massage over his balls.

"Gwen..."

I love the way he says my name with such desperation. He moans again, shifting on his feet.

"I'm going to cum," he whispers, releasing a soft, husky breath.

Anticipation courses through me. I've never tasted him like this before, and a part of me is a little nervous. What if—

A sweet, fruity flavor floods my mouth, and I automatically swallow. Jameson draws his finger along my cheek, getting me to look at him. Lust darkens his gorgeous green eyes, and I purposely lick my lips and hum softly under my breath.

"Was that okay?" he asks me, helping me to my feet. He engulfs me in a hug, snuggling me close.

"It was as sweet as your blood," I say. "Unexpected."

"And you're mouthwatering," he murmurs, touching me between the legs.

"If you keep talking to me like this, we're never leaving this shower." I graze my teeth to his throat. "You're going to beg me for a break."

He chuckles. "I highly doubt that. I'm sure to keep begging you for more."

"Is that so?"

A soft tap on the door interrupts our flirtation, and Jameson glares at the opaque glass. Light from the bedroom shines into the bathroom, and Jameson scoops me off my feet and spins me away. I hook my legs around him with a laugh, knowing that he wants nothing more than to ignore his brothers. I can spot their blurry figures through the glass, though I think they train their gazes to the floor.

"You two need to hurry up," Bronx says, keeping his voice even. "We have to meet the Crescents for breakfast. The humans of Twilight Peak have been captured and are being held for interrogation. We need to file for immediate transfers. We're giving the Greys' town to the Crescents as not to raise suspicions. Claim treason."

"Fucking mood-killer," Jameson murmurs.

I realize I'm just hanging onto Jameson, devouring Bronx's words. And with them comes a rush of confusion. I nearly forgot about last night and how Ronan pissed me off enough that I attacked him...but after that? I don't remember.

"Uh, Jamie," I whisper. "I don't want to go. Convince them for me, will you?"

He groans and sets me on my feet. Shutting off the water, he opens the door and stands naked in front of his brothers. They all look up but train their gazes past him to me. I place my hands on my hips, trying not to squirm as they drink in the sight of my naked body.

"Gwen doesn't want to go," Jameson says, grabbing a towel to hand to me. "I'm not making her."

"We have to stand as a coven," Bronx says.

Jameson twists to look at me. "Sorry, Gigi. I tried."

I glare at him. "Not very hard."

"I have to agree that it's important," Jameson says, wrapping me in the towel he still holds for me.

Twisting my mouth, I shift my attention to Bronx, Everett, and Mikkalo. They wait for me to open my mouth to argue. Instead, I do the only thing I can think of. I drop my towel to the floor and saunter over.

"Uh-oh," Jameson murmurs. "She's determined."

I bite my bottom lip to hide my smile. I close the space to Bronx first and hook my fingers to the front of his shirt. "Please don't make me," I say. "I thought that we could all spend a little time together. Last night was intense."

Bronx sighs. "Gwen."

I shift my hair from my shoulder. "Maybe I could feed you all."

Bronx clenches his jaw, his eyes flashing silver. His features harden, and he locks his fingers to my waist, pulling me against him. He caresses his lips to mine, sneaking his hands down to my ass. "You're torturing me."

"It doesn't have to be," I say, smiling.

"Yes, it does. My answer is still no."

"No?"

"Ah, hell," Mikkalo says. "Come on, brother. Look at our girl. We can't deny her. She is putting a lot of effort into not going."

Everett extends his hand to me, and I let him spin me into him. "What about a compromise? We give Gwen what she wants now and then handle things after. I'm sure Ronan won't mind if we're a bit late. He'll understand."

"Especially after last night," Mikkalo says, punching Everett with a smile.

I frown, turning to Mikkalo. "What's that supposed to mean?"

The four of them look at each other with various expressions. Jameson breaks first, tipping his head back to laugh. Mikkalo steals me from Everett and grins at me, leaning in to kiss me even as I narrow my eyes at him.

Everett stands behind me, pressing against me. "Your sexiness distracted me. I meant to ask how your head is."

"Our girl is perfect," Jameson says. "Woke up a little insatiable, but I took good care of her."

Heat flushes my skin, sending tingles through me at his words. He and Bronx close the circle around me, way too amused.

"Was I hurt?" I ask, shifting to look at Everett.

"Knocked both you and Ronan out," Everett says, pressing his lips together.

I suck in a breath through my teeth. "But you're laughing. You sure you didn't tear Ronan apart and only want to rush out of here to avoid more conflict?"

"Mik, bring up the feed," Jameson says, smiling wider.

"Is no place safe from you, Mikkalo?" I ask.

He chuckles. "Nope."

Everett swats him. "He's kidding. We don't spy on households. Ronan gave us access to ensure safety because of the attack. All of our room cams have been disabled too."

Mikkalo breaks our circle first to pull his com device from his pocket. Jameson wraps a towel around my body, nudging me toward the door to our bedroom. He plops on the edge of the bed and pulls me onto his lap. Mikkalo sits next to us with Bronx on our other side. Everett stands in front and peers down as Mikkalo taps a few buttons.

I stare in shock, embarrassment burning my cheeks. "How the hell do you guys even tolerate me?"

Mikkalo laughs. "Wait for it."

Covering my mouth with my hand, I cringe, watching the video of me yelling and tackling Ronan. Video me swings out and slaps the rugged vampire across the face for the second time.

"You will not disrespect me or my coven with your bullshit fantasies," I say through gritted teeth.

Ronan's eyes widen. "I've never seen anything like her."

The fact that he talks about me to my face, pretending like I'm not even there must set me the hell off. I raise my hand to slap the vampire again as my guys look down on us instead of ripping me away.

"You tell him, ball kicker," Mikkalo says on the feed.

Ronan snatches my hand, stopping me from hitting him again. I cringe again at the shrillness of my voice echoing from the com device.

"You fucker," I snap at Ronan, trying to yank my hand

away. I jerk my head to look at my guys. "Why are you all just standing there?"

Bronx rubs the back of his neck in the video. "You got it handled pretty well."

"I think I'm in love," Ronan says, letting me slap him with my other hand.

"What the fuck?" I ask.

"So back-world."

His words piss me off even now, and I dig my fingers into Mikkalo's leg in anticipation to see how my crazy ass reacts.

"Here it comes," Mikkalo says, linking his fingers through mine.

I gasp. Holy shit. I watch myself jerk my head back and slam it into Ronan's, head-butting him. In the video, Bronx doesn't even let me slump onto the vampire. Everett snatches me from Bronx and disappears from view.

"How am I still alive?" I ask.

"We'd have never let anything happen to you," Everett says, stepping closer, bowing to kiss the top of my head. "The Crescent Coven wouldn't fight us either. We outmatch them by quite a bit. Ronan is all talk, anyway. He wouldn't have done anything to jeopardize the shift in power we offered him for helping us."

"Fucking hell." Ronan's musical voice draws my attention back to Mikkalo's com device. The vampire props himself up on his elbows with a giant gash bleeding on his forehead. "How long was I out?"

Bronx holds his hand out to the guy. "Twenty seconds."

"Hell, no wonder you're sneaking around Zaire's back. She's something else. If you don't promise that feisty, gorgeous thing a Blood Vow, you bet your asses I will."

Mikkalo flicks off his com device before I can hear the rest of their conversation. I crinkle my nose, glaring at him.

"I want to watch the rest," I say.

He leans in and kisses me. "Not a chance. We don't need you to get all riled up again."

I nip his lip. "I wouldn't get riled up."

"Yeah-fucking-right, Gigi. You went from nervous to my badass babe in like two seconds. We need to keep as many alliances as we can." Jameson shakes my shoulders.

"That was only because of..." I groan and bow my head forward. Thoughts of Silas sneak up on me, and I can't stop the image of him with fangs flashing through my mind. I still don't even know how to deal with all of that.

Bronx squeezes my hand. "We'll figure it out as soon as we start the interrogations. But right now, we need to get dressed, keep charming the hell out of the Crescent Coven, and try not to murder anyone. Every alliance at this point is important for when we have to formally announce Zaire's death. The board will look to other rulers in our region to see if power should pass on to me or if they should open the empty board seat to someone else."

I blink a few times. "Wait, the board seat?"

"I'm next in line," Bronx says, remaining expressionless.

"Damn." I don't know why, but it was one thing with Bronx controlling the region. It's a whole other thing to think of him joining the board of Donor Life Corp. Just the thought of him working for the very ones I've always thought of as the enemy freaks me out a bit.

"Gwen, talk to me," Bronx says. "I can't decipher your expression."

I push off Jameson and get to my feet, keeping my back to the four of them. A dozen thoughts swirl through my mind. Closing my eyes, I inhale a few deep breaths. I don't want any of them to see that the idea bothers me.

A gentle hand touches my shoulder. "Gwen, please look at me."

I swivel to look up at Bronx but don't get a chance to open my mouth to say something.

The shock alarms blare, and all five of us drop to the floor.

7

SELFISH

MIKKALO HOPS TO HIS FEET first and scoops me up, helping me cover my ears. The guys never react to the shock alarms at home and watching them orient themselves freaks me out a bit. Bronx and Everett look to me to see if I'm okay before disappearing out of the room. Jameson tugs an unfamiliar dress over my head, probably from one of the staff members.

"Let me take Gwen," Jameson tells Mikkalo, shouting over the alarms.

Mikkalo hesitates, sucking in a breath through his teeth. I extend my arms to Jameson to encourage Mikkalo, reminding him it's my time with his brother, and I'm sure Jameson wants Mikkalo to be free to fight if he has to.

Relenting, Mikkalo hands me to Jameson and pulls his com device from his pocket. He taps the screen, bringing up the video feeds. The alarms shut off, leaving my ears ringing. Jameson holds me with one arm while he somehow manages to dress with a little help from me. I stretch to get a glimpse of whatever Mikkalo's looking at. I see figures blurring across the cameras as the Crescents, Bronx and Everett, and the household security team swarm the property.

Mikkalo releases a growl. "I see something. Balcony 216."

"On our way." Ronan's voice sounds from Mikkalo's device.

I realize he was talking to everyone scouring the property and not Jameson and me. Jameson adjusts me in his arms to stare at Mikkalo's com device. I swivel, knowing exactly what his sneaky-ass is trying to do by making it harder for me to see. I wiggle and stretch, silently fighting against Jameson without calling him out. He doesn't call me out either, just continuing to reposition me.

"Get ready," Mikkalo says. "It's a person. Can't tell if it's human or vampire."

I grab Jameson's face and pull his head toward my

breasts. The small distraction gets him to loosen his hold enough for me to link my hands to Mikkalo's tight muscles and pull the both of us to him. He doesn't even budge, also ignoring the fact that Jameson and I play our silent game. Jameson finally gives up on trying to stop me from watching the feeds, and I dig my nails into Mikkalo as a figure stands up.

"Ah hell," Jameson and I say at the same time.

Mikkalo zooms in on the figure. "Capture, don't kill. It's Silas."

Bronx turns his attention to the nearest security cam, looking directly in it so that we can see his face. His frown matches mine, a dozen dark emotions hardening his features. "As long as he doesn't put up a fight."

"We can use him, brother," Mikkalo says.

None of us has time to argue as Ronan leads his security detail into one of the rooms. They stroll past a couple in bed, frozen by surprise, and head toward the door to the balcony. I tense, fear and anxiety tightening my chest. Now that Silas isn't right in front of me, it's easier to think than let my dhampir half react. But seeing him as a vampire still fucks me up inside.

"Mr. Crescent, I come unarmed," Silas says, raising his hands.

No one gives him a chance to say anything more. The security detail captures him and throws a black bag on his head. Mikkalo clicks off his com device, not allowing me to see anything that happens next.

"When were you going to tell me that Zaire was dead?" Ronan paces around the circular black and white rug in front of a sleek, black metal and glass-topped desk.

I sit on a leather couch between Jameson and Everett while Bronx remains standing with Mikkalo by his side to back him up. Apart from Ronan, only his coven brother Nash is present, leaning against the far wall to silently watch everything unfold.

"I wasn't if I didn't have to." Bronx crosses his arms, standing taller than anyone. His broad chest and bulging muscles make him intimidating as hell...and super hot. There's just something about seeing him all hard-ass toward someone other than me that I love.

Ronan growls and spins to punch a hole in the wall. "Who else knows?"

"What's left of the Anderson Coven." How Bronx manages to stay calm and in control with the man who looks like he's about to have a coronary? I have no idea. I admire it though. Seeing him confident and unexpressive helps keep my nerves in check.

"Corona? Seriously?" Damn. Ronan looks offended as hell. I can't really blame him. I'd probably be pissed too.

"I'm not exactly happy about it either," Bronx says, flicking his attention to me. "He matched to Gwen's brother and grew suspicious. It accidentally came out."

"Is that why more than half of his coven is dead?" Ronan finally stops pacing. He slumps into the chair behind the desk, resting his elbows on the glass.

Bronx follows his lead and slides in the chair on the opposite side. "We didn't kill them. It was the unregistered coven involved in the attack on the Yorks."

"Shit," Ronan says. "Why now? What does that coven want? It's obviously not the region."

"You're right," Bronx says, tightening his jaw. He rubs his hand on the back of his neck and glances my way again.

Ronan follows his gaze. "It's her. They want her."

No one says anything, but my dumbass face reacts and frowns. Bronx sighs and gets to his feet to close the space to me. He holds open his arms and coaxes me to get to my feet. Enveloping me in a comforting hug, he lifts me up to carry me back to the desk to face Ronan.

"Gwen isn't a donor from gen. pop.," Bronx says, sliding his fingers through mine. Of course Ronan wouldn't know. Only the Andersons knew that Kyler and I were convicted criminals.

"I should've guessed," Ronan says with a sigh. "So was she a runaway from this coven? Entered the Blood Match Program to avoid a blood debt?"

"Not exactly." Bronx rests his chin on my shoulder. "We caught her in the city with her family trying to get donors out."

"She's a Blood Rebel?" Ronan's voice rises.

Mikkalo, Jameson, and Everett all close the space to us. Nash materializes at Ronan's side. Tension steals all the air out of the room, the heaviness of the situation suffocating me even though my chest heaves with every single deep breath I inhale.

"She is not, but her family was. The Barons believe they have claim on her, but they do not have a contract or ties to Donor Life Corp," Bronx says, his face softening.

"And now you're risking the entire region...for her? One donor? Come the fuck on, Bronx. Are you stupid?" Ronan smacks his palms on the desk, startling me.

Bronx releases a threatening growl. "She is ours!"

Oh, shit.

"Everyone, calm the hell down!" The sound of my voice not only surprises me, but it also surprises everyone else.

The door to the office swings open and the rest of Ronan's coven brothers enter the room. I rip free from Bronx's arms and hop to my feet, holding my hands out. No one moves, keeping their distances. All eyes land on me, and I try my best not to react as my human instincts decide that now is the perfect time to alert me to my possible demise as

I try to control a room full of angry, on edge vampires.

I turn to face Ronan, looking him dead in the eyes. It's a bold as hell move, locking eye contact like I am, but there is no way I'm going to let him talk about me like this, especially to my guys.

"You might think I'm some donor, but you're sorely mistaken. I was Blood Matched to Zaire Royale, and I am now a part of the region's most powerful coven. I am not a blood source, nor will I ever be. If you think that Bronx is making a huge mistake by not handing me over, then you're the stupid fuck. You think that an unregistered coven would start a blood feud if I were only that?" I keep my voice low to stop it from shaking. "Now, please. I need to see my brother."

A dozen questions flicker across Ronan's face, his brows pinching together to nearly blend as one. His light brown eyes search my face, trying to understand what makes me different, but I doubt he could ever guess.

"Under one condition, Ms. Royale," Ronan says, rubbing his scruffy jaw.

"Call me Gwen. You're strong allies to the Royale Coven, there is no need for formalities," I say.

He nods. "Okay, Gwen. If you want to see your brother, you must tell me. Why the Royales? Bronx has asserted his claim, and I can understand his reasoning in a sense, but what about you?"

"I love them. They're mine," I say.

"I'm not sure what that's supposed to mean. Are you looking for a Blood Vow? You realize that will require you to choose one of them to receive their bite—whether it be for love, loyalty, or an enhancement in status, you cannot choose all of them." Ronan turns his attention to my guys, the four of them remaining expressionless.

"I don't even know what that is," I say.

Ronan hums under his breath. "While I can see and understand their infatuation with you, I'm still unclear about you if it's not a Blood Vow you want. If you love them, then why not do the most ridiculously human thing and save them all the heartache? Stop them from making a huge mistake with this impending war. Why don't you give yourself over to the Barons to stop the destruction of the Royale power?"

Is he for real? I'm not a martyr. I'm selfish as hell. If I weren't, I'd have traded myself for my brothers. But it is more than about me. The Barons think I possess some sort of power that will help them rule the future or whatever. But I can't exactly tell this guy I'm a dhampir. Too many already know.

"Because I'm selfish." I break my stare to look at my guys. "Because—"

A beep from Ronan's computer cuts me off. His eyes turn to his screen, and he drops a few f-bombs, sliding his hand over the desk to swipe a bunch of papers to the floor. A strange smoky smell wafts through the air, and everyone looks at each other.

"The south side is on fire," Ronan says, tapping his fingers on the digital keyboard. "The sprinkler system has been disabled."

I fly off my feet and land in Bronx's arms. The Crescent Coven vanishes, leaving the five of us alone. Mikkalo, Everett, and Jameson unsheathe their weapons and head to the door. Bronx's muscles flex as he squeezes me tighter than usual.

Mikkalo brings up the video feed. "We have to go to Silas. He's chained in a room on the top floor. This was probably a distraction."

"I don't know, brother," Bronx says, his deep voice croaking with an agitated growl. "The Barons aren't stupid. They knew we'd catch Silas."

"Maybe they're trying to lure us out," Jameson says. "Or they think we'll go after Silas."

"A fire won't kill him," Everett says. "I say we leave him. Interrogating him isn't necessary."

All four of them look to me for my opinion. "I'm with Everett. I refuse to let those assholes think they can use my brothers against me."

"Damn straight," Jameson says, kissing me in Bronx's arms. "Let's just get out of here so I can continue to satisfy our girl for the rest of the night. She made me so hot with the way she spoke to Ronan about us."

"So, so hot. Maybe I can help," Mikkalo teases.

I stick out my tongue. "Or maybe it's the fire?"

Everett laughs. "Definitely not."

Bronx doesn't say anything and just holds me tighter. I'm nearly certain he's not going to put me down until he's sure it's safe. With everything going on, he's in over-protective mode. He doesn't have to tell me for me to know that Ronan's words might have gotten to him, but I don't think his sudden silence involves me.

Voices in the hallway outside the office draw our attention to the door. Mikkalo moves forward first, fully prepared to dismember anyone who dares try to fight us. A guy yells and stumbles—clearly human—and I watch as three more men and a woman help him to his feet. Ronan materializes, carrying a sword. He flashes his fangs in the direction he came.

"Bronx, we need help," he says. "Half our staff is in that wing. Something is wrong with them."

"Mind manipulation?" Bronx asks, tightening his jaw.

Ronan nods. "The staff is panicking, but they're running toward the flames instead of away. We locked as many as we could in their rooms, but there are far too many to retrieve alone."

Bronx turns to Everett, Jameson, and Mikkalo. "Help

the Crescents. I'll keep Gwen."

"Conrad will lead you there," Ronan says to my guys. He looks at Bronx. "You two come with me. The front is in flames, so we need to leave out the back."

"Be safe, brothers," Bronx says, letting me quickly hug them.

Everett, Mikkalo, and Jameson follow a short, silent guy with hair flowing past his shoulders. They disappear into the hazy air. Bronx shifts me so that our chests press together, and I tug his shirt up slightly to help filter the air. Bronx's bare stomach touches between my legs, and I really wish Jameson hadn't ripped my underwear.

"Dandelion," he murmurs.

"Blame Jameson."

He chuckles. "Or thank him."

I kiss his throat, laughing into the crook of his neck, so relieved that he finally finds amusement in something in this shitty situation. The world blurs around me as Bronx follows behind Ronan through a few hallways that look exactly the same. I don't know if it was made to confuse humans or what, but I'd be screwed if I got separated.

A small crowd of people blocks an opaque door in front of us. They bang on the glass, trying everything they can to break it. Ronan shifts and peers at us over his shoulder. He growls in frustration, his eyes flashing silver at me. He looks like he wants to scream a few choice words at me but doesn't because of Bronx.

"Move!" Ronan yells, drawing the people's attention away from the door.

A few bite marks decorate their bodies. They must've been personal donors to the coven and with them. It would explain why they haven't been mind manipulated. The people move away from their door and cling to each other. Ronan blurs away from us and rams into the door, shattering it. He waves to the humans, getting them to follow him out.

Fear prickles on the back of my neck, and I tighten my grip on Bronx. "Something's wrong," I whisper. "Don't go out there."

Bronx freezes a few feet from the door. "What's wrong?"

"I don't know. My fear instincts are going crazy," I say.

A soft growl comes from behind us, and Bronx draws his weapon from his sheath. He spins to find Nash in the hallway. My heart slides in my stomach, spotting the figure behind him. Silas pushes Nash forward, causing him to clench his jaw. Blood drips from the front of Nash's shirt where his heart would be. The five blossoms remind me of when Francisca had Jameson's heart, threatening to rip it out. Silas is about to do the same.

"You have sixty seconds, Mr. Crescent," Silas says, extending his fangs.

Bronx roars, jerking me in his arms. Silas and Nash distracted the both of us long enough that Ronan managed to stab Bronx in the back. Bronx spins with me, turning to Ronan. He shoves into us, using me to smash Bronx into the wall.

I scream out in pain, pretty damn sure Ronan broke some of my ribs. Hands lock around my waist in an attempt to rip me away from Bronx. Bronx swings his dagger, sinking it into Ronan's shoulder. Ronan punches me in the back, knocking the wind from me. Bronx twists again to protect me and takes another stab to the shoulder.

"You have to put me down," I say, heaving a breath.

Bronx relents, setting me on my feet. He spins around and power kicks Ronan, sending him flying into the wall. Silas releases Nash, and the two of them charge us. We're outnumbered, and Bronx is injured.

"Time to use your best weapon. Give me your dagger." I lose all my fucks toward the fact that I'm in a stupid dress without undergarments and charge toward my brother. I crash into him, knocking him back. Bronx hooks his arm around my waist and spins me. I slice the dagger through the air too fast for Nash to stop. The front of his shirt tears, showing off his thick body hair that I think might cover his abs.

"Bronx, this is pointless. I don't want to hurt you," Ronan says, stepping closer. "You're going to hand me Gwen. This can't end any other way. I will not let my city fall because of a donor."

"You asshole!" I say, glaring at Ronan.

"Don't take offense, gorgeous. You'd do the same thing in my position," Ronan says, brushing his fingers through his brown hair. "Unlike the Royales, I'm not willing to jeopardize those who count on me, even if it means I must bow to another."

Bronx releases a deep-ass growl, lacing his fingers through my hand. A figure blurs past the shattered door, setting off my fear instincts like crazy. I tense, darting my gaze from outside to the three vampires surrounding us.

"Gwen, I'll block them. I want you to run. I'll catch up," Bronx says.

"You want us to separate?" I ask, my eyes widening.

"It's what Laredo would have you do." Bronx's face remains expressionless, though I know his words are just loud enough for the others to hear.

Licking my lips, I nod my head. The fighting technique I practiced with Laredo was the only thing Bronx ever admitted to being good that I learned from my previous blood source. It's something vampires never expect. Who knew my stubbornness to do as someone says would come in handy?

"Get ready," Bronx says.

Ronan, Nash, and Silas close in, trying to surround us. Bronx curls his fingers into fists, tensing his muscles. He charges forward, spreading his arms wide while bowing. I rush past the four of them to the glass door, knowing that Bronx can't block all of them. Instead of running outside, I stop and drop to my hands and knees. Ronan trips over me and skids across the floor. I launch at him and jump on his back. He tries to overpower me, but I punch him in the throat hard enough to stall his breath.

Hands lock into my hair, ripping me away from Ronan. I scream and flail. Cool breath tickles my ear. Fighting sounds from behind me. Things crash. I can't turn to look. I think I hear more vampires.

"Get Gwen!" Bronx shouts.

"Tell them to back off, Gwen," Silas says into my ear. "If they don't, they're dead. So are the Crescents. All the humans here. If you don't, you'll be responsible for the collapse of an entire region. You'll never survive that. Everyone will want your heart."

I lock my fingers to Silas's, digging my nails into his wrists. "I'm going to kick your ass."

"Maybe you could before."

Jerking my head back, I attempt to head-butt Silas. He bends his neck, moving out of the way.

"Come on, Mr. Baron," Ronan says. "My brothers will hold them off. So will my security. Follow me."

Rage rushes through me at his words, and I narrow my attention on the vampire standing before us. Kicking my leg up, I surprise the hell out of him, managing to hook his neck by my knee. The force of my body throws Silas off balance, and he lets me go. He might now be a vampire, but I'm still a better fighter.

I manage to kick my other leg up, hanging myself upside down. A few strange-ass noises sound through the air, one coming from Ronan, and I hiss and swing my head back right into Ronan's junk. He drops me, and I land on my shoulders and flip over to get to my knees.

"Gwen, behind you," Mikkalo calls.

I don't turn to look, knowing that whoever is coming up will move too quickly to try to catch me when I'm not looking. Instead, I punch in front of me. Nash's knee buckles and he drops to the floor.

I crawl forward, my whole body begging me to rest for a moment, but I can't. Nash darts his arm out to grab me, and I let him. He hops to his feet, spinning me around. Ronan materializes in front of us with his arms open.

"You promise my guys will live?" I ask Ronan.

"Gwen!" Jameson yells.

Ronan nods, gathering me to him. "As long as they don't fight."

I wrap my hands around his neck. "Well, that's not going to work for me."

Linking my hand through his hair, I bend his neck and bite down as hard as I can, filling my mouth with his blood. He automatically shoves me away, taken by surprise. I spin on my feet and punch my fist into Nash's chest. His eyes widen as he freezes, staring at my fingers impaling him. The pain and desperation, the scent and taste of Ronan's blood, set me off. My dhampir side takes over, and I crush through Nash's sternum and tear his heart out.

Ronan releases a roar behind me. I swivel and throw Nash's heart at him, hitting him in the face. The Crescent brothers' shock halts them in place. Confusion washes over them as they realize what I've done.

"Damn it, Gwen. What did I tell you about ripping hearts out?" Jameson says, dodging past the guy I remember being named Conrad. "And biting? You know how jealous that makes me."

Bronx, Everett, and Mikkalo take advantage of Jameson's distraction. They team up and dismember another one of the brothers, one I don't recall getting his name. Ronan yells, trying to fly at us, but Silas materializes behind him and grabs him by the back of the shirt.

Ronan turns to fight him off, and I break from Jameson, rushing the asshole. Jameson still manages to beat me, and he rips Silas away from Ronan to hold Ronan to his chest. Fury darkens my vision, and my body moves without me thinking about it.

Ronan hollers as I punch him so hard that Jameson reflexively arches his back to avoid my fist breaking through the vampire's bones. Snapping his teeth, Ronan attempts to bite me. Jameson locks his head in place by pulling his hair and severs his head. Ronan's body drops to the ground, taking me with him.

My stomach rolls, nausea sneaking up on me.

"Bronx, what should we do?" Mikkalo asks.

He materializes next to me. "Let them go."

I heave a few breaths, the smell of the dead vampires' blood wafting through the air, mingling with the scent of burning. Everett helps me slide my arm from Ronan's body, and I can't stop my stomach from twisting.

"Watch out. She's going to be sick," Everett says.

The world blurs as Everett takes me outside and rubs his hand along the length of my back. "Take a few deep breaths. They're gone."

I clutch my knees and look at the burning mansion, at the people crying in the grass, and the destruction caused by my presence.

They might be gone now, but I know deep in my heart that this isn't over.

8

PROVOKED

"YOU SHOULD DRINK SOME MORE," Everett says, massaging his fingers into my shoulders.

I groan and bow my head between my legs, letting my hair cascade forward. My stomach twists, my mind whirling. Everything catches up to me, and I can't stop the anxiety and fear from making me sick.

Mikkalo leans between the seats and offers me his bleeding arm. "Here, Gwen. Let me."

I shake my head and turn my face away. "I don't feel so

good."

"Because you threw everything up," Jameson says, pouting at me. "Such a waste."

I groan a laugh. "Don't remind me."

Everett continues to stroke my back. "I know you're afraid of getting sick again, but you're going to be okay. The blood will make you feel better. You have some broken ribs, a knot on your head, and some bruising."

"Listen to your health keeper, dandelion," Bronx says from the driver's seat. "Don't be a pain in the balls. We need to keep your wild ass in check. An empty stomach and a few injuries will pull out your dhampir side in full force when provoked. We're almost at Corona's, and I probably wouldn't stop you from punching his heart out. I need you in control so that you don't."

I jerk upright and gawk at him in the rearview mirror. "No fucking way am I going to Corona's."

He tightens his features, turning into the hard-ass I know won't give me my way. "Yes fucking way you are. I know it's not ideal, but the Anderson Coven is the only ally that knows the things we do about you and the Barons." Bronx's eyes flash silver at me in his reflection. "No one will bother us, and their security is as superior as ours in Crimson Vista. We will be safe there."

"I still don't like it," I mutter, hanging my head to break my gaze away from his. "The asshole locked me in the basement."

He might have a good reason, but I still don't have to be happy about it. I know I don't need to remind them. They'd never forget any of the shit I've been through. I just want to make my feelings clear because it makes me feel better. It's bad enough I occasionally have to see Corona in Crimson Vista. Returning to the place he killed Kyler pisses me off on another level.

Jameson squeezes my knee. Out of the four of them, he's listened to me work through my feelings the most. "We'll make him stay there the whole time if you want."

I offer him a small smile. "I do."

"And it's just for the night while we call all the city heads in for a gathering. We need our region to prepare for future attacks. Having the Anderson Coven at our side will show unity and support, especially with what we have to deal with in regards to the board." Bronx taps the navigation screen and sets the autopilot on to meet my gaze. "We can't let the Barons turn more covens against us. What happened with the Crescents...I failed them."

His words hang in the air, and he scrubs his hands down his face. Even though he doesn't give many of his emotions away, I can tell that losing Ronan, even though he betrayed us, took its toll on him. I think Zaire's death is truly starting to sink in as well. I can't help feeling like shit. Not for either asshole, but for my guys. Their lives have changed so much since I came along, including losing people that have been around for more time than I can even comprehend. Longer than a human life.

I crawl between the seats and envelop Bronx in my arms instead of the other way around. He inhales a breath against the crook of my neck, savoring the scent of my closeness. I quietly hug him, giving him all the affection he wants until his muscles relax, and he manages to soften his sharp features. I can't fault him for doing what he thinks is necessary despite the bad feelings I have toward Corona. It's clear that he's far better at seeing things outside of us than I am.

"How much longer? I need to cuddle the hell out of all of you," I ask, shifting my legs on his lap to straddle him. "Tonight sucked and you deserve to get what you all want and need from me."

Bronx releases a soft chuckle. "Ten minutes, but you being here is perfect. I don't need more."

"I think you do. All of you." I stretch out my arm and pull Mikkalo closer. "And I can't wait that long."

Mikkalo leans in and hugs me to Bronx. "Me either, especially with how you rejected my offering. Will you please try again?" I should've known denying his blood might have bothered him.

I swallow, trying not to frown. Though my stomach clenches at the idea, I nod my head anyway. I know they desperately want to take care of me, and I don't want any of them to take it personally.

Mikkalo offers me a relieved smile and bites his arm a second time to hold it out to me. Everyone's gazes burn over my body, their anticipation even more intense than usual, probably because I've never refused their blood before.

Gliding my tongue across the ribbon of blood, I lick Mikkalo's arm and mold my lips to the puncture wound. I let the blood seep into my mouth instead of sucking, just testing to see if my stomach will behave.

It doesn't.

Nausea bursts in my belly, and I pull back and press my lips together. I breathe slowly through my nose, trying not to react. Forcing myself to smile, I meet Mikkalo's gaze and nod my head again and lick my lips.

"So good. Thank you. It helps," I say, sliding from Bronx to rest my head on Mikkalo's chest, knowing he wants my closeness after giving me his blood. His hands tighten around me, and I sink harder into him, so I don't risk meeting his eyes.

It doesn't stop Bronx, though. Bronx's eyes bore into me, studying my attempt to pretend I'm fine. I avert my gaze to the road in front of us, despite his furrowing brows. He doesn't call my ass out on the fact that I usually drink way more. I think Everett realizes it too, because he narrows his eyes a bit when I glance back at him.

"You can have more if you want," Mikkalo says, running his hand up my arm. They all know me so well.

I open my mouth to make an excuse, but a beep rings through the air, and Bronx takes control of the car to navigate through a well-guarded gate. There is security everywhere—more vampires than I have ever seen protecting the property, none of them I recognize.

A man with a giant-ass gun beams a light into the car, double-checking our identities. I glimpse at him for a second. His eyes rove over me as he scrutinizes my face. I try not to react, feeling gross under his gaze like he wants me to get out of the vehicle so that he can devour the rest of me with his stare.

Mikkalo gives him a warning growl, tugging a dagger from the dash compartment to point at him. The vampire backs up from the window and motions us to continue on. There are three more checkpoints along the road to the mansion.

Corona greets us outside, bowing deeply to my guys. I ignore him completely from Mikkalo's arms. Brooklyn materializes in the doorway, a dozen comments crossing her pinched face. She doesn't say anything, but I bet if I weren't surrounded by my guys, she'd probably blame me for everything.

"My estate is your estate," Corona tells Bronx, sweeping his arm toward the monstrous house. He remains expressionless, though his eyes quickly flick over me. I should be used to it. Every vampire I've ever come across can't help showing me attention, but it still pisses me off.

"Glad you said that," Jameson says, speaking up. He manages to grab Corona's complete attention, which helps suppress my nagging need to fly at the guy and inflict as much pain upon him as possible before someone manages to rip me off. "Our girl requested that you spend the duration of our stay here in the room you kept her in. I think it's a pretty fair request, all things considered."

Corona tightens his jaw without a word. His eyes flash silver, his annoyance as clear as my anger.

"That's absurd," Brooklyn says, huffing out a breath. "She is not the head of your coven and that sort of request is completely unreasonable and disrespectful to our coven's generosity."

Mikkalo tightens his hold on me, feeling my body tense. I glower at Brooklyn, though Bronx's hulking form mostly blocks me. She's lucky I'm feeling pretty in control of my deep-seated nature and don't hiss at her or some shit.

"It's fine, dear," Corona says to Brooklyn, putting his arm around her.

"But father, abiding by such a preposterous request gives the impression that you're beneath the donor. It's not only demeaning, but it will also weaken your stance as the head of our coven." Brooklyn glowers at me, her perfectly arched brows lowering on her forehead.

It's so weird to hear her speak to him that I ignore what she says, focusing on the whole dad thing. They look far too close in age for him to ever be called her father, unless it's some sort of game to them. I shiver at the thought. No thanks. I don't need those images in my head.

"What coven?" Jameson says, flashing his fangs and pulling me from my twisted thoughts about their term of endearment. "Last I checked, there were only a handful of you left. Without the backing of a large coven, the Anderson name does not hold enough power to properly run a city in our region."

She hisses at him.

I growl at her.

Bronx gets between all of us. "Settle down. I'm sure Gwen was joking about the basement, but I do request Corona keep his space. You too, Brooklyn. Gwen's been through enough and needs time to heal without the reminder of your coven's prior offenses."

I clear my throat, now fully hell-bent on making my feelings clear. "I wasn't kidding."

Bronx turns his attention to me, his lips pursed. I can tell he just wants to get settled and focus on other things, but I can't. I can't get past this situation. "Gwen—"

Holding my hand up, I cut him off. "No, Bronx. It might be easy for you to try to pretend that everything about this situation is normal and fine, but this asshole murdered my brother. He tried to imprison me. He wanted to use me not unlike the Barons. So, yeah. I'm really fucking serious about where I want him to stay."

"Your brother turned against you, you little bitch," Brooklyn says, her sharp words feeling as if they cut me open. "You cannot blame my father for taking advantage of the situation."

I open my mouth to respond, the edges of my vision shadowing, but Mikkalo relocates me. I land on my back on a bed, disoriented from the sudden movement. Dizziness washes over me, and I scramble to get to my feet, my stomach still not in a place to be put through this kind of turmoil.

Thankfully, I don't get sick.

Mikkalo stands in front of me, steadying me on my feet. I can't stop my face from reacting. I glower despite my anger not being directed at him. I'm angry with Brooklyn. Bronx too. I mean, what the actual fuck to both of them? Bronx for not backing me up and playing down my feelings like they're unwarranted by saying I'm joking and Brooklyn for standing up for a guy she is fine committing treason against. I guess that was before all this shit happened but still.

"Not cool," I say, sinking into his open arms. I'm so angry that I can't stop from shaking.

"I'm sorry, Gwen. I didn't want to risk you starting a fight that would end with Brooklyn's blood on your hands. Or Corona's. That would make me extremely jealous." Mikkalo brushes my hair out of the way to massage his fingers into my upper back, just touching the bare skin peeking from my dress.

I hug him closer, groaning into his chest, breathing hard in an attempt to engulf myself in his scent to try to settle my nerves. "You're fine. It was...Bronx."

"I'm still sorry. I know this whole situation is shitty as hell." Mikkalo nudges my chin to tilt my head up to him. He presses a kiss to my forehead before brushing his lips to the tip of my nose to smooth out my frown. He continues lower to softly kiss my mouth, and I hum and pull away.

"Don't get carried away. I'm not sure you want to kiss me like you usually do right now," I say, pouting my lip. If I can taste the lingering sweetness of vampire blood, I'm sure he can.

He chuckles. "I'm used to the taste of my brothers' blood on your mouth. Your mouth is delicious regardless."

I shake my head, twisting a smirk into a half frown. "This is different." Going down is far better than coming back up. I should know.

"Nah. I think you underestimate my need to see you smile. To take care of you. You have no idea how badly I want to help you relax and forget the world outside of us."

Mikkalo kisses me again, sneaking his hands up my dress, feeling the smooth, bare skin of my ass cheeks. "Especially knowing that there's nothing under this dress."

"Who knew my naked ass would be the thing to save me?" I say, trying not to think about the fact that it gave me an advantage in fighting Ronan.

"Gwen..." Mikkalo's soft smile disappears. My chest clenches at his sudden broody face. My guys spend so much time concerned over how I feel about shit that I go through that they suppress their own feelings. I know tonight wasn't easy on any of them.

I pull Mikkalo closer and rest my cheek to his chest to listen to his heart beating. "I'm sorry how things happened tonight."

"You don't need to apologize." He tugs me to the end of the bed so that we can sit down together and savor each other's closeness. "You're not to blame for anyone else's actions."

"I killed your friend." I swallow as I say the words, my throat tightening. I'm pretty sure if I had any friends, I might be upset if one of them killed them.

"This might sound fucked up, but I prefer that you killed him over the alternative. I can't lose you, Gwen. I'd rather see our region fall to pieces or ignite in flames than risk a future without you." He twines our fingers together, holding my gaze. "We might have claimed you as ours, but we also picked you over everyone else. I hope you know that."

"And I picked you." Because it's true. I might want to try to save the rest of my brothers, but if it came down to it, I'd pick my guys. I'd pick me. I don't care how selfish it is. Growing up as a supposed gift to humanity only to discover that the Barons think I'm some sort of prize for them leaves me really fucking bitter.

"You brought my brothers and me closer together than I ever knew we could be. Our coven has never been stronger." He bows into me for another kiss. "Which is why I always want to prove my love to you. My devotion."

I smile. "Mikkalo...you know you don't need to prove anything. I already know."

His words help loosen the knots in my stomach, and I snuggle him close, kissing him tenderly. He reacts to my affection, devouring every ounce of it like I've starved him the last few days as I spent my time with his brothers.

"I've missed you," Mikkalo murmurs, trailing his finger along my jaw. He gazes into my eyes with an expression that fills me up with everything I seem to need. I love the good weight of his stare and how it sends warmth and contentment washing through me.

I shift from next to him and onto his lap to give him my full attention. He can't resist playing with the hem of my dress, his desire for me growing with our closeness, how only fabric separates us from being together how we both want.

I rest my arms on his shoulders, only allowing a few inches of space between our mouths. "I've missed you too. Missed being with you. Alone. You have no idea."

A smile crosses his lips, his dark eyes lighting with the gesture. "Well, Jameson is prepping your dinner, so we have some time if you'll let me show you that I do have an idea. If you're feeling up to it."

I shiver at the thought, my body reacting with excitement. "Have you forgotten how tough I am?" I tease, sucking his bottom lip between my teeth. "I'm already feeling better. We definitely should take advantage of this alone time. I'm not sure I can wait...another hour?"

Purring from his throat, he squeezes my hips, guiding me to grind against him to feel what I do to him. "Everett will kick my ass if you're lying," he says, searching my face, his eyes trailing away from mine to drink in the rest of me.

I ease up a bit to rub his bulge. "I'll make it worth it."

He hums in his throat but doesn't make the first move. So I do it for him.

Easing off of him, I stand between his legs and hook my fingers to his shirt. I wince at the dull pain of lifting my arms, wishing my body would heal quicker. Mikkalo notices my reaction and grabs my hands before I can reach for his pants next. He studies my face, trailing his gaze to the rest of me like he can see beneath my skin.

"I'm fine, Mikkalo. Just sore," I say, knowing why he hesitates. "I promise. But I could be better…"

Mikkalo hooks his fingers to my waist. "You're bad."

I bite my lip. "I know. Now let me continue. I'm undressing you first."

He hums his desire. "Damn, you're so sexy when you talk to me like this," he says, reaching out to nudge the strap of my dress off my shoulder.

I bend down to unfasten his pants, the motion feeling like someone just punched a bruise. I wince at the sudden pain, annoyed as all get-out. Mikkalo sits straighter and gives me a thorough once-over, just as intense as Everett does. I squirm under his attention, failing to remain expressionless.

"I'm fine," I say again. "Don't look at me as if you'll break me."

"I'm not looking at you like that. But you're setting off my need to do what I can for you. You have to let me take care of you first." Mikkalo motions for me to join him on the bed. "Come here. Let me give you more blood. Neither of us will enjoy this if you're too stubborn to admit you're hurting."

He rests his back against the headboard and helps me nestle between his legs. I lean against his chest and turn my neck to meet him for another kiss. Easing me up a bit, he bites his arm and holds it in front of my face, gently hugging me to him. I'm surprised he chooses this position to allow me to drink, because I know how much he enjoys watching. I flare my nostrils at the scent. My stomach growls like crazy for the first time since we left the Crescent Coven's mansion. Now that I'm not a mess or on edge, the stress wears off. Mikkalo's touch definitely helps.

"I was starting to worry you didn't like my blood anymore," Mikkalo murmurs, moaning softly as I glide my tongue over his arm. Now the position makes sense. He was afraid of my reaction, so that's why he's not watching me.

I squirm between his legs, feeling his cock awaken even more against me, his desire so palpable that it sends a rush through me. "Definitely not the case. Like I said, I'm feeling much better."

"Yeah?" he whispers, nudging the other strap of my dress off my shoulder to kiss my skin.

"Mmmhmm." I savor the sensation of his tongue gliding over me. It never ceases to amaze me how good such a little thing could be.

"Then taste me." His words come out deep, sultry.

I can't resist any longer, my body begging me to hurry up to satiate the burning desire and need within me. I draw Mikkalo's arm to my mouth, licking the stream of blood threatening to spill. The subtle spiciness of his blood sets me off. I suck hard, and Mikkalo tightens his fingers to me, hugging me around my waist. I swallow and brush my tongue over his puncture wounds, practically making out with his arm. I can't help it.

He tastes so incredible—rich and velvety, satisfying.

His blood tingles down my throat, filling my belly with warmth. I had no idea I was this hungry, my mouth fully intent on devouring him. Mikkalo's moan hums against my shoulder, his hand mapping across my body like he can't help himself. I already feel tons better, the ache in my chest easily ignorable as his hand trails down my clavicle and to my breasts. He slips his hand into my bodice, grazing his fingers along my nipple. He gently pinches, and I cling onto his arm and sink more into his chest.

"I might need to call one of my brothers if you need more," Mikkalo says, sliding his other hand across my hip.

I shift and wiggle, so turned on by his blood and touch. I don't want to stop.

He hikes up my dress with his roaming hand to touch between my legs. I bend my knees a bit, spreading my legs wide enough so he can explore wherever he wants. I can't stop myself from moaning as he rubs my clit under his fingers, playing with me in such a way that I push more into him. It makes me suck harder, and he moans louder. I lose myself to the pleasure he arouses in me.

"You're so beautiful," he whispers. "I want to give you everything you need, but...I think you need more than what

I can give you now. Let me call Jameson."

"Nu-uh," I murmur against his skin.

It takes Mikkalo slipping his finger inside me to get me to release his arm. I sink against his chest, wiggling my body under the pressure he creates. He holds me still with his now free arm, exploring my body while kissing my heated skin.

"I'm sorry I got carried away," I say, with a moan, my chest heaving with my gasps. "You taste so good. Everything is so good."

He glides his tongue up my neck to my earlobe. "If you're still hungry..."

I shake my head, squirming more under the incredible pressure he creates, opening myself up more for him by hanging my legs over his. "You're what I need right now."

I tip my head back, and Mikkalo kisses my throat. He whispers his love for me into my ear, working me over with his fingers, feeling how much he excites me. I enjoy the sensation of his touch, moaning softly, barely able to stay still.

"I want you so much," he says, digging his fingers into my thigh. "I need you too."

I moan my agreement, wanting nothing more than for him to get me out of my clothes already. "Show me."

Shifting me to lie down, Mikkalo helps me out of my dress. He loses his pants next, and I stroke the length of his shaft, his boner practically throbbing as he flexes it under my fingers. I don't play with him long, fully needing to feel his closeness. He spoons me from behind, resting his raging hard-on between my legs, just teasing me with his tip as he continues to rub my clit, making my whole body tingle.

"Is this okay?" he asks, adjusting himself to align with my body.

"So good." My words come with a moan, and I reach behind me to dig my fingers into his hip.

He starts slow, just testing and teasing me, not letting me experience all of him just yet. I wriggle in anticipation and arch my back, pressing my ass harder into his pelvis. Moaning, Mikkalo squeezes my leg to hold me in place so he can thrust deeper inside me. I pant with the motion, my moan sounding every time our bodies completely meet. Our hearts beat wildly, and Mikkalo kisses the side of my throat like he can't help tasting my skin as he slides in and out, the pressure building from the position so intense that I grip the blankets just to hold on.

His love and desire crash over me, igniting mine even more. He knows exactly what I like, pinching my hip with one hand while caressing my nipples with the other. Neither of us cares how loud we are or that we're not in Crimson Vista. Nothing in the outside world can ruin such a perfect moment as we express our love for each other in the way we both crave and want and need.

Rolling me onto my stomach, Mikkalo manages to enter me even deeper, and I scream out in pleasure into the pillow. His intense passion collides into me in the best possible way as he embraces his deep-seated nature as a vampire, experiencing the same pleasure I do. He picks up his pace, thrusting just right that my body buzzes with my oncoming orgasm.

I smother my face in the pillows, my body exploding in the best possible way. Mikkalo moans, feeling my body clench and relax, reacting to the intense sensation he creates inside me. Whispering my name, he kisses my throat and then my shoulder blade, grazing his fangs in a way that makes me shiver until he finishes, pricking me with his fangs upon his release just for a taste.

His hands find mine, and he links our fingers together, keeping his weight off me but still cuddling me the way I like. Neither of us moves for a long while, relishing the sound of our rapid breathing and hearts beating. With Mikkalo so close, our bodies entwined, our love so palpable from the hot sex we had, I completely push away any lingering thoughts that don't involve how good he makes me feel.

If Jameson didn't knock on the door, I'm sure I'd ask Mikkalo to give into my desire again. And again. I know he wants to.

"Is Gwen asleep?" Jameson asks, keeping his voice low. "Bronx thought it would be best if I brought her food here."

Mikkalo shifts off of me, feeling my muscles suddenly

tensing in annoyance. He grabs the blankets and pulls them around us. I don't stay in bed with him despite his quiet plea not to respond to Jameson. Instead, I roll from the bed and stretch for a second, testing my body for the aches that are only as annoying as Bronx's suggestion.

Opening the door, I stand butt-ass naked before Jameson. His eyes widen, and he nudges me back to enter the room.

Kicking the door closed, he stares from me to Mikkalo, now sitting up. They share an indecipherable look with each other. I step between them and place my hands on my hips, raising my eyebrow at Jameson.

"You look so starved," Jameson says, licking his lips.

"She was pretty set on draining me," Mikkalo responds for me from the bed behind me. His husky, sultry voice turns me on more, and I squeeze my legs together at the thought of being with him again.

Jameson flicks his gaze to me and back to his brother, a smirk playing on his tight lips. "I see you figured out how to save yourself. You'll have to give me pointers later."

I crinkle my nose and whack Jameson on the shoulder. He nearly drops the tray of food. Spinning on his feet, he sets it on top of a dresser. Jameson doesn't back up when I close the space to him.

He remains utterly still, keeping his arms at his sides as I stand on my tiptoes and nip his neck, tasting the decadence of his skin.

Unable to control himself, he tries to hook his hands to my hips to pull my naked body into his. I press my hands to his chest, smiling while not letting him get what he wants. I can see he wants nothing more than to distract me.

He play-growls at me. "Tease."

I glide my tongue over my top lip, drawing his attention to my mouth. Stepping closer, I drag the collar of his shirt over to expose more of his skin. I suck the nape of his neck, fully set on messing with him, knowing how much he likes it.

"Do you know how dangerous it is to tease a vampire?" he murmurs, his fangs peeking from beneath his lips.

I rub my hand over his growing erection. "Mmmhmm, but it might be worse to tease a dhampir."

Jameson catches me by the waist and kisses me, nipping my lip before his own to blend the drops of our blood together.

My stomach complains at the fact that I don't bite him harder or move to a place I can get a better taste of his blood. And with his hands holding me in place, I'm not so sure I can.

I suck his lip again, pulling away to meet his silver flashing eyes. "Careful, Jamie. I'm starving, and it's still technically our time for..."

"Eleven minutes," Jameson says, his voice deepening.

"Give our girl what she wants," Mikkalo says, coming up behind me. He shifts my hair, kissing my shoulder again. "I'm going to start the shower."

I spin in Jameson's arms to kiss Mikkalo, and he draws my lip between his teeth, tasting the drops of blood seeping from Jameson's nip. I hum, feeling the hard length of his shaft tease me again, but he doesn't let me get carried away. He spins me back to his brother and heads to the bathroom, starting the shower.

"Bite me," Jameson says, lifting me into his arms. "I want your mouth all over me."

I grin and kiss him. "Want to join us in the shower?"

"Mikkalo, you better tell me no. Bronx wanted me to return right away," Jameson calls out.

Mikkalo pokes his head out of the bathroom door. "Like our girl said. It's still your time. If she wants to suck your neck in the shower, I think you should let her. She deserves everything she desires."

"You know you want to," I say, gliding my tongue down his throat. "You know I'm not alone in my needs."

"Bronx is going to kick my ass," he murmurs without breaking away.

I drag Jameson's shirt over his head and glide my tongue from the hard muscles of his stomach and over his peck. "He'll have to get through me, and there's no way I'll let him. You're mine."

"Damn," Mikkalo says from the bathroom.

"Her protectiveness is so hot, right? I love it." Jameson eases away to smile at me. "And you. A lot. I just thought you should know."

"Why do you sound like you think something bad is going to happen?" I ask, grinning at him. I fiddle with his pants, unclasping the button. I don't drag them down and instead glide my fingers into his boxers to play with his erection.

Mikkalo chuckles. "It might. I think I hear Bronx."

"Then you better hurry and lock the bathroom door." I laugh as Jameson rushes us into the bathroom, kicking the door closed with his foot. Mikkalo already stands in the shower, the steam engulfing the pretty small glass stall.

"Jameson." Bronx's voice muffles through the door, his deep voice full of annoyance already. "I need to talk to you."

I hold my finger up to Jameson's lips to stop him from responding. "He's not here, Bronx," I say. "If you want to leave a message with me, I might pass it on."

Jameson grins against my hand and drops his pants on the way to the shower. I kiss him deeply, sliding my tongue into his mouth.

Mikkalo makes room for us and soaks my hair, playing with the tresses as he adds in a sweet, citrusy-smelling shampoo.

"Hurry and bite me," Jameson whispers. "I think he's

ten seconds away from breaking our no entering uninvited rule. If you're sucking my neck, he won't risk interrupting."

"He's right," Mikkalo says, pressing his chest into my back.

Ohmyfuck, do I love the sensation of being squished between their slippery, naked bodies.

I turn my neck so that Mikkalo can reach my mouth for a kiss. "You're really okay with this?" I ask the both of them.

Mikkalo kisses me again, gliding his hand around to my stomach. "Mmmhmm."

Jameson tilts his head to expose his neck. "Fuck yeah. Way more fun than...all the other bullshit."

"Let's not talk about the bullshit," I say, reaching down to lace my fingers around his cock. "Now, take a deep breath. Bronx is most definitely about to charge in here."

Jameson releases a cross between a grunt and a moan as I sink my teeth into the sensitive skin of his neck. He drops me down a bit lower to feel how hard I make him without entering me.

Silence falls between the three of us. I savor the taste of Jameson's sweet blood and the softness of Mikkalo's lips on my shoulder.

I only pull back at the sound of another tap.

"Gwen, brothers," Bronx says, cracking the door an inch.

"You better lose the clothes if you take one step into this bathroom," I say, meeting his dark eyes. "This is a bonding experience."

Bronx growls in frustration. "Do you think this is some sort of joke, Gwen?" His question ignites fury inside me, poking at my already hurt feelings.

It was easy for Mikkalo and Jameson to distract me from the fact that Bronx had disregarded me earlier, but now that I'm looking at Bronx, his face hard as he suppresses his reaction, I can't stop from feeling like I'll explode if I don't give him a piece of my mind.

I don't get a chance to respond, though.

Mikkalo stiffens, his anger mirroring mine. "Get out, Bronx. You're upsetting our girl, and she doesn't need this. I just got her to cool off and eat. You're ruining it."

"We have shit—"

Bronx doesn't have a chance to finish his sentence. Mikkalo flies from the shower and at Bronx, the two of them breaking out into a fight.

Their arms fly at each other with punches they manage to avoid, but Mikkalo knocks a shelf of folded towels off the wall.

Jameson flicks off the water and grabs one of the discarded towels to hand to me.

"Bronx, Mikkalo, stop," I say, wrapping the towel around myself.

They don't listen, and Bronx shoves Mikkalo into the wall.

"Bronx!" I yell, fisting my hands. "Enough!"

He flashes his fangs at me.

He loses control.

9

TROUBLE

I CRASH INTO BRONX, KNOCKING him off his feet. He flips me over and gets on top of me. Gripping the front of his shirt, I force him to yank me up with him. His eyes flash crazy silver, but he doesn't direct his anger toward me. He tries grabbing for Mikkalo.

I pinch his chin. "Bronx, calm down," I say, trying to get his focus on me.

Bronx flashes his fangs at me again. He releases a scary-ass growl, darting his gaze away from me. Jameson risks yanking me away from Bronx, and Everett materializes between us and shoves Bronx into the wall.

"Get yourself under control before you accidentally hurt Gwen," Everett snaps, pinning him with two hands.

Bronx struggles and snaps his teeth at Everett. I've never seen him act like this toward his brothers. It pisses me the hell off. Because, what the fuck? I can handle his brooding annoyance and anger, but what I can't handle is his fury that has unleashed the part of his nature I've feared all my life. The part that screams at me to run for safety.

"He already did hurt our girl," Mikkalo says, pacing in a half circle like he's waiting for Everett to leave an opening so he can try to start a fight with Bronx again. I know he will try given the chance. My guys don't put up with crap in regards to me. They might manage to control their possessiveness with each other, but their protectiveness is another thing, like how Jameson threatened to murder Mikkalo when he thought I was out to take down the region.

Everett stiffens at Mikkalo's words and swivels to glance at me from over his shoulder. He drinks me in, starting from my face and working his way down inch-by-inch. I'm nearly certain he might try to steal my towel to see the skin I cover up and not in the way I like.

"I'm fine," I say, talking to Everett. "Mikkalo's not referring to my physical state."

Mikkalo closes the space to me and embraces me from

behind. I hug his arms to me, assuring he stays with me instead of letting his wild emotions get the best of him. My guys are definitely more reactive after any sort of intimacy. "Like that makes it any better."

"What the hell are you talking about?" Bronx asks, narrowing his eyes. I don't know if his genuine surprise makes things better or worse for my hurt feelings.

Mikkalo presses into me to inch closer to Bronx. "You—"

I elbow Mikkalo in the stomach to stop him from forcing me in the middle. "It's nothing."

"Gwen."

Spinning in Mikkalo's arms, I face him, getting him to stop arguing with one look. "I know you want to stand up for me, and I appreciate it, but I don't want to get into it right now, okay? I'll get over it."

He groans and rests his head on my shoulder. "Maybe he'd stop being a dick if he knew what a complete idiot he is."

Bronx curls his fingers. "You think I'm being the dick and an idiot? I'm trying to secure our region while you and Jameson are fucking around with Gwen. You're the head of our defense. Jameson is our communications lead. So if I have to be an asshole to protect our futures, then damn right I'll be."

Mikkalo lets go of me to charge at Bronx. Everett gets

between the two of them, and Jameson yanks Mikkalo back. My human fear instincts go off like crazy. I automatically step back. My move doesn't go unnoticed because everyone turns their attention to me. I clench my trembling fingers together. I should be happy that my sudden fear stops their fight, but it really sucks that it had to come to this. I hate that I can't control my body's reaction.

Bronx huffs a deep breath, closing his eyes. "You know what? You guys stay here with Gwen. I'll do things myself." Bronx disappears, slamming the door shut.

I know he left because of me, and it makes me feel a bit like crap, not because he hurt my feelings but because I know something is majorly up with him. He gets grumpy when shit gets out of control, but he never takes it out like this. And maybe we are in the wrong. But things could've been handled differently.

I cover my face with my hands, inhaling a few deep breaths to settle my tight nerves. "Someone should go after him."

"No fucking way," Jameson says. "He needs to cool the hell off. I was only gone for a few minutes—during my time with you, if I might add—and he acts like we've disregarded our jobs. Taking the time to give you what you need doesn't hurt anyone. It's dawn anyway. It would be worse not satiating your hunger."

I glance to Mikkalo.

"I'm with Jameson. Plus, if I go, one of us might not come back." Mikkalo swings his arm, punching the wall.

I startle, and Mikkalo swears under his breath and disappears into the bathroom. Without having to ask, I know he won't come out until his anger settles some. Unintentionally setting off my human rationale bothers the hell out of my guys, more so than it bothers me. The last thing they want is for me to be afraid.

Silence settles in the room, the only sound I hear is my heartbeat pounding in my head. Jameson digs through a dresser and pulls out some clothes. He dresses first, his shirt a size smaller than he'd normally wear, but it's sexy as hell hugging his body the way I like. He grabs a too big T-shirt for me and helps tug it over my head. It's long enough to cover my vagina, so I don't mention that he should find me some underwear or pants or something.

Everett soundlessly watches the two of us, and I close the space to him and fall into his open arms. He looks like he could use some of my affection. I don't think I've ever seen him get between Bronx and his other brothers, and I know it bothers him. Everett's usually pretty neutral unless someone does something that might jeopardize my safety and health.

"I'm sorry you had to intervene," I say, inhaling a breath of his calming scent. "I know you hate being in that position."

"The only reason I did get in the middle was because I was worried about you. My brothers should know better." He raises his voice just a bit, passively chiding Mikkalo and Jameson.

"I hope you know they'd never hurt me," I say. "You should be more concerned about me accidentally hurting them. They're not as tough as my wild ass."

Everett's blue eyes light up with his chuckle. "I suppose you're right. Next time, I'll let you handle them. Because really, I don't know what's worse. Getting between my pissed off brothers or not getting to enjoy the shower with you too." His words are intended to be a joke, but I can't help wondering if he did feel left out. Maybe Bronx too. We have our alone time and also some times where we're all together, but we never discussed anything else.

I pout my bottom lip. "I'm sorry I didn't invite you. It was a spontaneous idea."

Leaning in, he pulls me closer by the small of my back. "I was only teasing. You don't owe me an apology and shouldn't feel bad. Plus, it would've been kind of crowded."

I graze my pelvis to his. "We'd have made it work."

"While I enjoy any time you give me no matter who it's with, I love our moments alone, having you all to myself." Everett's breath tickles my ear. "I can't wait to be the reason you scream in pleasure."

I release a small puff of air between my lips, his voice

turning me on. "Mmm, me too."

Jameson whacks Everett on the back, cutting into our conversation. "Have you two not banged already? Because if you're waiting for the perfect moment, you might be waiting a long fucking time."

"Jamie," I say, narrowing my eyes at him. "Only I can break the rules." It takes everything in me to remain expressionless. Keeping our sex life a secret is mine and Everett's thing. I'm nearly certain he's never told any of them anything, and they just assume what they want.

Everett squeezes his fingers into my hips. "Gwen's right. Stay out of our business. We do things in our own time." Like pretty immediately. And sometimes during their times given the opportunity.

"Now might be good. You know, since Jameson mentioned it." I hop into Everett's arms and meet him for a kiss.

Jameson groans. "All right, let's not get carried away. You're going to learn that once you get our girl started, it's hard as hell to stop."

Everett slides his hands to my ass. "I'm willing to risk it."

"As her health keeper, you should really prioritize Gwen's needs. She hasn't eaten her human food all day, and she doesn't like when her dinner gets cold."

I frown. Food is the last thing on my mind. "I'm not hungry."

Jameson raises an eyebrow at me. "The hell you aren't."

"It's just...Bronx." A mixture of emotions swirls through me. "You've distracted me long enough."

"Let him work through his own shit," Jameson says.

I ease down from Everett's arms. "I don't like feeling like I'm getting between you guys. I just—will you help me find him, Everett?"

Jameson grumbles under his breath, knowing that my mind is set now that I managed to pull myself away from their attempts to distract me.

Flaring his nostrils, Everett looks at me like I've asked him the worst favor ever. But I already know Jameson and Mikkalo won't, and there's no way I'm walking around this place all on my own.

Just as Everett opens his mouth to respond, a chime sounds through the air. Everett pulls his com device from his pocket and rubs the back of his neck. "Bronx says not to. He wants you to stay here."

"Then he can tell me his damn self!" I shout the words, knowing that he's close enough to hear.

"Fuck, now he's done it," Jameson says.

No one tries to stop me as I stride to the door, though Jameson doesn't follow me like Everett does. I glance over my shoulder to watch Jameson cross the room to where Mikkalo has decided to shut us out as well.

"Bronx! You better face me." I strut down the long

hallway and fling open every door along the way.

Everett slides in front of me, blocking my way. "If you think you might want to rip his heart out..."

I glower.

It's enough that he steps aside. "You better come get Gwen, brother. I'm not getting in the middle." Everett grabs my hand for a second, drawing my attention to him. "Try to take it easy on him. He's under a lot of stress."

"No fucking way am I now. He can't just hide from me."

Everett disappears, leaving me alone in the hallway. I know he wouldn't abandon me if Bronx wasn't close by, so I stride down the hall and continue to thrust doors open. I find Bronx sitting with his back to me on a bed. He doesn't look at me, just slumps over with his elbows resting on his knees.

"Hurry up and get it out of your system, dandelion. I'd like to get some sleep." Bronx keeps his voice low.

"What the hell is your problem?" I stand in the door-way, bracing against the frame. "First you make light of my feelings about being here. Then when I'm finally starting to feel okay, you come in and accuse us that we don't care. And now you act like I'm the bad guy."

Bronx straightens his shoulders but still doesn't look at me. "This isn't about you."

I inch into the room and shut the door. "You're right."

"I'm doing everything I can to protect you and my brothers. Our region is at risk. People are dying. So, fucking sorry if I hurt your feelings or interrupted your good time. Kill me for wanting to keep the tension to a minimum during our stay."

I suck in a breath, trying to keep my anger in check. "You're such an ass. I came here to try to be here for you, but fuck, Bronx. You make it really hard."

Sighing, he bows his head more. "I'm sorry. I don't mean to take my frustration out on you. I just feel like a complete failure that it has come to this. This is the last place I want you. You have every right to be upset that I put you in this position and haven't done anything to retaliate for Corona's wrongdoings. Zaire would have sentenced him to death." Bronx flops back on the bed and stares at the ceiling. His voice comes out lowly as he tries to keep the conversation between us.

I shift my weight between my feet. "Zaire would have also turned me into a blood slave, so don't compare yourself to him. I'm sure you have things in control. This just sucks."

Bronx shakes his head. "That's the thing. I don't. I might have been first in line, but I never actually expected to step up in Zaire's place. I hate it. I hate that I can't figure things out or even plan things accordingly."

I shuffle across the room and sit on the edge of the bed.

"What are we even doing, Bronx? Is all of this even worth it? I don't want you to feel like this. I don't want to feel like this."

Turning his head, he finally meets my gaze. "What do you mean?"

I wave my arm around. "This. Look at what this bullshit has done to us. I never wanted you to fight with your brothers or think you're failing because of some psycho coven. I never wanted you to feel like you had to team up with a damn asshole because you worry you're not powerful enough without the backing of other covens in your region. You are powerful. Your brothers are powerful. You got this, and even if you didn't, we're going to be fine. We don't need this region. If anything, it needs us."

He groans and stretches his arms over his head. "How do you always know what to say to make me feel better yet also like an asshole?"

I laugh and shake my head. "You do the latter by yourself."

"I am sorry, Gwen. I'm just—"

"In serious need of some masturbation." I grin as I say it. "At least, according to some horny bastard that thinks it helps chill him out and deal with stress."

Bronx releases a loud laugh and reaches for me. I attempt to scramble away, but he catches me by my feet and yanks me to him. My back hits the bed, and he rolls on top of me. Tipping my head back, I avoid his kiss on purpose. He brushes his lips to my throat instead, trailing down to my clavicle. His fingers brush the hem of my long shirt and sneak underneath it.

I hum under my breath. "Sometimes I think you like to piss me off so that you can get me all worked up on purpose."

"Exactly," he murmurs, working his way lower. "That way I can take care of you how I want."

"And how's that exactly?"

Bronx releases a moan at the realization that Jameson failed to find me undergarments. I snatch his hand and stop him from trying to touch me. Pushing him off, I get on top of him and pin his arms above his head. He licks his lips, trailing his gaze to my hiked up shirt exposing my body to him.

"Nu-uh," I whisper, bending down to kiss his throat. "You're still in trouble."

"Am I now?" His fangs peek out from under his lips, his prominent erection pressing into me. I'd lie if I said I didn't enjoy making up with Bronx. His intensity ignites his passion so fervently that all I want is to make love to him.

I suck hard enough on his skin to leave a mark. "Mmmhmm. So much."

With one hand, I reach for the hem of his shirt and pull it off. His eyes flash silver, and he arches his pelvis, teasing me through his pants.

"How are you going to punish me?" He grins at me, his sharp features finally softening. He takes our role-playing so seriously that I can't help but continue to play along. He controls mostly everything in our coven and in his life that I know it's a relief to give me control in moments like this.

I roll my body, teasing him more. "I have a few different things in mind depending on the offense."

"What do I get for being a dumbass? I am sorry that I played down your feelings toward Corona. I didn't mean for you to feel like everything he did to you was forgotten. I haven't, and I won't ever." He breaks free of my hold to sit up and hugs me to him for a moment. "I hope you can forgive me."

I bob my head. "Maybe if you do make him sleep in the basement."

"He's already there. I don't care what Brooklyn thinks. He *is* beneath you. So is she."

Closing the space, I kiss him, wanting so much to give him all my affection. "You're in slightly less trouble now."

He chuckles. "That's too bad. I was looking forward to your kind of punishment."

I push him back. "You still have several other offenses to pay for."

A deep cross between a purr and a moan escapes his lips. "Don't go easy on me."

"I didn't plan on it."

I slide off of him and unfasten his pants. He raises his hips and lets me tug them down, leaving him in his boxer briefs. I kneel next to him, drinking in his rippling muscles. Shifting up, he tries to grab my hands to pull me back to him.

I wag my finger, chewing on my lip. "No touching yet."

"That's beyond punishment. That's torture," he says, leaning back to rest his hands behind his head.

"You just wait." I smile and nestle between his legs, taking a moment to appreciate how hot he is lying in front of me. It's easy to forget how tense our emotions run when he lets me do what I want.

Bronx never takes his eyes off me as I crawl forward and rest my hands on his waist, purposely digging my nails into his taut skin. I hold myself up on him as I bend down and use my teeth to tug his underwear over his erection. I kiss his tip, and he releases a hot breath. Straightening up, I lick my lips and finish undressing him with my hands.

"I want nothing more than to make it up to you, Gwen," he says, his voice coming out low, raspy.

"Don't worry. You will." I grin, loving how he tries to grab me again like it truly is torture that I keep space between us. "First, for interrupting my dinner before I was finished, you're going to let me bite you."

"Anywhere you want." Clutching my hand, he tugs me on top of him, letting me straddle his body. His cock flexes in anticipation, and I scoot up to let it brush against my pelvis. I lace my fingers around him and rub his shaft as I meet his gaze.

"Anywhere, huh?" I push my body a bit higher to bring his cock to my clit. I let him feel what his closeness does to me, teasing him a bit more without letting him enter me.

"Mmmhmm." He stretches out his arms and sinks into the bed, proving he's serious.

I glide my tongue over my teeth. "I know the perfect spot to satiate my needs."

Shifting up, I turn around to straddle him backwards. I purposely flash him in the process, easing my body onto his while squeezing his sides with my thighs. He props up and kisses my ass cheek, making me release a cross between a moan and a laugh.

"None of that now," I tease, shaking my ass, trying so hard not to laugh. I'm nearly certain I'm more ridiculous than sexy. "You can look but no touching."

"I think you underestimate my restraint."

I reach between my legs and grab his hands to link my fingers through his. It's a bit awkward, but I'm determined to tease him until he can't handle it. He moans as I brush my lips over his hip, sucking and gliding my mouth over his pelvis and around his cock. His hands tighten around mine, and I hum in my throat, knowing that he wasn't joking about his restraint. My closeness and teasing test him like crazy, and I love the hell out of it.

"I think here is the perfect spot for your punishment," I say, tracing my tongue across his thigh in the same spot he asked me to bite him before.

"I'm ready," he whispers, relaxing beneath me.

I take his cue and bite him hard enough to make him bleed. He releases the sexiest noise in existence and breaks my hold on his hands to grip onto my legs. The sweetness of his blood tantalizes me, and I suck harder, enjoying the tingles buzzing down my throat. Bronx sits up and hooks his arm around my legs, lifting my body just enough that he can kiss my clit. He draws his tongue over my heated skin, igniting my lust in a hot wave. I moan so loud that I'm sure the whole place can hear me.

Bronx leans back, lowering me so that I sit on his face, caging his head with my thighs. I ease my mouth from my bite mark and kiss my way to his balls. I gently suck them and draw my tongue around his shaft to lick up the length. I caress his tip with my tongue before sucking his cock in my mouth. He moans against my skin, the vibration feeling so incredibly good.

We work our mouths over each other, savoring our closeness.

"Don't make me finish," Bronx murmurs, using his

finger to add to the pleasure he creates.

I slide my mouth away from him and rest my head on his hip. "Wasn't planning to. You're still in trouble."

"Good," he says.

Gripping the blankets, I relish the sensations Bronx creates with his lips and tongue. He takes his time enjoying me, using his fingers to help get me off. I squirm as the intensity builds and builds until I feel like I'm on the verge of exploding.

Bronx's name comes out of my mouth with a moan as I orgasm. He holds me in place to keep me from flopping off him and slows down until my muscles stop their spasms. Nudging me down, he kisses my ass cheeks again, grazing his teeth along my skin.

"I could do that all day," Bronx says, helping me roll off his muscular body and onto the bed. "You're as sweet as your blood."

I catch my breath, lying flat on my back, staring at the ceiling. This wasn't exactly what I had planned to happen when I came storming in here but damn. "But you can't."

"Want to bet?" He shifts on top of me and rests his body between my legs, poking me with his boner to see how I react.

"I don't need to bet. It's part of your punishment," I say, grinning.

His eyes flash silver. "That's just punishing yourself."

"Possibly." I press my hands into his chest, stopping him from sinking into me though I really, really want him too. "And making you wait to enjoy the rest of me might also be a punishment to me."

He play-growls.

I smile wider, reaching down to ease his cock away, letting it lump on my pelvis. "I wasn't joking about you masturbating."

Cocking his brow, he studies my face to see if I'm kidding. I don't react, keeping my mouth in a tight line. I think he doesn't realize how hot I found him the first and only time I caught him jerking off, especially when he did it while watching me.

"You like that, huh?" he asks, his voice deepening.

I shrug without saying anything.

He hums under his breath and pulls me up so that we sit facing each other. My legs rest over his, our bodies close enough to touch. Leaning in, he kisses me deeply, sliding his fingers through my hair. His tongue slips into my mouth, and I can't resist scooting a bit closer.

"Start me off," he murmurs, breaking from my mouth to kiss my jaw.

Instead of stroking him, I position his body to mine and rock forward with a loud ass moan. My plan to tease him totally backfires, and I lock my fingers to his shoulders, letting him pull me closer, digging his fingers into my ass cheeks. I gasp at the pressure of the position, all my ideas of teasing him gone with each thrust of his body.

"Mr. Royale."

Bronx releases a guttural noise from his throat, and I screech at the man standing in the doorway. Mikkalo materializes behind him, yanking him out of the room. Something thuds against the wall, and the man yells out. Bronx lifts me off the bed with him, relocating me into the bathroom.

"Wait, please. Don't hurt him." The musical voice of a woman sounds through the air. "Gordon was announcing my arrival to Mr. Royale. I was under the impression he'd be alone and in need of some company."

"Who sent you? Was it Corona?" Mikkalo asks.

"Ms. Anderson."

What the hell? By Ms. Anderson, I know the woman means Brooklyn, because she's the last female remaining since I killed Francisca. And damn it, if I'm not annoyed.

Mikkalo clears his throat. "Return to Ms. Anderson and tell her your company isn't needed."

"Perhaps I can join you?" the woman asks. "Or maybe your brothers?"

"No," Mikkalo says.

"But, sir. Providing company to you or your brothers assures I get the transfer I need to be with the one I love," she says.

I frown. "Are you fucking kidding me?"

Bronx presses his finger to my lips. "Try not to overreact. We're not going to agree to her company. You know that."

"That's not it."

"Then what?"

"The situation Brooklyn arranged with that woman is so messed up. She had to have known you guys wouldn't have accepted the offer." I slide past Bronx to peer through the crack in the door and into the bedroom. "Super cruel to give her hope like that."

Jameson appears in my line of sight. "Brooklyn's going to lose her damn head for this, Bronx. Our girl is upset enough."

Bronx slides his hands around my waist. "I'll talk to her."

"She only did this shit to instigate Gwen. You know as well as I do that no coven would willingly transfer a female out of their household." Jameson keeps his voice low. "I bet Brooklyn's laughing her ass off at us. We can't let her get away with this."

"And what exactly do you expect us to do? Are you going to accept her company and bite her?" Bronx asks Jameson from over my shoulder.

"Fuck no. Mikkalo and I already decided to share a room with Gwen for extra protection. I know how awful this place makes her feel." Jameson meets my gaze. "I mean, if Gwen's okay with it. You guys kind of look like you're in the middle of something."

I rub my lips together. "I'd like that, Jamie, but with the five of us. I don't want you guys out of my sight now."

"That's a whole bunch of morning wood that will want you."

I blush like crazy and shake my head. "As much as my curious side would like to explore that crazy-good time, my human side says going there under this roof isn't going to happen. The last time we all..." My words trail off. I don't need to remind them about our bonding biting session and how the asshole Barons crashed what was one of the best, sexiest moments of my life.

"Damn, Bronxy. We gotta get our girl out of here and get home already." Jameson reaches through the crack and combs my hair behind my ear.

"Please! You have to let me." The woman's high-pitched voice makes Jameson wince and twist his mouth into a frown. "I need this. I swear you'll have a good time, Mr. Royale."

The woman starts full-on sobbing, and Mikkalo enters the room and tries to shut the door on her. She blocks his way, sticking her arm through the crack. She's lucky Mikkalo isn't some asshole, or she'd totally end up with a broken arm.

"Everett, do something," Mikkalo says.

I can't stand the woman crying, so I pull the door open wider. Bronx sticks to my back, and I'm pretty damn sure he's not letting me go. Or maybe he's using me as a shield to block his naked ass, not that he's ever been shy about that kind of thing. Or maybe it was just for me. Maybe now because of me.

"Mr. Royale!" the woman shrieks, waving her arm at Bronx. "I'll do anything. Please. I can take over where that little doll left off. I'm stronger than she is."

Either Mikkalo loses focus or the woman is damn determined, because she manages to squeeze her way through the crack. She starts stripping right in front of us, throwing her dress to the floor. Shock freezes my guys in place. I realize they all watch me as I watch her. And holy shit. She's been donating blood probably all of her adult life. Circular scars decorate her skin, darker than her tawny complexion. I can't even tell how many times she's been bitten.

The woman strolls closer, tossing her brown hair over her shoulder to expose her breasts. Jameson blocks her from getting close, and she surprises the hell out of him by trying to jump into his arms. With his reaction, I'd think she had some infectious disease to vampires. She falls a little too close to me and tries to reach around me to grab onto Bronx.

He growls at her. "I've been claimed. Do not do that

again."

"Vampires can't be..." She narrows her eyes at me. "You're the donor the staff talks about."

I don't respond.

She grabs my shoulders, making all four of my guys growl. "The traitor."

No one gets the chance to react as she yanks me to her, kicking my feet out from under me. Bronx rips the woman away from me and tosses her on the bed. My guys surround me, helping me to stand. They look ready to murder the woman for touching me.

Mikkalo yells out and swings behind him, knocking a man, the same guy who interrupted me and Bronx, away from him. The scent of Mikkalo's blood wafts through the air. I rush to get between him and the guy.

I don't see the woman launch from the bed, gripping a dagger in her hand, until it's too late.

She jumps on top of me.

10

REBEL INFESTATION

"I DON'T FUCKING THINK SO!"

Jameson rips the woman away from me. She screeches and swings her arm, stabbing him in the thigh. Swearing, Jameson disarms the woman and drops her. Everett flips her onto her stomach and restrains her.

"Corona!" Bronx yells, his voice bellowing so loud that I'm sure people across the region can hear him.

Everett scoops me off the floor and relocates me to the bathroom. Mikkalo joins us, closing the door and leaning his muscular frame against it. Kneeling in front of me, Everett inspects me inch-by-inch, waving his hand over my body without touching me.

"Do you hurt anywhere?" he asks, playing with the hem of my long T-shirt.

"No, I'm just a little shaken." I comb my fingers through his blond hair, pulling him to me by his head.

He hugs me from his spot, resting his cheek to my stomach. "Are you sure?"

I smirk. "Would you feel better if I showed you?"

"I know I would. This stab wound hurts like hell," Mikkalo says from his place in front of the door.

I can't stop the pout from puckering my mouth. "Oh, Mikkalo. Let me take a look."

"After you." He graces me with a flirty smile, which helps lighten the invisible weight pressing down on me.

"You make sure that door's in place. I'm not having any more rude interruptions." I suck my bottom lip between my teeth.

Mikkalo holds the handle even though it's locked. "No one would dare."

I give into them and slowly tug my shirt up, exposing myself. My skin prickles under the weight of their gazes, and I slowly twirl around. "Do I look okay?"

Everett gently glides his fingers over the small of my back. "Does this hurt?"

Now that he mentions it, a dull pain radiates from the spot he touches. The longer I stand here, the more my adrenaline wears off.

"A little," I say, answering honestly since he takes on his health keeper tone. "What's wrong?"

Everett bites his arm and holds it out to me. "She must've nicked you. It's already coagulating, but drink some of my blood in case."

A roar sounds from the bedroom, startling me. Everett shifts my shirt down, and Mikkalo flings the door open. A blood spot blossoms on the back of his shirt where the man attacked and stabbed him.

"Did you hear that, Corona? This rebel hurt our girl," Jameson says, thrusting his hand out at the woman, now wrapped in a blanket.

Corona's eyes dart to me, causing my stomach to twist. I can't even bear to look at him. It not only pisses me off but also just being near him makes me nauseated.

"I'll handle the both of them," Corona says, yanking the man toward him first.

"You assured me the rebels were no longer here," Bronx snaps, still standing butt-ass naked. "How can I trust you if you can't handle a simple task? You know the risk the Blood Rebels pose to our region. The Barons use them."

Everything happens so fast that I don't get a chance to act. Corona sinks his teeth into the man's neck hard enough to squirt his blood across the floor. The sight sends my stomach rolling. My body heaves in despair, and Everett spins me toward the toilet.

"Are you fucking kidding me?" Jameson asks. He's all sorts of growly, sounding like he's on the brink of starting a fight. I kind of hope he does. I want Corona to pay.

I get my shit together, wiping my mouth on my arm. I swivel toward the door to catch sight of Jameson kneeling next to the man, whom I'm nearly certain Corona just gave his final donation to.

"You monster!" the woman screams, scrambling to get the man's discarded knife from the floor. "You killed him!"

Corona snarls at the woman. She cries out and covers her face with her arms to shield herself. But it does nothing to protect her. Locking his hands to her head, he yanks her up and bends her neck. He extends his fangs longer than I'm used to, going in for the kill bite.

Something inside me snaps, and I rush forward. Mikkalo tries to block me, but I shove him, sending him into Jameson. Corona drops the woman to the ground and growls at me in warning, and then he snaps his teeth. I don't stop though. His crazy ass doesn't scare me. How dare he think he can just end someone's life like this. I don't care who she is or what she tried to do to me. I refuse to let this asshole murder another person, but especially on my behalf.

Bronx snatches me by the wrist and drags me toward

him. He locks his arms around me, stopping me from attacking. Everett gets in Corona's face and snarls when he flashes his fangs at me. Tension builds in the room, my guys ready to act on Bronx's order.

I buck in Bronx's arms. I'm so furious that I can barely see straight. "I want his heart. This weak alliance isn't worth it. Keeping him alive has no benefit. You have to!"

"Leave now, Corona!" Bronx yells, squeezing me even tighter. "Take the rebel with you but do not harm her. Do you understand? We need her alive."

I scratch my nails into Bronx's arms. "Bronx, no. He needs to die." I kick my legs, struggling against his strong hold. "Jameson! Jamie! Please. Do it for me."

"Fuck," Jameson mutters.

Bronx growls. "Don't act on rash demands, brother. And Corona, I *said* leave. Your presence isn't helping."

Corona offers a stiff nod and grabs the woman. Jameson follows Corona out, and Everett disappears after them, probably assuring Jameson doesn't act on my demand. I can't stop glaring at the door. If I can break free, I can do it myself.

"All right, Gwen. You have five seconds to calm the hell down," Bronx says into my ear. "You're not going after him. I will handle it."

"Not the way I need you to. Now let me go! You can't let him get away with that. He killed that man like he killed

Kyler." I thrash and drop to the floor, unsure if I broke Bronx's hold or if he dropped me.

"I'm sorry, Gwen. You have to trust me. He will be dealt with accordingly," Bronx says, bending down on a knee to gather me off the floor. "I swear. But right now, please, you have to chill the fuck out. Your eyes are flashing like crazy. I've never felt you so strong before."

I shove him away and try to get up. Kicking out his leg, Bronx knocks my feet out from under me. I land on my back and full-on hiss at him, the edges of my vision shadowing. My mind begs for me to take a breath and do as Bronx asks, but my body refuses. My dhampir mutation awakens in full force.

"Shit. She's out of control," Bronx says. "I need your help, Mik."

I point at Mikkalo. "Don't you dare help him."

I catapult to my feet and jerk my elbow back to stop Bronx from restraining me again. The force of my hit knocks the wind out of him, and he grunts. Spinning, I kick out and clock Bronx in the side. He snatches my leg and yanks me off my feet again. Instead of dropping me, he dangles me upside down. The action doesn't last long because my shirt falls over my head. Bronx tosses me to the bed, flips me onto my stomach, and straddles me.

He leans into me, sinking his weight against my body. Instead of pissing me off even more, the gesture somehow manages to calm my wild ass down. I feel his naked body pressing into my ass, my shirt hiked up a bit. And damn it if it doesn't turn me on. Bronx too.

"I need you to listen to me, dandelion," Bronx says, his words a whisper in my ear. "I have a plan for Corona, and it's killing me that you can't trust me to handle him."

I squeeze my eyes shut at his words. "I—I do trust you. But I don't know how much longer I can wait. I hate him. Loathe him. A part of me feels like it's dying even looking at him."

He groans in my ear. "I'll keep him away until the gathering. We just need to use him to show the city leaders that a prominent member of our region is on our side. After that, I will personally restrain him so that you can get your revenge."

"I don't want revenge. I want justice," I whisper. "What he did—"

"Was fucked up. I know. I don't take the murder of humans, even Blood Rebels, lightly. Neither did Zaire. His belief in the proper care of the population was one of the reasons he was invited onto Donor Life Corp's board. I don't know how much you know about the Donor Life Corp territory history, but it wasn't that long ago that the founder lost sight of our purpose to maintain civility the best we can, not only between our regions but also between the vampire and human population." Bronx eases off me to lie on his side. He doesn't let me get far and hooks his arms to my waist and positions me so that I face him. "He started a war that ended with the destruction of five regions over the course of a few months."

I furrow my brows. I had no idea about any of this. "Five regions? What the hell? Why?"

He flicks his gaze to Mikkalo, who still stands quietly guarding the door. "I don't know all the details, because Zaire wasn't allowed to share them, but what I do know is it involved the Divine Coven of Ombre Noire, a city now a part of the Vaduva Region, and Blood Rebels."

"Divine?" I ask. "That name sounds familiar."

"The former leader was the founder of Donor Life Corp. He massacred a huge Blood Rebel colony using outcasts. You might know the place as The Orchards or Red Canyon Crest Grove." Mikkalo draws my attention to him.

I widen my eyes. "Shit. I do. But Laredo said it was a huge shadow dweller colony unincorporated with Donor Life Corp. He said that no one gets in or out." I close my eyes, remembering the short conversation we had brought up because Grayson heard it was a human paradise. Laredo said that was exactly what vampires wanted humans to think, so they'd attempt to go there. I should've known Laredo lied.

Bronx reaches out and touches my face. "I know there are a lot of things you still don't know, but I will do my best to inform you. Some other time."

I glare at him, and he risks leaning in to kiss me. Snuggling in his embrace, I rest my head on his arm and just share the same breathing space as my nerves fully settle. Mikkalo sits on my other side and rests his hand on my hip, just wanting to be close.

Bronx sits up when he's certain I'm not going to try to go after Corona. I watch him slip back into his clothes and head into a wardrobe. The last room we were in only had a closet with nothing for me. I expect Bronx to come out with more too big guy clothes, but he hands me a cotton nightie with a lace trim and matching panties.

"I'll pick up more clothes for you in the evening. For now, you should try to get some sleep," Bronx says, combing his fingers through his hair.

"In another room." I nearly get sick again as I peer around and spot the dead man still on the floor in a pool of blood.

Mikkalo swipes the blanket off the bed to drape over the body. "Where Everett can give you another look."

"I'm fine," I say, trying to imagine anything else that isn't gore. "Just a little nauseated. I'll feel better when we get out of here, and I can get some solid food and a little more blood in my stomach."

Bronx helps me up. "Let Everett help, Gwen. He can feed you as well."

I sigh. "Okay."

"Good. I'll send him your guys' way and meet up with you after I make sure everything is taken care of."

"You'll assure the woman is safe?" I ask.

Bronx tightens his jaw and nods. "You can help me interrogate her later, along with the rest of the staff. We can't take any more chances. We have enough to deal with."

"What will you do with them after?" I can't stop the blip of fear tightening my chest.

"That'll be something we can all decide."

"I think it might be worth the risk," Grayson says, leaning his elbows on his knees. "If we can get to the community, we won't have to deal with shadow dwellers all the time."

"Yeah, Nathaniel said that vampires are caged. They bow down to us. There's also a huge compound full of women. They let the fiercest fighters live with them. A higher chance of finding a permanent supply of pussy."

Grabbing my silver stake from my jacket, I chuck it at Porter. It whacks him in the forehead. "Not for you, if you keep talking like that."

Porter jumps to his feet and rushes to me to retaliate. I jerk my leg up to try to kick him in the groin, but he grabs my foot and hoists me off the couch. I slam my back into the floor and roll a few times to stop him from tackling me and twisting my arm until I call mercy. Last time, I passed out from pain because I refused to let him think he could ever best me.

"Don't let him get you, little sis," Grayson calls. "Show him who's powerful enough to save even his dumb ass one day."

I catapult to my feet with a laugh. "Not if it raises his chances of a supposed endless supply of vagina. The last things we need are Porter's offspring running around."

"Aw come on, Auntie Gwen. You're going to need our spawn to back you up when we're all old as fuck," Silas says. "Your daughter will need a bunch of cousins too. The bigger our family, the better. Right, Grayson?" Silas appears in the doorway, offering me his cheesiest smile.

"My daughter? Yeah, right. You guys are a bunch of cock blocks." I pick up a pillow from the couch and swing it at Porter, stopping him from closing the space. "Hmm, of course if we did make it to this supposed paradise, you'd all be too busy with your endless supply of vagina that I wouldn't even have to sneak around to get my endless supply of dick. I hear the elders take their procreation seriously. Only the best, hottest, fiercest of all the dick welcome to try to impress a woman."

My brothers groan.

"I did not just hear you say that." Declan comes into the living room from the kitchen. "One dhampir Gallagher *is enough."*

"Get used to the idea, bro," Ashton says, following behind him. "Why do you think Mom and Dad had so many of us? I'm pretty fucking sure we'll be expected to do the same."

"I still don't want to hear my precious, innocent little sister talk about how she's thinking about fucking what sounds like an entire army of dicks. I don't care what the elders want. No way." Declan looks at me. "Seriously, Gwen. Expanding the dhampir population is not your responsibility. How about you concentrate on finding someone who will treat you like the gift to humanity you are and not a tool to start the next generation."

I laugh again. "Jeez, Declan. I'm only kidding. I don't want an army. Maybe just a few. A woman has needs too, you know."

"Gwen! Shut the fuck up." This comes from Silas.

"Seriously, Gwen," Grayson says, crossing his arms. "I don't want Laredo to hear you talk like this and get any ideas. I know you two have grown closer over the last few months."

I stick my tongue out at Declan. "Maybe you should get on Porter's case. He started it with his ridiculous, most definitely never-going-to-happen fantasy. Sorry if I have my own too."

Declan grabs Porter and puts him in a headlock. "You

fuckhead."

"Plus," I add. "Maybe I want Laredo to hear. No risk of procreating there."

Grayson's face twists in disgust, and he closes the space to me and shoves me. I stumble back, catching myself on the wall. "Don't be stupid, Gwen."

"Me, stupid?"

"Grayson, back away from Gwen." Laredo's voice cuts through the air. "She is only joking around to get a rise out of you because you and your brothers lack tact and respect toward the female population with your ideas for your futures."

Grayson stiffens, reaching for the stake in his jacket. Porter pulls his gun from his holster. Silas, Declan, and Ashton unsheathe their daggers. Kyler appears in the hallway with his own stake. All of my brothers turn to face Laredo, looking hell-bent on attacking him.

I sigh and strut in front of Laredo. "You guys, knock it off. Laredo was right. I was only joking. He knows he's not my type."

Laredo releases a soft growl.

"Now, put your weapons down. Laredo is my blood source, and he's not a threat. I really don't feel like having to hunt the shadows for a new one. He's raised my expectations on who I drink from quite a bit." I look at each of my brothers. "As for the other stuff, I doubt such a place exists."

Laredo drapes his arm over my shoulder. "She's right. It's a trap to lure humans into an out-of-control, infested area of shadow dwellers. The Orchards is the last place I'd ever take you."

My brothers get themselves under control and leave me alone with Laredo, though Grayson gives me a pointed look to warn me that our conversation isn't over. Lifting me off my feet, Laredo spins me toward the couch and plops down next to me. I shift to look at him, his eyes flashing silver.

"You lied to my brothers," I say, keeping my voice low.

He shrugs. "You don't want to go to The Orchards. Trust me. The Blood Rebels will use you. You were not far off on your assessment of how they'd treat you. You might feel like a queen among them, but they will take everything from you. Your father and mother left The Orchards to keep you from them. They'd have taken you away and raised you as a weapon and not the beautiful, exquisite woman you are. One I hope to win over soon enough."

His words send goosebumps over my skin. "Laredo, please. We've been over this. My brothers—it would never work. We are not compatible."

"We're more compatible than you think."

"What's that supposed to mean?"

He flashes his fangs and bites his arm, distracting me. I automatically take his offering and mold my lips over his arm and begin to suck.

Capturing me with his gaze, he says, "You will forget everything I've said. You will believe The Orchards are now for vampires."

I blink a few times, a strange feeling washing over me.

"I will die before the Blood Rebels get you."

11

STRESS RELIEF

SOFT LIPS BRUSH MY SHOULDER, drawing me from sleep. Bronx rests his raging morning wood between my legs, testing the boundary of my underwear. I squeeze my thighs together and trap him in place.

Opening my eyes, I stare at Mikkalo's sleeping face. His fingers curl through mine as we face each other. I can't see Jameson or Everett, but I can hear their soft breathing. I doubt it's been more than a few hours. A small line of sunshine peeks into the room from the tinted glass window, letting me know it's still day time.

Bronx slides his fingers over my hip and to the waist of my panties. I suck in a tiny breath as he tests to see if I'll let him continue exploring my body. I do. Easing my leg up a bit, I give him better access to my body. He rubs between my legs, arousing me.

"You're so tense," he whispers, keeping his voice so soft that only I can hear him.

I bite my lip to keep from moaning.

"Can I help you relax?"

"Your brothers are sleeping right next to us," I whisper.

"Exactly. Sleeping."

I wiggle my ass, pressing it into his hips. "Okay, but bite your arm for me."

Easing my head up, I let Bronx slide his arm under my neck. I glide my tongue over his blood, just tasting his sweetness.

He wastes no time and tugs my panties down. I latch onto his arm as he enters me, muffling any noise I make. A dozen sensations explode through me, Bronx's blood setting off my lust like crazy. His breath tickles my neck, and he kisses me a dozen times as he slowly rocks into me, savoring the feeling of my body.

Locking his hand to my hip, Bronx holds me in place, assuring I don't bump into Mikkalo. I gasp as the pressure builds. He grazes his teeth to my shoulder, his hunger mirroring his desire. I release his arm and kiss his sweet skin. My breathing quickens with his short thrusts, my mouth wanting nothing more than to scream out my enjoyment. I close my eyes, tightening my fingers around the sheets.

Cool lips brush against mine, and I release what sounds like a quiet whimper. I suck in Mikkalo's bottom lip into my mouth, kissing him more fervently. His lips break from mine, and he kisses my jaw, shifting lower to kiss my cleavage. He eases my bodice down and flicks his tongue over my nipples, and I cling to his head.

"Let me feed you," I whisper. "Both of you."

The subtle click of Bronx's fangs extending sounds in my ear. I twine one of my hands through his, squeezing his fingers as he bites me. Mikkalo silences my moan with another kiss. He trails his hand lower, running his fingers down my stomach to rub my clit.

I release another breathless moan, Bronx's thrusts and Mikkalo's stimulation bringing me to the brink of release. Mikkalo waits for my muscles to tense before he bites the top of my breast, letting my blood drip just enough to lick it off my nipple.

I moan so damn loud that both Jameson and Everett startle awake. Jameson sits up, meeting my gaze with a cocked eyebrow. He doesn't say anything, watching my face as his brothers pleasure me.

"Damn," Everett whispers, shifting toward the end of

the bed.

"Right?" Jameson risks leaning over Mikkalo to kiss me. "Talk about a wakeup call."

I giggle against his lips. "I'm sorry. I didn't mean to wake you guys."

Mikkalo eases his lips from my breast. "I'm glad you did."

Bronx moans, breaking away from my shoulder as he cums. He eases out of me and cuddles me close while he catches his breath. No one comments or anything, thankfully. I'm sure they're all thinking that they'd have done the same.

Everett massages his fingers into my calf. I wiggle my fingers at him, getting him to come closer. Mikkalo shifts a bit to let him pile in with us. Everett doesn't stay on top of me long, hooking his arm under me to flip positions. I laugh and land on top of him. He tugs me forward by my ass and kisses my thigh.

"If you can wait a few minutes, I can get in the shower and feed you and Jameson next," I tease, squeezing his head between my knees.

"I'm on it," Jameson says, disappearing into the bathroom. "And Bronxy, you're in charge of Gwen's human breakfast. Something hot like her. Savory, not sweet. Cheesy. No bananas."

Bronx reaches out and strokes his fingers along my

cheek. "I'll see what I can do." He shifts up and kisses me before whispering, "I love you, dandelion. You're my favorite kind of stress relief."

I shake my head with another laugh. "You better hurry. I'm starving."

"Mikkalo, go with him and help," Jameson calls, standing in the doorway, steam from the hot shower wafting in the room. "I don't trust the staff, especially after dinner last night."

Everett sits up with me, carrying me to the shower. I had nearly forgotten about the fiasco of dinner and the hair Jameson found in my pasta, thankfully before it touched my mouth. My guys found three more Blood Rebels who were excellent at pretending to be mind manipulated. And now, we're supposedly going to find out the traitor vampire who has been giving them blood today.

Everett sets me on my feet in the small glass shower where Jameson waits, covered in soap. I laugh as Jameson hugs me, sliding his chest against mine. Everett slips in behind me and grabs the shower sprayer to soak my hair. I laugh again as he sprays the rest of me, enjoying my reaction at the sudden change of the water stream that he sneaks between my legs.

"Your reaction to that is enough that I'm going to get a couple of fun things for us to play with during my time," Everett whispers.

I shiver, goosebumps prickling across my skin.

"You cold, Gwen?" Jameson asks, not hearing Everett. "I can't go much hotter before I burn our cocks off."

I snort and shake my head. "I'm fine."

He bites his arm. "Maybe a little blood will warm you up."

Both Everett and Jameson behave while feeding me and taking pleasure in washing every inch of me. I love how normal it feels just to be together like this. I think everything we've been through brought us closer than I thought possible. It was one thing for me to think about splitting my time between four vampires—I never really imagined how I would feel to share the time either.

"Before you feed us, I want to know how you're feeling," Everett says, combing my hair to push it onto my shoulder to cover both Bronx and Mikkalo's bites.

"I think I'm okay," I say. "Everything is pretty much healed."

He rests his head on my shoulder. "What about your stomach? You didn't eat much at dinner."

"Can you blame her?" Jameson asks.

"He's right. The whole thing grossed me out. Not to mention, I'm a bit nervous that someone will try to poison me." I didn't want to admit it, but if the Blood Rebels were determined enough, they could totally try.

Everett groans. "Luckily, your immunity is similar to a

vampire's."

"Except I have been getting sick."

"Most likely unrelated to your health," Everett responds.

I nod. "You're probably right. Everything about everything freaks and stresses me out."

Jameson links his fingers through mine. "We'll be home soon enough."

"I can't wait." I kiss him sweetly. "Now, you two let me feed you. It makes me feel even better."

Jameson hums. "Sure, that's it. I'm nearly certain you heard Bronx and Mikkalo return."

I smile against his mouth. "Don't be jealous. I react the same way when you bring me food too."

Everett presses his naked body to my back. "She's right. You know how much our girl loves to eat."

Jameson's fangs extend. "And so do I."

I hum and tip my head a bit to show him I'm ready whenever. Jameson sandwiches me to Everett to kiss me deeper. I can't stop thinking about both their erections touching me and what our naked bodies feel like together like this.

Everett holds me in place by the hips, and I hug Jameson, digging my fingers into his back. The two of them bite me—Jameson on the top of my breast and Everett on my shoulder, mirroring their brothers' marks on me. I moan, shifting on my feet, enjoying their lips and hands on my wet skin. This is the best start of my day that I've had. I mean, I love waking up to each of my guys and their affection, but there's just something about our slumber parties that makes me all sorts of happy and excited.

"You love this, don't you?" Jameson murmurs, bringing his lips back to mine when he's through drinking.

"How could I not?" I say, smiling through another of his kisses.

Everett pulls away from my skin, and I twirl to meet his lips next. He hugs me close, and I'm nearly certain he's going to suggest we take things further, but a tap sounds on the door. I sigh and ease away so that I can face the both of them. I hook my arm around each of their shoulders and rest my chin on the crook they make with their shoulders pressed together.

"Come in," Jameson calls out.

Mikkalo cracks the door open and smiles at me as I stare at him from over Everett and Jameson's bodies. I wiggle my fingers in a wave and watch him grab a towel off the hook to bring to me.

"If you're not ready to get out, I'll gladly join you," he says, grinning.

Jameson turns off the water. "You can take my place. I hear our girl's stomach and it sounds beastly. You know she always goes after me first, and I'll never make it out of here in time to meet the guests if she does."

I giggle and reach down to lace my fingers around his cock. "Maybe that's what I want."

Everett squeezes my ass. "Don't worry, Gwen. I got you. I'm not needed for that bullshit."

Reaching down, I stroke his boner too. "You guys are bad."

Mikkalo opens the shower door and holds a towel out for me. "You love it."

I smile. "I do as much as I love all of you."

Scooping me up, Mikkalo carries me to the bedroom, leaving Everett and Jameson to dry off. My breakfast sits on a bed tray on the nightstand. The delicious scent of bacon, eggs, and spiced potatoes wafts through the air. My stomach burns with ferocity, and I clutch my belly and jerk in Mikkalo's arms, nearly making me drop him.

"That smells so good," I say as Mikkalo sets me on the bed. I wrap my towel tighter around me. "I can't believe you made this."

Mikkalo twists his lips to the side and leans in to whisper, "I hope it's okay that I supervised the chef from start to finish. I might even have had a few different taste testers."

I raise my eyebrows. "That's thorough."

"Not risking Jameson trying to murder me."

Stabbing my fork into a piece of cut up potato, I bring it to my nose to sniff it. Not like I would be able to tell if something were wrong with it. All I can smell are the potent spices that make my stomach rumble like crazy. Mikkalo encourages me to take the bite, and I savor the explosion of flavor on my tongue.

"This is incredible," I murmur, covering my mouth while I chew.

"Good. Now eat quickly. Bronx is waiting for us." Mikkalo disappears and heads to the wardrobe. He pulls out a white dress and meets my grimace with a frown. "He also asked that you wear this."

Fucking hell. Not another damn bridal gown. "Ugh, why?"

"You're still Zaire's Blood Match and must be dressed like one even in his absence." Mikkalo drapes the dress in front of him, swaying the fabric. "And just think...I can rip it off later."

"Or I can." Everett winks at me, strolling from the bathroom with a towel slung low on his hips. He glides his tongue over his top lip, looking sexy as hell with his wet hair and sparkling blue eyes drinking me in. "Might I remind you that you'd be wearing a dress anyway, or did you forget our bet?"

I fake-glare at him.

"What kind of bet was this?" Jameson drops his towel just for me and turns around to grab a pair of boxers from a chest of drawers. Looks like Mikkalo also brought them suits to wear. The last thing I want to experience is a formal occasion with vampires outside of my guys, but I highly doubt they'll leave me alone to hang out in the room.

"Nothing," Everett and I say in unison and smile at each other.

"Gigi, you are lucky I have to greet the city leaders," he mutters, quickly getting dressed. And damn it does he look hot. I don't want him to go. He turns to his brothers. "I trust you to remember to make her lunch if I can't break away. Remember, no one but you handles the food. Got it?"

"Not even Gwen?" Mikkalo teases. He snatches my fork away from me and offers me another bite, noticing that I'm not shoveling food like I usually do. "Perfect. I love taking care of our girl."

I snap my teeth down on the fork and yank it away with my mouth. I set it back on the plate. "You've done enough. I think I can handle it from here."

Mikkalo kisses me. "You have until I get out of the shower."

I flop back on the bed and stare at the ceiling. Everett sits next to me in the towel, linking his fingers through mine. He gazes down at me with a worried expression, but he doesn't speak his mind. He doesn't have to ask to know that I'll take my sweet time so that I don't have to leave the room.

"Gwen, I know this fucking sucks—"

"Go ahead and get ready, brother. I'll make sure she finishes," Everett says to Jameson.

Jameson closes the space to me and squeezes my knee. "Behave. Call me if you need me."

The three of us watch him go. I take a few more bites of my breakfast and set it aside. Nerves tighten my stomach. Everett notices how little I've eaten and offers me another bite. I force myself to eat a bit more but shake my head when he offers me a piece of the bacon.

"Is it not how you like it cooked?" Everett asks. "I know how much you like bacon."

I scrunch my nose. "I'm just—it doesn't sound good. I might have drunk too much blood. If I eat anything else, I won't be leaving this bed due to a food coma."

Sliding off the bed, I drop my towel to the floor to purposely distract him from going in full-on health keeper mode. He hums under his breath and stands behind me, hooking his fingers to my hips. He kisses his bite mark, anything he was thinking now pushed to the back of his mind.

"Do you know how much I want to bend you over?" he asks, moving his hand to my stomach and pushing me a bit forward.

"How much?" I stand on my tiptoes to let him slide between my legs.

"All right, Gwen. No seducing Everett. We only have a couple of minutes, and I can already tell he'll want to ravish you all night." Mikkalo stands in the bathroom door, stretching his arms up to show off his muscular body. I love how brazen my guys are. I'm starting to think I only get a bit wild because of them.

"That sounds like a far better plan than getting into that dress," I say, smiling at Mikkalo.

He groans. "All right, Ev. I'm pulling the it's-my-time card."

Everett chuckles and nudges me toward where the white gown hangs on a hook. Mikkalo dresses as Everett helps me into the flouncy, floor-length dress. I laugh when he expertly adjusts my boobs to show off my cleavage.

"I know you hate the gowns, but you look stunning," Everett says.

"I wish you could wear your hair up." Mikkalo plays with my blond tresses, lifting them from my chest to run his finger over his mark on me. "I want the whole region to know you're our girl."

I trace my finger over his freshly shaved jaw. "I want that so much too."

Mikkalo's com device beeps, and he grumbles under his breath. I'm not the only one avoiding life outside this room. Everett snatches it from his hand and glances at the screen. He frowns as well. I try to attempt to grab it to see what's up, but Everett holds the com device over his head to give to Mikkalo out of my reach.

"If I give you an hour of my time, will you cover for me?" Mikkalo asks Everett.

"Whatever keeps our girl away," Everett says.

I narrow my eyes. "This better not be about the rebels."

Mikkalo remains expressionless. "It is."

"Then I don't think so. Bronx said—"

"Bronx felt bad for your fight. He'll tell you yes to anything for at least another week," Mikkalo says, flicking his gaze to Everett. "Me, on the other hand—"

"Will say yes for the rest of eternity." I grin and pat his cheek. "So let's go."

I don't get a chance to brace myself as Mikkalo scoops me into his arms. He hikes up my dress so that I can wrap my legs around his waist. I snuggle my face into the crook of his neck, teasing him by nibbling on his skin. The world comes to a halt, leaving my head spinning. I close my eyes as my mind catches up to my body.

"Mikkalo, shit. Get her out of here," Bronx says. "Didn't you read the fucking message?"

Mikkalo locks his fingers to the back of my head, preventing me from seeing anything. "I thought Jameson was just trying to protect Gwen by asking for Everett."

"What happened?" Everett asks. He stands behind me, being the only one I see.

"The traitor got to them." Bronx keeps his voice even. "I need you to examine the bodies."

"What the hell?" My voice cuts through the air.

"Mikkalo, out!"

I don't give Mikkalo a chance to relocate me. I shove against him with all my strength. Bronx must expect me to fight, because he catches me before I hit the ground and throws me over his shoulder. I jerk my neck up and catch sight of what they're trying to hide from me.

Motherfuckinghell.

"Gah-gah-gah." The strange guttural sound echoes through the air.

"One's alive. Quick, Ev," Jameson calls.

Bronx gives up on trying to protect me and carries me with him toward the collection of bodies.

"Gah-gah-gah."

"You," Everett says, pointing to an unfamiliar vampire. "Give her blood now."

"Wen. Wen." Another voice sounds out.

"Gah-wen. Help."

"Shit, they're all alive," Jameson says.

"Did you not check their pulses?" Annoyance laces Everett's voice.

Bronx clears his throat. "I didn't think the traitor would be stupid enough not to assure their deaths." He sets me on my feet, keeping me in place so that I can't get another look.

Mikkalo pulls me back to him. "Good thing. Stupid

was exactly what we needed to get this piece of shit."

"Gah-gah-gah. Wen-wen-wen."

I twist in Mikkalo's arms to peer at the people bleeding on the floor. A man stretches his arm out to point at me. He opens and closes his mouth, trying to spit the words out. I drag Mikkalo with me, moving closer. He whispers something too low for me to understand. My guys don't catch it either.

"Don't get too close, Gwen," Bronx warns.

I crouch down and study the man's mouth.

"Him," the man mouths.

"Him?" I ask.

A loud pop sounds through the air, startling me.

I drop to the floor.

12

REVELATION

"GWEN. GWEN." EVERETT TOUCHES MY back.

I scream, staring into the blank eyes of the man with a bullet hole in the middle of his forehead. Hands lock around me, and I flail as Everett picks me up and relocates me. I hit my back to the hallway wall and heave a breath.

"Kiss me," Everett whispers against my lips.

"Wh-what?" My voice quivers.

"Please."

A breath trembles on my lips as I lean in and caress my

mouth to Everett's. He tightens his hold on me, kissing me deeper until I stop shaking. Teasing my dhampir side proves to be a sure thing to either drive me wild or distract me. I feel if as long as I stay close to Everett, sharing his breath, that none of this bullshit is actually happening.

"Take her to the study," Bronx orders. "All of you stay with her. Do not separate. I'll handle this and meet you there."

Again, I don't have the chance to brace for my relocation. I steel myself, refusing to make a sound. Everett rushes me through the house with Mikkalo in front of us and Jameson behind. A few voices whisper through the air, but my guys ignore them.

"What a delectable treat," a masculine voice says, drawing my attention to the suddenly quiet room we stop in. "Is this the infamous Blood Match to Zaire?"

"Yes," Mikkalo says, speaking up.

The man smiles at me, keeping his fangs in check. "May I greet her?"

"Of course you may," I say, speaking for myself. "Mikkalo is not my keeper, and I'm sure he won't tell Zaire as long as you're not an asshole to me or ask for a sample of my blood."

"Don't touch her either," Jameson says, straightening his back to stand tall.

The man nods and offers me a low bow. "It's a pleasure

to meet you, Ms. Royale. I'm Carlsbad of the Cortez Coven and head of Onyx Canyon. Have you ever been?"

I shake my head.

"Consider this an invitation for you and Zaire. We'd love to have you." Carlsbad offers me another dazzling smile that lights up his honey-brown eyes.

"Thank you," I say, remaining expressionless. I know better than to act more than pleasant. From my experience with vampires, they can be major flirts, and that's the last thing I want.

"Why don't you allow me to introduce you to the rest of my coven?" Carlsbad asks.

I turn my attention to Mikkalo, and he subtly shakes his head. Without looking at Carlsbad, I say, "No, thank you. I'm not here to socialize without my Blood Match."

"Then why are you here, covered in tantalizing blood, if I might add." Carlsbad's eyes flash silver.

A hulking form materializes in front of me, and Bronx whacks Carlsbad on the back. He doesn't growl like I expect but instead, Bronx shakes the man's hand. A few other vampires, three men and a woman, stand to join Carlsbad.

One of the men looks to me, and I recognize him. Fear prickles through me at seeing Brentwood. He and Corona had started a blood feud between each other because of Silas. I know Corona was responsible for having to return his female donors back to him after they ran after Silas, but I never asked how it went. Obviously, they're both alive.

"Darling, Gwen," Brentwood says to me. "It's so nice to see you again. You look ravishing."

"And you should stop looking at me like I might be interested in being your personal donor." The words come out before I have a chance to think them through. I've been around my guys so much that it takes a lot of work for me to realize that these city leaders might take offense to my rebel mouth.

Brentwood shrugs without comment. He shifts his gaze to look behind me, and a shiver trails down my back. My fear instincts blare like crazy, and I automatically reach for Mikkalo and Everett's hands since they're standing the closest to me. I don't have to turn around to know that Corona hovers in the doorway. I close my eyes and concentrate on my breathing to stop myself from spinning to glower.

"Thank you for your patience this evening. I have arranged a feast in the dining hall to occupy your covens during our meeting," Corona says.

The only woman in the room apart from me raises her perfectly arched brows. "And why can't we join them and discuss matters over lunch?"

Bronx clears his throat. "Due to the nature of our gathering, and for the safety of our cities, I must insist on privacy. If you choose to share information with those closest to you, Brea, I must ask that you wait until returning home."

"Shouldn't Zaire be here?" Brea asks.

"Yes, he should. But unfortunately, he's not. As acting region head, it is my duty to prepare you all for a possible war brewing in our region." Bronx flicks his gaze to me. "I also have an announcement that you should hear first."

"What about the Crescent and Grey Covens? Ronan and Irvine would never miss a gathering," Carlsbad says.

"I will get to that. Now, if we may, please take a seat." Bronx strolls toward the desk and perches on top, sitting higher than the others who return to their seats.

Mikkalo and Everett guide me to a leather couch in the corner while Jameson joins Bronx. Corona closes the door to his study, choosing to remain standing with his back against the wood. Thankfully, he pretends like I'm not here. If only the other city heads would.

"What of the donor?" another man asks. "You cannot possibly trust her with our region's business. It's far too easy to break into her mind if she ever goes unaccompanied."

"Gwen doesn't," Everett says. "Ever."

"I still don't think—"

"Enough, Vernon!" Bronx's booming voice freezes everyone in place. "We don't have a lot of time. The longer you're away from your cities, the more at risk our region is."

Vernon growls. "Excuse me if I take our laws seriously."

Bronx launches at the vampire, dragging him off his feet. He slams his back into the wall. Vernon snarls, trying to snap his teeth, but Bronx is far too strong for the guy. I stare in awe, watching Bronx's muscles flex, his air of authority so palpable that it steals my breath in a good way. I always knew my guys would do their best to assure my safety but damn. Seeing Bronx in action turns me the hell on.

Everett digs his fingers into my leg, drawing my attention to him. "You like that?" he whispers too quietly for anyone else to see.

I blush like crazy and shrug.

He chuckles and pretends to wipe drool from my mouth. I bump my shoulder to his, smiling. And then I realize that none of the other vampires watch Bronx and Vernon. All their attention focuses on me.

"Ignore them," Everett says. "They're jealous that you've chosen me to show attention to."

I flick his shoulder. "You love it."

He wags his eyebrows without comment.

"If you question my authority again, you will lose Silver Rock," Bronx snaps. I realize that Everett distracted me enough that I missed what Bronx said before his threat. "It is more important than ever that all our cities have a strong alliance, but especially to the Royale Coven if you want our region to remain intact."

"What are you saying?" the last man asks.

"We're under attack, Arvin. Ronan Crescent is deceased. Irvine Grey, along with the rest of Twilight Peak, was also annihilated. Seventy-five percent of the Anderson Coven gone. And there will be more if we do not prepare. There are traitors in our midst—vampires and humans."

"Then where is Zaire? I demand he join us!" Brea says, her voice turning shrill. "He is our region head. He needs to get Donor Life Corp involved."

Bronx closes his eyes and scrubs his face with his hands. He doesn't respond to her right away, collecting his thoughts. Without having to ask him, I know this is it. This is the moment that he will announce his brother's demise.

"Zaire cannot join us," Bronx says, darting his gaze to us.

Mikkalo tugs me off the couch and pulls me past the group of vampires to take his position at Bronx's side. Everett rests his hands on my shoulders, and I glance around at the various expressions crossing the faces of all the cities' heads as they realize the extent of Bronx's admission and wait for him to confirm their suspicions.

"It is with great sadness that I announce the leader of the Royale Coven lost his life in battle." Bronx remains expressionless.

Inching my way closer, I touch my hand to his as he rests it behind his back. He squeezes my fingers, his body rigid as the announcement sinks in.

"As first in line, I've stepped up as head. I must ask that the rest of you support the shift in power. I plan to announce my run for the free board seat in less than a week," Bronx continues. "If you do not back me, I can't promise things will end well for our region."

"As leader of the Anderson Coven, I support the power shift to Bronx Royale," Corona says.

Bronx turns his gaze to Corona. "Thank you, Mr. Anderson. To show my appreciation, I'd also like to formally announce the union of our covens."

"What?" My. Damn. Mouth.

I drop my hand from Bronx's and take an automatic step away from him. Everett tightens his hold on me, stopping me from trying to flee. Hurt and anger storm through me, my whirlwind of emotions threatening to send me into an uncontrollable rage. I knew that Bronx humored the idea of joining their two covens, but I thought it was a joke or a way to keep Corona in line. I'm so not cool with this bullshit.

"It would be an honor to blend bloodlines," Corona says, ignoring my reaction.

Everyone does.

The small group of people applauds, and Brentwood stands up. "You also have my support, Mr. Royale. I look forward to seeing the strengthening of our region while putting a stop to the rise of our enemies."

Bronx nods stiffly. "Thank you. I'd also like to reassign the Crescent and Grey areas. For those of you who show support, I'll divide the population among you."

"And if we don't?" Vernon says, scowling.

"You may stand against me in front of Donor Life Corp," Bronx says simply. "But mind you, it will not go over well."

"I also offer my support," Vernon says, surprising me.

"As do I," the remaining city leaders say.

They all stand up and bow deeply to Bronx. I ease back, pushing Everett with me. Their sudden closeness sets me off even more. With Bronx's announcements, I don't even want to be here.

"What of Zaire's Blood Match?" Brentwood asks, turning his attention to me. "Perhaps you'll consider a generous offer to take her from your household."

Bronx growls. "Absolutely not."

"Are you sure?" Brea asks.

Baring his teeth, Bronx says, "Enough. Gwen is *mine*."

I pace circles in our suite in my bra and underwear. There is no way I'm putting on another white dress. As long as I stay like this, no one will try to drag my ass out of here to supposedly celebrate. The last thing I want to do is celebrate. I'm pissed off. Beyond pissed off. I'm about to turn into a raging bitch, and no one will be able to stop me.

A tap sounds on the door.

"The only person you better send in here is Corona," I snap. "Because I'm in a terrible mood and don't want to risk ripping your heart out."

"How about we bone or something? That always makes me feel better," Jameson says through a crack in the door.

"Seriously, Jamie?" I ask, stopping to glare at the door.

He risks entering the room and stops in his tracks. Inhaling a breath, he drinks in the sight of me, staring at my glittery heels to the sheer white, sexy bra and thong I wear. My bloody dress rests in a pile on the floor.

"I'm so fucking serious now that I see you." Jameson shrugs out of his suit jacket and sets it on the dresser. "Because, damn. Gigi, you're so hot."

I purse my lips.

His tie comes off next. "Bronx wants us present in the dining room, but I don't give a shit now. I'm going to ravish you." Closing the space, he swings the tie over my head to pull me against him.

Gripping his dress shirt, I rip a couple of buttons free to expose his chest. "Is that what you think?"

"Mmmhmm."

I snap my teeth at him. "I could hurt you."

He snatches my hands and pulls them over my head. I don't have a chance to react as he ties his tie around my wrists, restraining me. "I'll assure you don't."

The suite door suddenly swings open, and Everett enters the room. He closes the door behind him and hesitates, seeing the two of us. A look of desire crosses Everett's face, sending my heart racing like crazy.

"Gwen's a little tied up. Tell Bronx she doesn't want to join him," Jameson says.

Everett licks his lips. "Bronx said I can't return without her."

I scowl. "Why? Because I'm *his* girl now?"

Jerking my arms, I manage to rip the tie from my wrists.

I spin on my heels and stroll to the bed. I flop on it, burying my face into the pillows. A solid body lands on top of me. Jameson shifts my hair and kisses my shoulder.

"You're not only his girl, Gigi," he murmurs. "If you were only his girl, there's no fucking way I'd ever do this."

Jameson glides his tongue over my neck and kisses a trail to my spine. I sink harder into the bed under his weight, enjoying the sensation of his mouth on my skin. The bed shifts as Everett joins us. He laces his fingers through mine, kissing each of my fingers, and works his way down to my wrist.

"I hope you know that Bronx only said that to make a point. You're very much all of ours," Everett says.

"Still. It pissed me off," I say, trying not to raise my voice in annoyance.

Jameson shifts lower, spreading my legs. "And we'll

help hold him down while you kick him. You did warn him of the consequences, even if he was doing it for show." His fangs graze my thong, but he continues past to kiss my ass cheek.

"What about the other thing? Was he joking about that too?" I ask, squirming the lower Jameson's mouth goes.

"What other thing?" Everett asks, hooking his hand to my leg to roll me over onto my back. He cradles my head on his lap and plays with my hair.

Jameson rests his elbows on both sides of my legs, staying propped up to look at me. He doesn't say anything and stops his quest to memorize my body with his lips. I sling my arm over my eyes to cover my face. I tense with my annoyance.

"Seriously? I know you're not that oblivious." Anger sharpens my voice. I can't even bring myself to look at either of them.

A knock sounds on the door, and Mikkalo enters without waiting for a response. He rubs his lips together, staring at Jameson between my legs, and Everett combing his fingers through my hair.

"You were supposed to be dressed," Mikkalo says, keeping his gaze locked onto me. "Everyone's waiting."

"I'm not going," I say.

"But Gwen, it's important." Mikkalo closes the space and sits on the bed. "We need to be there as a coven, and we can't leave you here."

"Bronx has Corona, doesn't he?" I immediately regret my comment.

Shocked silence greets me as the three of them gape at me. How the hell are they even surprised?

Groaning, I lift my leg over Jameson and roll onto my side. "What?"

"You're angry," Jameson says. It's not a question.

"Of course I'm fucking angry!" I sit up. "Did you guys know?"

Their silence speaks volumes. They did, and they kept it from me. I know if I don't get up and do something, I might blow up even more.

I'm sure they might've had their reasons, but right now, I don't want to hear them. I don't want to think about any of this anymore.

I get off the bed and stride to the wardrobe. I shrug into another damn white dress and glance at my reflection. My eyes flash silver at me, and I inhale a few deep breaths, trying to get my shit together.

Nothing works. I'm losing control.

Stomping from the wardrobe, I ignore their stares as I head to the bathroom. I splash water on my face and then grab a glass from the sink. I purse my lips, keeping my gaze on the floor, and head back to them, now all sitting on the edge of the bed.

I hold the glass to Mikkalo. "If you want me to go out there, I need blood. It's your time, so please fill up my glass."

"Gwen," Jameson says. "Please. Let us—"

I turn my attention to Jameson, and he closes his mouth. His eyes flash silver at me. He swallows, his Adam's apple bobbing with the gesture. Something in my eyes makes him nervous, because he bites his arm and extends it out to me.

"No, Jamie. You don't like to put it in the glass, and that's how I want to drink it right now." I try to keep my voice even, but my heart aches, my chest tightening. The quiver in my voice makes the three of them frown.

"Gwen—"

Mikkalo reaches out and flicks Jameson on the shoulder. "Don't push her."

"She's quite angry," Everett adds.

Biting his arm, Mikkalo fills the glass with his blood and hands it to me. I turn my back to hide from the weight of their stares. Taking a sip, I down the blood in a long swallow and set the glass on the middle of the carpet. I tighten my jaw with the wave of warmth washing through me.

I head to the door and stand until Mikkalo checks the hallway. "Don't be afraid to celebrate because of me. At least someone should enjoy themselves."

None of them responds to my comment.

I let Mikkalo lead the way in silence. The stroll down the hallway feels like a death march.

If only it didn't feel like mine.

13

PARTY CRASHER

"YOU'RE A BLOOD MATCH, TOO?" A young guy in a white tuxedo slides up next to me as I shovel another bread roll in my mouth.

"That obvious?" I ask, covering my mouth with my hand. I swing the hem of my gown back and forth, sweeping the floor.

He chuckles. "Fortunately, white looks beautiful on you."

A soft growl sounds from where Mikkalo hovers. I keep

my gaze trained on the floor, not even bothering to look at the guy. I can feel a dozen gazes on me, but the most intense of all burns over me from Bronx's place talking to Brentwood. I haven't acknowledged him at all, or anyone for that matter, except for now with one of the only humans not lying on a table as a blood source.

"Be careful what you say," I murmur. "Someone might think you're flirting with me."

"I don't give a damn. Let them. If my Blood Match fails to protect me, I get automatic exemption status." The guy bumps his shoulder to mine.

I jerk my head up and meet his gaze with wide eyes. Mikkalo materializes a few feet closer. It's one thing about how they react to other vampires, but I can feel the tension between me and my guys so intensely that I worry.

"You can't get exemption if you're dead." I step a foot away. "And I don't want to be responsible for such a thing."

"You could always intervene. I'll help you. You help me." Shifting his feet, he tries to close the space again. "Don't you want to reunite with your family?"

"No," I say, lowering my voice. "Even if I did, I couldn't. I'm not a volunteer."

The guy lifts a brow like he doesn't believe me. And why would he? I had no idea that a forced entry to the Blood Match Program was possible. Donor Life Corp would probably never make that information available to the general donor population. It's supposed to be some great program.

"What's that supposed to mean?"

"Gwen." Mikkalo strolls up to me and puts his hand on my lower back. He doesn't acknowledge the guy at all. "Bronx would like you to join him."

We both know he's full of crap. If Bronx wanted me to join him, I'd have heard him ask. All he does is continue to discuss his strategy to split up the two areas without any complete divisions, keeping human families together. At least that's something.

I peer at the guy from over my shoulder. "It was nice to meet you."

"Likewise, Gwen. If you ever change your mind, I'm sure we'll see each other at some other party. The Dukes love a great gathering," the guy says.

Mikkalo nudges me away from the guy, guiding me to the other side of the room. He doesn't say a word to me as I plop into a chair at a table with a guy in a speedo sitting on it cross-legged. He greets me with a smile, and I force one back, feeling awkward as hell. Bite scars pepper his body with a couple of fresh ones from this evening. I've heard of donor buffets, but I never imagined them to be like this or that the humans participating might actually enjoy it. Some of the people even dance with a few of the vampires.

"You're new to exclusive donations, aren't you?" he

asks, swiveling on the table to face me. I really wish he hadn't. From my position, his bulge points right at me from his speedo. "May I offer your mister a taste? He looks rather hungry."

I can't control my glower. "No, you may not. He's mine."

Mikkalo releases a strange, sexy noise from his throat. I flick my gaze to his, and I can see him struggling to hide his smile. It makes it hard for me to control my own, which annoys me more. I'm supposed to be mad at him. I *am* mad at him.

I burn daggers at him and turn away, flipping my hair over my shoulder. "And right now, I want him to starve."

"Makes for more fun later, huh?" the guy asks.

"They wish."

That gets a groan out of Jameson. I can't stop the smug-ass grin from crossing my mouth, which I quickly hide with my hand. The guy studies me for a long, awkward moment. I clear my throat and swivel in my chair to glance at the rest of the party.

"My name's Howie, by the way." The guy stretches his legs, getting them uncomfortably close to me.

I bob my head. "Gwen."

"I'd offer you a compliment, but I'm nearly certain I'd meet my final donation," Howie says.

"I highly doubt it."

"So does your mister treat you well?" Howie scoots forward and hangs his legs off the side of the table.

"Yes. What about you?" I dart my gaze to Mikkalo, but he doesn't look at me. Having to make small talk with Howie feels like some sort of punishment. All I want is to go back to the food table and shove more rolls into my mouth.

"This job is a dream. My family only has to make half the usual gen. pop. donations. We get a large apartment in the city. And the best part? I only have to work once every six weeks, if you can even call this work. All the food I can eat, socializing, good music." To prove his point, he slides off the table and gets to his feet. Howie starts dancing right in front of me, not giving a shit about anyone or anything around him. He wiggles his hand out to me. "Come on, Gwen. You should dance with me."

I shake my head. "No way. I don't feel like it."

Howie wags his finger. "Oh, come on. You look bored as hell. Just one song."

Sighing, I push to my feet. Howie's right. I am bored as all get-out, annoyed with the entire night, and can't stop thinking about how my guys purposely disregarded my feelings toward Corona. How Bronx stakes a claim on me.

I start slow, swaying my hips. With my heels and dress, I can't move like I want to, so I hike up my dress a bit and lift my foot onto the chair. I don't get a chance to unbuckle the strap before Mikkalo does it for me. Neither of us says anything to each other. Howie claps his hands and shakes his ass. A laugh bubbles from my throat. I've never seen anyone move like him before, and it's both amazing and hysterical.

So I copy him.

I'm pretty sure I look dumb as hell, but he was totally right about needing some entertainment. A part of me is upset that I'm dancing with this dude instead of my guys, because I hate feeling this way. Yet another petty as fuck part of me hopes they wish they were the ones dancing with me. I want them to realize that they can't just assume they can do things and hope that I forgive them after the fact. And this bullshit Corona invite? I don't care if it was to show unity. It feels far too legit. I could've used a warning instead of getting thrown off guard.

"I can't stand this any longer," Jameson says. "I'm risking it. I need to be all up in our girl's space."

I spin around, sending my hair flying out. I catch Everett grabbing Jameson by the shoulder to stop him from coming to me.

"Don't do it, brother. This is the first time I've heard her laugh all night. She needs space, and you need to respect that no matter how hard it is." Everett keeps his gaze trained on me, though I try obviously not to stare at the two of them. "Plus, it's better to wait until she's done. Dancing is proven to put her in a better mood."

"But—"

"As her health keeper, I insist," Everett says.

Jameson growls at him and skulks past me to the other side of the dance floor. The sneaky bastard keeps his eyes on me the whole time and starts dancing with a small blend of vampires and the table donors. He dares me with his green eyes to try to resist joining him, so I guarantee it and turn my back.

"Damn it, Gigi. I hate this." Jameson ignores Everett's warning and grabs my hand to spin me toward him. "We need to talk about this bullshit. Now."

My throat tightens at his comment, and I stop dancing. "I can't."

He leans in, getting close to my ear so that no one overhears him. "I don't like you when you're angry at me."

I stiffen. "And I don't like you when you keep fucking secrets from me, Jameson, especially in regards to the asshole who not only took me away from you and imprisoned me but also killed Kyler and separated my brothers."

"Gwen, you have to—"

I pull away from him. "I don't have to do anything right now." My emotions get the best of me, and a heavy pit forms in my chest and sinks into my stomach. I never knew this kind of anger and hurt could make me feel physically sick. Turning to Everett, I meet his eyes. "I don't feel so good. Please take me back to the room."

"I'll take you, Gwen," Mikkalo says. "You don't have to pretend to be sick. We've been here long enough."

My head starts to pound, and I wobble on my feet. "I'm not pretending. Something doesn't feel right."

Everett materializes in front of me and touches my face. "Why don't you feel good?"

I squeeze my eyes shut, a dizzy spell competing with my sudden headache. "I—" Closing my eyes, I wait for my head to stop spinning. My stomach lurches, and I cover my mouth with my hand. A cool glass touches my lips, and Everett's sweet blood tantalizes my senses.

"Hey, Gwen? Can you open your eyes and look at me?" Everett's gentle hand touches my cheek.

I flutter my eyelids open, realizing we're no longer at the party. "What happened?"

Everett shines a light in my eyes. "You fainted."

"How long have I been out?" I ask, my throat burning. My voice comes out hoarse like I might have screamed.

"Maybe thirty seconds." Everett tilts my head up and offers me the glass of blood again. "Do you still feel bad?"

I purse my lips without drinking and nudge his hand away. "Can I have some water instead?"

He studies my eyes for a second. "I'd like you to drink my blood first. You didn't drink very much of Mikkalo's before the party."

"But I don't need blood. I need water. Something solid to eat."

"Dandelion, stop arguing with your health keeper." Bronx's voice cuts through the quiet room, and I jerk upright and spot him standing with Mikkalo and Jameson next to the door.

My head spins again from the fast movement, and I flop back. "You don't all need to be here. Go back and enjoy your celebration."

"You're our girl. We're not going anywhere until we're sure you're okay," Bronx says, strolling closer to look down on me.

I glower at him, and he takes an automatic step back. "Are you sure I'm not just *your* girl?"

Bronx laces his hands on the back of his head, messing with his hair. Staring up at the ceiling, he blinks a few times, his jaw shifting. Every muscle on his body tightens. As each second passes, he steels himself a little more. All of the softness he carries toward me hardens, and he finally turns his gaze back to me. The heavy silence presses so hard into me that it feels as if the weight of the entire universe crushes me, breaking each bone in my body while liquefying my heart.

"I know you know that I only said that to get the city leaders to back off," Bronx says, tightening his mouth. "You can't hold that against me. Any of my brothers would have said the same thing if they were in my position. Right, brothers?"

I huff a breath. "Don't ask them to take your side."

"I'm not!" Bronx shouts, flashing his fangs at me.

Mikkalo pulls Bronx back, and they growl at each other. "Don't yell at her. Just fucking apologize and make up. You've ruined my night with Gwen enough already."

Bronx fists his hands. "I have nothing to apologize for. I did what I had to do, and I would do it again, all right? Gwen knows she comes first to me. Everything I do is for our coven and too fucking bad if she doesn't always like it."

"Wow." I can't stop the word from escaping my mouth. "I guess I shouldn't be surprised."

Bronx sighs. "Gwen, come on. You're being unfair."

I shake my head and slide off the counter Everett had put me on. It's now that I realize we're in a kitchen, probably where the human staff prepares everything for the other humans on the estate.

Without responding to Bronx, I turn to Everett. "Please take me back to the room. I'm still not feeling so great. Maybe it was something I ate. This is just a bit too much right now."

"Want me to get you anything, Gwen?" Jameson asks.

"No, thank you, Jameson. I'm just going to rest."

Bronx blocks the door out. "You can't just fake sick and leave. We're not done talking."

Everett surprises me by getting into Bronx's face. He flashes his fangs and grips onto the front of his dress shirt. "You're not her fucking health keeper. If she says she doesn't feel well, I believe her. She passed out. Her normal flush has yet to return. And honestly, you're making it worse. So get out of our way. If she's feeling better by the start of your time, you can work your shit out then. If not, then too bad."

Bronx flares his nostrils and raises his hands in surrender, letting us past him. Picking me up, Everett cradles me like the bride I'm dressed as. We don't even get a foot away from the door before Bronx, Mikkalo, and Jameson start shouting at each other. I've never heard any of them so angry, and I hate I'm the reason. I hate that I can't just suck it up and let it go.

Everett carries me at a human's speed in silence. I rest my head on his shoulder and just listen to the muffled party noises trickling through the hallway. On and off, Everett glances at me, his expressionless face sometimes breaking its mask with a pout. But he's quick to clench his jaw every time it tries to betray him.

"Gwen," he whispers, his voice barely a breath tickling my ear. "I'm sorry. I truly am. I'm an asshole for ever agreeing to the union. It wasn't all Bronx's decision to keep that official announcement from you."

I inhale a shuddering breath, my resolve cracking.

Blinking away my burning tears, I try to remain composed. Being angry I can deal with. It was my anger that protected me. Now with Everett's admission, a whole shit-ton of hurt swells inside me. I don't even know how to deal with it. Laredo never allowed me to. He took it away before I could even get a chance to wallow in pity.

"But why did you?" I ask, my voice quivering. "You guys said we were a team. I feel like I'm no longer a part of it. That's a huge problem for me."

"Gwen, you are. You are so incredibly important to me. To us." He stops in the hallway and looks at me. "I love you."

I give in to the affection he craves and meet him for a whisper of a kiss. "I love you, too. I just want to get past this, you know? Being here...it's messing me up."

"It's only for another day."

I sigh. "It's more than that. It's—"

A door opens, and a guy stumbles out, cutting off my thought. I stare at the guy from earlier—the guy who was also a Blood Match—fall to the ground. He tips his head up and releases a loud-ass laugh. Everett tightens his hold on me and turns away, continuing to stroll with me down the hallway toward our suite.

Something smashes on the floor in front of us. Glass sprays across the hall. Everett stiffens and spins around. The Blood Match guy swipes another vase off a decorative table and throws the flowers on the floor. He waves it around, laughing again. A strange expression crosses his face. And then he chucks the vase at us.

Everett spins and shields me with his body against the wall. The vase shatters by his feet. Releasing a low growl, Everett shifts to look at the guy over his shoulder. A silver candelabra hits Everett's arm.

He snarls this time, turning to set me on my feet. Pain erupts in my foot as a piece of glass slices my heel.

"Ouch, fuck," I say, lifting my foot. Blood drips from a small cut.

"Uh-oh," the guy says, pointing at me with wide eyes. "You failed to protect your Blood Match. You know what that means."

Everett loses his shit.

14

FUTURE ARRANGEMENTS

SLAMMING THE GUY'S BACK INTO the wall, Everett lifts him off his feet by his throat. The guy continues to laugh and cough, not even struggling. Fear pours through me. Everett extends his fangs longer than I've ever seen him do. And fuck. He's going to kill this guy.

"You better h-hurry, Mr. Royale. My mister will come at any second," the Blood Match guy says.

Everett snarls.

"Everett, stop! It's what he wants. He's trying to get his

contract broken." I step around the glass and touch Everett's shoulder. "Please, don't do this. I'm fine."

Heaving a few deep breaths, Everett relaxes under my touch and drops the guy to the ground. The guy hits his knees and shouts but not in pain. His crazed laughter turns into something that sounds straight out of a back-world horror movie, igniting my fear instincts not unlike when being stalked by a predator.

"You bitch," the Blood Match guy mutters. "We're supposed to have each other's backs."

I narrow my eyes from over Everett's shoulder. Everett hugs me, still trying to calm his racing heart. "What you're doing is stupid. My contract can't even be broken. I'm a criminal. I was convicted of being a Blood Rebel." I regret my admission immediately.

A dozen thoughts flash through the guy's eyes, his body turning rigid. "You could still help me."

I shake my head, tugging Everett back with me. He doesn't look at the guy, but I know he's aware of the guy's every move. "No. Even if I could, I wouldn't. You chose to Blood Match. You gave in to the offering of Donor Life Corp."

The guy flies to his feet to rush us. It's taking everything in Everett not to attack the guy. If I wasn't digging my fingers into Everett's sides, he would. Instead, he just keeps with my movements, acting as my shield. He could snatch me away and relocate me, but he must suspect that I don't want that. I'm pissed at this guy, and he's going to get a piece of my damn mind.

"I did what I had to," the guy says, swinging his fist. Everett pushes him, and the guy punches the wall. He howls and shakes out his hand. "My family needed me. My sister got pregnant with her fourth child and wouldn't have been able to give enough to satisfy the donation laws. The father just up and disappeared. Donor Life Corp would've taken my nephew."

I blink a few times, trying not to let his words get to me. I knew there were some fucked up laws in regards to blood donations and procreating. Donor Life Corp focuses a lot on population control—the more gen. pop. donors, the more power a region has—but they also have limitations to prevent one region from overpowering all the others. Laredo explained it as a way the board keeps the peace. I never really asked my guys about the details. My love for them allowed me to grow distant.

I don't respond to the guy and tug back to look at Everett. "Maybe you should help him. You can say he attacked me. Just don't kill him."

"Gwen, he's lying to you. The Royale Region raised the number of people one donor could provide for to four children due to the lack of growth. We're a new region. The only restrictions lie within vampire households. The gen.

pop. are rewarded for having children." Everett holds my gaze, his blue eyes assuring me that he speaks the truth.

The guy groans in frustration. "You're going to believe a blood sucker over your own kind?"

I ease from Everett's arms so that I can face the guy. "Yes, actually."

"You fucking idiot." The guy swings out at me, but I block his punch.

Snatching Everett's shirt, I stop him from going after the guy. "Don't. He's baiting you. I can handle him."

"You're sick, Gwen. I'm not jeopardizing your health to prove a point. Let me take you to our room. You've given this asshole enough of your time," Everett says, keeping his voice low.

"Just another minute," I say. "I don't want him purposely provoking someone else. He'll get himself killed."

The guy tips his head back and releases another peel of laughter. "That's cute. I'm a dead man, anyway. My mister plans to give me my final donation so that he can reapply to Blood Match. I guess I wasn't good enough for him."

I frown. "They can do that?"

"Vampires do whatever the hell they want," he snaps. "For being a supposed Blood Rebel, you're delusional to think anything different."

"I'm not."

"You are, blondie. I bet this asshole manipulated the

crap out of your head to make you think it. I bet all you ever do is feed and fuck him, right? The perfect little Blood Match."

"Shut up."

He gives me a smug as hell look. "I'm right, aren't I?"

Anger pours over me, and I clench my fingers into my palms. The guy's cocky expression suddenly shifts to confusion and then to fear. He takes an automatic step away from me. Bending down, he swipes a chunk of glass from the floor at holds it up. I don't have to see myself to know that he poked my nature enough that my dhampir side peeked out.

"What the fuck?" he asks, his hands trembling.

"Shit." Everett rushes the guy and lifts him off his feet again. "Don't move. Don't speak."

A low growl sounds from behind me. I don't get a chance to react as a man grabs me by the waist and yanks me into his hard chest. I tense at the sound of his fangs extending.

"Let go of my Vic," the vampire says, his low, throaty voice sending fear through me as he speaks to Everett.

Everett ignores him. "You will forget what you saw."

The vampire roars in my ear, and my body automatically reacts. I elbow the vampire hard enough that he releases me, thrown off by my strength. I spin and face him, shadows edging my vision. The strange vampire startles at the sight of me. Without thinking, I launch at him. Pain erupts in my hand before warm blood and other vampire guts swallow my fingers. I punch the wall behind the guy, the weight of his body just hanging on my arm, dragging me to the floor.

"Oh, fuck," I whisper. "What have I done?"

"Damn it, dandelion," Bronx says, appearing in the hallway.

Mikkalo and Jameson rush to grab the dead vampire from the floor. They vanish without a word, taking the body with them. My body trembles, my breath quickening. Everett drops the Blood Match guy—Vic—and rushes to me.

"You okay?" Everett asks, searching my face.

"What have I done?" I repeat, swallowing the burning in my throat.

"You just gave that man exemption," Bronx says, his deep voice remaining even.

"I what?" I stare at the blood staining my dress instead of meeting Bronx's gaze.

Bronx squats down next to me and holds out his com device for me to look at. "He Blood Matched just before Donor Life Corp added stipulations. There won't be a bid within his match's coven to see if someone wants to fulfill his contract. The man gets exemption."

"Oh."

"Everett, take him back to the party and alert the Dukes. Tell them that Ontario tried to use his Blood Match to get to Gwen and decided to fight me instead of surrender to an investigation." Bronx lifts me into his arms, not giving me a choice. "I'll take Gwen."

I open my mouth to argue that I don't want him to take me, but the world blurs. Bronx sets me on my feet in the bathroom and turns on the shower for me. He doesn't say anything, just giving me a long once-over.

My emotions run rampant, and I know if I try to say anything, my voice might catch. Anger no longer grips my chest, though sadness remains clinging to me.

So I turn my back and tug down the side zipper on my dress without a word. The bloody gown drops to the floor along with my bra and thong, and I step into the shower without inviting Bronx to join me.

I close my eyes, letting the hot water cascade over me. Bronx remains in the bathroom like he doesn't trust something not to happen to me if he leaves me alone for a few minutes, even if he stands on the other side of the door.

Something snaps inside me as I replay everything over and over again in my mind. I can't stop the tears from bursting from my eyes to join the steady stream of shower water. I try my best to suppress my sobs, but it's too much. I feel more overwhelmed than ever. And I hate it. I hate feeling like this.

I sink down to the floor and curl my knees to my chest and cover my face with my arms. "Why didn't you tell me you were going to make the coven union official?" I ask, tilting my head to look at Bronx through the foggy glass.

Bronx doesn't respond to me.

"You know how much I hate Corona. You promised that this alliance was only temporary and to appease the other city heads," I continue. "But making it official like that? That's not temporary. You lied to me."

The shower door cracks open and Bronx reaches in and shuts off the water. He quietly helps me to my feet and wraps me in a towel without a word. His silence digs deeply into me, leaving what feels like a Bronx-sized hole inside of my heart.

"We're supposed to be a team." I hug the towel around me and stand in front of Bronx. His dark eyes flash silver at me, and he tightens his jaw, still not saying anything. And it drives me crazy. So I push him, even though he doesn't budge. "Say something, Bronx."

"No. Not without my brothers." His soft voice rips me open, and instead of getting mad, I start crying again.

"This isn't even about them."

I push past him and head back to the room. Bronx remains in the doorway to the bathroom, watching as I dress in the cotton panties and nightie he must have picked out earlier for me to wear after the party.

Flopping on the bed, I pull the blankets around me and hide under the pillows. My mind whirls, and I try my best to relax. A heavy pit grows in my belly like my heart dropped from my chest, weighed down with my hurt.

I toss and turn for a few minutes, knowing that there is no way I will fall asleep. Sitting up, I twist the blanket in my hand and turn my gaze to Bronx. His expression gives nothing away. I wish it did. I wish I could know what he's thinking.

The thought nags me so much that I decide to flat-out ask him. "Tell me what's on your mind. I want to know what the hell you're thinking."

Bronx tightens his jaw and swallows. "About how I wish you wouldn't be such a pain in my nuts."

"Are you kidding me?" My voice rises. "You're responsible for your own damn pain or annoyance or whatever. Don't you dare put that on me."

Groaning, he crosses the room and sits on the far corner of the giant bed, keeping as much space as he can between us. "You're right. I am. You're just not making it easy."

"What's that supposed to mean?" I inch closer because he doesn't look at me.

"Gwen, I'm doing the best I can." Leaning his elbows on his knees, he bows forward. His shoulders slump as he finally gives me a reaction that isn't sharp and steely, making me feel like I'm the only one feeling anything at all. "You have to understand. I might've been first in line, but I was not prepared to be our coven leader, let alone the leader of an entire region. I wasn't prepared to have you drop into my life either."

I scoot the rest of the distance to him and hang my legs off the bed. "I know that. I know you're doing what you can, but you've forgotten that you don't have to do this all yourself. I'm here too and you purposely chose not to include me. You know how much I hate Corona."

He closes his eyes. "I know."

"I'm not cool with any of this. Do you know what it would mean for me if you blend bloodlines?" My hands tremble at the thought.

"I'd never allow him to stake a claim on you. We will transfer your contract before we go through with the union." Bronx sits up to meet my gaze.

My forehead wrinkles with my frown. "You're actually going to do that?" The thought tightens my chest. We discussed this when I allowed the four of them to claim me that we wouldn't put any of their names on my Blood Match contract.

Bronx sucks his top lip into his mouth and nods his head. "I know it's not ideal, but it's the best way to assure your safety."

I want so badly to argue, but he's completely right. It

helps that I feel more confident in our relationship that I don't think a measly signature will change anything. But the thought still bothers me. "Who?" I manage to ask.

"Do you want to pick?" He swivels his body so that we face each other.

"Hell no." The response escapes my mouth without me even thinking about it. Because really...that can't end well. I don't want to hurt anyone's feelings by offering my contract over, even if it means nothing to all of us.

"I guess we'll have to work it out then. Obviously, we all want it," Bronx murmurs, slowly moving more as he blends our personal spaces together.

"If you guys think you're going to fight over it—"

Bronx shakes his head. "We won't."

"Then how will you pick?" I ask.

"Possibly a competition."

Oh, boy. I can only imagine how fiercely competitive the four of them will be. I'm almost afraid of the idea.

"I'm on board with that." Everett's voice trickles through the room as he cracks the door open. Mikkalo and Jameson follow behind him. "Maybe we can time to see who gets Gwen to orgasm the fastest."

My mouth falls open.

Jameson licks his lips. "It's on."

The four of them grin at each other before turning all their attention on me. And damn them. I love and hate being under all their hot intensity. I squirm, my heart picking up pace. Just the thought turns me on, even though it's the most ridiculous suggestion for a competition I've ever heard.

I scramble back, diving onto the bed to cocoon myself in the blankets. "Stop right there, Jamie."

He glares at me. "It's the fairest way, Gigi. We all know each other's strengths and weaknesses when it comes to stuff like combat, strategy, mind manipulation, blood drinking, and even driving. But making you cum? That's unpredictable and totally how I want to spend the day."

My cheeks flush. "Still have to say no. I'm not in the mood for that kind of marathon. I kind of feel like going to sleep."

"Damn," Jameson says.

I chuck a pillow at him. "Damn straight. You can't just come in here and think you can get away with distracting me, especially with—"

Bronx lunges toward me and covers my mouth with his hand, stopping me from talking. I nip his palm, but he doesn't pull his hand away. Everyone stiffens. A few seconds later, I hear the soft muffle of voices coming down the hall.

A tap on the door soon follows. "Brothers, may I have a moment of your time?"

I shake my head, pelting Bronx with strands of my hair. "Tell him no," I mumble into his hand.

"It'll only take a second. It's about the coven union arrangements," Corona says, cracking open the door without permission.

Bronx sinks onto me, pushing me deeper into the bed to restrain me. "Close the door and give us a minute. Gwen is sick."

"Sick? That's impossible. Dhampirs don't get ill," Corona says.

I bite Bronx's fingers hard enough that he jerks his hand away. "Like you would fucking know!" I can't help myself.

"I know more than you think, Gwen." Corona pushes the door open completely, narrowing his gaze at me. "You'd be surprised what kind of information you can find out if you're powerful enough to manipulate a dhampir gene carrier's mind."

I tighten my jaw. "Kyler knew nothing." This fucking asshole.

He gives me a cocky grin, getting under my skin in the worst way possible. "That you know of. I happened to realize he had a block on his mind, and I broke it."

Anger rushes through me. "Get out!"

"I will when I'm through discussing our coven arrangements." Corona turns his attention to Bronx. "So, may I please have a minute?"

I expect Bronx to deny him. To yell at him. To do something to get him away from me. But he doesn't. All he does is shift off me and get to his feet. He doesn't even glance at me as he closes the distance to Corona.

"Make it fast," Bronx says, clenching his hands. "We've had a long day and need rest for our trip back to Crimson Vista."

"I just wanted to inform you that I went ahead and filed the paperwork for our union with Donor Life Corp," he says, smiling.

"You did what?" Bronx asks. "I haven't even informed the board of Zaire's death."

"But I thought since you announced it—"

No one has a chance to react as I fly from the bed. I land on top of Corona, pinning him by smashing my hand into his cheek.

I prepare to take his heart.

15

WARNING BITE

CORONA JERKS HIS HEAD AND sinks his fangs into my hand. I scream, punching out my fist. But I don't hit him. Bronx hauls me off Corona. The two of them growl at each other. Mikkalo, Jameson, and Everett close the space around us.

I smile through my watery eyes, clutching my hand. This was the moment I've been waiting for. My guys will tear him to pieces. They'll surely let me take his heart now. They never let anyone get away with hurting me.

"Leave us," Bronx snarls, his voice reverberating through my bones.

"What?" I ask, surprise stealing the warmth from inside me.

Corona exits the room and slams the door shut. No one goes after him. No one says a word. Bronx sets me on my feet and turns his back away from me. Everett closes the space and grabs my hand, inspecting the two puncture wounds.

"It's not deep," Everett says, touching my aching skin. "Just a warning bite."

"Just a warning bite? Are you fucking kidding me?" Jameson releases a scary-ass growl, looking ready to chase down Corona.

"It hurts like hell," I say, pulling away from Everett. I turn to Jameson and show him. "Look what he did. You can't let him get away with this."

Bronx reaches inside his jacket and unsheathes a dagger, but Mikkalo shocks the hell out of me and blocks the door. Everett joins him, the two of them standing off against Jameson and Bronx.

"Mikkalo? Everett? What are you doing?" I ask. "Let them through. You can't let him get away with this. He hurt me."

Mikkalo jerks his attention to me, his eyes flashing silver. "Gwen, I love you, but shut up."

Whoa.

"Are you fucking kidding me?" I yell, anger rushing over me. "You're supposed to be on my side. I'm supposed to be your girl yet you're letting that monster get away with everything, including biting me."

"Gwen, stop. I know what you're doing." Mikkalo risks inching away from the door while Everett stands firm. "And I know why. I get it. I want to go after him as much as everyone, but it will destroy everything we put into place."

"I don't care! He needs to die!" I lose my shit, my anger getting the best of me. I can't believe this is happening. I can't believe Corona gets to breathe a second longer. "I can't just go along with this anymore. I can't!"

Silence falls over the room, my strangled sobs the only sound in the air. Bronx and Jameson freeze, the fiery anger gone from their eyes. Mikkalo punches the wall, cracking the plaster. Only Everett steps into my space. He quietly bites his arm and holds it out to me. My insides twist, and I deny drinking his blood.

I can't think about eating or drinking or anything for that matter as Corona continues to live. The man isn't stupid. He purposely submitted the coven union request so that my guys couldn't back out. He purposely did it to announce Zaire's demise before my guys had the chance. What all of this means? Probably that we're fucked. I can't imagine the board taking kindly to this, considering that my guys lied to the face of Viorica Vaduva.

"Gwen, you need to eat or drink. You're losing color. Your eyes are flashing silver like crazy. The bite mark isn't even coagulating." Everett's words draw my attention back to the puncture wounds on my hand. I hadn't even noticed that they drip blood all over the place.

"Then treat me like a donor," I say. "Give me a bandage."

My knees wobble as I shuffle toward the bed. It's like my body has had enough, and it wants nothing more than for me to check out and give it a break. My mind agrees. I slump onto the bed and curl my knees to my chest.

"Gwen," Everett repeats, sitting down beside me. "You're scaring me. Please, just let me take care of you."

I don't respond to him.

I can't.

My eyes close, a comforting numbness washing over me.

I never felt such relief.

"What's the matter, my little dhampir?" Laredo asks, scooting closer to me.

I sigh and lean my elbows on my knees. "The usual. My brothers planning things without asking for my opinion."

"Is this about heading south?" Touching my knee, Laredo draws circles over my skin with his finger.

"Yeah, kind of. I just...I want a break. I'm tired of traveling." I twist my lips to the side and look at him. "Is that so wrong?"

"No, it's understandable. We haven't stayed anywhere for more than a week since leaving your home. It was bound to catch up to you." He bumps his shoulder to mine. "Perhaps a drink might help change your mood."

"Or maybe if we just up and left for a while," I say. "Have you thought about it? Taking me somewhere alone?"

His eyes flash silver. "All the time."

"Then let's do it." I get to my feet and offer my hand to Laredo.

He chuckles and links his fingers through mine, allowing me to pull him toward the front door of the shack. Cool night air engulfs us, and I stride toward the old van hidden under a green tarp.

"I like this side of you, Gwen," Laredo says, stopping to spin me toward the van. He presses my back into the cold metal. "Once your mind is set, it's set—whether or not you're wearing pants. But I don't mind."

I glance down and laugh, realizing I never did finish getting dressed. I was so pissed off that my brothers didn't include me in their vote of where we were heading next. Everyone knows I hate that shit.

"*Fuck. Change of plans,*" I say, pushing him away from me to head back inside. "*I'm just going to knock the shit out of my brothers until they comply.*"

He laughs. "*Ah, come on. You can't get my hopes up like this and then back out.*"

I raise an eyebrow at him. "*You would really face my brothers' wrath when we got home?*"

"*Who said we'd come home? Think about it, Gwen. You and me, the world at our feet. You're only going to get stronger, you know. You were born to carry power unlike anything the world has ever seen. It's why my coven covets you so.*"

"*What do you mean your coven?*" I ask, searching his gaze.

"*They want to do the same as your brothers. Keep you locked away without a choice in your life. But not me. I will figure out how we can both be free.*" He touches my cheek. "*When you're truly ready. I won't accept a promise less than a Blood Vow.*"

"*What's that?*" I suck in my bottom lip, devouring the information he gives me. I don't think he's ever been so open in his life. I mean, a coven? He never mentioned it before.

"*Your love and loyalty forever, my dhampir. You'd let me transform you into who you were meant to be.*"

I frown. "*Wait, are you saying you want me to trans-*"

form into a vampire?"

"Not exactly. But either way, it'll set you free."

I gasp and sit upright, my mind whirling. Cool hands grab my cheeks and stop me from flailing about. Everything hurts—my body, my head, even my heart. I can't shake the uneasiness brought on by my memory of Laredo, one he had stolen away.

"Shit," I whisper, thinking about his mention of a Blood Vow. That's another thing my guys like to tiptoe around, and now it all makes sense. A Blood Vow is offering to sever mortal bonds to transform a donor into a vampire. But I know I can't transform. From the memory, it seems as if Laredo knew that too. He bit me with the idea of setting me free but how exactly? What was he expecting to happen?

"How are you feeling?" Bronx's big hand touches my leg from on top of the blanket. "You scared the hell out of Everett."

I don't respond right away and stare at the familiar light fixture of the suite I share with Bronx in Crimson Vista. How long have I been out? There's something un-nerving about being relocated unaware. It's even worse than getting moved at vampire speed.

"What century is it?" I ask, rubbing the heels of my hands into my eyes.

Bronx chuckles, the lightness of his voice filling up the ache in my heart. "You've only been asleep for a few hours.

It seems with everything that happened we haven't been tak-ing proper care of your human needs. You were dehydrated. I guess you did need that glass of water you asked for."

I stretch my back. "I could've told you guys that blood can't replace my other needs. I just don't have to eat or drink as much."

"Everett's kicking himself. He drew some of your blood to run some tests just to be safe. I hope it's okay that he gave me some of his time," Bronx says.

"Depends. What about you? Are you kicking yourself?" I keep my voice even.

"Right in the fucking balls, dandelion." He props him-self on his elbow to get a better look at me since I don't shift onto my side. "You'd be impressed."

I release a laugh that explodes through the air, surpris-ing me. Slapping my hand over my mouth, I muffle the loud-ass noise and glare at Bronx. "Don't do that."

"Do what?" he asks.

"Make me laugh. I'm still pissed off at all of you." I nudge his chest with my knuckles.

"That makes two of us," he says, his fangs peeking out from beneath his lips.

"You're mad at *me*?" I sit up, half expecting for my body to give out on me and send me crashing back to the bed. "How can you possibly be mad at me?"

He flops on his back. "Where do I even start? For one,

your stubborn as hell ass won't even give me the chance to explain myself and my decisions. Instead, you accuse me of putting you beneath me. And two, you attacked Corona and provoked him so that he would bite you, knowing well enough that it would trigger me to want to murder him."

I growl at him. Full-on, throaty, predatory growl. "I fucking did not provoke him on purpose. You're such an ass even to think that."

"How can I not? Both Mikkalo and Everett said you smiled like you knew. Then you went and tried to use our nature to get your way." Bronx gives me a pointed look like he knows he's right.

I jump on top of him and shake him. "You ass! How about you try not smiling when you think you're finally getting the justice you've been denied over and over by the ones who are plenty capable of providing it."

"Gwen, I told you—"

"Just stop it. I get it. You're doing what you think is best for the coven and region. But don't you dare accuse me of purposely letting the guy I hate most in the world bite me. I would never, and I mean never, go that far. I don't even want him within a mile of me let alone let him sink his teeth into me." I inhale a few deep breaths through my nose.

Bronx slackens under me. "I'm sorry, Gwen. You're right. You wouldn't no matter how much I try to convince myself to make me feel better about letting him live."

"You shouldn't feel better," I snap. "You should feel like shit."

"I do," he says, his voice lowering. "And that's why I'm not going to compete for your Blood Match contract. I don't deserve to have that kind of claim on you."

My breath catches at his words. "Bronx, don't talk like that."

Sinking into him, I slide my arms under his neck to embrace him despite our disagreements and anger. Because even if I'm mad or upset, it doesn't change how I feel about him. I love him. I love all my guys.

"You deserve me just as much as your brothers," I whisper. "The only reason I'll accept you backing out of getting my contract would be because you don't want it, not because you don't think you deserve it."

"Dandelion," he murmurs, tilting his face up to mine. He doesn't meet our lips together, though. "I want it more than anything."

"Then you better give your damn all in whatever competition the four of you decide on," I say. "I expect nothing less from all of you."

"I'm nearly certain the competition will be what Jameson suggested," he teases, sliding his hands around my hips to push me down just a little until I can feel the hardening of his cock between my legs. "Maybe you'll let me practice."

Fuck. Me.

I shiver at his words, his suggestion getting me wet already before he even does anything. He licks his lips and leans up to kiss me. His tongue tastes the seam of my lips as he wastes no time deepening our kiss like he's been starved for my affection. A fiery need erupts inside me, and I react to his furious desire with my own, wanting nothing more than to let my body control me to get what it needs to push the rest of the world away.

Bronx rolls me off him and breaks from my mouth, licking his way down to my breasts. He kneels between my legs and tugs the nightie over my head.

I moan as his tongue flicks over my excited nipples. "I hope you covered me up before you paraded my ass around Corona's."

He nips my breast. "What kind of asshole do you think I am?"

I flop back and squirm against the pillow, enjoying the sensation of his tongue continuing to glide down my stomach. "Only the stubborn kind that loves denying me what I want. Who I also think likes to piss me off so that we can make up like this."

"I definitely don't like you getting pissed at me. Not like that," he says, his voice lowering. "It killed me. Still does. I just want to do everything I can to make it up to you."

I ease my hips up to let him tug my panties off. "This is a start."

He hums against my pelvis and works his lips down until he kisses my clit. And damn does it feel amazing. Closing my eyes, I moan through the sensations he creates by sucking and licking over my body in a way that has tingles exploding between my legs.

Stretching my arms, I comb my fingers into his hair, playing with his short, soft strands. I can't stop wiggling and shifting, the pressure growing more intense. Grasping my hips, he tries to hold me still, but my body doesn't want to cooperate. I practically smother him with my thighs when I reach my release. I jerk back, trying to clutch the pillow to cover my face. Bronx snatches it before I can, loving nothing more than to hear my scream of pleasure.

I gasp, trying to catch my breath. Bronx slides up to sink his weight against me to hug me until my heartbeat slows enough that it doesn't feel like it'll escape my chest.

Hooking my fingers to his shirt, I don't give him long to cuddle me, my mind fully set on things just getting started. Bronx's eyes darken as he kneels between my legs. He unfastens his pants and tugs them down enough to tease me with his prominent erection through his boxer briefs. He rubs himself, licking his lips just watching me watch him.

"I love when you look at me like this," he says, tugging down the hem of his underwear to give me a show.

He strokes his cock more, and I can't stop myself from arching up to get on my own knees. I lace my fingers around his girth, taking over to feel how hard I make him. He moans, easing onto the bed so I can finish undressing him.

Pulling me closer, he adjusts my legs over his. Our bodies meet, but he doesn't enter me. I don't let him quite yet. I tease him, just rubbing his tip against the slick wetness of my arousal, enjoying how his muscles flex in anticipation.

"You feel so good, Gwen," he murmurs, bowing his head to my shoulder. His hands tighten on my hips, and he rocks me a bit to sink a little more inside of me.

I moan my enjoyment, adjusting myself until we align completely. I sit on him, his pelvis meeting my thighs. He guides my body in the rhythm he wants, thrusting deep into me with every swing of my body.

I kiss his shoulder, sucking hard enough to leave a mark. Teasing his skin with my teeth, I nip at him, my whole body humming with starvation for his affection and love and blood, everything he can give me to satiate me on every level.

"Gwen," he whispers, bending his neck. "You can bite me. It feels so good."

"I want to savor your skin a little longer." I kiss his shoulder and work my way to his neck. I suck his earlobe into my mouth.

Bronx moans, tightening his fingers on my ass. He squeezes, sending a burst of electricity through my body. Picking up speed, he pulls me to him harder and faster. I gasp over and over into the crook of his neck until my need to taste him grows so intensely that I can't resist.

"Ready?" I ask, kissing the sensitive spot on his neck.

He stretches his neck more, silently giving me permission.

Blood floods my mouth with my bite, and I moan as I swallow. My body buzzes with a desire so intense that I lose myself to the feeling of Bronx inside me, the sweet taste of him, the love we share.

Pushing me back, he lands on top of me. I break my mouth from his skin to meet him for a kiss. He kisses me deeper, plunging his tongue into my mouth, not even caring if his blood still stains my lips. I keep my legs hooked around him and move in sync with his thrusts until he slows with his finish.

"I love you," he says, resting on top of me, our bodies warm with flush.

"Even when I infuriate you?" I relish his skin against mine, how his heart thumps against my chest. "Because I love you regardless."

Tilting his head up, he graces me with a smile I haven't seen on him in a while. I can't even remember if I've seen his face carry so much happiness.

"I'm going to try my best to do that less." He tucks strands of my hair behind my ear. "And so you know, yes. I love the hell out of you, even when you infuriate me. Even when we can't agree on something. Even when you're stubborn as fuck and don't listen. That's how I know I'm madly, sometimes possessively, and endlessly in love with you."

I grin and kiss him, nudging him onto his back. He lets me get on top of him, and I straddle his body. "Keep talking like that, and I'm going to want more...you know, with all my pent up frustration."

"We can't have that now, can we?" he says, his eyes flashing silver.

His cock pulses between my legs, and I grind against him, just feeling his length until he looks ready to flip me off him to have his way. I don't let him. Grabbing his hands, I pull his arms up and pin them. He releases a play-growl and nips at my shoulder when I continue to wiggle and tease him until I finally guide his erection into place.

A knock sounds on the door, drawing our gazes from each other. Mikkalo clears his throat. "I really fucking hate interrupting like this, considering how glad I am you two made up, but we have a problem, Bronx."

"How serious?" he asks.

I crinkle my nose. "Can it wait a couple of minutes?"

Bronx cocks his eyebrow. "Gonna need longer than that, dandelion."

Mikkalo groans and thuds something, probably his forehead, against the door. "I'll try to stall, but the Vaduvas are adamant in delivering a message directly to you."

"Viorica's here?" Bronx asks, propping up on his arms. "You should've told me she entered the city."

"It's Heidi and Merrick. And no, I shouldn't have. There was no way I was going to ruin our girl's fun. Not for them." Mikkalo cracks the door. "So, what do you want me to do? Stall them?"

Bronx groans and hugs me. "I need to handle this. I don't want them around longer than necessary."

"I guess I should get used to all the rude interruptions, huh?" I sigh a long breath through my nose. "I can only imagine things getting busier. I mean, that's why you guys gave up some of your hobbies."

Bronx shakes his head. "I'll never be too busy for you. Wait here for me, and I'll be as quick as possible."

The elevator dings, and Mikkalo stiffens. Bronx grabs his clothes and shrugs them on, abandoning me in bed. I barely have time to pull the blankets around me before soft laughter draws my attention to the door.

"How *divine* of you, misters Royale. Were we interrupting something?" The brunette, who I remember is named Merrick, stands tall to peek over Mikkalo's shoulder and into the room.

Bronx tightens his jaw. "That is none of your business,

Ms. Vaduva."

"No shame in having some fun with poor, poor Zaire's Blood Match. I can't blame you for not letting her go to waste." Merrick wiggles her fingers at me. "She looks delicious. Is she?"

"Maybe you should ask her if she finds Mr. Royale to be the delectable one," the red-haired vampire, Heidi, says. "I never took you as someone who would give over control to a donor."

"Enough. What has you two here before sundown? Is there an emergency with the board?" Bronx asks, absently massaging the bite mark I left on him.

Heidi flashes her fangs. "That's yet to be determined. We're here to inform you that the board requests your coven's presence in Midnight Valley at midnight."

"Midnight?" Bronx asks. "We'd have to leave now."

The two beautiful vampires nod. "So pack your bags," Heidi says, smiling like it brings her great pleasure to interrupt our lives.

Merrick points at me. "You too, Ms. Royale. We're here to escort you."

16

THE WIDOWS

I STARE AT THE LONG stretch of sprawling hills that go on for miles. It's been a while since I've traveled by day, and I nearly forgot how colorful the world is. The aqua sky stretches into a never-ending blue without a single cloud in sight.

Bronx tightens his arms around me as I sit on his lap. Everett sits beside us, and Jameson and Mikkalo in the middle row with the two Vaduva sisters in front of the sleek vehicle. Knowing Bronx, he's probably annoyed as hell that we have to trust them to get us into another region safely. It's been a while since the Barons have messed with us, and I think they're what the five of us suddenly think about now that we're outside the safety of our city.

"Do you want something to eat?" Everett asks me, keeping his voice low. "Jameson packed your breakfast to go."

My stomach growls, answering for me. "Will we be much longer? I can wait."

Everett shrugs. "I don't know. It's been a while since I've been to Midnight Valley. I want you to eat, though. And drink water. We don't need a repeat of last night."

"What happened last night?" Merrick asks from the front.

Everett stiffens with annoyance. "We took Gwen to her first gathering. She was having too much fun that she forgot to drink water and fainted. She's still not a hundred percent feeling good." That's a flat-out lie. We all know I feel fine, but normal humans tend to take longer to recover.

Heidi glances at us in the rearview mirror. "No wonder Zaire wouldn't let you apply to Blood Match. You can barely keep the poor thing alive."

I dig my fingers into Everett's hand, stopping him from reacting. He inhales a sharp breath through his nose. Heidi and Merrick both smile, knowing that they got to him. I'm nearly certain that's why Mikkalo and Jameson pretend to sleep. I shift on Bronx's lap and sprawl my legs over Everett's to do the same. If I purposely ignore them, they'll get bored.

I touch Everett's cheek. "So what's for breakfast?" I hope my question distracts him enough to let their snark go.

"I'm sure he hopes it'll be you." Merrick laughs, her voice sounding velvety and smooth.

I fake smile at her. "If he doesn't spill anything while he feeds me, I might just let him have a taste."

Merrick blinks a few times, trying to compose her surprise. I'm sure she didn't expect that to be my reaction to her comment.

Heidi laughs this time. "I like this one. Maybe we can convince Mother to revert her contract to the old laws. That way we can invite her into our household. She might fit right in."

All four of my guys growl, the sound so intense that I cover my ears to try to get my bones to stop shaking. The two women don't react how I expect, but instead they continue to laugh and joke. They get great joy in getting on people's nerves and playing with insecurities.

"I don't know about that. I require a lot of attention." I keep my voice even and serious to pretend like I don't know what they're doing by messing with my guys.

Merrick swivels in her seat and meets my gaze. "I highly doubt that you need as much as you think. I've read your file."

"My file?" I press my lips together as not to frown. "Most of that was speculation."

"You mean you weren't attached to an outcast?" Heidi turns on the autopilot to turn in her seat to face me as well. My guys remain silent, acting aloof and allowing me to speak for myself.

"Attached? No. He was rather clingy. My brothers fed him once and he wouldn't go away." I don't look at either of them as I say the words, allowing Everett's breakfast prep to hold my attention. He mixes fruit into a container of yogurt the way I like and scoops up a little for me to taste. I hum and nod. "That tastes different."

"Pineapple," Everett murmurs. "Do you not like it?"

"No, it's delicious. Almost as good as you." I try not to cringe at my comment. I've been all over Bronx that I didn't necessarily want the Vaduvas to realize that I'm close to all of them. My guys warned me a dozen times how unnatural it was for a coven to share a human, considering I wouldn't produce enough blood to feed them exclusively like my contract says I have to.

"You were always obsessed with pretty donors, weren't you, Everett?" Merrick asks. "Bronx better be careful. She speaks to you in a way that only someone with an attachment would. Have you been secretly giving her your blood behind your brother's back? I know Blood Rebels like that kind of thing, thinking they have some sort of power."

Damn her and using the whisper voice I shouldn't be able to hear.

"She's referring to the day we caught her," Everett mutters. "And so you know, Bronx has not placed his claim on her."

Bronx stiffens under me, and I know the conversation heads in a direction that none of us want it to go. I sink more into Bronx and motion to Everett to feed me some more of the yogurt. Mikkalo and Jameson feel the brewing tension, because they both straighten their backs in their seats.

"It's only a matter of—"

"Whoa, shit!" I say, pointing out the windshield.

Both Merrick and Heidi jerk back toward the road to see nothing. I just needed to get their attention off the subject.

"That thing was huge," I add, leaning forward in the seat.

Jameson chuckles softly, loving how I totally freaked out the Vaduvas. "Have you never seen an owl, Gwen?"

I try not to laugh. "That thing was *not* an owl."

Heidi shakes her head, rolling her eyes in the rearview mirror. Merrick whispers that she highly doubts I'd actually fit in with their coven, her attention now drawn elsewhere. I puff a breath through my lips in relief, the tension evaporating the closer we get to the towering wall of a city I can barely make out from my position.

Heidi turns off the autopilot and slows at the massive gate with dozens of human security personnel with a massive arsenal of weapons like outcasts would attempt to invade the city with the sun shining. We made it here faster than I expected, but I guess my guys need extra time to prepare for their midnight meeting.

Heidi navigates into the city, and I twist in my seat and gawk out the tinted window. Humans stroll around the streets, walking all over the place. I don't think I've ever seen a city like this in the day. We always had to stick to the night because of Laredo. Midnight Valley fascinates the hell out of me. Everything looks so normal apart from watching the human population avoid the shadows of buildings as best they can. If there are shadow dwellers around, I don't see them. I know not all vampires live the same life like my guys or the Vaduvas, but I'm sure in a city like this, they have their vampire-only sections. It keeps the human populace in control as long as they think they're relatively safe.

"This is crazy," I whisper, trying to keep my voice low enough not to be heard by the Vaduvas. "Is Crimson Vista like this? There are so many people."

"Yeah, pretty close. A bit smaller," Bronx responds in my ear. "Every working adult has a job to keep things running. Would you like to explore it in the day sometime?"

I shift and meet him with wide eyes. "Really?"

Bronx shrugs. "I think we can handle the shade, especially to see your eyes light up like they are now."

A strange squee sound escapes my lips, and I can't stop myself from bouncing a bit on his lap. Heidi drives along the massive wall, obscuring the view on my side. I squirm, trying to look out the back window for a better view until Bronx nudges me toward Everett to stare out his window. From Bronx's hard-on, I'm sure my wiggling is utter torture since we can't do anything about it.

Everett slides his arms around me, keeping me in place. He didn't even suggest that I buckle the restraints, and I wonder if it's because he worries about me needing a quick escape with him. He always weighs what's a greater risk and decides from there. Luckily for us, Heidi slows down the vehicle outside a half-demolished skyscraper, the top floors long gone.

"There are sun blankets under the seats," Heidi says, smiling over her shoulder. "We'd take you to the garage, but it's pretty busy this time of day. I'm not in the mood to listen to a bunch of complaints."

She's talking about shadow dwellers.

It's a strange concept to think about. I know that my guys deal with a lot of vampire issues in Crimson Vista, but they keep me pretty far removed from it. All I know is that shit happens between covens, vampires can be petty as fuck, and they're sometimes not much different than humans when it comes to getting the authorities to do something. They have laws just like the donor population.

"It's fine," Bronx mutters, grabbing a blanket to cover his exposed head with. "I don't want to have to sever a bunch of heads of those who'd like to test my power."

My guys finish preparing for the dash to the awning of the tower while the Vaduvas cover themselves for the few seconds the open doors will expose them to the sunlight. I twist to straddle Everett, allowing him to cover me in the blanket with him. The moment we're hidden, he kisses me deep enough to turn me on. He doesn't pull away until we're out of the car and under the awning.

"Mmm," he murmurs against my mouth. "I've been dying to do that since we left home."

I grin and kiss him again until Jameson tugs the blanket off us. I wag my finger at Jameson. "Hey, I wasn't finished."

Everett chuckles, shading his eyes. "We'll get alone time soon enough."

Setting me on my feet, Everett turns toward his brothers. None of them rush to enter the building, just taking in the sight of the city. I risk toeing the line between the sun and shade and stick my hand out to feel the heat of the day warm my skin.

Mikkalo gives me a small nudge toward the sun. "You can go into the sun for a minute. We're not ready to go inside yet."

I swivel to look at all of them. "Really?"

Bronx nods. "Just stay close."

Bouncing on the balls of my feet, I stare at the bright sunlight in front of me. I never thought I'd be this excited about something so simple, but it feels so familiar, like how my brothers and I played outside the bunker in the sunlight during the day, even getting sunburned in the process. But none of us cared.

I take a breath and step forward, tipping my head toward the sky. My eyelids turn red under the bright light, and I soak the heat into my bones, pushing away the cold dread clinging to me. It's easy to forget that our lives might change forever in only a few hours if the board decides against Bronx filling Zaire's position on the board, though that might change our lives as well.

"One more minute, dandelion," Bronx says from behind me.

"Yeah, it's getting hot as hell out here," Mikkalo adds.

I snap my eyes open and glance around the city in front of me. I start to turn around when I spot a familiar face staring at me from across the street. Rubbing the heels of my hands into my eyes, I try to wipe my brother, Ashton, out of existence. He remains standing, staring at me like he can't believe I'm here either.

"Gwen?" His voice trickles to me as he steps closer.

My feet react without consulting my mind, and I dash forward farther into the sun. Bronx swears under his breath, and Jameson calls my name.

"It's Ashton," I call, glancing over my shoulder.

Mikkalo releases an annoyed growl. "Gwen, stop. Let him come to you. Don't make me go into the sun."

All I do is turn and hold out my finger to him, telling him to stay where he is. "I'll be fine. It's just twenty feet."

Strong arms hook onto my waist, dragging me back into the shade. Ashton yells my name, and I watch him rush toward us, not even caring that Mikkalo hugs me against him, flashing his fangs at me for a second as he composes himself.

"Don't hurt her! Please! I'll do anything," Ashton says, raising his hands. And then he braves stepping into the shade, proving how fearless he is even though he was taught to be smart. "I'll give you my blood. Just, please."

The desperation in my brother's voice gets Mikkalo to set me on my feet. Ashton shuffles closer, rolling up his sleeve. A purple-green bruise decorates his inner elbow from what might have been a blood donation and not the bite kind. He extends his arm out to Mikkalo, who just stares at him with a raised brow.

I grab Ashton's arm and pull his sleeve back down. "He's not going to hurt me or bite you. None of them will."

Ashton doesn't look at any of my guys directly, but he

doesn't take his attention from them. I can't blame him if he doesn't believe me. The last time I saw him, he helped my brother fight Everett. He will always think the worst first.

I shift on my feet and look at Ashton and then to Bronx. "Can he come inside with us?"

Bronx gives a stern nod without saying anything. No one does. Offering my hand to Ashton, I tug him along inside. My guys surround us like a wall of muscle, and I can't stop myself from smiling at Ashton. He looks good with his hair cut and neatly trimmed beard. He was healthy before, but he looks even fitter now, comparable to Declan, who has always been a bit more muscular.

"I'm so happy to see you, Ash," I say, smiling at him again. "I was worried about you."

He eyes me and leans closer, brushing his lips to my hair. "You think you were worried? I thought you were being held captive and turned into a baby-making machine."

I scoff, surprise pinching my face. "What? Why the hell would you think that? You knew I was with the Royales."

His brows scrunch together, lowering so much that he squints. "We have a lot to talk about if we can get a moment alone."

Mikkalo clears his throat. "That will not be happening."

I jerk my attention to him. "Mikkalo, seriously?"

"Hell yeah I'm serious. So far, all of your brothers have been pretty shitty toward you." Mikkalo flashes his fangs at Ashton. "I'm sure he's not any different."

Ashton risks meeting Mikkalo's gaze, but neither of them says anything. They just study each other, trying to figure out what's going on.

Ashton obviously had a specific idea in his mind of what was happening to me. Mikkalo probably thinks Ashton's in cahoots with my other brothers, but I don't think he is, especially if he's in this city and acting like a donor from the general population.

I reach out and rest my free hand on Mikkalo's shoulder. "Will you please not base your opinion of Ashton on the actions of my other brothers? And as for privacy..." I turn my gaze to Bronx. "It's technically not your time to decide."

Bronx peers at me over his shoulder, narrowing his eyes. "Oh, no you don't, dandelion. No one is undermining Mikkalo's judgment. He's the head of our security for a reason."

"Fine, then I am." I flick Mikkalo's shoulder. "I demand privacy. At least thirty feet."

He meets me with a fake-glare, knowing that thirty feet isn't even real privacy but only pretend since they can hear anything my brother says at a whisper. But Mikkalo catches on to my sneaky-ass strategy to get Ashton to talk to me. I doubt he will if he thinks someone will overhear. None of us really knew the extent of super hearing before, and my guys rock at narrowing noises though a lot of vampires tune shit out.

"Twenty-five feet," Mikkalo says, turning to walk backward.

"Forty," I counter, trying not to grin like crazy.

Ashton's gaze penetrates the side of my face as he watches me negotiate. If I could hear his thoughts, I'm sure he'd be exclaiming, "What the fuck?" I know it's what I'd be thinking if he was casually arguing with a vampire.

Mikkalo sighs dramatically. "Okay, fine. Forty feet. But I swear, Gwen. If he even looks like he's going to hurt you, I'll kick his ass out. From the balcony."

Ashton squeezes my fingers. "I assure you, Mr. Royale, I'd never hurt my sister. It's why I am now a registered donor in Midnight Valley."

I peer at Ashton, everything inside me begging for him to continue. But Mikkalo gives him a look that screams to shut the hell up, and Ashton droops his shoulders and glowers at the floor.

We stroll the rest of the way to a small guest room on the fourth floor, taking the elevator instead of the stairs. The room is barely the size of our closets in Crimson Vista, the bed made for a single body.

"Stay here for a second. I'm going to find out where

Zaire's suite is," Bronx says.

Jameson peeks in the room. "Damn straight, you better. Our girl is a bed hog. Everett will be on the floor if you don't."

I laugh and smack Jameson's shoulder. Ashton inhales a sharp breath, fully prepared to jump between me and Jameson as if he thinks Jameson will try to hurt me. The reaction is enough that I tug Ashton a few feet away.

"Ashton, I have something I need to tell you," I say, shifting my weight between my feet.

"Just wait, Gwen," Everett says, speaking up for the first time since we entered the building.

I shake my head. "No. He's freaking out." Turning my attention from my guys, I meet my brother's gaze. His brown eyes look just like Declan's, and the longer I stare at Ashton, the sadder I feel, because I miss my other brothers too. I don't think Ashton and Declan have ever truly been apart.

Ashton links his fingers to the back of his head. "Of course I am. Vampires fucking ruined our family!"

Slapping my hand over Ashton's mouth, I stop him from saying anything more. "Stop, Ash. Our family was already ruined before the Royales caught us. They have been nothing but amazing to me since I entered their household. I will not allow you to talk badly about them. I love them."

Ashton doesn't respond how I expect. Instead of glowering in disgust, he slumps his shoulders. Tears fill his eyes, but he's quick to swipe them away before they fall. I can't stop from gawking. I've never seen him cry ever.

"God, Gwen. Please tell me they feel the same. Tell me you're happy. That you get what you need without anything in return," he whispers, throwing his arms around me. "I've been so worried about you."

Confusion lines my forehead. "Um, what?"

He releases a soft laugh. "I sound crazy, don't I?"

"Just a bit. You screamed that the Royales ruined our family but then asked if they loved me...why?" I grasp Ashton's chin so that he looks at me.

He tightens his jaw. "I didn't say the Royales. I said vampires. I'm talking about another coven, Gwen. One far worse than we could have ever imagined."

My heart sinks into my stomach. "You know the Barons."

His eyes widen. "Fuck, you do too."

I swallow, trying to stop my voice from breaking. "They tried to claim me."

"Shit," he whispers. "You don't belong to them. You have to know that. The contract was never signed. Dad wouldn't do it."

"I know," I say. Swiveling, I meet my guys' gazes. Bronx appears in the hallway, striding toward us. I can tell he's heard everything Ashton's said so far, and he wants to know more. "Plus, I have a contract already. I belong to the Royale Coven."

"What?" he asks.

I smile, showing Ashton it's a good thing. "They also belong to me."

17

FAMILY REUNION

BRONX MANAGED TO GET US into the board member-only floor of Midnight Valley's Blood Match Center. According to my guys, it's as new as the one in Crimson Vista. I try not to think about the fact that some humans are currently taking the dumbest test in existence to see if they Blood Match with a vampire.

The lobby was pretty empty, so I imagine it's not much different. People—like the crazed guy at Corona's—only enter the program out of desperation. The fact that there were only two humans in sight kind of makes me feel better about this region. It shows that the general population is doing well enough.

"Are you sure you don't want anything to eat? Jameson is an excellent cook. He learned just for me," I say, stabbing at one of the small breakfast sausages on my plate.

The second we were settled, Jameson called the human staff to bring food that he could prepare himself. I couldn't stop laughing at how surprised the man was that it was Jameson cooking. I guess they don't see much of that.

"I'd learn anything for you." Jameson kisses the top of my head, hovering behind me like he'll swoop in to steal my fork at any second just to feed me himself.

Ashton tries to remain expressionless. "I'm fine. I had an early dinner."

I nearly forgot that he'd be on a human schedule. "Maybe dessert?"

"Like I said, I'm good."

"Suit yourself," Jameson says. "This will be the only time a vampire will ever cook for you."

I laugh and roll my eyes. "Not if we take him home."

Silence fills the room. My smile fades with the realization that my guys might not want to—or they can't—take Ashton from Midnight Valley. He is a registered donor here after all.

Ashton reaches across the small table and rests his hand

on top of mine. "Gweny, I'm not leaving. I like it here."

My guys audibly release their breaths. I flick my attention to Bronx, his obvious relief over my brother's words annoying me. I know we haven't had the best luck with my other brothers, but they can all obviously see that Ashton is different. Joining the gen. pop. of a city proves it. No Blood Rebel would ever do such a thing. They'd rather die trying to escape wearing one of the shiny silver bracelets like the one adorning Ashton's wrist.

"Don't get me wrong," Ashton continues. "I love you, little sis. I want nothing more than for us to have a normal life together, but it's not possible. We both know that."

He doesn't have to say I'm a dhampir for me to know that's what he's referring to. I haven't told him yet that my guys know. He's about to find out, though.

Everett bites his arm and partially fills a glass. He hands it to his brothers who take their turns to add their blood until the glass is filled to the top. Ashton watches Everett hand it to me, and I smile and kiss Everett.

I slowly sip the blood despite wanting to gulp it. "Mmm," I say, smiling at my guys. It's a habit of mine to make sure to tell them how good their blood is. "Just what I needed."

It weirds Ashton out. I can tell by his grimace. "Gwen, can I be honest?"

"As long as you don't say something stupid that could

hurt my guys' feelings," I say, drinking more blood.

He clears his throat. "How are you able to do...this?"

Shit. I thought he was going to ask if they knew I was a dhampir. "What do you mean?"

"You're with all four of them." Ashton glances to each of them before turning his attention to me. "Like a relationship. I don't get it. It's—"

"Not weird. It's the best thing to have happened to me. And so you know, I told them I was a dhampir. They love that about me." Might as well get it all out there.

"But, the four of them?" he asks again. "Are you...having sex? I mean, with all of them?" He grimaces and scrubs his face. "Fuck, I'm sorry. This is weird. I don't really want to know, but I have to know."

"Why do you have to know? My sex life is none of your business." Awkward tension builds through the room.

"I know. I know," Ashton says.

"Then why the hell ask?" Jameson says, speaking up. "You're making our girl uncomfortable. We don't discuss this kind of thing between us. It's one of our rules. Only Gwen can bring it up, and she obviously doesn't want to."

"I don't mean to, I swear. It's just—you're vampires. You're not known for sharing, especially if intimacy is involved. Gwen's last blood source even had a contract that stated she couldn't have sex with anyone." Ashton thunks his head on the table without looking at me.

My muscles tense at his admission. "You knew about the contract?"

"We all did, Gweny." Ashton doesn't look at me as he admits the truth. "And so you know, I didn't agree with it. Both Declan and I fought with Grayson about what it meant for you."

Tears blur my eyes. "You did?"

"Of course I did. I hated everything about the situation. It wasn't fair not to include you in things involving your life." He gets up from his seat and comes around the table to envelop me in his arms. "And so you know. I don't agree with what Grayson is doing now. When he told me— I lost it. It's why I'm here. I would rather spend the rest of my life as part of the general population than do anything that would mess up your future."

"What do you mean?" Bronx says, pulling up a chair. Jameson, Everett, and Mikkalo all do the same, joining us around the table.

"You said you met the Barons and they tried to claim Gwen," Ashton says. "Do you know why?"

"They want her caged for her regenerative blood," Mikkalo says. "They know she's a dhampir."

Ashton releases a strangled laugh. "I wish. That's only partially true. It's worse."

I frown. "What could be worse than that?"

"They think you will bear power for them, Gwen."

Pulling back, he meets my gaze. "As in, spawn more dhampirs. More dhampirs mean more blood."

"And more blood means more power," Mikkalo says with a groan. "Not to mention dhampirs feed on vampires."

"The likeliness of Gwen having a symptomatic carrier is pretty slim," Everett says, speaking up.

"Not if she has eternity to do so," Jameson says.

Dread trickles down my back as a dozen thoughts swirl in my head. This was one of the reasons Laredo made sure I stayed out of rebel hands. He thought the same thing. It's why my parents turned their backs on the elders. Now, I realize it's also why Laredo kept me from his coven too. At least, I think. Unless he wanted me and the power I can supposedly bear all to himself.

"So fucked up," I whisper under my breath. "Why would Grayson agree to this? He was supposed to protect me."

Ashton shrugs. "I don't know. He wouldn't give me a reason other than he was doing this for our futures. I said I didn't want any part of it, and the next day I woke up here."

Bronx scoots his chair closer and pulls me onto his lap. I hug him, burying my face into the crook of his neck. "We're never going to let that happen, Gwen."

"Yeah, Gigi. We already have plans, remember?" Jameson hugs his arms around the both of us.

I laugh, remembering that I joked with him about only

wanting kids if it was with him. "Damn straight."

"Don't instigate him, Gwen," Everett says. "He asked me for information on all the options there are out there last week."

Jameson whacks Everett. "He's kidding. I only asked about the probability of the occurrence."

I groan. "Okay, okay. Enough."

"Please, yes. I can't think of Gweny like that," Ashton says.

Bronx shifts me on his lap. "You want to help assure it?"

Ashton tightens his jaw. "You want to open my mind."

Nodding, Bronx says, "With your permission. Maybe they blocked something that we can use."

"I'll do anything for Gwen."

Everett stands behind me, resting his hands on my hips. Softly, he brushes his lips to the skin peeking out from my dress. My choice of outfit doesn't go unnoticed by him, and he sneaks his hand under the hem to squeeze my ass cheek.

"He'll probably be out until after my brothers return. Maybe even past our meeting time." His whisper tickles my skin as he uses his nose to move my hair out of the way.

I tilt my head, sliding my hands down my sides until I can reach behind me to graze my fingers along his zipper.

"What are you suggesting?"

"That we don't let that dress go to waste. It is our time for a bit."

I spin in his arms and jump up. He chuckles as he catches me and kisses me deeper. "I was hoping you'd say that."

He hums and lowers me just a bit so I can feel the hard length of his boner. "Yeah?"

"Unless you feel like doing something else."

The face he gives me makes me laugh, his expression speaking volumes about how there is no way he even wants to consider doing something else. He carries me to the bathroom since it's the only place with a door. Snatching a towel from the rack, he drapes it over the sink and plops me down to stand in front of me.

Lifting my hips, I let him tug down my panties enough to rip the sheer fabric. Everett drops to his knees and eases my legs open, pulling me a bit closer by my hips. He ducks under the skirt of my dress, and I moan so loud at the sensation of his tongue flicking over me.

"I missed you," I whisper, hiking my dress up to run my fingers through his blond hair. "I can't wait for all this bullshit to be over." I gasp as he continues to explore me with his mouth. "I just want a night of nothing to do but you."

He eases away and smiles at me. "That's my plan. No

way will we stay here all night. I've been looking forward to some alone time."

I grab him by the shirt and pull him up. "You have some now."

"A bit of my brother's time isn't enough," he whispers, tugging down the strap of my dress to kiss the top of my boob.

I unfasten his pants and pull his erection out to rub my fingers over. "Especially because they're going to catch on one of these days."

He spreads my legs wider to fit his hips between them. "Maybe sooner than later. I heard the elevator."

I guide him inside me, moaning and leaning forward to rest my forehead on his chest. "You better hurry."

"Never."

Everett rocks into me, starting slow, just enjoying how my body feels. I clutch onto his shoulders to hold myself in place, capturing his gaze. His blue eyes drink me in, his bottom lip puffing out with his quiet panting. I suppress my loud ass mouth as soft voices trickle through the door.

"Gwen, Everett, you in there?" Bronx taps the door without trying to open it.

"Mmmhmm," I respond, the sound of my voice whispery, breathless.

"Do you need something?" Everett asks.

"The board changed the meeting time to eleven. I

wanted to brief Gwen to make sure she's ready to face them."

Everett narrows his eyes at the door. "Damn it."

Bronx taps the door again. "It's important, Gwen."

My groan turns into short bursts of moans as Everett picks up speed. I laugh, his sudden exuberance knocking my ass into the sink. I oomph at my head hitting the mirror, and it cracks with Everett's thrust.

"Shit," he murmurs, reaching around to protect my head.

My giggle turns into another moan. "The faucet. My back," I manage to say.

"Fuck." With his other hand, he lifts my legs to rest on his shoulders and turns me slightly so I lie diagonally across the round sink.

I laugh again.

His face lights with a smile. Neither of us is willing to stop despite the small space. I hadn't realized how much I needed Everett's closeness until now. It makes everything going on with Donor Life Corp and the board seem not so important. Nothing is important in the universe apart from the feelings we share, the passion, the love.

I give up on trying to be quiet, Everett's deep thrusts dragging out all sorts of noise from me. His position hits me just right that I reach the point of release, and I arch my back with my orgasm. Everett nearly loses his hold on me, and I screech and laugh, my back hitting the door as he props me up, continuing until he finishes.

He hugs me close, kissing my gasping mouth, stealing my breath. "That was hot."

"So good," I say, smiling as I draw his lip between my teeth. "I can't wait for more time with you."

"What if we test Bronx's patience?" he teases, raising his voice loud enough for his brothers to hear.

"All right. If that's going to be the case, make room. We're all joining." It's Jameson who pushes against the door.

I moan at the pressure of Everett still between my legs. "Jamie, don't stop."

He groans. "Damn it."

I tip my head back and thunk it on the door with a laugh. "As much as the idea excites me, it's probably better if we wait until we're safely in Crimson Vista to explore such an adventure."

"It kills me to say this, but I agree with Gwen," Mikkalo says.

Everett shifts me away from the door and gently sets me on my feet. We quickly clean up in the tiny shower, and I stroll from the bathroom in only my towel to retrieve another pair of underwear before slipping back into my dress.

It should be awkward that the three of them just listened to Everett and me getting it on in the bathroom, but no one says anything. Jameson does fist bump Everett. I give the both of them a whack on the back.

"You don't need to congratulate him, Jamie. We do it all the time." The words kind of just fall out of my mouth. Embarrassment burns through my cheeks as Bronx, Mikkalo, and Jameson look at me and Everett.

"You sneaky bastard," Mikkalo says, shaking his head.

Everett only smiles.

I raise my hands. "Okay, that's enough." Turning to Bronx, I shuffle forward and get him to open his arms so I can slide into them. "What did you want to prepare me for? Are you sure I have to meet the board?"

His eyes dart to his brothers. "That's not all. They want us to be prepared to announce who gets your Blood Match contract. We're all going to have to choose."

18

DONOR LIFE CORP

MY GUYS ENGULF ME IN a hug, just squishing me between their bodies like I'll fall apart otherwise. I think they need the love more than I do, so I continue taking turns kissing them. While I'm annoyed and pissed off at the board for throwing the whole you-better-decide-who-gets-the-girl at us sooner than we wanted, I'm not as nervous as I thought I'd be. The Blood Match contract is just that—a dumb contract. A piece of paper won't do anything, and it's not like I follow the laws anyway. I love each of my guys in my own way, and I know that whoever gets it won't cause problems.

"Are you sure you don't want the final say in who gets your contract?" Bronx asks me for the third time. "We won't get upset."

I rest my head on his shoulder. "Nope. I'm not having that decision hanging out there. You need to work it out. It's better this way."

"Gwen is right." Mikkalo rests his chin on my shoulder. "I don't like admitting this, and I'm sure I'd get over it, but I'd be disappointed knowing that she won't pick me."

I purse my lips. "Who says I wouldn't? You can't assume. Plus, I have picked you." I wiggle between all of them. "And you, and you, and you."

Everett squeezes my hand. "I think Gwen's contract might be best with me. I am her health keeper."

Oh, boy. That's a lot of suddenly tense muscle bunching around me.

"I'd be okay with that," Jameson says, "but I think I might be best considering I can not only take care of her dhampir needs but also her human ones. Gwen enjoys me cooking for her."

I'll give my guys credit. They manage to keep their voices even, treating this like an open and fair discussion.

"I'm getting pretty good at that too. If I get her contract, I can assure you she'd be safe. I'll rework all our defenses to guarantee no threat gets even within a foot of our girl." Mikkalo smiles at me with the idea. His eyes light up at just the thought of planning our future around him possessing my contract.

"It would be more beneficial for Gwen's contract to go to me. As our coven leader and hopefully a new board member, I can use my influence to persuade the board to change and create laws that would protect and benefit our girl." Bronx tightens his jaw. "I think it's already what the board expects. First in line usually takes the contract."

Jameson flashes his fangs. "Just because it's what they expect doesn't mean anything. You piss off Gwen more often than not. You do things she doesn't agree with. You—"

Bronx growls. "You put her life in danger all the time, Jameson. One of the stipulations is to guarantee protection."

"He's right, brother," Everett says. "Gwen almost died on your watch."

"Have you forgotten she was kidnapped on yours?" Mikkalo says, narrowing his eyes.

Ah hell.

I try to push against Mikkalo and Everett's chests as they close in to get into each other's faces. "Guys, please."

Everett reaches over me and nudges Mikkalo with his fist. "You threatened to murder her, Mik."

"I thought she was—"

Jameson flicks his other shoulder. "That's no excuse. You took things into your own hands without even informing us. Had I not intervened, you'd have made a huge fucking mistake."

The heat of their sudden anger as they throw mistakes and accidents involving me in each other's faces burns through me. I try to break out of their circle, their throaty, angry voices spitting out incoherent words with their fury. My fear instincts blare like crazy, my mind begging my body to get the hell out of the middle of them, but it's like I'm caged between four solid walls.

"There's no fucking way I'll agree to that," Mikkalo says.

I miss part of their conversation, my head pounding, my heart racing wildly. Closing my eyes, I try to ignore their comments to each other. Every time they mention something terrible they think one of them is responsible for, it cuts deeply in me. Because none of them are responsible. Not for Zaire trying to bite me, not for the outcasts trying to claim me. None of them is responsible for Mr. Bevaldi's actions, Corona's, Kyler's, and the Barons. Yet somehow, they each manage to push the events toward each other.

I can't take it anymore.

Flinging out my hands, I smack all of them across their chests, finally getting them to take a step back. I gasp a breath of air like their closeness suffocates me. And maybe it does. How they can suddenly fight each other after everything we've been through squeezes my heart.

I drop to the floor and curl my knees to my chest. Everyone freezes, their anger turning to worry as they look at me. I ignore them and rest my chin on my knees. I never wanted this to happen. It's why I didn't want to choose.

"You guys promised I wouldn't get between you," I manage to say, my voice barely sounding over a whisper.

Silence falls between the four of them. I don't look up and wait for them to get their shit together. Jameson kneels beside me first and engulfs me in a seriously good hug that I savor, feeling his love.

"I'm sorry, Gigi. What I said...it was bullshit. I know. I just love you so much that I can't help myself sometimes." He kisses my temple and pulls me to him until I sit between his legs, facing him. "I want your contract—like really fucking want it—but you're right. I made you a promise, and I intend to keep it. Your love and affection are enough for me. I don't need to have a piece of meaningless paper."

I release a relieved breath and lean in to brush my lips to his. "Thank you. And that's how I feel. A contract means nothing unless it ensures that you provide breakfast in bed daily." I tilt my head up to look at Mikkalo. "The best bubble baths and full body massages."

Mikkalo joins us on the floor. "I'll write one up immediately."

I laugh and wiggle my fingers at Everett. "Also one to ensure that my body's needs are satisfied on every level."

Everett hums in his throat, getting on his knees. He kneels behind me and combs my hair away to kiss my neck. "I think I can handle that."

Tipping my head up, I meet Bronx's handsome, brooding face. "And from you, I want one that guarantees that you satiate my dhampir side—on every level, of course."

Bronx's eyes flash and he licks his lips, taking me up on my invitation to kiss me. "I already planned on it, dandelion."

I smile against his lips. "Good. And as for you four, I will give what each of you needs whenever you need it. Blood, body, mind, and soul. I'm your girl."

"Hell yeah, you are," Mikkalo says, smothering me with his affection, squishing me between his brothers with his muscular arms.

"And we're your guys," Jameson says. "At your disposal for anything."

Bronx eases back to look at his brothers. "Unfortunately, we still need to give the board an answer. As much as I want Gwen's contract, you are all too important to me. So I'm not going to ask for it."

"Shit," Jameson says, shaking Bronx's shoulder. "That's what I was going to say."

"So, Mikkalo or Everett?" Bronx asks.

Mikkalo and Everett shake their heads. Everett says, "Perhaps we can arrange the transfer of her contract another way—the way we originally wanted to get it."

"You want us all to apply to Blood Match?" Jameson asks, tilting his lips down. "Think the board will go for it?"

Bronx scrubs his hands over his face for a moment. "We can ask. It's a better idea than anything else we've come up with."

I shiver at the thought of having to go through the Blood Match process all over again. The dumb questionnaire, the health exam, the blood draw? All it does is bring up terrible memories for me.

"Gwen," Bronx says softly, touching my cheek to grab my attention before my thoughts consume me. "Is that okay? The results won't change anything between us."

I press my lips together, my chest tightening as I think over his words. I can tell all of them want to do it this way. And because I don't want to pick, and they obviously can't pick between them, I guess I'll have to suck it up.

"If this is what you want, then I'll do it," I say, swallowing the knot in my throat.

Jameson slaps his hands and rubs them together. "Fuck yeah. I finally get to prove that I'm one-hundred percent your body match." His enthusiasm lifts me up and settles my nerves.

I raise an eyebrow at him. "You guys better not rub any

of the results in."

Jameson chuckles. "Sorry, Gigi. That's the one thing I can't promise."

"Me either," Everett says, whacking Jameson on the shoulder. "I'm about to prove Jameson that he's one-hundred percent wrong."

My hands tremble as I stand within the circle my guys create around me outside of a set of dark wood, double doors. Cool air trickles from the vents, helping combat against the nervous sweat attempting to drench the underside of my hair. Quiet voices sound from within the room, and I squint my eyes like it'll suddenly give me better hearing.

"Just a couple more minutes, Gwen," Bronx whispers. "We'll hopefully get this over with fast. The board is known for their swift decisions."

"And lack of patience. None of them actually like to get together like this all the time, let alone have to travel from their regions," Mikkalo says.

I groan. "Ah, hell. If they're already annoyed, it's not going to be good."

Everett brings my hand to his mouth. "Annoyance doesn't affect their judgment."

"They will always do what they feel is best for Donor Life Corp even if they don't necessarily agree," Jameson adds.

I bounce on my feet, continuing to stare at the door. I wonder if I will the board to hurry up, the universe will respond and have the door swinging inward in three, two—

"My brothers." Corona's sharp voice cuts through the air, stealing my breath.

I jerk my attention toward the elevator to see him lead Brooklyn and the two other guys, I never bothered to learn their names, that make up the rest of the Anderson Coven into the lobby. Bronx steps away from me, using his massive, muscular frame to block Corona's view—or maybe mine—as he greets the asshole with a proffered hand.

"I hadn't expected your arrival," Bronx says, keeping his voice even.

I stand on my tiptoes and glare at the Anderson Coven. Anger suppresses any nerves I had about meeting the board. Now, all I can think about is all the ways I can break one of the chairs to ram one of its wooden legs through the bastard's heart.

"Neither had I." Corona risks flicking his gaze to mine. He smiles, the sharpness of his face leaving my heart cold and hard like a piece of ice hanging in my chest. "A few of the Widows summoned us."

Before Bronx can respond, the double doors swing inward to reveal two women and two men sitting at a giant glass table. I recognize Viorica from her surprise arrival in

Crimson Vista, but I haven't seen any of the other board members before.

The other woman gives me a long once-over, drinking me in as I stand facing them since my guys turned. Glittering diamonds sparkle from her ears, neck, fingers, and wrists. Her long, dark hair cascades over her bare shoulders in waves. She's stunning. I can't take my eyes off her to even look at the other two guys, who I can feel give me equal attention as she does.

Viorica stands from her seat, getting me to break my stare on the woman. She saunters around the table to greet Bronx. He offers her a deep bow and his brothers follow his lead. Corona's coven joins in. I remain standing stiff and only offer her a short nod. She doesn't acknowledge me, treating me as if I'm not even here.

"Thank you for joining us tonight," Viorica says, acknowledging everyone as a group. "Please, come in and take a seat."

Viorica disappears and reappears at the table, using her vampire speed. Touching the small of my back, Bronx leads me into the boardroom and guides me toward a small sitting area in the corner with a view of the city through the tinted glass.

I take a seat, crossing my legs at my knees, and rest my hands on my lap. My guys flick their attention to me as they sit beside the Anderson Coven and across from the board.

The man on the end—a guy with long blond hair, a neatly trimmed beard, and a broad, muscular body winks at me. I can't help my reaction to the forward board member. He laughs at my frown but clears his throat when everyone looks at him.

"If you must say hello to Ms. Royale, hurry up, Mr. Goldman," Viorica tells the board member.

He suddenly materializes in front of me, cocking his head to the side. "It's a shame Zaire didn't have long to experience such an exquisite donor."

It takes everything in me not to uncross my legs and kick him in the cock. I think Bronx must notice my sudden urge, because he comes up beside the man and drapes his arm over his shoulder.

"It truly is. Gwen would've made him quite happy," Bronx says.

Mr. Goldman's lips split into a smile. "I can assume you've been enjoying his assets?"

I open my mouth to tell him that I'm not a piece of property, but Bronx releases a fake as hell laugh, humoring the guy. I just gape at the two of them as they share a silent conversation with their eyes. Bronx reaches out and touches my cheek, pushing my hair behind my ear without a word.

"All right, you've had long enough. Some of us don't want to be here all night," Viorica says.

"She's right. I have far better things to do than draw

out something longer than necessary," the other male board member says. "There will be no need to prove your capability of filling Zaire's vacant seat. We know you and your coven have done an excellent job in building the Royale Region."

I sit straighter at the man's words.

"Thank you, Mr. Woodsman. I take the leadership of the Royale Region seriously. It is my number one priority," Bronx says.

"Which makes you the perfect candidate," the woman beside Viorica says. "Zaire made an excellent decision in making you his first in line."

Bronx's eyes light up, though his jaw remains serious. "That is kind of you to say, Ms. Aku."

She leans in her seat and extends her hand to rest it on top of Bronx's. "What have I told you? Please, call me Zara. No need for formality, especially with your advancement to the board."

I inhale a small breath. "Fuck yeah," I whisper under my breath.

I must not be quiet enough, because the woman turns her attention to me and raises a perfectly arched brow.

"All we need is one final vote of agreement in front of your coven as witnesses," Viorica says.

"All who agree that Bronx Royale will fill the open board seat, raise your hand," Mr. Goldman says.

The four board members all raise their hands.

Mikkalo, Everett, and Jameson break their steely expressions and grin at each other. Corona reaches over and pats Bronx on the back. I cringe a little, even imagining his touch. The fact that he's here makes me nervous as hell.

Viorica nods her head and gets from her seat, striding to the desk positioned on the opposite side of the room from me. She swipes a stack of papers from her desk and sets them in front of Bronx.

"While we're here, we'd also like to inform you that we've approved your request to merge the Royale and Anderson Covens. Please read over the contract and if you agree to continue with the union, you will blend your bloodlines as we bear witness tonight." Viorica clicks a pen and sets it on the stack of papers.

My heart ricochets around my ribcage, threatening to throw itself from my body. Fear pours through me in icy waves. The sudden silence filling the room unnerves me. I shift on the seat, unable to stay still. No one looks at me. No one acknowledges that they can probably hear my heart freaking out from clear across the room.

Bronx rests his elbows on the table and glances over the top page of the prepared contract. He gives nothing away, his eyes drawing lines across the papers. I stare at him, hoping that the weight of my gaze gets him to look at me, but he doesn't. Neither does Jameson, Everett, and Mikkalo.

This can't be happening. They can't possibly go along with this.

Bronx turns his gaze from the papers to the board members. "The only thing I disagree with is your suggestion to make Corona first in line. I have already chosen Mikkalo, considering he is the best suited and most knowledgeable of the infrastructures of every coven in our region. Corona recently had a dispute with another one of our city heads, so putting him in the position of first in line will cause unnecessary tension."

The board members glance to each other in silent conversation before Zara says, "Mikkalo will make a fine first in line. We accept your request to change the position."

Corona flares his nostrils and straightens his back. I expect him to argue, but all he does is flick his gaze to me. He smiles, purposely getting under my skin like he knew how relieved I'd feel, and he doesn't think I deserve such a feeling.

"Very good. Then I accept the contract and agree to proceed with the coven union." Bronx signs the paper and hands it to Viorica. "I'll submit my new coven member's titles after I fully prepare their contracts."

"Within the week, please, Mr. Royale," Mr. Woodsman says, leaning back in his chair.

Bronx nods.

Mr. Goldman waves his hand. "Hurry now and finalize

your union. I'm sure you'd all like to be on your way to celebrate."

Bronx extends his fangs longer than I've ever seen them. I tense at the flash of silver in his eyes as he settles his gaze on me. We stare at each other in silence, my body and mind on the verge of a meltdown. He remains expressionless and gets to his feet.

"Corona, welcome to the Royale Coven. It is an honor to have you by our sides," Bronx says. "Please, give me your arm."

Extending his arm, Corona smiles at me without looking at anyone else. I scoot to the edge of my seat, my legs shaking so much that my whole body bounces. I twist my fingers together in panic and anticipation.

"Bro—"

Jameson presses his hand over my mouth, silencing anything I could possibly say. I watch in horror as Bronx bites Corona on his arm to blend their blood. Corona releases a low grunt, his eyes flashing silver, and then the two of them hug. Mikkalo and Everett hug Corona next, and the sight of it twists my stomach.

I cover my mouth with my hand, trying to force my belly to chill the hell out before I get sick in front of the board.

Bronx continues to Brooklyn and bites her next along with the other two guys. He welcomes them all to the Royale Coven and they hug like he did with Corona. Tears burn my eyes, every bad thing in my life crashing over me. A part of me feels like it dies. The one thing I didn't want, the one person I hate most in the world, has managed to invade my life. What that means for me? I have no idea. All I know is that if Corona dares even to think he can act as if he didn't murder my brother or imprison me, I will punch his damn heart out. If Jameson didn't grip me tightly, I would fly across the room and do it now.

"Congratulations, Royales. We look forward to the continued progression of the Royale Region. I expect you to accomplish great things together," Viorica says, genuinely smiling for the first time tonight—the first time I've ever seen her do something other than look bored, annoyed, or angry.

I groan and cover my face with my hands.

"Oh, the Blood Match," Zara says, her feminine voice cutting through the agony clinging to every molecule on my body. "We almost forgot. Will you be taking her contract, Bronx?"

I jerk my head up and meet Bronx's gaze. It's the first time he's looked at me since the board threw the coven union at him. My mouth trembles, and nothing I do can stop the pout from crossing my face. The last thing I want now is to deal with this—to participate in the Blood Match Program all over again.

Bronx clears his throat. "Actually, my brothers and I were hoping we could use the program to determine who she belongs with. We like her equally and would like the opportunity."

"As long as you don't ask her to decide, I think we can agree with that," Viorica says, keeping her eyes on Bronx.

"Seriously?" I can't stop the comment from escaping my mouth. I mean, I know I didn't want to make the decision, but it pisses me off that she thinks I don't deserve to make it.

Viorica appears in front of me and looks down at me. "I'm very serious, Ms. Royale. There was once a time I'd have considered allowing such a thing, but there are far too many possible outcomes that can happen from your decision. The Royale Coven will not be torn apart because of a donor."

"That wouldn't happen," I snap.

Viorica flashes her fangs at me. "Mr. Royale, get the donor under control."

Jameson tightens his hand around mine and grabs my chin, getting me to look at him. "Never talk to Ms. Vaduva like that again." While he doesn't show it, I can tell having to speak to me this way kills him. He's as angry as I am.

I swallow and nod. "My apologies. Retaking the test will be fine."

Viorica doesn't say anything as she returns to her seat.

She laces her fingers together and rests her hands on the table. No one says anything for a minute, waiting for her to respond. Her drawn on silence digs into me worse than Corona's constant gaze in my direction.

Viorica sighs. "I'll oversee the process myself. Whoever is interested in inheriting the Blood Match contract of Ms. Royale, please remain seated. The rest of you may be excused."

The three other board members disappear along with Brooklyn, leaving behind my guys, Corona, and the two other vampires who just joined our coven. Jameson releases a soft growl under his breath.

"No fucking way," Jameson says. "They do not have the right to apply."

Viorica holds her hand up to stop him—or anyone else for that matter—from arguing. "I can see why you feel that way, but because they are now formally your coven brothers, they have the same rights as you under the Donor Life Corp law."

Bronx slams his hand on the table. "I'm taking Gwen's contract. I've decided against allowing anyone else to have her. She is mine."

"We agree," Jameson, Everett, and Mikkalo all say in unison.

"Fine by me," I say, drawing Viorica's attention to me. Because there is no fucking way I'm going to risk having my contract to pass to one of those other fuckers.

Viorica shakes her head. "I'm sorry, Mr. Royale. You had the opportunity to claim her and you did not. My decision stands. Anyone in your coven is welcome to apply."

19

BLOOD MATCH

I PACE IN FRONT OF THE computer, ignoring the list of questions glowing on the screen. If I don't take the damn questionnaire, I can't Blood Match. It's quite simple. I'd rather risk pissing off a board member than even risk the possibility of ending up with a former Anderson. Because fuck.

A knock on the door startles me. I swing my gaze to the small window, half expecting to see one of my guys, but a blond vampire with green eyes peeks in. She smiles without her fangs and waves at me like I can actually open the door. There isn't even a handle, and my handprint turned the palm pad bright red with a buzzer that basically screamed a big nope, you're not escaping so easily alarm.

The door swings open and the cute blonde drags a dark-skinned female human in behind her. The two of them smile at me as the vampire shuts the door. I take an automatic step toward the wall. I was uneasy enough that Viorica separated me from my guys, but now I'm flipping out because I don't know what to do.

"You shouldn't be in here," I say, keeping my back straight. "I'm in the middle of an exam."

The female human tugs away from the blonde and steps closer. "You don't have to be afraid. My Sammy won't hurt you."

"*Your* Sammy?" I ask, my forehead lining with my confusion. This is the first time I've ever heard a human claim a vampire that wasn't me.

The vampire giggles, the sweet sound really throwing me off. She sounds child-like, but she definitely doesn't look it with her petite yet curvy body accentuated by the tight cut of her sequin dress.

"Evora's my Blood Match," Sammy says, smiling at the beautiful woman who might be my age. "Of course I'm hers."

"All righty. That still doesn't explain what you're doing

here." I cross my arms over my chest. "Like I said, I'm in the middle of an exam."

Evora twirls her finger at the computer screen. "You mean you're at the beginning." She glances at Sammy. "She hasn't even started."

"Oh, no," Sammy says, materializing next to me. She bends down and looks at my screen. "You should've been finished already. You've already had twenty minutes longer than the last time you took the questionnaire."

"So," I say. "Maybe I don't want to re-take it."

"My mother will not be pleased." Turning to Evora, Sammy says, "Come on. We have to tell her and the Royales that Gwen has decided against complying."

Evora stops the pretty vampire from pulling her away. "Wait. Just give her a minute. You know what Viorica will do."

I swallow, my nerves getting the best of me. From the sound of it, the vampire belongs to the Vaduva Coven. "And what's that?"

"Mind manipulation." Sammy pouts her bottom lip like the thought pains her. She actually kind of annoys me. She can't possibly understand what it's like to experience something so invasive.

I glower. "My guys would never allow it."

I regret my words immediately at the expression Sammy gives me. She raises her eyebrows and steps closer to me to gaze deeper into my eyes.

"That's why Mother's so adamant," Sammy says, whispering the words more to herself. "You like them all."

"The Royale brothers are pretty cute," Evora says.

I shrug. "So. What does that have to do with anything? They've all been kind to me. Except the Asshole Andersons. Those fuckers manipulated the Royales."

Sammy brings her hand up to my mouth. "Shhh! You can't throw around those types of accusations, especially with a newly expanded coven."

I clench my fingers into fists. "It's not an accusation. It's the truth. Corona killed my brother. He separated my whole family. He's only doing this to test Bronx's power."

Sammy sucks in her bottom lip into her mouth in thought. "If you dislike Corona so much, there is no way you'll match with him. You have to trust that you'll end up with the person you belong with. Evora is proof that the program works."

"I don't trust anything Donor Life Corp does," I mutter.

"Then trust yourself and the one you want to match with."

I close my eyes, her words doing nothing to stop the rolling in my stomach. "What if I want to match with all four of them?"

Sammy and Evora glance at each other in silent conversation. "That's a strange thing to desire," Sammy finally says.

"Why?" I rest my hand on the table, my knees suddenly wobbling.

Sammy closes the space to me and wraps her arms around me without answering my question. The edges of my vision darken. My mind whirls, making my stomach feel worse. I heave, my insides threatening to come out.

"Gwen? You don't look so good," Sammy says.

I slump into the chair. "Get Everett."

The word barely escapes my lips before the door swings open. I dart my gaze from Sammy in search of Everett, but a man in a white coat rushes into the room. He strides across the room to my side.

He shines a light in my eyes. "Ms. Royale? Your misters expressed some concerns about your health and asked me to take a look at you. Is that okay?"

I groan and cover my face with my hands. "I want Everett."

"Everett can't come," Sammy says. "He'll be disqualified for interference."

The world goes dark for a few seconds. Voices trickle to me, prodding at my consciousness. Someone jostles me around as they lift me into their unfamiliar arms. Whoever carries me is much warmer than I'm used to. Softer too.

"Put her down there," another voice, a female, says.

"Please assure the Royales that we have everything under control. I don't trust them not to intervene. I'd hate for them to be disqualified." It's Viorica. Why she would care? I can't help but wonder.

"Ms. Royale." Cool fingers touch my cheek. "Can you open your eyes?"

I flutter my eyes open to stare at Viorica. The same human in the white coat tucks a blanket around me and quickly hooks me up to a couple of machines to check my vitals. The stark white room smells sterile, almost chemically, and it makes my stomach churn.

I lean over and gag. Luckily, I don't throw up. Not like there is much inside me. I couldn't bring myself to eat much before the meeting.

"When was the last time you ate, Ms. Royale?" the man asks.

I stare at the light on the ceiling.

"Gwen, please answer Dr. Ruiz," Viorica says.

Swallowing, I hesitate to assure my stomach isn't going to protest. "When we got here."

Dr. Ruiz pulls a com device from his jacket and taps the screen a few times. "I'll have the kitchen prepare you something. If it's okay, I'd like to draw your blood and run some tests to make sure there aren't any underlying issues. Your vitals look good."

All I can do is nod. It's not like I can deny him.

"I'd also like to use your original Blood Match results due to the time constraints," Viorica says, speaking up. "I doubt much has changed since you've last taken it."

"But—"

"You've had plenty of time." She meets me with a glare, daring me to argue. "If you were serious about the process, you would've already completed the questionnaire. I'll inform the Royales of the situation and your current status. Once the doctor assures you're fine, we will meet in the lobby for your Blood Match results."

Viorica disappears without giving me a chance to beg her to please let me do it. Because in this moment, I realize that Viorica is wrong. I have changed. I'm a completely different person than the Blood Rebel they brought in kicking and screaming. I'm not bitter and angry. I have more life experience, forged with my guys, and it surely would show in how I match with them.

"Ms. Royale, I need you to lie back. I don't want to risk you toppling over on me again." Dr. Ruiz draws my attention to him. On a metal rolling tray, he fiddles with blood draw equipment.

"Do you have to? I'm feeling much better already." I swing my legs off the bed.

"Gwen, please do as he asks," Everett whispers from the other side of the closed door. "I'm right here in case. We just want to get you home."

I nod even though he can't see me. The doctor takes my gesture as me changing my mind about arguing and rolls over a stool to my side. I flop back and close my eyes, doing my best to ignore him.

"Ouch, fuck," I say, trying to jerk my arm away.

Everett's growl reverberates through the quiet room.

Dr. Ruiz stiffens. "I'm so sorry, Ms. Royale. Your vein is hard to find. May I please try again?"

Jameson groans. "Are you kidding me? What kind of doctor is this?"

"Calm down, brother," Mikkalo says.

I bite my lip to try my best not to react as Dr. Ruiz attempts to draw my blood again. He wiggles the damn needle under my skin, and I cringe, unable to stop my mouth from whimpering. Everett's the only one who has ever drawn my blood, and I wish it were him.

Something crashes in the hallway, startling Dr. Ruiz. I tense. The door flies open and Bronx stomps into the room with his fangs flashing. Everett beats him to me, causing the doctor to jump away. Dr. Ruiz spins and covers himself protectively.

"Bronx, please," I say, my voice cracking. "I'm fine."

Everett carefully extracts my blood and kisses the spot on my arm like always. Bronx relaxes and sets the doctor on his feet when he realizes I'm okay. I try my best to keep my shit together. Everyone's on edge enough, and they don't need me adding to it.

"You guys have to go," I whisper. "You can't be here."

"The hell we can't. You're our girl," Jameson says, pulling me into his arms for a hug. "I don't care what anyone says or what the dumb results of a test might indicate. You. Are. Ours."

His certainty helps ease the nerves still bunching my stomach.

"Plus, everything is already submitted, so it's safe," Mikkalo says.

"We wouldn't have risked getting disqualified." Bronx wraps his arms around both me and Jameson. "There is no fucking way your contract will pass on to Corona or any of those other assholes."

My lip quivers. "But what if—"

He brings his mouth to my ear. "I will slaughter them. They think they can play games, but your life and our love aren't to be messed with."

Mikkalo squeezes in. "Not to mention that you will punch out their hearts."

"So try not to worry." Everett stretches over Jameson and meets my lips. "We're going to take care of the paperwork, get Corona in order, and still have time to celebrate privately."

"Privately?" I tease, reaching my hand out to pat his cheek. "I'm nearly certain I need attention from the lot of you."

Mikkalo chuckles. "Hell yeah."

Dr. Ruiz clears his throat, drawing my guys' attention to him. He cowers under the weight of their glare, and I feel a little bit bad for him. He was doing his job, after all. "Please excuse me, Misters Royale, but I need to get Ms. Royale's blood to the lab."

"Go straight there. Stop for no one," Bronx commands, opening the door for him.

Dr. Ruiz hurries out of the exam room, his clomping footsteps fading down the hall. Without his nagging presence, I sink into Jameson's arms until he scoops me off my feet and nuzzles his mouth against the crook of my neck.

He kisses my throat. "It's one thing having you spend time with my brothers, but I wanted to set this whole city ablaze knowing you were with a damn Vaduva and then an amateur health keeper."

"Me too. The whole region," I whisper. "Though Sammy wasn't that bad. She was...sweet? I don't know how to describe her. She didn't scare me. She kind of actually tried to make me feel better about this shit show."

"At least that's something," Bronx mutters under his breath.

All of their com devices chime at once, and they break away from me. I stay in Jameson's arms, locking him in a death grip that makes him chuckle. He stretches his arms out and swings his hips back and forth, showing his brothers how I refuse to let go.

Mikkalo laughs. "I love when she's clingy. Give her here."

"You can try to take her," Jameson says, stroking the length of my back.

Everett comes up behind me and sneaks his hand under my dress. I squeal and bounce against Jameson, loosening my hold on him. Everett hooks his arms around me and drapes me over his shoulder, giving his brothers a view of my ass as my dress hikes up.

Bronx kisses my ass cheek. "Works every time."

I wiggle and laugh. "Careful, Bronx. Once you get me started..."

"We gotta get out of here," Jameson says, play-smacking my ass.

Everett lowers me in his arms and cradles me against his chest. I rest my head on him, listening to the sound of his steady heartbeat. It keeps my wild emotions under control, and I savor the protective circle my guys create, taking me out of the room.

The world blurs with Everett's speed, and he doesn't slow until we reach the long, wide hallway that leads to a lobby. Dozens of voices sound through the air, sending a wave of ice over me to steal the warmth I just got back.

Everett sets me on my feet and motions for me to walk

in front of him. I force my legs to move, but my feet drag the closer and closer I get to the noisy lobby. Bronx gently rests his hand on my back, putting enough pressure to keep me going. The four of them remain expressionless despite the sudden quiet falling through the room upon our arrival.

One of Corona's children, or whatever the hell his twisted self referred to those beneath him in the Anderson Coven, pops up in front of me. My body automatically reacts, and I swing out and punch him in the throat before kicking him between the legs. He drops to the floor, his eyes bulging as he flashes his fangs at me.

"Oh, Mother. I really do like her." Merrick's voice draws my attention to the group of female vampires sitting in a circle with their chairs facing each other. "Not jumpy at all. I don't think I've ever seen a man drop to his knees for a woman so fast."

Viorica doesn't respond, but her lips pull up into a small smile.

Jameson leans into me. "Get that sexy ass of yours in control. The last thing we need is for a Widow to offer you a Blood Vow to join their coven. They enjoy ball kicking. Throat punching. Basically everything you do. So quit it."

I grin at him. I can't help it. "I highly doubt it but okay."

Something grabs my leg, and I freeze as the dumb Anderson asshole tries to retaliate. His teeth get within an inch of my flesh before Jameson kicks him hard in the gut, sending him rolling. His power and strength obviously outmatches the guy, because the guy pushes to his feet and straightens his shirt, choosing to glower at me rather than to pick a fight he can't win.

"I'm going to take pleasure in teaching you your place," the asshole mutters under his breath.

He disappears across the room to settle against the wall. What a coward. He can't even stand up to his own threat.

I narrow my eyes at him. "I look forward to it. That way I can assure someone worthy of me inherits it after I rip your heart out and eat it for dinner."

He growls in response.

I flip him off, ready to drop a whole bunch of swears at him.

A cool hand grasps mine, the sickly familiar scent of Corona overwhelming my senses as he gets into my personal space. None of my guys react to his forward gesture, and I nearly lose my resolve at the sensation of his thin, dry lips caressing the top of my hand.

"Lovely Gwen, I do hope you're prepared for the life I have planned for you," he says, attempting to capture me with his gaze. "Unlike my brothers, who'll be dominated by…regional affairs, I'll now have all the time in the world to shower you with everything you could ever want and desire."

My heart slides into my stomach at his certainty. "I'm not going to match with you." I keep my voice low to stop it from hitching.

He smiles like I've said the silliest thing. "You don't sound so sure."

"Corona, leave her alone," Bronx warns. His chest presses into my back as he looks at Corona from over my shoulder.

"Relax, brother. I'm only trying to prepare Gwen for what is to come." He squeezes my fingers to stop me from yanking my hand away. "You can't honestly think that you're a better match for her. You might know her on a physical level, but there is more to this ravishing woman than what teases me from under her dress. I learned quite a lot about her from her brother. They are alike, you know. I did match with him after all. If applying to match with Gwen wasn't so expensive, I'd have considered matching with her instead."

I can't stop my face from reacting. His words stab inside me at the mention of Kyler and what he could possibly know about me.

Again, I try to pull my hand from him. "You're wrong. I'm nothing like my brother."

Corona's eyes flash silver. "Maybe now, but not before. Not when you originally entered the Blood Match Program. And I believe it's fate that Viorica decided to use your original test."

Ohmyfuck.

Shoving my hand against his chest, I manage to push him away and break free of his hold. Panic grips me, stealing my breath away. I swing my attention across the room until I find Viorica in the same seat, watching me like everyone else does.

I rush toward her. "Ms. Vaduva! Ms. Vaduva, please. I have to retake the test."

She licks her lips, flicking her gaze behind me. "I'm sorry, Ms. Royale. I already told you that—"

Something dark comes over me, and I rush the vampire. Growls and hisses rip through the air, setting off my fear instincts like crazy. Glass shatters behind me, and a thud booms as a body hits a wall.

Viorica raises her hand to stop her daughters from intervening. I drop to my knees in front of her, bowing my head. I never thought I'd bow down to a vampire in my life, but I can't think of any other way to get around this. If she uses my original test to pick who gets my contract, I'm afraid Corona's right, and I'll end up with him. I can't let that happen. Not even for a minute. It would destroy my guys. They might not show it, but they're as nervous as I am. They have the same fears I do. We're all afraid that I won't match with them.

"Please, I'm begging you." I blink the tears from my

eyes, my desperation getting the best of me. "Please."

A strong hand locks on the back of my dress and hoists me to my feet. Without having to look, I know it's Corona.

"My apologies, Ms. Vaduva—"

The world flies out from under me, and I spin through the air. Bronx roars as he lands on top of Corona, the sight of Corona lifting me off my feet setting him off. Mikkalo catches me, whirling me away from the fight that breaks out between Corona and Bronx.

"Stop immediately or you'll be disqualified," Viorica says. Her sharp voice freezes me to the core and also stops Bronx and Corona in their tracks.

"I insist you do disqualify Bronx," Corona says, flashing his fangs.

"You son of a—"

I don't have time to think things through, my body taking over under the wave of fury crashing over me. I shove against Mikkalo's chest and launch off him at Corona. I catch Corona off guard, colliding into his back. The two of us hit the floor, but he manages to roll over to pin me beneath him. We skid across the tiles, and I jab my hand against his face to keep his fangs from getting near me.

"Don't you dare fucking bite her!" Jameson yells, his form blurring as he rushes toward us.

I manage to grab the front of Corona's dress shirt in one hand. With my other, I jam my fingers hard enough into his chest to impale him. He freezes, his eyes widening and his body stiffening on top of mine.

I scowl at him, digging my hand deeper into his chest. His blood pools against my palm, and he attempts to scramble off of me, but I don't let him go. I can't. He set off my very dhampir nature and my body is fully set on seeing this through. I want nothing more than to rip his heart out and taste his bitter blood one last time as I snuff his miserable life out and get the vengeance for my brother that I deserve.

Bronx and Mikkalo stand above me, ready to drag Corona off. They hesitate, probably noticing my eyes. Everett kneels on one side of me, and Jameson takes the other. The four of them keep everyone in the lobby away.

"It would be in your best interest to let me go," Corona whispers, his breath sending a shiver through me. "If you do not, your secret will be discovered. No donor is capable of ripping out a vampire's heart. You will be caged."

I squeeze harder, feeling his skin give a bit under the pressure of my hand. "I don't care."

"Gwen, please," Everett says softly. "Even if they don't discover what you are—what you plan to do? It's punishable by death. We can't lose you."

His pleas are enough to snap some sense into me. I take a breath and ease my hand from Corona's chest without pulling his heart free. His life for mine isn't worth it. Not only would I jeopardize myself, but I'd also risk my guys' lives too. They'd never allow anyone to sentence me to such a fate. They'd fight and die by my side. I know they would. Their expressions prove it.

Corona smiles a cocky grin and pushes to his feet, leaving me on the floor. He buttons up his black jacket to hide the punctures my fingers made in his shirt and then returns to his seat next to the other former Andersons.

Viorica sighs and stands, sauntering across the room toward us. I expect her to yell at me or something, but she doesn't glance our way as she strolls to the reception area where a man sits behind the counter and types on a digital keyboard.

"How much longer, Mr. Erikson?" she asks, her voice rising in annoyance.

Mr. Erikson turns his computer screen in her direction. "The doctor is entering her health stats now."

She nods and returns to her seat.

It takes Everett pulling me off the floor to realize my body decided just to plant itself in the middle of the lobby. He quickly wipes my bloody hand the best he can on his jacket. Mikkalo and Jameson close in on me, obscuring the other vampires' view of me. Bronx leads the way, heading toward the last few seats left in the crowded lobby.

"Mr. Thompson?" the receptionist calls, and I turn to peer behind me.

A guy my age casually strolls toward the counter with his hands hidden in his pockets. He makes eye contact with me and smiles. I try not to let my confusion scrunch my face. It takes me a moment to realize that the lobby isn't crowded because of me. Some of the vampires must be waiting for their Blood Match results.

Everett tugs my hand until I pull my attention from the guy. I sit on Everett's lap, doing my best to ignore Corona's blatant stare as he watches my every movement from only a few feet away.

"Because donors scarcely volunteer for the program in this region, the Vaduvas only bring in applicants once or twice a month," he murmurs into my ear.

"Congratulations, Mr. Thompson. You've Blood Matched eighty-four percent to Mr. Vegas of Grand Valley."

I glance at the screen on the wall that displays all of the donor's stats along with a picture of a beautifully handsome vampire that suddenly appears at the counter. Mr. Vegas signs the paperwork and disappears with his new blood source without so much as a word. It happens so fast that I wonder if the donor even gets a chance to say goodbye to his family.

"Ms. Royale, your results are in," Mr. Erikson says, waving his hand to me.

Hesitating, I remain on Everett's lap, my nerves getting

the best of me. Bronx stands and offers his hand out. Dread flows over me in an icy stream. I can't do this. I can't find out my fate, not with the possibility that I'll end up in Corona's grasp.

The second I'm on my feet, I flick my attention around the lobby, looking for the nearest exit. If I run, my guys will follow. I won't give them a choice but to run away with me. They'll understand why.

Taking a deep breath, I slowly shuffle my feet in the direction of the counter. As long as I make it past the Vaduvas, I can reach the door. I doubt they'd chase me. I keep my eyes locked on the floor, counting each tile until I reach ten and inch just past the Vaduvas' circle of chairs.

I bolt for it. Pushing as fast as I can on my feet, I race toward the exit. Bronx groans from behind me, but he doesn't call my name.

A security guard materializes in front of the door and blocks my way. I pull my arm back to swing into a punch strong enough to knock the guy back, but a cool hand locks on my fist. Bronx tugs me away and wraps his muscular arms around my shoulders, turning me toward the reception desk.

"You always have to be a pain in my balls, don't you, dandelion?" he says loud enough that the whole room can hear.

Jameson chuckles. "She wouldn't be Gwen if she

wasn't."

"Everyone's going to think you don't want to match with us with the way you attempted to escape." Bronx stops pushing me when we reach the counter.

I glare at him. "I wasn't trying to escape. I need to use the bathroom. I thought it was there."

"You must have to really go with the way you ran," Everett muses, joining me and Bronx.

Scrunching my nose at him, I say, "I do."

"Then let's hurry and get this over with," Jameson says.

He and Mikkalo get behind us, creating a semi-circle around me. The former Andersons have the nerve to get close, standing a couple of feet away to also get a clear view of the giant screen on the wall behind the receptionist.

"Are you excited, Ms. Royale?" Mr. Erikson asks, smiling at me. He clicks a few of his digital keys. "I just love a good Blood Matching, knowing that two perfect pairs come together."

I thunk my elbows on the counter and lean in. "No, I'm not. I don't believe this dumb test can pair me with my supposed perfect match. I've already found them through fate, time, and a lot of special attention."

My guys all smile at me, and then Bronx wags his finger at the guy and says, "Please proceed so we can get on with our night."

Mr. Erikson smiles and nods, tapping a few more keys.

He leans in a bit toward his screen, his soft features suddenly hardening. He swallows audibly as he looks over what I assume are my results.

"Well?" I ask. "Are you going to show me?"

The man's heartbeat picks up speed, making me nervous as hell. "Just a moment, Ms. Royale. Something went wrong, and I'm trying to figure out if this is an error on my part."

Viorica materializes behind the man, startling him. She holds his chair in place so that he doesn't roll back into her. He points out a few things on the computer, his face twisting even more into a frown. Viorica flicks her gaze to me, her eyebrows lowering. She runs a hand through her gorgeous red hair and shakes her head.

"What is it, Viorica?" Bronx asks. "Did she equally match with more than one of us?"

"Huh? Something like that is possible?" My voice rises in anticipation. I never even thought of the possibility, but I'd be ecstatic if that happened...unless it was with Corona.

"Possible but not probable. It has only happened once." The soft voice comes from behind me, and I twist to look at Sammy.

"And also why Zaire had eliminated the option of allowing more than one coven member to apply at a time," Bronx says.

I bob my head. I knew that. It was one of the reasons

my guys were pissed off at him, because he chose to apply to Blood Match with me, which disallowed the rest of them from doing so.

"So, what are the results?" Everett asks, inching his way toward the end of the counter. He looks ready to risk going around to peer at the computer himself.

Jameson does, standing next to Viorica to read over the screen. His whole face scrunches, a dozen indecipherable emotions crossing his expression. He pales, his knuckles turning white as he grips the back of Mr. Erikson's chair. If I didn't know any better, I'd think he was about to be sick.

"Fuck, it's one of them, isn't it?" I ask, my heart crashing about my chest, ready to expel itself to save me from discovering that my future with my guys is over. My stubbornness to retake the questionnaire might have ruined everything.

"Just fucking tell us already," Bronx says, his hand tightening around my waist. He's preparing to run with me. I can feel it in my bones. He won't accept the results if my contract doesn't transfer to him or his brothers.

With a shaking hand, the receptionist taps his keyboard, lighting up the wall in front of us. The same ugly-ass picture from my original matching pops into view. I cringe, my insides churning, my whole body wanting nothing more than to give out on me.

A bunch of stats appears on the screen, and I clutch onto Mikkalo's hand, knowing that my match will pop on screen next.

But it doesn't.

In big, bright, flashing letters, the screen announces that I've been disqualified.

I don't have a Blood Match.

20

DISQUALIFIED

EVERY VAMPIRE IN THE ROOM gathers around the counter to stare at the glaring disqualification sign plastered across my picture. I don't know whether I should be thrilled or freaked the hell out that this happened. What does getting disqualified even mean? Since I'm a convicted criminal, will my guys have no choice but to send me to auction like they had intended to do with my brothers? Could they just buy me then?

I hate the thought of being treated like property.

"So, will someone tell me why I've been disqualified and what that means?" I finally ask, breaking the tense, eerie silence overtaking the room.

Viorica glances toward Everett. "To be able to Blood Match, you must be in optimal health."

I blink a few times, fear gripping my chest. I hadn't considered the possibility that maybe my dhampir mutation showed in my blood work. This is bad. Really fucking bad. The board will want to run tests. They'll want to cage me.

"Gwen is in optimal health," Everett says. He pushes through the Vaduva sisters and strolls around the counter to get a better look at the computer. "I give her regular health checks, monitor her blood donations, dietary habits, fitness. She's healthier than most humans who enter the Blood Match Program."

"Well, it's obvious you've missed something, Mr. Royale. What, exactly? You tell me. I'm not a practitioner. I don't know what this means." Viorica points at the computer screen, her mouth tightening.

"She did faint," Sammy says, speaking up from beside her sisters. "Maybe she's caught a virus."

"As long as it's not something serious, she can go through the process again," Heidi adds. "We've allowed it before. It'll take, what, like two to three weeks?" She looks at Everett, and I wonder if she's the health keeper among the Vaduva Coven.

Everett rubs his jaw and swallows. He glances from the screen to me and back to the screen. I can't tell if it's something bad or something fucking awful, but whatever it is, Everett doesn't want to tell anyone.

He clears his throat. "Because the status of Gwen's health is sensitive, as her health keeper, I'm requesting privacy to inform her."

Corona releases a growl. "Blood Matches don't get privacy. Just tell us how long until we can do this again?"

Everett snarls at him, lunging to jump over the counter. Viorica grabs Everett's shirt and drags him back, spinning him toward the wall. The two of them flash their fangs at each other until Everett composes himself.

He tightens his jaw and says, "Please, Viorica. This isn't something to be taken lightly. Allow me to inform Gwen in private or only in front of people she's comfortable with."

Viorica relaxes her shoulders and nods. "I'll allow it, but I insist that I must be present."

Everett darts his eyes from Viorica to look at me before each of his brothers. "I suppose that will be okay."

Viorica turns towards me. "Ms. Royale, please follow me to my office. You may allow anyone you like to join us." Turning to the crowd, she adds, "As for the rest of you, please excuse yourselves. You will be contacted when and if Gwen's contract gets transferred. You will not be needed since we have your applications.

Corona slaps his hand on the counter. "I demand to be present. This involves my coven."

His coven? Yeah-fucking-right.

Viorica shoves Corona into the wall so fast that it takes me a second to realize she's moved from her spot by the receptionist. Lifting him off his feet, she scowls at him, looking ready to treat him like a donor and bite his neck.

"Must I remind you that Bronx is your coven leader? And as for Ms. Royale's results? It will only be your business if you match with her. Until then, leave. You will respect your superior's request. Do you understand?"

"Thank God," I whisper to myself. I never thought I'd actually like another vampire outside of my guys, but I have to respect Viorica.

Corona disappears, and his former coven mates follow. The Vaduva sisters leave next, and I find myself strolling behind Viorica toward the elevator as Bronx tugs me along. My brain can't stop thinking about the results, and I kind of wish Everett had just shared them. The anticipation turns my stomach upside down.

"Are you allowing everyone present into the room?" Viorica asks, meeting my gaze.

I look at my guys. "Yes, they're the only ones I'm comfortable with."

Viorica allows us into her office, decorated like some antique back-world library I've seen in a few movies. Floral printed chairs rest in a cluster around a circular table with a painted vase full of blooming lilies in the center. A golden chandelier hangs in the center of the room, casting soft light over the plush rugs. Dozens of bookshelves display old books that look more decorative than anything. A huge, dark wooden desk with a modern chair takes up one of the far walls along with a floral sofa.

I gaze at the paintings of gardens as I stroll to where Viorica takes a seat in the sitting area. She motions for me to sit across from her. Everett slides onto the last chair, leaving Mikkalo, Bronx, and Jameson to stand. I don't think Jameson could sit if he wanted to. He fidgets with his suit jacket and sways his weight from foot to foot. Mikkalo crosses his arms over his broad chest, his frown clearly showing his annoyance. Like me, he probably would have just rather heard the results in the lobby. As for Bronx, he gives nothing away. If anything, he looks relieved that I was disqualified, which helps with my own nerves. It might not be a big deal after all. Maybe it was the universe's way of giving me the chance to retake the tests properly so that I don't end up with Corona.

Viorica hands Everett her com device, and he sets it on the table. I lean forward and read my stats. I'm five pounds heavier now than last time, probably from all of the food Jameson likes to stuff me with or maybe the added muscle I've gained from strength training with Bronx and Mikkalo.

"What are we looking at?" Viorica asks, beating me to it. "Is it a virus? Do I need to prepare my city for quarantine or is it something else? How long until we can settle your inheritance?" She doesn't pause between questions to let Everett answer. "I will notify the rest of the board immediately."

Everett taps on the screen and brings up my results from my blood test. "Your city is safe. I wasn't lying about properly caring for Gwen. She isn't sick."

"Huh?" I ask, unable to understand what the names and numbers of the tests mean.

"So what is it? How long will the disqualification show on her application?" Viorica hunches forward, looking annoyed as all get-out that Everett doesn't just tell her.

"I'm not sure," he says, keeping his voice even. "Depends when Gwen's last menstrual cycle was. I don't recall her telling me, and she has not had one under our care. I thought perhaps it was due to the stress she was under upon her arrival."

Viorica looks to me. "Ms. Royale? Please tell your health keeper what he needs to know."

Everyone turns to me, and heat flushes my cheeks. "I don't know. Before I Blood Matched..."

"You *don't* know?" Viorica asks. Something strange crosses her face, and she jerks her attention to Everett. "Wait, Mr. Royale. Why do you need to know that? Are you suggesting that Gwen is...?" She doesn't finish her thought.

Everett nods.

Viorica intakes a breath.

"What the fuck are you implying?" Jameson asks. "You just need to say it. I'm not following."

Everett leans across the table and takes my hand. My whole body tingles as my own thoughts consume me. I don't know a lot about the human body or medical stuff, but I do know that there might be only one reason Everett wants to know when my last period was. And it's completely bat shit crazy.

"Gwen, you're pregnant," Everett says, meeting my gaze. His blue eyes flash silver. "That's why you were disqualified. You cannot be a Blood Match and sustain a vampire."

"What the actual fuck?" Jameson's voice rises through the room. "That's impossible. How the hell can she be pregnant?"

I stare at him, the same thoughts crossing my mind.

"It seems Gwen and possibly one of your staff members have some explaining to do," Viorica says, smirking at me.

"I—" I snap my mouth closed without denying such an accusation. I'd never sleep with a staff member. I've never been truly alone.

Viorica gets to her feet. "Due to the nature of this situation, I'm going to leave Gwen's contract unclaimed during the duration of her pregnancy. I'd advise you to interrogate your staff if Gwen doesn't give you the information you desire."

I swallow the burning in my throat. "And after?"

Viorica meets my gaze. "That will be up to your official Blood Match to decide. I'm sure if your match chooses to do so, and with the proper fees paid, I'm sure the board will agree to grant your heir exemption. I can't imagine your future match wanting to deal with...that." She points at my stomach.

Ah, hell. I still can't believe it. There has to have been a mix up. I'm not pregnant. Vampires don't procreate like that. They transfer vampirism through venom.

Offering her hand out to Bronx, Viorica says, "If you'll excuse me, Mr. Royale. I do have plans for the rest of my night. Please keep me updated about your situation, and I'll see you at the next board meeting."

Bronx shakes her hand. "Thank you, Viorica."

"Again, welcome to Donor Life Corp. You can show yourselves out." Viorica disappears from her office, leaving the five of us alone.

The second the door clicks closed, Jameson practically pounces on me. He kneels in front of me and gets between my legs, pulling me close to press his ear to my stomach. I comb my fingers through his hair, tugging him away. The gesture surprises the hell out of me, considering he looked ready to blow up a minute ago.

"Gigi, I'm freaked the fuck out," he says, snuggling me again. "How did this happen? I wanted to attack Viorica for even suggesting you'd sneak around with the staff. You'd never do that. You can't eat them."

I release a cross between a laugh and a whimper. "There has to have been a mistake." Turning to Everett, I say, "You have to test me again."

He bobs his head. "We'll get this figured out."

Mikkalo releases a soft growl, drawing my attention to him. "What if it happened at Corona's? I'm going to murder him. If one of his staff—"

I stretch my arms up to him, getting him to move closer. "Nothing happened there. I was left alone and starved."

"You can't be certain. If he used mind manipulatio—" Mikkalo picks up the vase from the table and thrusts it at the wall, shattering it.

I gasp at his thought.

Bronx grabs Mikkalo by the shoulders. "No, I don't think so. His staff all checked out. His coven wouldn't cover something like that up. The guy would've been slaughtered." His words make me feel a teensy bit better.

Combing my fingers through my hair, I push it from my face. "I don't want to think about Corona's anymore. I want to go home."

Jameson scoops me up and adjusts my legs around him. "Me too. Why don't we check on your brother and then get out of here?"

I frown. "Shit."

Jameson nuzzles his nose to mine. "Don't feel bad about forgetting about him. You're under a lot of stress, which we need to cut out immediately. I also need to look into your new dietary needs."

I pout my lip. "Don't get ahead of yourself. This is a mistake."

"It has to be." Bronx meets my gaze from over Jameson's shoulder.

"Not necessarily." Everett rubs his hand on my back. "We don't know much about the dhampir mutation. Maybe she's compatible. We don't impregnate female vampires because of our regenerative nature and our bodies fight against foreign cells. We don't impregnate humans because we're incompatible and technically two different species. But Gwen is half. Her mutation might allow it."

"Her brother did mention the Barons desire to use her to procreate," Mikkalo says, speaking for the first time.

"You're not suggesting they actually wanted to procreate with me," I say, tilting my lips down in a frown.

Bronx's expression mirrors mine. "Their coven is responsible for your family's dhampir line. Maybe they knew."

Jameson shifts me in his arms. "Maybe your brother might be able to help us now."

I hug him tighter. "Fucking hell. Then let's get him."

I almost fear that we'll discover Ashton missing from our room when we enter the hallway that leads to our suite. Jameson refuses to let me walk, and I can't help thinking about what the hell is in store for me, if my results were right.

"Stop stressing. He's in there," Jameson says like he can read my mind.

"You think that's what she's stressing about?" Mikkalo asks, nudging Jameson with his knuckles.

"One of the things," he responds, kneading his fingers into my back.

I lean away from him so that I can cup his cheeks in my hands. "Jamie, can you please stop reminding me? We don't even know for certain."

He caresses his lips to mine. "Doesn't matter. I'd rather be safe than sorry."

Everett whacks him on the back. "Knock it off. You're going to be the one to stress her out. Or smother her. As her health keeper, I insist you keep your thoughts to yourself and treat her as you normally do."

"I am," he murmurs.

I nod. "He's right. He rarely lets me down."

That gets a chuckle out of Jameson. Resting my head on his shoulder, I let him carry me the rest of the way into the room. To my relief, I find Ashton standing in the kitchen, making breakfast. I'd usually eat dinner a little later, but the familiar scent of his cooking has me wiggling in Jameson's arms.

"Your eating habits are starting to make a lot more sense now," Jameson murmurs, finally setting me down.

I play-smack his chest. "Oh, shut up. My eating habits have nothing to do with..." I stop talking, feeling Ashton's gaze on my back. I swivel on my feet and smile at him. "Hey, Ash. I'm glad to see you up. Are you okay?"

He waves his spatula. "Strangely, yes. Want some pancakes?"

I stroll to the small kitchen and take a seat on a barstool. "I almost forgot you were as good a cook as Porter."

Ashton offers me a sad smile. "I was the one to teach him, you know."

He sets down a stack of pancakes in front of me. I pick one up with my fingers, waving it around to cool it off before I take a bite, not even using a fork or waiting for the syrup Jameson grabs from the cupboard, knowing I like things super sweet.

"I didn't. He claimed he taught himself," I say.

"Of course that dickhead would."

I can't stop myself from smiling. Something feels incredibly normal, sitting here and talking to my brother. My guys stay close, but none of them say anything or join the conversation. They may be waiting for me to acknowledge them.

"We might have a lead on him. Right, Mikkalo?" I ask, swiveling to look at him.

Mikkalo nods. "As long as Corona doesn't do something stupid."

I frown. "Fuck."

Ashton turns from the stove and sets down another plate on his side, choosing to stand to eat. "Are you planning on punishing him? I remember that the Barons had mentioned he knew about Gwen."

Everyone greets him with silence.

"Surely you will, right?" he asks, glancing at me. "I know Gwen well enough to know she'd want that, especially from whichever one of you she matched with."

I clear my throat. "I didn't match."

He frowns.

"I was disqualified."

"I don't understand. You qualified before. You should have again." Ashton looks at my guys. "Right? It's not like she suddenly aged out."

I groan and thunk my head on the counter. I know we

were going to ask Ashton about the possibility of me getting pregnant by a vampire, but I really—and I mean fucking really—don't want to tell him. He was always worried that my fate would end up with me as a baby factory or some shit. He even said so before he allowed Bronx to see if he could unlock anything the Barons might've wanted to hide from us.

"Just say it, Gigi," Jameson says.

Ashton rests his hand on mine. "You can tell me anything, Gwen. I love you unconditionally. You're my baby sister. It's what Dad would want from us. He'd be furious to find out about Grayson and Silas's betrayal."

Tilting my head up, I pout my lip at him. "Looks like you don't have to worry about the Barons caging me and forcing me to become a baby maker."

"You're sterile?" he asks, keeping his voice calm.

I bare my bottom teeth to him. "No, pregnant." Waving my hand at my guys, I add, "By one of them."

I expect a look of total confusion or shock. I expect Ashton to laugh maniacally and to tell me he doesn't believe me—that the possibility is utterly and completely bullshit. I hold my breath, praying to the universe that he'd react in the way I hope. That he knows it's impossible for me to get impregnated by a vampire.

He doesn't do any of that. All he does is scrub his hands down his face and turn away from me to stare at the dirty skillet on the stovetop.

"It's ridiculous, right?" I ask, my voice low as to not break. "Everett's going to test me again when we get back to Crimson Vista. We can't exactly trust a health keeper that could barely find my vein to draw blood. It's most likely a clerical error."

Ashton heaves a breath. "You've been having sex with all of them, Gwen."

"I told you I'm in love with them," I say, like it could make it better. There's no way I'm mentioning that I succumbed—or more like completely embraced—to my blood lust even before I had some major feelings

"Unprotected sex," he says.

Jameson makes a strange noise from his throat. "There is no other kind of sex in our territory. The last time a condom was made was...decades ago."

Ashton turns around and glowers. "You could've pulled out."

My cheeks burn with so much embarrassment. I'm nearly certain I'm going to explode into flames and die with any kind of response that Jameson comes up with. Or any of my guys for that matter.

Mikkalo grabs Jameson by the shirt and drags him from the room, stopping him from what I can sense might be a string of shouts that the entire Vaduva Region might be able to hear. Bronx inches closer to me and laces his fingers between mine, quietly supporting me while I try not to break down.

Everett leans his elbows on the counter on the other side and meets Ashton's gaze straight on. "Pulling out is not a guaranteed way of preventing pregnancy. But that doesn't really matter now. None of us knew that we were compatible to procreate with Gwen. Had we known, I assure you we would've taken better precaution."

Ashton only nods, his anger fizzling out with Everett's words.

"So, it is what it is," he continues. "What I want to know is how you knew of the possibility."

Furrowing his brows, Ashton rubs his scruffy jaw, mulling over Everett's question. He turns his attention to me, giving me a long look, training his gaze to my stomach like he can possibly see what's going on inside of me.

"I—I just remembered. The Barons told me. It's why they want Gwen. It's weird. Like I have two different memories of the same situation." Ashton strolls from the kitchen and plops onto the barstool next to me. "I think Bronx's mind manipulation worked, but I'm still a little confused."

I let go of Bronx's hand to take my brother's. "Things will be weird for a while, but if you say the Barons told you I could get knocked the hell up by a vampire, that's the memory I'd believe."

"It's why they want you, Gwen. Apparently, whatever

thing is inside of you will be as powerful as hell."

"Did he just call one of our future kids a *thing?*" Jameson asks, his voice echoing through the door.

I can't stop myself from laughing in exasperation. Not only because I'm damn sure Jameson's already currently all in for whatever comes of this unexpected situation but also because the Barons had the nerve to think that I'd just let them impregnate me and "bear the power" or whatever they said, which now makes a whole lot of sense.

"So powerful that it could change the balance of the world," Ashton says. "And like I told you, I wanted nothing to do with the future they want with you. I couldn't just accept the deal that they made with Grayson and Silas."

I purse my lips. "What deal exactly?"

"They were going to bring them into the Baron Coven. All of our brothers who agree. Silas was transformed to set the deal in motion. If they get ahold of you, Grayson will be next. The rest of us were to follow after—" He reaches out and rests his hand on my belly. "This happened."

"Fuck," I say. "They're a bunch of psychos."

Ashton squeezes my hand. "You can't tell anyone else, Gwen. If the Barons find out...I'm afraid for you."

"We won't let anything happen," Everett says, his voice sounding more certain than I think I could ever feel.

"Damn straight," Jameson says, opening the door to come back into the room.

A chime rings through the air, but only Mikkalo pulls out his com device to look at the screen. He stiffens, darting his gaze to Bronx.

"We have to go," Mikkalo says. "There's been another attack on our region."

Ashton swears. "The Barons?"

Mikkalo surprises me by nodding to let him know his thought is right.

He gets to his feet. "I'm coming with you."

"I'm sorry, Ashton. You can't. You belong to the Vaduva Region," Bronx says.

"I don't care. I have to go with you. I can't just leave Gwen now. Things are different. Clearer," he says. Ashton grabs my hand, proving he's serious. "And if the Baron's attacked your region, they know about Gwen. They have to."

"You can't do anything to help us," Mikkalo says.

He scowls. "I can do more than you can."

"How?" Jameson asks, flashing his fangs.

Ashton straightens his shoulders. "I can tell them that I've changed my mind. I'll tell them I want to join them. And when they allow it, I'll kill every last one of them."

"You can't do that alone," I say, frowning.

He offers me a smirk, like I'm dumb for even believing that he thought he could. "I'm not doing it alone. Your coven will help me."

21

MINI BEAST

"WE NEED TO TAKE HER home," Jameson says, hugging my arm to his chest. "It's too dangerous to take her back to Brentwood's."

Bronx flicks his gaze to me in the rearview mirror. "I'm not leaving her."

"What, so is everything going to be a group activity from now on?" Jameson squeezes my hand as I sit on Everett's lap.

Mikkalo swivels. "I don't know, brother. Are we? You

look fully set on never leaving Gwen's side."

"I guess we have our answer," Jameson snaps.

I groan and twist to rest my head on Everett's chest. I wish I could pull down the seat and look at Ashton, but we've barely passed through the gate to leave Midnight Valley, and my guys won't risk getting caught with him. If there is one sure way to piss off a vampire, it's taking a blood source from their gen. pop. donations. The last thing we need is to anger the vampire who might actually have a mindset that will fall in our favor.

"All right. Everyone needs to relax. I agree that we shouldn't take Gwen home. We need to stay together." Everett runs his fingers up and down my arm. "Not just for our safety but for our sanity. I don't know about you, but Corona really fucked me up with insisting to Blood Match."

Mikkalo shifts and knocks his fist into Everett's knee. "You're not alone in your feelings. But still, it's easier to protect Gwen in our own city. I'm with Jameson."

Bronx releases a breath. "All right, dandelion. What do you want? You're the tie breaker."

I close my eyes so I don't have to look at anyone's reactions. "Sorry, Jameson. Mikkalo. I don't want to separate unless it's just to our rooms. I think we should stay together outside of our city until we can take care of the threat. I'll worry too much otherwise. I like to know where you all are so I can protect you myself."

Jameson groans the longest, most dramatic breath I've ever heard. He shifts and awkwardly rests his head on my lap, half crouching on the floor. I laugh and link my fingers through his soft hair, tugging his head up before he tries to stick his face under my dress.

"You will not be protecting us, Gigi," he murmurs, managing to escape my hold. Instead of attempting to get under my dress again, he nuzzles his face into my belly. "Not in your condition."

"My condition? I'm not suddenly some fragile donor. I can still kick your ass." I snatch the hem of my dress and tug it over his head to distract him from whatever the hell he's thinking. "Nothing has changed since yesterday."

He kisses my thigh. "Everything has changed. Yesterday none of us knew you were going to be a mother and carrying one of our babies. Kill me for being protective."

Silence falls between the five of us, and Bronx slows to go through the final checkpoint outside the city. Ten minutes pass before Jameson slides to the middle of the backseat and tugs the lever to get into the trunk. Ashton lies on his side with his eyes closed. I can't blame him for falling asleep.

"Just let him," I say. "Keep the hatch open in case."

Jameson does as I ask and leaves the seat down, remaining squished against Everett. Everyone continues to keep their attention on me more than usual, and I know a lot of questions flit through their minds. Questions I have no desire to ponder if I don't have to.

The sweet scent of Jameson's blood trickles through the air, and my stomach roars like all it takes is a single drop of his deliciousness to unleash my wild side. Jameson sucks in a breath through his teeth and quickly presses his bleeding arm to my mouth without vocally offering it to me first.

"We should've given you blood before we left," Jameson murmurs, stroking his fingers over my legs until I scoot onto him so he can hug me from behind while I drink. "Pretty sure that wasn't just your stomach growling."

"Jamie," I murmur as I swallow, the burning in my stomach subsiding, though I can't get myself to let him go just yet.

He hums softly against my shoulder. "What do you think the baby will favor? Human or vampire blood?"

I yank back from his arm. "Nu-uh. We are not discussing this. We don't even know if it's a sure thing."

"Gwen, I know you're scared—"

Bronx smacks the dashboard, setting the car into autopilot. "She said she didn't want to discuss it, Jameson. I know this threw all of us off, but I need you to get your head together and push everything aside for now until we're safely home. We don't know what we're dealing with, and I'm counting on you. We all are."

Bronx's growly voice startles Ashton awake, and he

peers at me from his spot lying in the trunk. He doesn't attempt to move, probably sensing the tension. I consider crawling back there with him.

"I'm sorry if we can't all be as emotionless as you, Bronx," Jameson snaps, flashing his fangs. "This is why I wanted to take Gwen home. I don't want her anywhere near anyone. We have to rearrange our priorities. I know you're now officially a board member, but I need to know that we come first. Our girl is too important. That little mini beast in her belly is too important. Who cares about everything else."

"Mini beast, Jamie, really?" I ask, gently knocking my head into his chin.

"As wild as its mother. I can already tell. I wonder if this is why you're always insatiable. If it drinks vampire blood—"

"Jameson," Bronx warns. "Enough."

Jameson growls. "Obviously some of us won't be getting up for daytime feedings."

Swiveling on his lap, I meet him with wide eyes.

He shrugs with a smirk. "Don't worry. You've trained me to stay up all day already. I'll be fine doing it."

I tip my head back, releasing an almost maniacal laugh. Just the thought of any of my guys feeding a baby gives me a major case of giggles. I know I drank blood all my life growing up—from a bottle as an infant to a cup until I turned eighteen and met Laredo—but it's hard even to imagine.

"Damn does our girl like that idea," Mikkalo says, grinning at me.

"Well, I do love sleep," I say. "Almost as much as eating."

"More than sex?" Everett whispers.

I bump my shoulder to his. "Obviously not."

Ashton clears his throat from his spot in the trunk, and because of his silence, I nearly forgot he was with us. I force myself to smile and motion for him to climb into the backseat. Jameson gives him a hand, and Ashton settles in beside Jameson.

"We're almost there," Bronx says like he expects Ashton to ask. "The Hunters are on the edge of our region. It's pretty quick to get to from Midnight Valley."

Ashton bobs his head. "Anything I should expect?"

Mikkalo meets my brother's gaze. "From what I can see on the video feeds, the Barons didn't wreak as much havoc on Sky Canyon as they did other towns. The Hunters only had three casualties. All vampires."

Ashton rests his hand over mine. "And you think it's a good idea to go there?"

Jameson throws his arm out. "See, Bronx? Even Ashton sees the problem."

"It's what they expect. We can't change our usual protocol or they'll change their plans. We just have to be ready." Bronx glances at Jameson. "We are strong enough to handle it, especially with our girl."

"He is right about that, Jameson," Mikkalo says.

"Mmmhmm," Everett adds.

"Plus, they'll also expect that we picked up Ashton. They'll try to go after him too. It's what we need if we want Ashton to help us from the inside." Bronx gives Ashton a look like he had better not mess up. "It's what will help Gwen and...our baby."

"Weird as hell to say, right?" I ask.

"Not weird, dandelion. Just different. Not something any of us ever expected." Bronx's sharp features soften as we stare at each other. "I've never even been around a human child since I was a human myself."

Jameson slaps him on the shoulder. "It's going to be great."

"That's easy for you to say," I mutter. "I'm the one the mini beast is growing inside of."

"And the one who has to push it—"

I elbow Everett. "Don't remind me."

He smiles and kisses my cheek. "It's an amazing thing."

"Then you do it."

All my guys laugh, and I groan and shimmy forward between the seats and into the front with Mikkalo. He slides his arms around me, and I sprawl my legs across Bronx's lap.

Bronx rubs his hand over my shins.

"Too much?" he asks, trying not to smile.

I fake glare at Jameson and Everett as they grace me with their best smiles. "No more talking about you know what. Got it?"

"Got it," they both say in unison.

"Good."

Mikkalo leans into me and kisses my cheek until I shift to meet his lips. I savor his spicy sweetness, my own desire playing off his. No one says anything as he deepens our kiss. I slip my tongue into his mouth and explore his with mine, feeling his body awaken under me.

"You're the most incredible being in the world, you know?" he whispers against my lips, pulling back only to smile. "I love you."

I grin. "I love you too."

I meet Ashton's gaze from over the seat. He stares at me with confusion wrinkling his forehead. I try not to let him get to me and stay cuddled up with Mikkalo.

"Gwen, I know I'm probably never going to get another minute alone with you, so I'm just going to be forward and ask you... Are the Royales always like this with you? I mean, I know you all have an obvious connection, but it feels so unnatural almost. I've never seen anything like it." Ashton tries not to react under the weight of my guys' sudden attention on him.

I bend forward to look at him better. "What do you mean?"

"They're quite affectionate, and not in the way that makes me think they're only trying to charm you to get you to give them blood or sex." He shifts awkwardly, sliding more into the door to put two inches of space between him and Jameson. It doesn't help that Jameson burns his gaze into the side of my brother's head while my brother ignores him to continue to look at me.

"They are, aren't they?" I ask, smiling at each of them. "But so you know, it's not always this grossly romantic." I lift my leg and poke Bronx's chin with my knee. "This guy doesn't like to give me my way all the time."

"Which infuriates the hell out of her," Mikkalo says with a laugh.

"And her stubborn ass drives me crazy." Bronx smiles with the words. "Always getting into trouble."

I stretch forward and hook my arms around his neck to pull him close enough that I can whisper in his ear. "I'm still waiting for you to spank me one of these days." I say the words too quietly for anyone to hear but Bronx.

He purrs deep in his throat, tightening his fingers on my legs. "Gwen," he whispers softly.

I grin and press my finger into his lips to keep him from trying to kiss me. "Nu-uh. You need to keep your shit together and not get distracted."

He play-growls. "Don't think I won't save this thought for later, especially now."

I give into him for a kiss. "Better not."

The car suddenly jolts, and Mikkalo holds me in place as we bounce in the seat together. The rough terrain must scare Everett, because he reaches between the seats to take me from Mikkalo.

"What's happening?" Ashton asks, bracing against the back of Bronx's seat.

"We're entering Sky Canyon. Looks like the Baron's took out the main road," Bronx says, taking the car off autopilot. He taps a few buttons on the dashboard, and the ride smooths out. "Everyone stay on guard. We're meeting Brentwood south of the town on the outside of the wall. He's put the place into quarantine. No one goes in or out until we personally complete the sweep."

Mikkalo's com device chirps. He draws his finger on the screen. "Change of plans. Head to the east wall. There is an access tunnel that'll drop us into the groves."

Bronx turns the wheel and navigates the hard-packed dirt where Mikkalo directs. "Something happen with Brentwood?"

Mikkalo tightens his jaw. "Yeah, he betrayed us."

Jameson swears. "A repeat of the Crescents?"

"Looks like it." Mikkalo continues to stare at his screen, flicking through different feeds of the city. "Here, Bronx. I need you to grant me access to the private feeds."

Bronx presses his finger to the screen and it turns green for a split second. "The board works fast."

Mikkalo nods. "Which Brentwood doesn't realize. Donor Life Corp hasn't announced your acceptance of the board position. He probably thinks we can't access anything without permission or Zaire's help."

"That asshole," I say, hunching forward. "The first thing you should do as region leader is pick new city heads. The ones we currently have suck."

"The Barons must've offered the Hunters something they couldn't refuse," Jameson says.

"Like they'll spare their lives? Give them power?" I say, throwing the thoughts out there. "Because if it's those things, I'm about to offer them the same a second before I kick their balls and punch their hearts out."

"Uh-oh. No sudden movements," Jameson teases. "Gwen's going wild."

I flick him, not finding his amusement funny. "Damn right, I am. I'm pissed off. First, we had to deal with Corona. And then the board. Now this? I just want to go home."

I punch the back of Mikkalo's seat, and he jerks forward. My hand rips right through the leather and frame before sinking into the cushion. Everett snatches my hand, inspecting my bloody knuckles. He presses his cool fingers into them but doesn't say anything as he stares at Bronx.

Jameson and Mikkalo do too. But Bronx and Ashton look at me.

"We can't take her out there like this," Jameson says, trying to keep his voice even though it raises in pitch a notch.

"The hell you can't. I'm done with this bullshit. These assholes can't even get whatever sick fucking thing they wanted from me." I curl my fingers into fists. "So just drive to wherever the hell the Barons are waiting."

"No damn way, Gigi," Jameson says.

"I agree with my brother," Everett says.

"Same," Bronx and Mikkalo say in unison.

"Which means majority rules," Jameson says.

I glare at him, looking all smug as hell now that he gets his way. I shift and turn my back toward him, and he hugs me even though I remain stiff. He even has the nerve to bite his arm again to offer me blood.

"If you think your blood will chill me the hell out, you're wrong, Jamie," I say, pressing my fingers into the puncture wounds to stop them from bleeding.

"I don't think, I know," he grumbles, attempting to get his arm close to me again. "And if you're too stubborn to let me satiate you, then let Everett. Please, Gigi. We can't risk the uncertainty you create, especially not now. Think of—"

"Don't you dare say it," I snap.

"Our family." He nudges me until I face him. "We

can't keep each other safe if we're worried about you."

I purse my lips at his words and silently lace my fingers around his arm. "Damn you."

Mikkalo chuckles. "You're getting pretty good at that, Jameson."

"I've kind of had to. I can't just submit to that sexy mouth of hers and die a happy man. I love what's in store for our future too much." Jameson combs his fingers through my hair.

"You're ridiculous," I mumble. "And sweet."

Bronx slows the car to a stop and cuts the engine. He swivels in his seat, and I look past him to stare out the window. A couple of hundred feet away, a towering wall divides the town from the road that disappears into a forest of trees.

None of us gets the chance to exit the car before a figure blurs in front of us.

I point at the vampire rushing our way.

The guy stops at the hood and slams his hands on the metal.

He screams my name.

22

IMPURITY

BRONX AND MIKKALO ABANDON US in the car. Jameson crouches and motions for Ashton to get in the middle and hands him a dagger. Everett does the same for me, easing me off his lap to hide me on the floor. He adjusts the front seat to give me more room and shields me with his body.

"Give me Gwen. You can't keep her. She doesn't belong to you," a guttural, almost manic voice says.

I shiver and clutch onto Everett's leg. "Fuck off. I don't

belong to you either." I know I shouldn't say anything, but I can't help it.

Bronx and Mikkalo both growl. I can't see anything from my position, but something slams against the car, shaking it.

"If you leave now, we won't kill you," Bronx says, his voice sharp enough to cut someone. Hopefully this douche.

"I can't. Not without Gwen. I will not let Freeport have her. He doesn't deserve her. Neither do you." The vampire releases a strange, animalistic noise unlike anything I've ever heard. "Gwen? Gwen, I know you can hear me. My name is Morgan Baron. I'm the protector of the Gallagher dhampir bloodline. Please, you have to come with me."

Are you kidding me? Everett tries to keep me down, but I straighten up enough to peek at the guy staring at me from the windshield. Every time Bronx and Mikkalo close in on him, he evades their tactics and disappears.

"I don't care who you are. I'm not going with you," I say, meeting his gaze through the side window.

Jameson flings the door open fast enough to knock the guy back. Mikkalo and Bronx manage to capture him and haul him to his feet. They each hold one of his arms, restraining him. Jameson closes the space with a dagger drawn and ready to sever the guy's head.

"Gwen, please. Don't be stupid. If you don't come with

me, my brothers will get to you. You don't want that to happen." He struggles in my guys' hold but doesn't even flinch as Jameson aims the knife at his throat, cutting Morgan as he stretches forward in an attempt to get a better look at me.

"We won't let that happen," Bronx says with a snarl. "Brother, end him."

"Wait, wait!" Morgan yells, thrashing. "Gwen, please. You have to be careful. You don't want to birth a future with convoluted power. That's what will happen if you stay. The bloodline must remain pure. To humor a life far beneath you will only end in tragedy."

I freeze at his thinly veiled words. "Jameson, wait."

Morgan's hazel eyes widen in relief. "Yes, please. Listen to her."

Everett locks his fingers to my arm when I attempt to sit up fully to exit the car. Morgan snarls and snaps his teeth, like even seeing Everett touch me sets him off. It only makes me want to touch Everett more. So I do. I use Everett's love of my affection to get him to pull me into his arms. I kiss him softly, clutching his face in my hands.

Morgan screeches, his anger probably loud enough to alert the entire town. "Stop that! You'll ruin her!"

"Shit, don't let her go," Bronx says.

Everett locks his hands around me, but my sudden fury allows me to overpower his strength. I drag him out of the car with me without giving him a choice on whether or not to follow me. He would anyway, but I return his grip on my hand just as fiercely that I'm sure his fingers are as numb as mine.

"Damn it, Gwen. Stay back," Bronx says.

Jameson shifts to peer at me from over his shoulder. "Seriously, Gigi. We've humored him long enough."

"Just a minute more." I strut up to my guys but stay behind Jameson, using him as a shield.

Morgan sighs a breath, his hard features softening at my closeness. "You're so enthralling. As perfect as the last time I saw you. Practically glowing."

I scowl. "Shut the hell up and listen carefully." Pushing against Jameson's back, I attempt to burn Morgan with my gaze. "Whatever you think you're doing will not end well for you or your brothers. I know everything about the contract that I never signed. About your twisted idea for my future. The promise your coven made to my brothers."

"Your future will be everything you want," Morgan says. "You'll see. What you feel now toward the Royales is a fleeting emotion. You couldn't help yourself. It's part of your very nature to bond with power, but they're not good enough, Gwen. You need someone stronger."

Morgan's words dig into me, prodding at the savage inside me who wants nothing more than to rip his heart out.

"My love for the Royales isn't fleeting or temporary," I

say, my voice whispery and sultry, heated with my fury. "It will only grow stronger. So will our power."

"Please, Gwen. They're not worthy of you. You deserve a better future."

I dodge around Jameson and grab the front of Morgan's shirt to get in his face. He stills under my grasp, his eyes darting around my face to drink in every inch of it. He puffs a small breath through his mouth like my closeness affects him in a way that leaves him breathless.

"What I deserve is to be left the hell alone," I say, twisting the fabric of his shirt to tighten around his neck. "Whatever plans you or your coven had will not happen. It's too late."

Morgan's fangs peek out from beneath his lips. "It isn't."

"Uh, yeah. It is," Jameson says, interrupting. "She will not be birthing any power for you or whatever the hell you think. What she will be doing is living the best life of our making as a family. The only thing she'll be birthing is...what did they used to call it? A bundle of joy? And it's ours."

Morgan's eye twitches.

Jameson wraps his arms around me and tugs me away. Morgan thrashes again, yelling incoherently.

"Gwen!" he screams. "Gwen, you can't do this! You can't sully the bloodline."

I jerk away from Jameson to close the distance to Morgan again. Swinging my fist, I clock him in the face, sending his head jerking sideways. Bronx and Mikkalo hold him tight, not saying a single word while I sock the douche again. And again.

"Don't you dare imply that our kid will be anything less than perfect. It isn't an impurity." I knee him in the stomach. "And I don't care about your bloodline."

Morgan remains stiff, his eyes widening at my words. "No. This can't be."

"What can't be? That we knocked her the fuck up?" Jameson asks. "Because hell yeah we did."

Jameson's lucky I'm not through showing this douche where I think his place is.

Morgan roars, startling me. I automatically step away, and he thrashes so hard that Mikkalo loses his grip on him. Bronx swings Morgan off his feet and into the side of the car. He doesn't get far before my eyes are on him again. It takes all four of them to pin him down, his fury now fueling his strength. I dash closer and glance down at him.

Morgan meets my eyes. "If you think my brothers will stop because of this, you're wrong."

I launch at him, punching him hard enough in the chest to shatter his sternum. He bucks and yells, but I don't stop. I can't see anything beyond the red tint hazing my vision. I can't feel anything beyond my fury.

A gentle hand touches my shoulder. "Hey, Gwen. Gwen, he's dead. We have to go."

Bronx lifts my trembling body into his arms and hugs me against him. Fear squeezes my chest as I replay Morgan's words over and over again. I know he's right. The Barons won't stop, not unless they're dead.

"Take a breath," Bronx whispers. "We're fine. Everything will be okay. We got you."

I swallow the burning in my throat. "We have to get them."

"We will."

"Right now."

Bronx sets me on my feet outside the car to peer down at me. "We have to strategize. I really think our plan with Ashton will work."

"Fuck," Jameson says, drawing our attention to him.

He stares into the car and at the empty backseat.

Ashton is gone.

Swiveling on my feet, I search around the dark area. Maybe Ashton lost control over his fear instincts and chose to run and hide. It wouldn't be the first time he's done it. But who am I kidding? He's not the sixteen-year-old who did that, scaring the hell out of Dad. He's a twenty-four-year-old man with more experience than me when it comes to handling fear.

"Where is he?" I ask, yanking Bronx with me to check

on the other side of the car. "Ashton? Come back here. Everything is okay."

My guys surround me, creating a protective circle as we assess the area without getting too far away from each other.

"How did this even happen? We were twenty feet away." I scrub my hands over my face.

"We were preoccupied," Mikkalo says, frowning.

"One of us could've been killed." I try to stay calm, stepping close to Mikkalo to embrace him. "It would've been so easy."

Bronx twists and slams his fist into the roof of the car, denting the metal. Fury flashes silver in his eyes, and he heaves a few breaths. "Come on. We have to move."

Instead of getting into the car, Bronx squats down and motions for me to get on his back. Everett helps me position myself for the best hold on Bronx. Pulling out his com device, Mikkalo flicks through the feeds. He remains expressionless as he studies the area. Jameson stands close to him, watching from over his shoulder.

"Fuck, someone must've picked up on the douche screaming," Mikkalo says. "The Barons are separating."

"Do they have Ashton?" I ask, nerves bunching my stomach. "Are they going to surround us?"

Mikkalo continues to study the feed without comment.

Everett strokes my back as I rest my chin on Bronx's shoulder. "Ashton will be fine. This was part of our plan, remember?"

Releasing a groan, Jameson points at Mikkalo's com device. "There he is."

"Shit," Mikkalo says. "This isn't good. It wasn't a Baron who took Ashton."

I frown. "What do you mean?"

"It was Lady Tori," Jameson says.

Furrowing my brows, I try to process the name to see if I remember it. The second it dawns on me, I release a string of fucks. Lady Tori was the woman who controlled the women on Brentwood's staff. She was the one trying to help Xochitl get pregnant by way of Silas. And now she has Ashton.

I lick my lips. "What do we do?"

Mikkalo stares at the screen a bit longer. "I don't think your brother is in any danger. We should go after the Barons that we can while they're separated. Some of them outmatch us individually, so we need to stay together."

Jameson shakes his head. "No, we need to go after Lady Tori. She could have heard us talking. Maybe that's why she took Ashton. If she manipulates his mind and finds out about the dhampir mutation—"

"Shit," I murmur. "Jameson's right."

"All right, dandelion. We'll go after him first. Our element of surprise is over anyway. If Lady Tori heard the Baron scream, it's probably why the rest of them dispersed."

Bronx hugs one of his arms over mine to assure he has a firm hold on me. "Mik, lead us in. Jameson, follow behind."

Jameson plays with my hair. "You got it. I'm always here to protect that sexy ass of hers." He gives my ass a little squeeze.

"Don't forget about Bronx's sexy ass too," I murmur.

The four of them laugh, the lightness in their voices helping to ease the fear and worry clenching my heart, refusing to let it go. Everett takes his place next to Bronx, and Mikkalo takes off at a vampire's speed. I clutch Bronx tighter, turning my head to protect my eyes from the wind. Pitch darkness engulfs us, and I tense. Stale air makes it hard to breathe.

Mikkalo's com device illuminates the darkness in front of me. I shouldn't be so nervous. I've entered too many tunnels to count to get into cities. But now? I don't know. I'm not as brave as I used to be. Or maybe I've just smartened up since I no longer live life like a constant death mission. I can't. Not knowing that there's a chance I'm responsible for bringing something scary beautiful into our coven.

"We got two outside the tunnel. One on each side of the mouth," Mikkalo whispers, keeping his voice too low for the outside world to hear.

"Everett, take Gwen." Bronx releases my arm so Everett can pull me into his arms. "Jameson, back up Mikkalo. Distract them, and I'll surprise attack."

Soft moonlight trickles in from outside. Everett shifts me onto his back to keep his arms free. We stay with the others until we reach the passage out. Everett turns to face his back to the side of the tunnel, sandwiching me in protectively. I inhale slow breaths into his shoulder, trying to get my heart to settle before someone hears it.

"Do you need me to distract you?" Everett whispers, reaching his hand up to touch my cheek.

I hug him tighter. "Don't even start. Look what happened because of all your guys' need to distract me."

His shoulders shake in a silent laugh. "Which means now's a better time than ever."

I graze my teeth to his shoulder. "You're so bad."

"It's going to be amazing, Gwen. I hope you know that." He twists his neck more to brush his lips to my cheek.

I inhale a long breath through my nose. "It's a lot to take in. It's like—I never thought it possible. Not like this."

"Don't let Jameson hear you or he'll give you his 'nothing is impossible' speech." Everett strolls a few feet away from the wall and toward the mouth of the tunnel.

I close my eyes and listen to the soft voices of Bronx, Everett, and Mikkalo. "He's going to gloat so much."

Jameson enters a foot into the tunnel and motions to us. "Damn straight, Gigi."

Everett strolls at a human's pace until cool, fresh air engulfs us, making me take an automatic deep breath. The grove looks like many of the others I've come across in my life. The sweet citrusy scent of oranges wafts through the air. A couple of rows away, I spot another kind of fruit I don't recognize.

A tree branch rustles, and I stiffen on Everett's back. Bronx emerges from between two trees peeling an orange only to throw the skin on the ground. He breaks it apart and handfeeds me a piece.

"I can wait to eat," I say, despite my possessed arm already reaching out to snatch the fruit from him.

Bronx doesn't let me take it, offering me a single piece again. "But you shouldn't have to."

Soft footsteps draw our attention from each other. Mikkalo materializes next to a tree a few feet away. Something strange crosses his face. My heart slides into my stomach at the sudden heavy scent of his blood.

He drops to his knees and falls face first on the ground. Several daggers impale his back, his blood pouring out of him, leaving him too weak to fight. Jameson swears and rushes toward him. He doesn't get a foot within Mikkalo's reach before a figure blurs next to him.

"Fuck!" Jameson yells, twisting to grab at his back.

A dagger stabs between his shoulder blades, but the vampire who did it disappears too quickly to catch. Bronx growls next. He catches a vampire by his shirt and throws him at the ground.

"Brentwood!" Bronx snarls and slams his fist into the familiar vampire's face.

Brentwood flashes his fangs at Bronx. He manages to twist and sit up, biting Bronx in the arm. I screech in anger from Everett's back. Bronx jerks his attention to me, leaving himself open for a split second. It's long enough for another vampire to rush him and stab him in the back.

Brentwood doesn't try to attack Bronx. Instead, he catapults to his feet and zooms in our direction. Everett tenses and swipes his dagger out. Brentwood dodges to the side. Everett spins to protect me, and I grip him as tightly as I can. The blurring of the world as Everett spins and dodges Brentwood sends my stomach into my throat.

Several growls sound through the air. My fear instincts go off like crazy. It takes everything in me not to throw myself from Everett to run away as fast as I can. But I don't have to. He runs into the trees in an attempt to get away. In normal circumstances, he would never leave a fight, no matter how powerful his opponent was. But now? I think my fear rubs off on him.

"Everett!" Bronx yells.

Everett drops to his knees and skids across the dirt. A vampire flies over us, trying to attack us from the side. My arms burn with pain as Everett's weight squishes them into the dirt, giving me road rash.

He quickly rolls and lands on top of me to take a dagger to the gut. The strange vampire grins like a lunatic getting pleasure from our pain. Everett kicks his leg, managing to knock the guy away long enough to launch to his feet. The vampire cuts us off and stabs Everett again, causing him to flinch. Neither of us has a chance to react as someone latches on to the back of my dress and yanks me away.

My scream echoes through the night.

"Shhh, little dhampir," Brentwood says into my ear. "It won't be long now."

Several vampires blur through the trees. Everett beheads two guys faster than I've ever seen him do so. Bronx and Jameson appear from the trees, blocking two other guys. Jameson jams a knife into one of the guys' neck, sending blood cascading across the dirt.

"Brentwood, let her go," Bronx says.

A cool blade touches my throat. "Stay back, Mr. Royale."

Bronx tests Brentwood and steps forward.

My throat stings from the small nick of the blade. "Stop, Bronx."

Stopping in his tracks, Bronx drops his dagger to the ground to show he's not a threat. It does nothing to get Brentwood to loosen his hold on me. Everett and Jameson follow his lead, and they stand together.

"What did they offer you, Brentwood?" Bronx asks.

"Power," Brentwood says, keeping his voice even. "But

I denied them. I swore my loyalty to you and the Royale Coven. They killed three of my best security guards. Took several of my females."

"Then what are you doing?" Bronx says, his eyes narrowing in anger.

"I'm doing what you promised to do," he snaps. "Stopping the war on our region."

"You think it'll stop if you hand Gwen over to them?" Jameson says, speaking up.

Brentwood heaves a few deep breaths, his chest pressing into my back. "You think I'm stupid? I'm not giving her to anyone. She's the reason they're here in the first place. I'm saving you. Our region needs you. But her? No."

Panic grips me, and I reach for the blade, cutting myself in an attempt to pull it away from my throat.

"No, no!" I plead, my blood spilling down my arms. "Don't do this."

"Hurry up, Brentwood," a feminine voice says. "The Barons were spotted circling. Our security will be slaughtered."

Brentwood stills his hand. "I'm sorry, Gwen. You were such a pretty donor."

"Wait!" Everett says, rushing closer. "Lady Tori, please. She's with child."

"Liar!" Brentwood yells. "You'd never let a donor get in reach of her."

I wiggle in his arms, feeling his hold on me loosen just a bit. "He's not lying. I was even disqualified from Blood Matching."

Everett pulls out his com device. "Look."

Lady Tori steps closer to get a better look at the device. She brings her hand to her mouth. It's enough to make Brentwood hesitate. Turning her gaze to Brentwood, Lady Tori confirms what we've told her with a nod. Silence draws between us, Brentwood's hand shaking so much that he nicks my neck again.

"Brother, please. I'll take her. We'll find someone to drain in her place—take the person's head. Assure they can't tell. Perhaps Agatha. They're similar sizes, and she refuses to expand the population." Lady Tori inches closer, treating Brentwood like a wild animal. Extending her hand out, she silently asks him to give her the knife.

"We have no choice. The Royales will never let you take her. They'll kill me the second I let her go." Brentwood growls in my ear. "If I'm to die, I won't do so in vain. At least I can save the region."

"Brentwood," Bronx says. "Killing her will not save our region. Your death will still be in vain. "

"It won't!" he yells, tightening his hold on me again. "It'll save you and my coven. Everyone. You've lost sight of things."

"Brother, hurry. Give her to me. They're coming." Lady Tori dashes at us, risking Brentwood slicing my throat.

I brace for the pain, knowing that even if he does it, I won't die. I'm a dhampir. I can survive it. It's the only thing stopping me from begging for my life now. If he does it, he'll run and my guys can get to me. But only if he does it soon.

"Just do it," I say, anger rising in my voice. "You want to kill me? Fucking fine. I knew I'd always die by a vampire's hands, and I'm not going to beg for my life any longer."

"Gwen," Bronx says, his voice shaking.

I meet his gaze. "I love you. I love all of you."

"Damn it, Gigi. Knock that shit off." Jameson flashes his fangs at Brentwood. "You have three seconds to release our girl. If you do, we'll let you live."

Brentwood shakes his head and pulls me back with him. "I'm sorry. You will thank me."

Something crashes into Brentwood from behind, sending him falling into me. I manage to yank the knife from my throat before we hit the ground. Lady Tori hisses and appears above us. She tugs Brentwood off of me only to lock her hands into my hair. She yanks me to my feet.

"Gwen, don't fight. Go with her," Bronx calls, drawing my attention to him. He dodges away from a blur that moves too fast for me to catch sight of.

Lady Tori doesn't get the chance to take me far. Brentwood appears in front of us and jabs a dagger at my stomach. I recoil to protect myself. Lady Tori spins me around and takes a knife to her back. It's enough to slow her down to where Brentwood circles back to face me.

"They will die because of you. Is that what you want?" Brentwood asks, snatching my hand. He drags me toward him. "I can save them."

"And so can I." Swinging my arm, I punch him hard enough to send him tumbling back.

Brentwood doesn't release me and drags me with him. I land on top of him and punch him in the face with my free hand. Something blurs in front of me. A familiar, creepy vampire materializes near us.

"My sweet Gwen. You look like you could use some help." The vampire, who I think is named Cortland, glides closer and extends his hand to me.

I try my best to suppress my fear instincts. "No. I have it under control."

He smirks at me. "Well, I insist."

I don't have a chance to scramble away. He locks his hands around me and hoists me to my feet only to throw me over his shoulder. I link my fingers to the back of his shirt and scratch my nails into his back. He only reacts by lowering me off his shoulder to force me to face him.

He leans in so closely that I can feel the scratch of his beard on my chin. His breath mingles with mine, and I squeeze my eyes shut. He's too close. His mouth too close to mine. My whole body trembles. I haven't felt this vulnerable in my life.

"My brother has a claim on you, but I'd risk stealing you away to keep you to myself for a while. The power we can create together will be far superior." Cortland rests his forehead to mine. "I'll make you rather happy."

Leaning back, I spit in his face. "I already bear power, you asshole. You're too late. I've given my future to the Royales."

He growls, the noise vibrating over my lips. "I think you misunderstand the extent of what it means to bear power."

I snap my eyes open, braving to look into his black depths. "I don't. I know exactly what it means. Morgan confirmed what it meant."

He stiffens. "You saw Morgan?"

"And took his heart."

He flashes his fangs at me, extending them so far that they graze my bottom lip. "How could you betray our line? How could you risk everything?"

I open my mouth to snap at him, but he surprises me by jerking his head and sinking his teeth into my shoulder. I scream out, my vision darkening. Pain explodes through me as his venom burns through my skin and into my blood.

"No matter. That should fix things."

"Wh-what?" My head lolls, and I can't stop myself from resting it on his shoulder.

"Shhh, rest now, sweet Gwen. I'm taking you home."

"No," I whisper, the venom threatening my consciousness.

"No!" Brentwood roars, choosing to fight instead of run.

Cortland spins to face the vampire, blocking my view of him. The two snarl at each other, and Cortland shifts me in his arms, but he's not fast enough. Brentwood yanks me away by my hair. Throwing me to the ground, he gets on top of me. A hot pain erupts between my shoulder blades, stealing my breath.

"Do that and die!" Cortland yells.

"I'm already dead."

Brentwood's weight sinks into me as his body drops. His dagger rams into my back and I scream.

The last thing I hear is my name.

The pain turns all-consuming.

23

FUTURE HEIR

"I TOLD YOU I DON'T have her, Thaxton." Laredo's voice murmurs through the thick wood of the trunk. It's the third time he's brought me onto his coven's estate, leaving my brothers in the small colony of Blood Rebels that trade blood for protection from Donor Life Corp.

"But you know where she is," a masculine voice snaps, putting me on edge.

I cover my mouth with my hand to muffle any possible noises I unintentionally make.

"If I did, I still wouldn't tell you. What you plan to do will backfire," Laredo says. "Even Rochester recognized the danger. Why do you think he didn't present her the contract? Why do you think he went as far as trying to force her into a donor contract?"

"Because when it came down to it, Rochester didn't care about us. All he cared about was himself." Something thuds, possibly a fist into a wall. "We should've taken care of him the moment he insisted he move into the Gallagher household. He was far too caught up in Gwyneth's sacrifice that he couldn't see anything beyond trying to replace her."

"Well, lucky for us, Gwen did take care of him."

"But now she's gone. You know how important she is. With her, we can rise and overtake the Donor Life Corp territory. Power is shifting. We must act, and we can do so with Gwen. What she's capable of, what we can create with her, will change the foundation of our world. You know it can't keep going on like this. The rebels grow stronger than ever. If they get ahold of any dhampir bloodlines, they can use it against all vampires. We must get to her." Thaxton's desperation rings so intensely that it's nearly palpable. I hug my knees harder into my chest. He's right about the rebels. They think dhampirs will take back the world, that we're humanity's gift. But what he wants? I don't even know.

Laredo groans. "You know dhampirs are quite wild. The likeliness of getting her to cooperate is slim. She'll *probably eat your heart."*

"Don't underestimate me, brother. She will listen. She will understand."

"And if she doesn't?"

"I will make her."

My body jostles as I hit the ground. It's enough to startle me from unconsciousness, and I sit up and gasp. My eyes burn with tears, my body swelling with pain. I gag, my stomach reeling. Jerking sideways, I vomit blood all over the ground.

"Come any closer and I'll kill you." The rumble of Cortland's voice does nothing for the state of my stomach.

The soft sounds of light footsteps draw my attention to a blurry form coming out from behind a tree. "Then kill me. Gwen is hurt. She needs medical attention."

A gargled cry escapes my mouth at the sound of Everett's voice.

"She will heal," Cortland says.

"She's lost too much blood. Her wounds aren't coagulating. Please, you have to let me help her." Everett's pleas pull at my heartstrings.

I gag again, trying to get my arms to push me from the ground. My body doesn't cooperate, and I roll onto my stomach and use my legs to push me a foot forward in the dirt.

"She's mine," Cortland says. "Do anything stupid, and

I will kill you."

"You can take her after. Just let me help her."

Everett and Cortland wage a staring contest that Cortland breaks first. He materializes next to me and lifts me to my feet to turn me around. I struggle for a minute until Everett's gentle hand touches my back. I have no idea what he's doing, but just his closeness is enough to calm me down.

"She was stabbed in the back," Cortland says.

"Anywhere else? Her abdomen?"

"My heir is fine." Cortland touches his hand to my stomach.

Screaming out, I jerk my head forward and sink my teeth into his chest. Just hearing him trying to stake his claim makes me lose my shit. My sudden strength throws him off, and he stumbles a few feet.

"Now!" Everett says, rushing toward me. He takes advantage of Cortland's distraction as he jerks his attention toward Bronx and Mikkalo flying from the grove.

Cortland doesn't get three feet from his spot. Bronx grabs the front of his shirt and swings him off his feet. He thrusts him into a tree, the crash so hard that the trunk cracks and branches thunk to the ground. Mikkalo grabs him and spins him around, hooking his arm around his throat. Jameson materializes in front of him and punches him in the gut.

"Gwen, hey. Look at me," Everett says, touching my chin. "You don't want to watch that. Let me give you some blood."

I swallow the burning in my throat. "You're o-okay."

He offers me a smile. "Tell me what hurts. You got stabbed?"

"Brentwood." My voice comes out barely a whimper. "My neck hurts the most."

Everett carefully combs my hair from my throat and inhales a sharp breath. His cool fingers touch the puncture wounds, but it does nothing for the pain of the venom. "Shit."

"It's b-bad, isn't it?" I ask.

"I'll get you fixed up right away, but you must drink first." Everett bites his arm and offers me his blood.

My stomach clenches, and I dry heave, unable to get myself to latch onto his arm. I press my lips together and shake my head.

"She's going to starve with you. The power she bears is now mine. It'll want nothing less than the pure blood of a Baron," Cortland calls. He releases a grunt as Jameson punches him again.

"What is he talking about, Everett?" Bronx asks.

"He bit her with venom."

Bronx roars and hits Cortland so hard that it knocks Mikkalo back too. Mikkalo dodges out of the way, and

Bronx shoves Cortland into the nearest tree. He swings his fists in rage over and over again, spilling Cortland's blood all over the place.

"He was trying to purify the bloodline," I murmur.

"What the actual fuck?" Jameson shouts.

"You are not worthy of her." Cortland flashes his fangs at Jameson. "None of you are worthy. Her future is mine. You don't have a choice now. She will die without me."

Jameson punches him again, his anger refusing to allow Cortland a swift and merciful death. Everett clutches my cheek, attempting to force his arm to my mouth to get me to drink his blood. My body reacts uncontrollably again, and I thrash, my stomach wanting nothing more than to come flying out my mouth.

"Let me try," Bronx says, extending his bleeding arm to me.

I attempt to taste his blood, but my body convulses once more. Panic slashes through me. If Cortland is right, I don't know what I'll do. I need vampire blood to survive, but there is no fucking way in hell I am going to live off of him.

Releasing a loud laugh, Cortland flings his arm, sending blood spatter across the three of us. My nostrils flare, my breath heaving. A guttural sound rips from my throat, loud enough to make Everett and Bronx stiffen.

"My Gwen. You know you want me. You yearn for a

taste. All you have to do is break free."

Jerking my arm, I elbow Everett in the sternum. He drops me only to have Bronx catch me and spin me in his arms. I snap my teeth, trying to bite him as a way to escape. Because Cortland is right. I do want him. I want to drain every drop of his blood.

"Don't let her go, Bronx," Everett says. "I have an idea."

Everett slides in front of me and blocks my view of Cortland. The silver in my eyes reflects back to me from the glassiness of his blue gaze. Bronx squeezes me tighter into his chest, his muscles flexing with every buck of my body. I can't stop trying to break free. I want this to end. I want Cortland to pay.

"Gwen, I know you're panicking, and you don't know what's happening to you, but will you trust me?" Everett asks, touching my cheek.

"You need to let me go. Cortland was right. I'm going to die without his blood." My voice echoes through the air.

Everett risks closing the space even more. He leans an inch away from my mouth, doing his best to block out the rest of the world from my vision so that it's only me and him. "I want your permission to bite you with my venom."

Bronx growls. "Are you kidding me?"

Everett licks his lips without taking his eyes from mine. "Yes. That baby is a Royale. If Cortland used venom to mess with Gwen, our venom might help counteract what he did."

"It could risk our girl's health," Bronx says.

"What else can we do? We can't lock up that asshole to feed to Gwen when she's hungry. I'm not cool with that," Jameson says. "I'm with Everett. Our girl is tough."

Mikkalo groans. "No. It could cause more damage. I'm with Bronx."

Everett looks at me. "None of our wants matter. It's Gwen's choice." Brushing his lips to mine, he risks kissing me. "It's your decision. I'll be gentle."

My heart pounds wildly in my chest as I think about his words. Could I really handle more venom? What if it doesn't work? What if Mikkalo is right and it makes things worse? What if—none of the what-ifs matter. I can't live my life like this, tied to a Baron by need for his blood. I can't.

I open my mouth to tell Everett to do it, to bite me with his venom, but a few loud beeps cut through the air. Bronx stiffens and pulls his com device from his pocket and stares at the screen, his eyes not giving anything away.

Footsteps sound from within the grove, and we all shift our attention. My heart ricochets around my chest at the sight of Thaxton emerging from the trees with Silas by his side. The memory of Thaxton's conversation with Laredo trickles through my mind, and I replay it over in my head. Now I know this is about more than trying to gain the power to take hold of a region. It's about the whole Donor Life

Corp territory. About Blood Rebels too.

"I suggest you free my brother, misters Royale," Thaxton says, waving his hand at Cortland.

"No," Jameson says, waving his dagger. "You can watch him die."

"Then all of your cities will perish. Vampires and humans won't stand a chance." Thaxton pulls out a device from his pocket and taps the screen.

The world around us quakes, and Bronx lifts me off my feet and grabs onto the nearest tree trunk to stop from toppling over. The scent of smoke trickles through the air a moment later, and all my guys' com devices chirp again.

Everett pulls his out to look. He blinks his eyes to hide whatever thought is on his mind and then whispers, "That was the north side."

"You have five seconds to release Cortland or the east side will fall next," Thaxton says. "The rest of my coven is currently making their way to your other cities. If you do not obey me, they will be destroyed."

Bronx nods his head at Mikkalo and Jameson, and the two of them push Cortland. He falls on his knees, weak from their beating, but he manages to get back to his feet. Slowly walking past, he drinks me in from head to toe, taking pleasure in making me uncomfortable.

"Now as for Gwen," Thaxton says. "We're taking her home. You've had enough fun with her."

"Fuck no," Jameson says. He rushes toward us to take his position in front of me to shield me. "Destroy the entire region. I don't care."

Thaxton smirks. "As you wish."

Another explosion booms through the air, causing the ground to tremble. Screams echo through the night, digging into my heart.

"The south will be next," Thaxton says.

I raise my hand up. "Wait, no. Don't."

Thaxton hovers his finger over his device. "You will come with us?"

I bob my head. "Yes."

Jameson grabs my hand. "No, Gwen. I'm not letting you."

"What choice do we have? They'll kill thousands of people. Hundreds of thousands. You really want me to live with that? What will I tell the mini beast? That I thought I was worth far more than an entire region?" I lick my lips. "And what about the aversion to your blood? That asshole bit me with venom."

Thaxton inhales a sharp breath at my words. "Is it true?" he asks Cortland.

Cortland nods. "I took care of it."

"Temporarily." Thaxton stiffens at his response. From the look on his face, I realize he hadn't intended to say the word out loud.

"Did he just say temporarily?" Jameson asks.

"He did," I say, my voice coming out as a whisper.

Bronx loosens his hold on me, and I dash away from him and toward the Barons. Silas steps in front of Thaxton, a strange look crossing his face. Mikkalo grabs my hand and propels me forward instead of trying to pull me away. Jameson and Everett split up and rush around to come at Thaxton and Cortland from the side.

"Get the device," Mikkalo says to Bronx, who charges next to us.

Thaxton turns to flee, but Mikkalo's quick to throw me. I land on Thaxton's back and wrap my hands around his neck to hold on. He runs backward, trying to knock me off. Mikkalo steps between me and a tree and blocks the force. He sandwiches me to Thaxton, and I tear into the crook of his neck, my blood hunger consuming me with my fury.

Fruity blood fills my mouth, sending tingles down my throat. The action freezes Thaxton in his place, his nature unable to resist the allure I have on vampires. Bronx grabs Thaxton's device and then shoves a knife into his chest.

Cortland materializes behind Bronx and yanks him back by the shirt. Thaxton manages to get his shit together and jerks his head back, head-butting Mikkalo from over my shoulder. I automatically release Thaxton, and he bolts to where Silas limps, trying to escape Everett's wrath.

"Gwen, come with us," Silas says, his voice hoarse. "Please. You're family. We don't want to hurt anyone, but you're too important."

Thaxton and Cortland charge Everett, forcing him to abandon Silas. Jameson materializes next to us, his arm limply hanging at his side.

"No, Silas. I made my decision. You call yourself my family, but you gave up that right the moment you let them transform you. You're not my family. The Royales are. We're creating a future together." I touch my stomach. "One I'm going to make sure you're never a part of."

"Gwen," Silas says. "Please."

I shake my head and hold my arms out to Bronx to pick me up. "We have to end them. Right now. I want their blood."

My guys position themselves, obeying my desire to finish this. Jameson charges first, his dagger aimed to kill.

The Barons turn and run.

They disappear into the tunnel that leads out of the town, and Mikkalo brings up the feeds to try to track their movement.

"The explosions must have taken the tower out. I can't access the feeds," Mikkalo says.

We rush through the pitch darkness of the tunnel. My heart pounds in my ears, my mind begging my body to keep up.

To get it together so that we can finish it. The Barons and their so-called powerful bloodline must be drained.

The world slows as fresh air engulfs us.

"Shit, they're gone," Mikkalo says, linking his fingers on the back of his head.

Jameson's chest rises and falls with his quick breaths. "We can track them. We still have a few hours until the sun rises."

Bronx shifts to cradle me like a blushing bride. "It's not enough time. They'll probably call upon the others to regroup and strategize. We need to alert our cities."

"Not to mention handle the destruction here," Everett adds. "It's our duty."

I bob my head. "You're right. They won't go far. We'll get another chance."

Jameson closes the space and hugs me. "We can split up."

"No," I say. "I told you that. Never again."

Bowing his head, he kisses my forehead. "Okay. Whatever you want."

I rest my head on Bronx's chest. "I don't know what I want, but let's start with our region. I wasn't joking about wanting to protect our people."

My guys surround me, engulfing me in a group hug. I savor their closeness, breathing in each of their scents, gathering their strength to carry with me.

"I hate to admit this, but I think the Barons were partially right. You're going to change and create an amazing future," Jameson says.

I smile. "No, we are."

Bronx kisses my temple. "And no one will stop us."

24

SO IN LOVE

I SIT IN EVERETT'S BED with my back propped against fluffy pillows. A sheet covers me up to my neck as I listen to Everett speak with someone in the hallway. Jameson sleeps on the couch, his soft breathing the perfect background noise to keep my heart calm.

Bronx and Mikkalo have been in Mikkalo's suite since we arrived back in Crimson Vista, working on strategizing against future attacks. With Thaxton's stolen com device, we managed to put a halt on any more invasions from the

Barons...at least for another night.

The door quietly cracks open, and Everett meets my gaze with a smile. "I have someone I'd like you to meet, Gwen. He was the top obstetrician and also the best neonatal specialist in the former Bellamy Region."

I swallow. "I don't know what that means."

"He oversaw the birthing unit of his medical center and will assist us throughout your pregnancy." Everett steps into the room and motions for a rugged, tawny vampire wearing a white coat and slacks into the room. "This is Rio Mercy from the Mercy Coven of Shadow Hill Pointe."

Rio offers me a friendly smile without his fangs. Something soft shines in his dark eyes, and I stare at him, trying to assess him before he even speaks. "It's nice to meet you, Ms. Royale."

I bite my lip and turn my gaze to Jameson. Rubbing his eyes, he gets up from the couch and heads toward the new vampire, offering his hand out to him.

"Thanks for coming by, especially under these strange circumstances," Jameson says, glancing at me.

A blip of fear clenches my chest. "How much does he know?"

"Everything in regards to your health." Everett remains expressionless. "It was a hard decision to make, but I don't specialize in pregnancy or pediatrics. We weighed the pros and cons of revealing your heritage, and the risk of others discovering the truth is far less important than assuring you and our child get the best possible care."

My heart flutters at Everett's words, and I bob my head, feeling lighter at the love in his words. Everything about this situation feels like a dream.

Rio strolls behind Everett. "You have my word that your secret is safe with me. No one, not even my coven brothers, will know of this. As far as anyone is concerned, you are purely human as is the fetus."

Jameson sits on the edge of the bed. "We call it the mini beast."

I shake my head with a laugh and swat him on the leg. "Let's hope that's not the case. I'm pretty sure I'm nearly too wild for you to handle."

Rio and Everett work together to bring in all sorts of medical equipment from the hallway and set up a makeshift exam area in the sitting area of the room. Jameson scoots closer and pulls me onto his lap so I can rest my back against him.

"Want to try to drink my blood again?" he murmurs, brushing my hair from my shoulder with his nose.

I shrug. "We can try."

The second he bites his arm and holds it out to me, I scrunch my nose. My stomach twists at the small drop that touches my bottom lip. "Maybe later."

"This really fucking sucks." He groans and buries his

face into my hair. "I hope you have a plan, brother, if Gwen doesn't drink vampire blood soon."

Rio stiffens slightly at Jameson's words, but he composes himself quickly. Turning his attention to us, he says, "Aversion to certain foods is common during pregnancy. So is nausea, fatigue, among a whole list of things you can read over with Gwen. I wouldn't worry as long as you keep her hydrated."

"And if all else fails, we'll catch a Baron. Silas will be the easiest target." Bronx pokes his head into the open door and smiles at me.

Mikkalo follows behind him and comes straight to me to lean down and kiss me softly. "How are you feeling?"

I shrug. "I've been worse. The bite mark still hurts, but my back is pretty much better."

Rio's brows pinch together. "Bite mark? You're not using her as a blood source, are you?"

Bronx puffs out his chest, his frame blocking me from meeting Rio's gaze as he looks at me again. "We did before we knew."

"And Gwen is quite different. She regenerates almost as quickly as a vampire. I think her blood regeneration is even greater. She's producing more than a normal pregnant human does, which would explain her fainting spells." Everett hands Rio a chart. "You can see the results of the tests I've recently run and also what Donor Life Corp had on file to see her previous history."

"What about the bite? If what you say is true, it would be healed, or am I mistaken?" Rio asks.

Everett rubs his hands against his scruffy cheeks. "It was a venom bite. Those take longer to heal on Gwen just the same as us."

Rio intakes a sharp breath. "We need to assess the fetus immediately. If Gwen's transitioning while pregnant, her body might not be strong enough. Her life might be at risk." Rushing to the equipment, he blurs around, getting the different machines to come to life.

Everett blocks him for a second. "While I am a bit worried about the effect it could have on her pregnancy, I don't think it'll harm Gwen. She can't transform. The only noticeable change has been the aversion to our blood. Even then, I think it might be temporary."

"I would still like to start the exam immediately," Rio says, looking at me. "Ms. Royale, please come take a seat on the exam cot."

Jameson carries me in his arms across the room and sets me on the inclined cot. My guys surround me, barely giving Rio any space. They're all just as anxious as I am, but no one says it. I do my best to suppress my nerves. The calmer I am, the calmer they will be.

Everett assists Rio, taking my vitals and measurements, along with a picture of me standing sideways to capture my growth visually. When I sit back on the cot, Rio pulls a strange machine over with what looks like a clear belt the size of my torso.

"This machine will provide a visual of your uterus so that I can determine how far along you are, Ms. Royale. I know some human rebel health keepers have obtained back-world medical equipment. If you're familiar with the antique technology, this would be comparable to an ultrasound but far more superior." Rio motions for me to sit up, and he places the clear, cold, almost jelly-like band around my torso under my shirt.

A huge projection lights up the wall, and I automatically reach for Jameson and Mikkalo's hands because they stand the closest at each of my sides. Bronx touches my knee, staring at me instead of the projection. I offer him a nervous smile, baring my bottom teeth. I can't tell what the hell I'm looking at. The screen is a collection of weird shadows and nothing that even resembles a child.

Rio adjusts the belt on my waist and taps on his com device. A bright light illuminates from the belt turning it from clear to white, and then Everett drapes a dark blanket over me to cover the nearly blinding glow.

"Holy shit," I mutter, tensing. The blurs on the screen clear in the weirdest image I have ever seen in my existence.

Rio chuckles. "Just a second, Ms. Royale. I need to magnify the scan."

Rio draws his finger across his com device with the same image that projects on the wall. My guys remain utterly silent, and now even Bronx stares at the screen. A moment later, Rio draws a red line around what I can only describe as a freaky-ass creature.

"Fuck, it is a mini beast," I whisper, tightening my fingers around Jameson.

Everett and Rio both laugh at the same time at my words. Nudging Jameson away, Everett leans down to me and cups my face with a smile. His eyes shine with a dozen indecipherable emotions before he kisses me softly.

"That's not a beast," he says, pulling away to smile. "That's our baby in the embryonic stage."

"You're measuring at five weeks along, Ms. Royale," Rio says, tapping away on his device. "And so far, everything looks like it would in a donor pregnancy."

"So this is really happening?" Mikkalo asks, sounding like his question is more toward the universe than any of us.

I cover my eyes with my hand for a second. "I can't believe it either."

"When will we know who the father is?" Jameson asks, his Adam's apple bobbing in his throat. His eyes dart to mine. "Or will we not?"

"I guess we have a lot of things to discuss," Bronx says, shifting on his feet.

I tug my fingers free from Jameson and Mikkalo's

death grips. Rio quietly excuses himself, and Bronx and Everett close in on me. I open my arms and attempt to hug them all at once. We don't break apart for what feels like forever, but I don't mind. I want nothing more than to remember this moment exactly how it is right now.

"But maybe that can all wait for a bit?" I ask, fidgeting with the blanket. "I'd much prefer to enjoy this. Maybe celebrate."

"Hell yeah," Mikkalo says, smiling widely. "We're having a baby."

"I don't know about you guys, but I'm excited as hell," Jameson says, brushing his lips to my forehead.

"Me too," Everett says, kissing me next. "But also a little bit scared."

"I'm terrified," Bronx and I say in unison. We both laugh and then fake pout and hug each other.

Mikkalo embraces me last, shimmying down to press his ear to my belly. "I'm in love," he says, kissing my stomach through the blanket.

"Same," Jameson, Everett, and Bronx say at the same time.

I grin at them. "More than I ever knew was possible."

I lie between Jameson and Everett on the bed. Bronx's arm stretches over Everett's head to hold my hand. Mikkalo breathes softly from the other side of Jameson, and I inch upright just a bit to smile at his sleeping face.

Jameson meets my gaze. "You hungry yet?"

"I don't know. I feel fine, though. Not out of control or anything," I whisper against his lips. "I just can't sleep."

"How about we watch a movie or something? I can try to feed you again." His anticipation sharpens his features, and he looks like he's silently begging me to agree.

So I do. "I'd like that. But let's move to the sitting area. I don't want to wake your brothers."

Jameson helps me ease off the bed, and the two of us stroll hand-in-hand to the comfy recliners of Everett's seating area. I pull a blanket off the back of the chair and wrap it around me while watching Jameson pull out a few things from the small refrigerator tucked away in the cabinet.

I get up to let Jameson plop into the recliner and then I sit sideways and balance a plate with a muffin, banana, and cup of fruit and yogurt on my lap. Jameson turns on a movie, keeping the volume down so it's just a whisper of noise through the air. Neither of us watches it. I focus on eating while Jameson focuses on handfeeding me, just enjoying our moment of early morning quiet together.

I gulp an entire glass of water, the liquid helping to cool the burning in my stomach from the lack of vampire blood. If Jameson knew how hungry I still am, he'd start to panic. The last thing I need is for him to feel like something is wrong with him because I don't really want his blood. It's not that he tastes bad now, I just...it's weird.

So before he can ask me, I swivel on his lap to straddle him and distract him with a kiss. He devours my affection, deepening our kiss, exploring my mouth with his tongue. The sweet taste of his lips awakens my desire, and I can't stop myself from yanking his T-shirt over his head. Mine soon follows, and he trails his lips away from mine and down my neck, taking his time to glide his tongue in a way that sends goosebumps over my skin. He sucks my hard nipple into his mouth, rolling his tongue over it before showing attention to my other breast.

I tip my head back and close my eyes, my breath quickening. Jameson drags his finger down my body, tracing my curves until he reaches between my legs. He tugs my panties aside and touches me, feeling the slick warmth of my lust for him.

"Let me take care of you," he whispers. "I've missed you. Everything has been so tense. I just—"

I cut off his words with a kiss. "I've been dying to feel your mouth all over me," I say, sucking his lip hard between my teeth. "But I also want my mouth all over you too."

He hums in his throat, his hard-on flexing under me. Without another word, he reclines the chair completely and eases me back until I lie between his legs with my feet resting at each side of his hips. Licking his lips, he watches my face as he undresses me completely and tosses my panties to the floor. He motions for me to turn around and tugs me by my legs as he lies flat.

A quiet moan escapes my mouth as he starts slow by kissing my thigh. I straddle his face while resting my cheek on his hip, just enjoying the pleasure he elicits from me. Playing with his boxers, I tug his erection out and lace my fingers around it. Jameson moans between my legs, the vibration of his voice sending a need through me to give him as much pleasure as he does me.

I twirl my tongue around his tip, just tasting the sweetness of his skin. Cupping his balls, I rub my finger over the soft skin while I suck his erection into my mouth as far as I can. I tighten my lips just a bit, gliding him in and out of my mouth.

"You're amazing, Gwen. Feels so good," he murmurs, taking a minute to enjoy my mouth on him.

He continues tracing his tongue over my body, licking and sucking, creating different sensations that drag moan after moan out of me. I squirm, my body begging to hit my point of release a second before a rush of tingles explodes through me. I pull away from Jameson, my body tightening with an intense orgasm that has me sinking my teeth into Jameson's thigh.

He grunts and clutches my hips, releasing his own moan as I suck on the bite, filling my mouth with his blood.

"Fuck yeah. Don't stop. Drink what you need."

A dozen emotions roll through me, and I relax on top of Jameson, drinking his blood, letting it quench the need burning inside me. To my relief, my stomach behaves, my body going wild under the taste of him.

"Mmm," I murmur, continuing to suck even though the stream of blood turns into a trickle.

He digs his fingers into my hips. "If you want more, let me wake up one of my brothers."

"I need so much more," I say, nipping his skin again. "Please. I'm starving."

"Hell yeah. I'll feed you, Gwen. I'm up," Mikkalo says from the bed.

Jameson grazes his fangs against my ass cheek to get me to pull away from him. "Let me sit you up...on me."

I lick his cock again and only stop when he sits upright and lets Mikkalo flip me off of him and onto my feet. Sliding his hands around me, Jameson turns me around to face Mikkalo and tugs me onto his lap.

Mikkalo smiles and kisses the moan from my mouth as I sink onto Jameson's boner. I reach for Mikkalo's pajama pants and grip the hem to pull them down enough to play with him while Jameson rocks me against him.

I pull Mikkalo closer until he stands between my legs. Licking my lips, I suck his cock into my mouth, teasing him with my tongue. I slide my hands around him and dig my fingers into his ass cheeks. Mikkalo moans, and I tilt my head back, resting it on Jameson to glance up at him.

"Let me get lower," Mikkalo whispers, playing with strands of my hair.

I pull away from him, and he kneels so that I can kiss him again. Breaking my lips from his mouth, I trail kisses to his neck and to his shoulder. Reaching down, I stroke my fingers over his boner. Jameson picks up speed, thrusting harder into me. I moan and bite my teeth into Mikkalo's shoulder, filling my mouth with his blood. I swallow, humming as warmth blossoms through me. Jameson tightens his hands on me with his climax. I gasp, sliding off him to push Mikkalo back. I straddle him, rolling my body hard and fast until he cums as well. Jameson joins us on the floor, and the three of us catch our breaths. Jameson cuddles me from behind, kissing my shoulder while Mikkalo hugs my arms to his chest.

"You got our girl to eat." Bronx's sultry voice draws my attention away from Mikkalo.

I sit up and smile at him. "And I feel so much better now."

Everett props himself up on his elbows and gives me the best smile. His blue eyes sparkle in the soft light of the nearly silent movie playing on the projection screen. He and Bronx devour me with their gazes, sending another wave of lust through me.

Bronx's eyes flash silver. "You still hungry, dandelion? I'd love to satiate you if you are."

I grin at him, knowing it's more than about feeding me. He and Everett stare at me with the same desire I do them. I don't know if it's because of all the shit we've been through or if it was because I was terrified that I wouldn't want their blood again, but what I do know is I need them both now. I want to be with each of them the way they desire.

I squeeze Mikkalo and Jameson's hands. "Will you two check to see if you can get ahold of Lady Tori again? If she has my brother..."

"We're on it," Mikkalo says, pushing up from the floor. He extends his hand out to me and helps me to my feet.

Jameson hops up and lifts me into his arms, kissing me tenderly. "Take it easy on my brothers, Gigi."

I giggle and comb my fingers through his hair as he carries me to set me on the bed with them. "We've already determined that to be impossible."

Bronx crawls to me and kisses my shoulder. "The way we like it."

After Mikkalo kisses me, he and Jameson disappear from the room, probably heading to their rooms to get ready before doing what I ask. Everett wastes no time, sliding off the bed to stand in front of me. Bronx tugs me farther onto the bed, and I drag Everett with me.

"I want you," Everett whispers, bringing his lips to mine. "I need you."

I chew my lip, drinking in his handsome face, sharpening with his desire. Bronx murmurs he's good with anything I want, and I nod to Everett. He kisses me again, shifting me to roll over to face Bronx. Bronx helps me lie on top of him, adjusting my legs to straddle his while giving Everett space to kneel between them.

Bronx strokes his hands up and down the length of my back, both nerves and excitement rushing through the three of us. While we've done stuff together, this still feels so new. So good.

Everett rests his hands on my back, his hips easing my legs open wider. I moan so embarrassingly loud as Everett thrusts into me. Bronx kisses me, caressing his fingers over my breasts, shifting me up enough to suck my nipples. My skin buzzes, my emotions running wild. I feel so hot and sexy, so wanted and loved.

Bronx links his fingers to my shoulders to hold me in place to assure I get to experience every crazy intense sensation Everett's thrusting creates. I suck on Bronx's neck, leaving a hicky without breaking his skin.

"Take what you need," Bronx murmurs. "I want you so badly to bite me. I want to take care of you and our baby."

I release a strange coo sound, so much happiness flowing through me that I hug against him for a moment, savoring his arms around me as Everett pleasures me. Bronx slides his hand lower and rubs my clit to turn my pleasure into full on ecstasy. I scream a moan with my orgasm and bite Bronx, giving him what he wants. Everett finishes soon after, resting against me.

"I'm so madly and deeply in love with you," Everett whispers into my ear. "I promise you that our lives will be everything you've ever imagined and more." He eases off me and helps me sit up.

I spin around to face him, hugging him while I bury my face against his sweet skin. "I love you too. So much."

Bronx shifts to hug me from behind. "If you're tired..."

Turning my head, I smile. "Tired? I feel amazing. I want more."

He releases a deep purr sound in his throat, spinning me around so fast that I screech and laugh. My back hits the bed, and Everett pulls my head on his lap, running his fingers through my hair. Bronx stretches my legs up and holds them against his chest while tilting my hips up. Pressure builds between my legs as he teases me with his tip, just enjoying how wet and excited my body is.

The click of Everett's fangs sounds in my ears, and I smile at him as he bites his arm to offer me his blood. The second I latch on, Bronx rocks into me, the pressure of our bodies connecting pulling a loud moan from me that I release Everett's arm.

Everett bends down and kisses me. "I'm going to run you a bath."

I bob my head with another moan, turning my full attention to Bronx. His eyes flash silver with his desire. He looks so sexy, his muscles rippling, his arms flexing. He thrusts into me harder and deeper until my moans come in short, quick bursts. His face scrunches with his orgasm, and he nestles between my legs to catch his breath. My body hums, my legs slightly aching but in a good way that reminds me how much I love my guys, how perfect we are together. How amazing the life we've created really is.

"I love you, Gwen," Bronx whispers, kissing me sweetly.

I smile and snuggle against him. "I love you too."

Everett emerges from the bathroom and opens his arms to silently ask Bronx's permission to lift me from the bed. But we don't make it to the bathroom. Mikkalo and Jameson enter the room, the looks on their faces sending fear through me. I tense in Everett's arm, a dozen thoughts about Ashton running through my mind.

"What's wrong?" I ask, my voice quivering.

Everett returns with me back to the bed to sit down. "Gwen, try to stay calm."

"Ashton's fine but the Barons got to him," Mikkalo's quick to spit out. "He managed to reach out to them in Sky Canyon."

"Then why do you guys look like someone died?" I ask, wringing my hands together.

Jameson sits next to us on the bed. He turns his gaze to Bronx. "We received a notice from the board. They've called a mandatory meeting. We have to travel to Midnight Valley immediately."

Bronx frowns. "Does it say what it's about?"

Jameson tightens his jaw. "You. Something came to the rest of the board's attention and they want to discuss it. If you fail to show up, you'll be removed. We're supposed to bring Gwen."

"Shit," I say, looking at the four of them. "It's the Barons. It has to be."

A chime sounds through the air, and Bronx stiffens. His com device glows from the nightstand, and he shifts and scoops it up. Tapping the screen, he answers an incoming call, keeping it private instead of projecting it on the wall.

Bronx's face twists into a frown. "Ashton? Where are you calling from?"

I scramble to get next to Bronx. Everett quickly drapes a blanket around me. "Are you okay?"

Ashton turns his gaze from Bronx to me. He furrows his brows. "I'm fine, Gwen, but I called with a warning. The Barons want the Royales to return you to them or to prepare for a region takeover."

Bronx growls. "We'll take our chances."

"You don't understand. They're not going to attack your region anymore. They've registered their coven with Donor Life Corp. They've inherited Sky Canyon from Brentwood."

I blink. "Wait, what? They're a city head now?" The call drops, leaving me in confusion. I turn to my guys. "What does that even mean?"

Bronx's jaw twitches. "I don't know. I've accepted the board position. They don't just replace people because someone new wants the position."

"Unless you die," Mikkalo says, frowning with his words.

My eyes widen. "Don't be morbid. I'll destroy the damn universe if anyone tries."

Jameson huffs a breath and hugs me. "I'll help."

Another alert pops onto Bronx's phone and he stiffens. "Fuck," he mutters under his breath. "It's from Brooklyn."

"What did she say?"

"Looks like the Barons might get their wish after all." Bronx holds his com device up for us to read. "Corona has formally accused me of treason."

Epilogue

FIGHT FOR THE REGION

I PACE IN THE LOBBY of the Blood Match Center in Midnight Valley. Every few minutes, a new coven of vampires arrives, filling the place so much that half the people have to stand. A few humans mingle with the vampires, and I refuse to meet any of their gazes. My nerves bunch in my stomach, my anxiety threatening to spill its contents all over the floor.

"This cannot be good for the mini beast," Jameson whispers to Everett. "I think you should take her to Bronx's suite until this is over."

I jerk my attention to him and glower. "Don't you even think about it. I'm not going anywhere."

Jameson sticks out his bottom lip in a pout. "At least come sit down. You're making Mikkalo a nervous wreck."

I stop in place, and Mikkalo bumps into my back. I hadn't realized he was shadowing me so closely, but I guess there was no way he was letting a foot of space fall between us in a room full of vampires pretty much only here to witness the shit show going down.

"Brothers," a familiar voice says, sending pain shooting through my heart. "What an unfortunate evening. Let me know if there is anything I can do to show our leader my support."

I tense and swivel, meeting Corona's gaze. He remains expressionless, giving nothing away.

Before anyone can react, I launch at him and knock him off his feet. I lock his hands over his head and scream in his face, fury stealing all good sense from me. The noisy room falls silent, and Mikkalo, Everett, and Jameson growl, the deep noises reverberating through my bones.

I shove my hand against Corona's heart. "You're dead! Dead! You can't come in here and pretend like you're even worthy of being a part of the Royale Coven. You're a traitor and a fraud. A weak, powerless asshole. You won't get away with this, accusing Bronx of treason."

Corona snarls at me, and I jab my nails hard enough to his chest that I pierce the fabric of his dress shirt. "I'd suggest you get your donor off of me unless you'd like me to act on my rightful authority under Donor Life Corp law."

"Beautiful Gwen, allow me to help you to your feet," Freeport says, his shadow falling over me.

I don't get a chance to react as Everett lifts me from Corona and spins me away. Mikkalo and Jameson unsheathe their daggers and get into fighting stance. All eyes drink us in, devouring the drama unfolding.

I glower at Corona. "You can't touch me. The law protects me from all punishment until the birth of my child." I squirm in Everett's arms. "Now let me down. I'm going to kill him. I don't care. He deserves it."

Whispers trickle through the air, the revelation of my pregnancy causing a wave of shock and speculation to explode through the gathered crowd. Corona gawks at me, his wide eyes showing me that he had no idea.

Freeport releases a small growl. "So my brother was right? You carry an abomination to the Baron bloodline."

Snatching Everett's dagger from beneath his jacket, I throw it with perfect accuracy, sinking it deep into Freeport's chest. He startles, taken by surprise. Gasps turn into loud uproars. Several vampires yell that someone should take my final donation immediately.

And then a man flies at me, flashing his fangs. He tries

to grab a hold of me, but a figure blurs between us, and he drops to the floor—at least his body does. Viorica flares her nostrils, gripping the severed head of the vampire by his long brown hair.

"Ms. Royale, please come with me," Viorica says, chucking the head into the wall.

"Only if Mikkalo, Everett, and Jameson get to come too," I say, tightening my grip on Everett in case she tries to rip me away.

"Only because I'm in no mood to argue." Viorica spins on her heels and click-clacks toward the elevator that will take us up to the floor with the meeting room.

Everyone—including Freeport and Corona—watches us as the elevator doors close. I release a ragged breath and groan, my shot nerves relaxing a bit. Without the presence of so many vampires, my human instincts can finally chill the fuck out.

"Ms. Vaduva, you have to believe that Corona set Bronx up. Corona's the traitor." I wiggle enough in Everett's arms that he finally sets me on my feet. "Bronx is a great leader. He cares about our region."

Viorica keeps her eyes trained on the elevator door. "Please do not assume that I'm foolish or stupid enough to believe a man who can't even manage to keep his children loyal to him."

I open and shut my mouth, trying to think of a response. "I'm sorry," I finally say. "I didn't mean to offend you. I'm just—all of this is bullshit."

Jameson slaps his hand over my mouth. "Please accept my apology on Gwen's behalf. She's going through a lot."

Viorica raises her eyebrow. "Do not speak on her behalf. We are alone, and due to these circumstances, I'll allow Gwen to speak freely. Her assertion and confidence are quite admirable."

I pull Jameson's hand from my mouth. "Thank you, Ms. Vaduva."

"Please, call me Viorica. Bronx informed me of his desire to propose a Blood Vow to you after the birth of your heir. If such is the case, there will be no need for formalities." Viorica flicks her gaze to my guys, looking for a reaction. From their reflections in the mirrored walls, they don't give her one.

The elevator comes to a halt, and Viorica steps out before us. I have to jog to keep up with her brisk pace. My guys surround me protectively all the way to the double doors of the board room. It swings open upon our arrival, and I spot Bronx sitting at the enormous table with the three other board members. I start to run to him, but he gets up and meets me half way, pulling me into his arms.

"Are you okay?" I ask, cupping his cheeks. "What's going on?"

Bronx kisses me without responding. I feel the weight

of the board's stares on the side of my face, and I ease away and flick my attention to them. Zara offers me a smirk while the two men look ready to pull their hair out from annoyance, like my very presence bothers them.

"Please take a seat, misters Royale," Viorica says, motioning to the table. "We have a few things to discuss, and it is of utmost importance that our conversation remains between us."

Zara turns her gaze to me. "This means you too, Ms. Royale. We expect your misters to take the proper precautions to assure no one manipulates your mind."

"Gwen already consumes our blood regularly for that very reason," Bronx says, speaking up. "With the current blood feuds besieging our region, we've found it necessary."

"Very good," Mr. Goldman says, nodding to Bronx. Now that we sit at the table, he looks less annoyed and more...I don't know. Concerned? It's hard to tell under his sharp expression.

Viorica links her fingers together, resting her hands on the glass table. "So, it has come to our attention of the recent events occurring in your region. Bronx has informed us of a recently registered coven threatening a siege of the region."

Bronx's eyes flash silver. "They've killed several of our city heads. Turned others against us. They want us to give them Gwen."

"Do they own a Gallagher blood debt?" the other man, Mr. Woodsman, asks.

"No. But even if they did, she is last born. Her four remaining human brothers would inherit it before she did," Bronx says.

"What happened to the other two?" Zara asks.

Mikkalo leans on his elbows. "Corona killed one and the Barons transitioned the other."

"An unauthorized Blood Vow?" Mr. Goldman throws up his arms in exasperation.

"That is concerning," Viorica says. "So is the unrest in your region, Mr. Royale."

"It must be handled swiftly." Zara turns her attention to me. "Can you tell us anything else about these Barons?"

I press my lips together. "They want power."

Viorica sighs. "Obviously."

"No, I mean, more than to take over the region. They want to destroy Donor Life Corp," I say.

The four board members apart from Bronx all laugh, like just the idea is ridiculous.

"It'll take more than one coven to overthrow the Donor Life Corp territory," Mr. Woodsman says.

I want so badly to tell them that they have a plan. But there is no way in hell I'd ever tell them that the plan includes me and my dhampir mutation. Instead of arguing, I just nod my head.

Viorica stands up and peers at all of us. "Do the members of the board find the accusations against Bronx Royale unfounded?"

"Yes," all of them say.

"Does the board agree to the re-evaluation and shift of power in the Royale Region?" Viorica asks.

"What does that mean?" I can't stop the question from escaping my mouth.

"They want to remove all city heads and transfer power to new covens, possibly sending some from their own regions," Mikkalo whispers to me.

"Yes," the board says, answering Viorica's question.

"All right. Due to the sensitive nature of the situation, I must ask the entire board to join me in the announcement. Please take five minutes to prepare your security heads and meet in the lobby."

The five of us are left alone in the board room, and I exhale a long breath as relief washes over me. I had expected the worst from the situation. I expected to have to channel the wild beast within me to destroy the whole board. What I didn't expect was for the board to side with us and to stand up for Bronx. To let me speak before them.

"So what the hell with the Blood Vow?" Jameson asks, turning to Bronx. "We agreed that we would not propose such a thing."

"I'm sorry, brothers," Bronx says, meeting each of their

gazes. "They needed a good reason as to why I didn't just hand Gwen over and be done with it. They had to know that I don't consider her just a possession."

"It better not have been one based on love," Mikkalo mutters, his shoulders tense.

Bronx shakes his head. "Loyalty. The actions of the Barons and the Blood Rebels made her loyalty easy to prove. She chose us. It was enough."

"And what about the fact that she can't transform?" Everett asks, keeping his voice low.

Bronx sighs. "We'll figure it out."

"Later," Mikkalo says. "We have to go. The board will arrive in the lobby soon."

Bronx picks me up, and the five of us head to the lobby in silence. Murmurs sound through the air only to silence under our arrival. Not even a few seconds later, the rest of the board materializes in front of us.

Viorica wastes no time, straightening her back and calling the crowd's attention. "We'd like to announce that we've found no evidence to support the accusations of Mr. Corona Anderson."

Corona growls. "It's Mr. Royale."

Zara steps forward. "Due to the lack of loyalty and the obvious ulterior motives, we've voted to annul the union between the Andersons and Royales."

Corona flashes his fangs and glares at me. "You better

tell the board you want to keep me in your coven. You don't want me to share your secret now, do you?"

My heart stalls before picking up in overdrive.

"What secret?" someone in the crowd asks.

Freeport materializes behind Corona, and he stiffens, his eyes widening. The scent of his bitter blood trickles to me, my sense of smell now stronger than ever. I don't have to see it to know that Freeport stabs a knife into Corona's back in warning.

I clear my throat. "That I'm pregnant."

"Something that the board is aware of," Viorica says. "And none of your concern. Mr. Royale granted Ms. Royale's request for an heir before her Blood Vow." It's a flat out lie, but the words are enough to settle the crowd.

Whatever Freeport does is also enough to stop Corona from continuing to speak up.

"Now, if we may continue with no further interruptions," Mr. Goldman says.

Viorica nods at him. "After looking into recent events occurring in the Royale Region, we have decided to do a complete re-evaluation of the city heads."

Gasps and growls sound through the air, setting off my human rationale like crazy. Bronx holds me tighter, rubbing his big hand up and down my back to suppress my out of control nerves.

"Based on what?" a guy asks, standing from his seat.

"Outsider influence." Viorica meets Freeport's gaze. "Because you did not trust your region leader and have purposely tried to jeopardize his position on the board, Donor Life Corp has convicted all Royale Region city heads with treason. You will be executed immediately."

Outrage bursts through the room, people pulling out all sorts of weapons. Bronx spins me toward a wall, and my guys surround me protectively.

"I'd like to motion for an appeal." Freeport's deep voice sounds through the air, silencing the angry crowd. "I'd like to remind the board that it is the leaders of the region's cities' right to make decisions that best protect their donor populations. None of the city heads have acted out against Mr. Royale but were doing what they thought necessary to protect their cities."

"Against you!" I yell.

"Me?" Freeport raises an eyebrow. "No, that is untrue. I have proof that all recent attacks were caused by Blood Rebels. Mr. Royale has done nothing of the situation and has even allowed many rebels to go freely without the proper consequence."

Bronx stiffens, tightening his hold on me. "What proof?"

"Videos, witnesses, even some of the rebels," he says. "And due to the severity of the situation and because I am the new head of Sky Canyon, I demand the board allow me to contest Mr. Royale's position as board member to apply for the position myself."

The board remains expressionless.

"Or do you not follow and uphold the very laws you've created?" Freeport asks. "How will your own city heads trust you?"

Viorica and the board look to each other in silent conversation for a moment, and then Viorica turns to Bronx. "I'm sorry, Mr. Royale. I'm afraid we're going to have to grant him the ability to apply."

Bronx tightens his jaw. "I understand."

"Do you want to challenge his request to maintain your position?" Viorica asks.

"I do," Bronx says, looking to his brothers. "The region is mine."

"Very well. We will meet again in thirty days to settle the future of the Royale Region," Viorica says. "This meeting is adjourned."

With her words, the crowd disappears. Bronx runs at a vampire's speed, relocating me to his suite. Mikkalo, Jameson, and Everett surround us, and they all try to speak at once.

"Stop," Bronx says, raising his hand. "I've made my decision. I can't let the region go. It's more important now than ever. For Gwen's sake."

"But to challenge that asshole? He's from before the

uprising, Bronx," Jameson says, throwing his hands up.

"It means nothing," Bronx snaps.

"Are you kidding me? We can't risk losing you," Mikkalo says, smacking him on the back.

My blood chills, my mouth going dry. "What? What does he mean by losing you?"

Bronx groans and links his fingers behind his head without responding to me. Mikkalo and Everett turn their gazes away, not wanting to tell me either. Snatching Jameson's hand, I force him to look at me.

"What does he mean, Jamie?" I ask, staring into his green eyes.

Jameson's eyes glass over for a second before he composes himself. "A challenge is a fight for power. It's a fight to the death."

To be continued...

Thank you so much for reading *Rebel Match!* Don't forget to check out *Rebel Heir*, the fourth book in *The Royale Vampire Heirs* series. Also, if you love the *Vampire Heirs* world and haven't checked out *The Divine Vampire Heirs* and *Academy of Vampire Heirs*, what are you waiting for? The Divines and Kings are waiting.

THE MATES OF MAGAELORUM WORLD

The Pack Mates of Lunar Crest:
The She-Wolf Games
The Wolf-Mate Trials
The Omega Hunt
The Witch Chase

Fated Mates of the Dragon Clans:
Caged by Her Dragons
Freed by Her Dragons
Saved by Her Dragons

SEVEN SINNERS WORLD

Her Personal Demons
Her Deadly Angels
Her Darkest Devils
Her Sinful Saints
Her Twisted Sinners

About Ginna Moran

GINNA MORAN IS a writer from sunny Southern California. She started writing poetry as a teenager in a spiral notebook that she still has tucked away on her desk today. Her love of writing grew after she graduated high school, and she completed her first unpublished manuscript at age eighteen.

When she realized her love of writing was her life's passion, she studied literature at Mira Costa College in Northern San Diego. Besides writing novels, she was senior editor, content manager, and image coordinator for Crescent House Publishing Inc. for four years.

Aside from Ginna's professional life, she enjoys binge watching television shows, playing pretend with her daughter, and cuddling with her dogs. Some of her favorite things include chocolate, anything that glitters, cheesy jokes, and organizing her bookshelf.

Ginna Moran loves to hear from her readers so visit her online at www.GinnaMoran.com. You can also find her on Facebook, Twitter, and Instagram. To stay up-to-date on new releases, sign up to her newsletter. You'll not only get exclusive access to extra stories, but you'll be able to participate in monthly giveaways!